THE
PRETTY
ONE

BOOKS BY CLARE BOYD

THE
PRETTY
ONE

CLARE BOYD

Bookouture

Published by Bookouture in 2021

An imprint of Storyfire Ltd.
Carmelite House
50 Victoria Embankment
London EC4Y 0DZ

www.bookouture.com

ISBN: 978-1-83888-710-0
eBook ISBN: 978-1-83888-709-4

This book is a work of fiction. Names, characters, businesses,
organizations, places and events other than those clearly in the
public domain, are either the product of the author's imagination
or are used fictitiously. Any resemblance to actual persons, living or
dead, events or locales is entirely coincidental.

For Simon

Isn't it odd – we can only see our outsides but nearly everything happens on the inside, said the mole.

Charlie Mackesy, *The Boy, the Mole, the Fox and the Horse*

PROLOGUE

2012

I ran screaming with excitement down the corridor. My baby sister toddled after me, falling on her nappy bum. I pulled her up, and slipped in my socks, laughing and sliding, yelling about getting a new sister. A big sister. A big sister who was going to live with us forever. She was called Bay and she was arriving today. Like a parcel.

We had met her three times before. She was eight years old. She had a black fringe that she combed down flat to meet the tops of her pink plastic glasses. She played Monopoly with us over and over and didn't notice when I cheated. And her best friend was knifed in the leg.

Every minute since I had woken up, I had asked Mum whether it was ten o'clock yet. At ten o'clock, Bay's mother would be dropping her off at the train station. Her mother wasn't coming to the house. We weren't quite sure why she didn't want to meet us and have a cup of tea (that's what I had overheard Mum saying to Dad).

'It's such a shame, isn't it?' Mum had also said, in a whispery voice.

'Believe me, it's not,' Dad had said.

'You can't say that,' Mum had said, giving Dad one of her naughty smiles.

'I can. I was married to the woman, remember?' Dad had said, holding his cup out for more tea.

And I had tried to imagine Dad being married to someone who wasn't Mum, and it was impossible.

When Bay finally arrived, I noticed that I was as tall as her even though I was younger. Dad was carrying her small grey rucksack for her, probably because her arms were as thin as pencils and might not have been strong enough to carry anything. I felt quite big and strong next to her.

'Can I help getting your other stuff from the car?' I asked, wanting to be super-helpful, dying to know what toys she had.

Dad put on his cross face. 'No, Nell. This is her only bag.'

'Oh,' I said, staring at it in wonder. How could she have just one small bag? I imagined how big my bag would be if I had to go and live somewhere else forever. I hated the thought and felt terribly sorry for Bay.

'Nell and Iris, do you want to show Bay her new room?' Mum said, giving Bay such a lovely smile. I felt a bit tearful, in a happy way.

We had become shy since Bay had walked through the door. Iris was sucking her thumb. Bay looked sad to be here and that worried me. I wished I hadn't asked about her other bags. I didn't want her to be sad. I wanted her to love us as much as we loved her. I wanted her to love our home as much as we loved it.

Upstairs, Bay sat down on her new bed. She took out her comb from her pocket and began combing her fringe down. She wasn't looking around her new room. So I pointed to all the things we had done to make it special for her. Like the cuddly rabbit on her pillow that I had bought with my own pocket money. And the fluffy pink rug that I had spent days choosing with Mum online. I pointed at the little purple fairy that was supposed to be from Iris, even though she was too little to choose a proper present. It was a good-luck fairy.

I waited for Bay to say how much she liked all these new things, which I had secretly wanted for myself.

Iris climbed on the stool and pressed her forehead against the windowpane. Her hair stuck out all over the place.

'Horsey,' I said to her, pointing to Pippa the horse in the field across the road. I was trying to get Iris to say her first word.

'Where's your room?' Bay asked. There was still no smile and it was beginning to worry me.

I dragged her next door. Iris and I were sharing now. At first, I had hated the idea of sharing with my baby sister, who was only one. I was six and way too grown up to have to share with a silly baby in a cot, and I knew I'd miss seeing Pippa the horse outside my window. But Mum had told me to think about Bay's feelings over my own and to remember that she had never had her own bedroom before.

'I wish I had this room instead,' Bay said.

'But it's smaller than yours,' I said, a bit confused. I might have even scratched my head.

Her grey eyes through her glasses looked watery and I began to panic.

Before I could do anything, Bay ran out and slammed her new bedroom door. The sign that I had chosen, saying *Sweet Dreams*, fell off the hook.

Iris unplugged her thumb from her mouth and picked up the sign. I snatched it from her and tried to reach the hook where it was supposed to be. If I asked Mum or Dad for help, I would get in trouble for upsetting Bay again.

I crept into the room that used to be mine and sat next to my little big sister Bay on the bed, pulling Iris onto my knee, telling Bay not to cry. But I felt so disappointed and guilty, I burst into tears too.

PART ONE: HOME

Present Day

CHAPTER ONE

Anna

A man with white-blond hair was staring at my three girls, and it was starting to wind me up. Normally I'd be the last person on earth to cause a scene, especially in an art gallery, but I was fighting back a deep-seated motherly urge to say something very loud and embarrassing.

For now, I concentrated on the golden cross-hatching of the artwork on the walls of the gallery, but I remained wary of him as we moved to the next exhibit. In a self-conscious whisper, I read the pamphlet to the girls. 'The weaving workshop at the Bauhaus in 1919, where Anni Albers studied, was dubbed the "Women's Workshop", in spite of its progressive ideals of equality'. I faltered, noticing the man was coming closer. He stood too near to us. I continued reading, picking up from where I'd left off. From the corner of my eye I saw him lean in to his male companion and point in the girls' direction. It was galling that he didn't appear at all sheepish about his leering, or notice my dirty looks. To him, I guessed I was just a vague forty-something irrelevance in unfashionable jeans.

It wasn't surprising that the girls were drawing attention, though. I looked them over now with a wave of pride. They were gorgeous. I wasn't biased. Not one bit.

Admittedly, Nell's favourite T-shirt was way too short and her jeans too tight. Since turning fifteen, she had become curvy, and her limbs had grown long and a little artless. There were clumps of yesterday's mascara on her eyelashes, but her blue eyes were guileless, like an unsheltered sky. The blonde baby hairs around her forehead had not been tamed into her high, thick ponytail and the wisps gave her an angel-like quality. Her heart-shaped lips were never quite closed properly over the gap between her two front teeth, as though she was permanently in awe of the world around her, poised to gasp or smile in surprise. She was still innocent and perfect, and she was all mine.

Iris had not washed or brushed her hair before we'd come out, which was my fault, considering she was only ten years old, yet she looked impossibly sweet, with her sticky-out ears, long, skinny legs and big feet. A little frowny and a little scruffy, she would always be the baby of the family. Perfect. All mine.

And Bay, my stepdaughter, looked exactly how I myself would have wanted to look at her age, almost seventeen. The back of her head was shorn, and at the front, her black fringe was swept to the side, tucked behind one small ear. Her tiny mouth was buttoned up, naturally red and bitten. Her eyes were green in one light, grey in another, yellow even in some, and had a sad little droop at either corner. Although her body was diminutive, narrow, especially compared to Iris and Nell, she knew how to dress. Today she wore a button-down black cardigan and high-waisted corduroy slacks. The cloth bag she had bought the last time we'd come to the Tate Modern was worn, weighed down elegantly by her Moleskine notebook and pen, and by her phone, of course.

Looking at Bay now, I couldn't help thinking back to the day she had arrived to live with us: the grubby, sullen child who had obsessively combed her long black fringe to meet the top of her glasses. The change in her had been hard won. Perfect. And she was almost all mine.

The mismatched threesome stared up at the piece of art. Bay moved over to hold Nell's hand. They often held hands, like Italian teenage girls. Little Iris pushed between them to get a better look.

I glared at the white-haired man and dragged the three of them off to the swatches of material that were hooked to the wall, marking the end of the exhibition.

'You're allowed to touch these,' I said to the girls.

Iris looked up, nuzzling into me. 'Won't we get in trouble?'

The material I chose was rough and scratchy. It was harsh on my fingertips and I looked for a softer fabric. 'You won't get into trouble. Feel them,' I said. 'Anni Albers thought we should use our sense of touch much more often.'

I thought about touch. Since the girls were small, I had luxuriated in the softness of them: their cheeks, their backs, their palms. The feel of their hair through my fingers. The sensation of their lips on my cheek. When they came to me for a hug, they might nestle into my middle or pull at my face or play with my hair or reach for my hand; it was the kind of touch that gave me life.

Remembering the man, I looked around for him. If he used *his* sense of touch anywhere near this lot, he'd have his creepy eyes poked out.

It seemed he had gone. I noticed that Nell was texting on her phone. 'Nell. Put that thing away,' I said, wishing I could take her phone from her and turn it off forever – except of course when I needed to reach her. She stuffed it in the back pocket of her skintight jeans. 'Sorry,' she said, ambling over to the skeins of yarn that hung like ponytails from hooks. She smoothed her fingers through them and cooed, placing one against her cheek.

Then I noticed the man again. He seemed to be approaching Nell, putting his hand into his black satchel. His gleaming high-top trainers squeaked on the polished floor as he walked. I noticed the seat of his trousers was almost at his knees – a look I associated with a man much younger – and a small bald patch was showing through his crispy white-blond hair.

The clack-clacking of the hand loom in the documentary film that was being projected onto the wall grew loud in my head, like teeth gnashing. I hurried forward to get to Nell first.

Bay pulled my sleeve. 'Check this out, Anna,' she said, showing me an arty close-up on her phone of the frayed edges of a fragment of material.

'Great shot,' I said, barely glancing at it as I reached for Nell.

'Come on, Nell, let's go and get some cake,' I said, holding her arm, beckoning the other two over. 'Bay! Iris! Come on, now.'

Pushing them on by the smalls of their backs, I hurried them out and through the gift shop, refusing all their requests for postcards or fridge magnets, promising we would come back later. *When the horrible man was gone.*

We settled at the shiny table in the café with the black floor and read the menu. I felt warily relieved, and not entirely confident we had lost the staring man for good.

'That was a brilliant exhibition, wasn't it?' I said.

Iris unzipped her rucksack and pulled out her 1974 *Beano* annual. Nell took out her phone and showed Bay her latest TikTok. They were head-to-head, talking as though they shared a secret language. The metal table wobbled as they scrolled.

'I thought it was so amazing to see all those little crosses in her notebooks, didn't you?' I continued, knowing I was talking to myself.

I scanned the room, wondering if it would be crazy to collar a stranger and share my thoughts on the exhibition. Yup. Completely crazy. I picked up my napkin and began folding it into a flower, and thought about Dom, who had chosen not to come. I thought about the skeins of yarn and the roughly hewn swatches and wondered which he would have been drawn to. I guessed he might not have touched them at all. Art exhibitions weren't Dom's favourite pastime, and I had given up trying to persuade him to come on our yearly London trips. Having a beer and watching the football without the girls disturbing him was what he had chosen to do today. I understood. He'd had a stressful week cooped up in the office.

'Excuse me,' a man's voice said.

The white-blond man was suddenly next to Nell. He was handing her some kind of pink flyer. I read the leaflet upside down. *YOU'VE BEEN SCOUTED!* it said in bold capitals.

'Hi, I'm sorry to disturb you guys,' he said. His skin had a taut, shiny quality and his lips looked as if they'd been injected with something nasty. Briefly he glanced at me before snapping his full attention back to Nell. 'I'm David, and I'm a scout for Take One models. Can I ask your name, hon?'

'Nell?' she replied, as though she wasn't sure any more.

'Have you ever considered modelling, Nell?'

She blinked at him, awestruck. 'No,' she said, before looking to Bay, who was giving him one of her haughty glares.

'Nell's only fifteen,' I said apologetically, hoping that settled the matter. I knew only too well how cut-throat that industry could be. It housed someone from the past whom I had left behind long ago. I didn't want Nell to be any part of it.

'Are you "Mum"?' David said, making quotation marks in the air.

'Yes,' I said, nodding.

'Great to meet you, Mum. I know this is big for you too, right? Has this ever happened to Nell before?'

'No, never,' I said. I didn't like the idea that anything was actually 'happening' to her.

'Well, get used to it. She'll be asked again. But Take One is the best in the business. The bookers in the New Faces division are like second mums to their girls.'

'Oh,' I said. Why would Nell need a second mother? I thought.

'Why not pop in to meet them? See what you think. What about you, Nell? Would you like to come in to see us?'

'You think I could be a model?' she asked.

'The bookers will make the final decision, but I think you'd have a great chance of being taken on. Your look is to. Die. For! Like a young Brigitte Bardot!'

It wasn't the first time I had heard the comparison. My mother had pointed it out to me once. The observation had alarmed me, as though it alienated Nell from me, made her too different. She would always be my squidgy-thighed baby, my little companion, who had eaten well and slept well and smiled early. I had told Mum she was biased. All grandmothers thought their granddaughters were beautiful.

'Who's Brigitte Bardot?' Iris piped up, very seriously. She placed her hands on her closed annual, as though David might steal it, and waited for his answer.

'Brigitte Bardot was a French film star in the sixties. And one of the most beautiful women to ever have walked the earth!' David said.

'Is she dead?' Iris asked coolly.

Bay answered her. 'No. She campaigns for animal rights and has hundreds of cats and looks like a fright.'

I laughed.

'Thanks so much, David,' I said, taking the flyer from Nell and folding it away into my handbag. 'It's lovely of you, but Nell will be starting her final GCSE year after the summer holidays and so she won't have any time to be a model, I'm afraid. I'm so sorry.'

His brow furrowed into a waxy crease. 'These days, the New Faces desk have a strict policy that their girls don't miss out on *any* school.'

'Honestly, thank you so much for your interest. I'm sure she's really flattered, aren't you, Nell? But it's a no from us.' I looked at Nell and shivered at the change in her expression. The god of thunder had taken up residence inside her and was poised to wage a hundred-year war on me.

Then she turned her pretty face up to David, blinking back the anger. 'Thank you,' she said politely. 'I can't really believe it. Thank you so much.'

I felt guilty for shutting the idea down before giving her the chance to respond and enjoy the compliment.

'Believe it, honey!' he said, then turned to me. 'She could be a star with a face like that.'

'Thank you. That's very kind,' I said. 'It was a pleasure to meet you. There's a lot to think about.'

'Okay, folks. Great to meet you, Mum. And Nell.' He did not so much as glance in either Iris or Bay's direction. 'You have my flyer, hon,' he said to Nell. 'All the deets are there if you want to call and fix a date to meet the team.' He winked. 'Hope to see your face on the front cover of *Vogue* some day.'

As he walked away, I met three sets of eyes at the table, worrying about each of them, trying to second-guess their reactions.

'Well, wow. What do we think about that?' I said.

Because of Brigitte Bardot and the mention of cats, I guessed Iris would take the opportunity to ask for a kitten again, rather than think too hard about Nell modelling. Bay would be protective, perhaps also feel ugly, even though she was beautiful, in a quieter way. And Nell would look to Bay for guidance. For everything she did, she needed her big sister's approval.

'Oh my God!' she said to Bay.

'Wow!' Bay said.

Nell thrust her hand in my direction. 'Can I have the flyer?'

I brought it out of my bag and handed it to her. While she read, I read it too, upside down.

CONGRATULATIONS!
You have been scouted by TAKE ONE MODEL MANAGEMENT.

Take One is responsible for scouring the UK to find fresh and distinctive faces to make it big in the fashion industry.

Thanks to the passion of our scouting team – all DBS-checked – and the perseverance of our bookers, Take One's books are bursting with talent, as seen on worldwide campaigns and catwalks. Our New Faces team has launched the careers of the biggest names in the business and look forward to making more dreams a reality.

Please email:

scouttalent@takeonemodels.com

www.takeonemodels.com

44 (0)20 7352 8670

'That guy must have left his glasses at home or something,' Nell said modestly.

I laughed. 'Clearly he's blind as a bat.'

Bay forced a smile, but her eyes were grey and overcast. I could not tell whether she was harbouring difficult feelings or simply thinking through what had just happened. In the early years, she had been a gloomy child; hurt would lurk inside her for days until she exploded, wild with it. I was wary of this still.

Nell glanced at her uncertainly, and Bay looked back at Nell. The two of them shared a communication that the rest of us weren't part of, like the telepathy of twins.

'Like you said, Mum, there's no way I'd be able to fit it in. Not with all the exams coming up this year,' Nell said.

'I think that's very grown up,' I told her, though I quietly worried she was saying what I wanted to hear. Or what Bay wanted to hear.

She began folding the flyer into her rucksack, but Bay leant over and snatched it from her and screwed it into a ball.

'Give that back,' Nell said hotly, prising it out of Bay's hands and flattening it out.

'Ow,' Bay said, rubbing her hand. 'You need to cut your fingernails.'

'Stop it, you two,' I said, shooting them both warning looks. Nell's blue eyes flashed with indignation as she zipped the flyer away.

'Can we get a kitten, Mummy?' Iris asked, left field.

All four of us laughed.

'Trust you, Iris,' Nell said, reaching over to ruffle her hair.

'Daddy is still allergic to them, poppet.' I squeezed her hand, feeling eternally sorry that I could not provide her with the pet she so wished for.

We ordered four lemonades and four chocolate fudge cakes, and I managed to sustain at least ten minutes of discussion about Anni Albers. But Nell didn't eat her cake with her usual gusto, and didn't even jump down my throat when I mentioned the evils of social media. She was brooding, in a slumping, sultry way, and she didn't immediately pick up her phone and text her friends to 'spill the tea', as they described gossip. I wanted to ask her why she seemed sad, but equally I was scared of doing so. She had agreed that she would be too busy with schoolwork to start modelling, and it was the right decision. If I opened up the discussion again, doubts might creep in. I knew a little bit about the fashion industry, and what I knew was not good. She was too young to be thrust into that world. I wanted her childhood to continue as it was – a little sheltered, perhaps, but safe and contained – and as much as I sensed there was a tussle inside her right now, I knew she wouldn't regret the decision long-term.

Arriving at our station, with the short platform and the weeds growing over the metal fence, hearing the wood pigeons and the scuttling of small animals in the hedgerow, was a blessed relief. London's energy had been wearing.

Our sunshine-yellow car smelt of old crisps and the seats were covered in mud, but I loved it. I was looking forward to getting home and making a cup of tea.

Quiet appreciation spread through me when I saw the bell tower of the little church. I turned right past the primary school and the cricket green and the old oak tree, which was the majestic centrepiece of the village. Moving out of London after Nell was born was the best decision we ever made.

I pulled up into the narrow space outside our terraced house, and inched the nose carefully forward until it was almost kissing the outside wall of the front room. The wellies were upside down on the wooden rack by the front step. The wood was stacked up in the porch. The key nearly snapped off as I pushed it through the stiff bit of the turn. The smells of herbs and spices and washing powder filled my head as the four of us squeezed into the hallway, kicking our shoes off and chattering.

'We're back!' I called out, getting my phone out, feeling guilty that I hadn't called Mum yet today.

With the phone pressed to my ear, I found Dom on the sofa watching telly with a beer in his hand. I waved and put the kettle on. He waved back, barely taking his eyes off the screen. Whatever he was watching was more interesting than our return. He would probably only half hear the day's news by zoning in and out of my conversation with Mum. It was better that way, easier for me to play down the modelling thing and make out that David had been some weirdo from an unsuitable agency. I didn't need him to get excited about it and ruffle Nell.

'Hi, Mum. Sorry. We're home now,' I said into the handset, leaning into the counter. I pictured her alone on the sofa, grateful for my call, with her milky eyes and her strong jaw and her swollen knuckles. 'How's it going?'

I exhaled contentedly as I listened.

We were home. Everything was as it should be.

CHAPTER TWO

Nell

'What a weird day,' Bay says, following me upstairs.

'I know, right?'

'What are you going to do?'

'Dunno,' I say. 'Mum doesn't want me to, so I guess that's that.'

'She's right. You really need to focus on your GCSEs.'

What I *need* is space, I think.

'I'm just going to call Jade,' I say, and I back into my bedroom, closing the door. I know Bay only wants to help, but I need some time to work it all out for myself.

Bay pushes through the door. 'There was this girl in Year 11 who was a model and she only did jobs that didn't objectify her. I really admired her for it.'

'Yeah? Actually, I'll call Jade later. I'm going to head out on my bike,' I say, thinking on my feet, retying my ponytail. I hurry downstairs, stick my trainers on and call out to Mum. 'Mum! I'm going out on my bike to meet Matthew!'

'See you in a bit!' Mum calls back.

Outside, I stand up on the pedals, the wheels roll and the wind blows my worries away. My whole body is lighter and faster on the bike. I bunny-hop off the pavement and whizz past the playground, over the green and into the woods. I stop and look around to see if anyone is about, then I text Matthew, hoping he might be able to come down. While I wait for him to get back to me, I clean up the jumps to make sure they are safe for the little ones who ride here, moving sticks and debris, checking the older kids haven't dug out bigger gaps between the take-off and landing.

Then I plonk myself on the fallen tree trunk and take the crumpled flyer out of my pocket. What am I supposed to do with it now? Stick it into a weird scrapbook about the amazing life I *could* have had?

I should screw it up again, like Bay did.

It's obvious Bay has decided that modelling is a bad idea, and maybe she's right. She probably thinks it's anti-feminist, or something like that. But I'm a feminist too. I believe women will change the world one day. I like to be positive about our future. Bay can be a bit negative about that stuff. But she is normal most of the time. She didn't mean to be a Debbie Downer. When I remind myself of what kind of life she had before she came to live with us, I get why she finds it hard to imagine that things will turn out okay if you just believe. The stories she told me about her mother were horrific. I remember wanting to un-hear them when she first told me, and I hugged her super-tightly. It explains why she can be weird and unpredictable sometimes.

To be truthful about today, I wanted to say a big fat *Hell, yeah!* to David, who had the strangest lips I had ever seen. Maybe he puffed them up with collagen because he'd been bullied when he was little? Everyone has their stories. Mum always says you should never judge a person from the outside, and I try to live by that. Funny, though, on the way back home, Mum said that the models on the flyer looked a bit pouty and big for their boots. I couldn't believe she was judging them from the outside! And I told her she was a total hypocrite. Iris said to her, 'You got burned!' like an American rapper, and Mum laughed, admitting she had been in the wrong and that they were probably lovely girls.

Reading the flyer again, I try to imagine being one of those girls in the teeny-tiny photographs. What would it be like? I get my phone out and go on Instagram to follow Take One Models Official. They have 402K followers! The girls on their feed are stunning and uber cool, kind of sultry and lanky. Compared to them, I'm like a stupid kid. Obvs David is a crackhead. He didn't notice the massive breakout on my chin or the gap in my teeth.

But Dad is always telling us to follow our dreams, and not make the same mistakes he made (whatever they were). So I get back on my bike, deciding I badly need to get Dad on my side and change Mum's mind. She's a big softie underneath it all, just a bit overprotective. I wish she trusted me more, though. My besties Mint and Jade drink vodka and vape and have, like, five secret Insta accounts behind their parents' backs, and Jade's even slept with her drip of a boyfriend, while the worst I've ever done is have a couple of beers and kiss a few guys. I did go a bit further with Max, almost all the way, but losing my virginity scares me. I am totally not ready, even though I'm fifteen years old, and I guess I should be. I know it sounds cheesy, but I just want to wait for the right guy.

I check my phone. Where is Matthew? He would know what I should do. Knowing Matthew Michaels, he would probably remind me that it is okay to follow your dreams as long as you don't hurt anyone along the way. I have a big think about Bay. A few bad memories crowd out my pea brain. I push them away. It's stuff from the past that I really don't have time for right now.

It's important to live my own life, right? No regrets. Mum's mum, Granny Berry, has so many regrets. It's all she ever talks about. Mum told me she was hospitalised for a nervous breakdown once, years ago, way before I was born, and I get the impression that Mum worries it might happen again some day. It's a really sad thought.

I imagine being powdery and wrinkled like Granny, in an old people's home, watching the rain dribbling down the window, saying to the nurse who wipes my bum, 'I could have been rich and famous when I was young, you know, dear! I could have bought the fastest mountain bikes that ever existed and travelled to Madeira and California and the Alps to ride those radical trails! But I didn't because my mum and my half-sister were pissy about it.'

Matthew texts me back when I'm almost home.

See you in half an hour? Just closing up for Mum. I'll bring Fantas.

I could go back to meet him, but I'm too keen to talk to Dad. I stop to reply.

Sorry. Gotta go. Tomorrow? Xxx

The Fantas are warm anyway.

I grin. He's so anal about the temperature of his drinks.

Lamo xxxx See ya xxxx

I arrive home and find Dad round the back, washing moss out of the flagstones with his jet wash thing – his birthday present last year from Mum. It makes a racket, though it isn't half as loud as his leaf blower.

'Dad!'

He looks up and smiles at me with that archy-eyebrow thing he always does. 'What's up?'

'Did Mum tell you what happened in London?'

He points the jet in my direction. Cool rainbows pop up through the spray.

'*Dad!* Stop it!'

I sound annoyed, but I kind of love it when Dad's dumb like this with me.

'So, we were in the art gallery and—'

He sprays me again.

'*Dad!*'

Every time I try to tell him what happened, he sprays me, so I just shout it out.

'I WAS ASKED TO BE A MODEL!'

He turns off the jet wash and takes off his cap. His hair is mashed into his head, and a clear drip of something wobbles on the end of his nose. Gross. I hope it's sweat, not bogey.

'I know. Mum told me.'

'Ugh! Why didn't you just say? You're *so* annoying.'

I give him the flyer and he reads it, super-slowly. While I wait for his reaction, I bite off too much fingernail. Ouch.

'Mum didn't say it was one of the top agencies,' he says. He frowns in the direction of the back window, where Mum is usually standing at the kitchen sink. I'm not saying she's chained to it or anything, but honest to God, she spends a lot of time at that sink.

'She probably doesn't want me to get big-headed,' I say, which is a bit mean, so I add, 'And she thinks I'll mess up my GCSEs, but I totally won't.'

'Let's go talk to her about it.'

He sounds stern, like he's going to tell her off or something. Now I feel bad for her. I don't want him to be cross with her. I don't want anyone to be upset about anything ever. Keeping everyone happy is my job in our family, but it's knackering sometimes. Before Bay arrived, I didn't have to think about it much. I just got on with being me. Bay changed me. Perhaps she made me think of myself less. That's a good thing, I guess. I've always put her feelings first. But sometimes I just want to do what I want to do and not care about whether it upsets her or anyone else. Like modelling. Modelling could be my thing. Mum just has to *relax*.

CHAPTER THREE

Anna

While the kettle boiled, I scrubbed off the porridge that had hardened like cement on Dom's bowl. I didn't mind so much today. Some days I did mind. Minded so much I wanted to throw it at his head. Today, thinking and scrubbing was a good combination. The Take One flyer was on my mind. In the café, I had noticed how impulsively Bay had screwed it up and how viciously Nell had prised it out of her hand. Their exchange kept replaying in my mind. They didn't argue much these days, not any more.

In that first year, they had fought endlessly. The passionate and enthusiastic Nell had turned into a ball of stroppiness and overreactions. Bay had been small for her age, and frighteningly vulnerable, crying or being sick at the smallest of things, and demanding an awful lot of attention. I understood that Nell had been usurped as the eldest child – I really *did* understand that – while also knowing it was vitally important to reinforce in her the values of empathy and patience and kindness; reminding her that Bay had not been given such a fortunate start in life. The messages had slowly been absorbed. Evident on the train earlier, when she had pulled me up on my unkind remarks about the models on the flyer. It had been stupid of me to make such superficial judgements, but I had been trying to shut down the modelling idea completely and make out that the girls in the photos were different to Nell, different to us.

The porridge was being stubborn today. But it wasn't worth asking Dom to rinse his bowl. He could get touchy about being told to pull his weight around the house. Nagging – my mother had told me once – sent husbands like Dom into the arms of other women.

Iris laughed out loud at something on her iPad.

Out of the window, I could see Dom spraying water on Nell. As he laughed with her, he looked happy. He turned towards me, squinting through the window. Though our eyes didn't meet, the glass deflecting any connection, his smile faded and his lips puckered into a pout. His looks were boyish still, with his crop of black hair and his small mouth and his eyes that changed colour like Bay's.

Baby rainbows shot through the water jets. When Nell laughed with abandon, she looked five years younger. She and Iris had both inherited the blue-eyed-blonde-hair combo from me, and the Bissett-Lee strong jawline, passed down through my mother's bloodline. My mother liked to remind me that it was too square on me and yet perfect on Nell. It gave her a grown-up face, framing her soft, pretty, blossoming features. But she was still a child. I feared that modelling could take what was left of that innocence. My college years in London studying millinery had opened my eyes to the fashion industry in a way that had made me want to shut them tight again.

The brass handle of the conservatory door rattled. Nell had still not mastered the pull-back-hold-and-twist manoeuvre – even though she had lived in this house since she was two years old and had come in and out of that door twenty times a day with requests for Ribena or biscuits. I dried my hands and went to open it. Dom was standing behind her, reading the flyer, oblivious to Nell's struggle. We had disagreed about this conservatory for years. Dom wanted rid of it, saying it was falling down. It was true that the frame had woodworm and the panes were loose, but I loved using it as my workshop, as long as I plugged in the blow heater and wore lots of cardigans, even in summer. And it doubled as a quirky dining room when we had guests.

'Hi, Mum,' Nell said. Her smile was lopsided and hesitant, and I immediately dreaded the confrontation.

Dom's trainers squelched over the kitchen floor and he sat himself down next to Iris on the sofa in his damp, moss-splattered jeans. It had been my mistake to choose light grey cushions. With the money from a small windfall from my great-aunt's will, I had become starry-eyed about a new sofa's potential to transform our chaotic living habits into those of a neat, minimalist family, as seen in Scandinavian design magazines. How naïve! We had also bought a flat-screen television and a woodburner with the money. The flat screen was a little too large for the small space, and I often got a crooked neck after a film, but the woodburner had revolutionised the winters. Every year, as soon as the first autumn leaf fell, I built a fire and felt less depressed about the encroaching darkness.

'You never said it was Take One models,' Dom said to me.

'Didn't I?'

'You said it was some weirdo with white hair.'

'Oh. I thought I'd mentioned it.'

'He was blond!' Nell said.

Dom got up from the sofa and sat on the bar stool next to her, leaving behind a wet brown patch on the cushion. 'I think it's worth a trip up to London to meet them. Don't you?' he said.

I didn't want to explain in front of Nell the reasons why modelling made me uneasy. I preferred to discuss those fears with Dom alone.

'I'm just a bit worried that it's quite a lot to take on in her GCSE year,' I said, rather half-heartedly.

Bay came in and almost sat down on the wet patch. She noticed it just in time and settled at Iris's feet instead, having tidied away some old newspapers, resting her phone on her knees and scrolling, endlessly scrolling. 'Year 11 is full on, Nell,' she said. 'Don't you remember how stressed I was?'

Nell didn't turn round when she replied. 'All I want is to go and meet them and see what the deal is, that's all.'

'The deal is,' Bay retorted, 'that the modelling industry is full of pretentious pri...' she looked at Iris and rethought, 'prats, and you'd go on loads of castings and loads of shoots with weird, druggy, skinny models, and because you're only fifteen, Anna would have to give up her life and chaperone you everywhere, and even though they say you'd never skip school, if there was a great job paying loads of money, of course you'd skip school. And if you skip school in Year 11, your GCSEs will suffer, for sure.'

'My GCSEs won't suffer,' Nell said quietly, tight-jawed, picking at her cuticles. Her right knee jiggled up and down. The tension of earlier was still there between them.

Iris laughed out loud again. With her earphones on, she was oblivious to the edginess of our conversation.

'Okay, you two,' I said, silently agreeing with Bay. 'Dad and I will discuss all this later.' I dropped teabags into five mugs, glancing over to Dom, who was looking at his phone again.

'Their website's impressive,' he said.

Nell untucked her hair from behind her ears. 'I'd never skip school, Mum. Promise.'

'It's a big decision. For all of us,' I said. 'Especially if Bay's right about the chaperoning. And remember, Bay's got her A levels coming up, too, and I've only just started earning from my hats again.' I felt it was safer to stick to the logistical issues for now.

'It wouldn't affect Bay! And I wouldn't ever let it get in the way of your hats,' Nell said.

Last summer, Nell and Bay had helped me clear out the conservatory and fill it with my millinery equipment. We had lugged in my Victorian sewing desk, picked up at a car boot sale for £20, and

placed my hat block and trimming turntable on top. Underneath
it I had arranged my various felts in the drawers. They had sifted
through my three hatboxes, where I kept my woodblocks, felt
hoods, rolls of Petersham for the trim, silk for lining and a box
of feathers. When they had commented on how beautiful they
thought my sketches were, I had been ridiculously grateful. I didn't
know why, but making hats made me happy inside, and they had
always recognised that.

'Your dad and I will discuss it later,' I repeated gently, looking
to Nell and then to Dom, hoping he would back me up, for now
at least. Until we had discussed it properly.

But his lips tightened and he said to Nell, 'Look, I'll take you
into London myself, we'll scope out the agency, and then if you
like them and you promise to do all your schoolwork, you can
maybe do some modelling in the holidays. Okay?'

Nell squealed and threw her arms around him. 'Really, Dad?
Oh my God!'

My stomach seized up. Beyond Nell and Dom I could see Bay's
mouth draw in like Dom's. Her shaky little fingers tugged at the
shorn back of her head. She and Dom were the spit of each other,
with those big ever-changing green eyes of theirs and their pursed
pouts. Sometimes she wore her black hair swept back in a similar
style to his and she'd look appealingly androgynous, but now it
flopped over half of her small face.

'Oh. There's no milk,' I said. 'I'll just pop out and get some.'

'Do you want me to get it for you, Anna?' Bay called out after
me. She was always helping out, but now I needed to be alone.
For everyone's sake.

'No, it's okay, darling. I'm happy to go.'

Nell bounded up behind me as I was getting the house keys.
'You're not angry with me, are you?'

'No, of course not,' I said, unable to meet her eye.

'You are! I know you are!'

'I'm not, darling, I promise you.'

'I never want anything to get in the way of your hats. Especially as you're doing so well now.'

'I know that, poppet. It's not about my hats.'

'Anyway, they might not even want me. David said there were no guarantees.'

'If you went along, I'd want you to get in, silly.'

'I can still tell in your voice that you're cross.'

I picked up a strand of her hair. 'Stop worrying about me, poppet. I'm not cross with you, I promise.'

Nell glanced over her shoulder at the closed kitchen door. 'Don't be cross with Dad either,' she whispered.

'I won't. I'll be back in a minute.'

My body was a cage. Anger stalked behind its steely bars. I walked towards the village shop and noticed that I still had my slippers on. I couldn't turn back. If I saw Dom's face, it would unlock me. I needed to calm down before I could set eyes on him again.

It was still light outside, and warm. The sun was low behind the old oak tree, casting a vast shadow across the grass and across my mind.

Dom had undermined me, like giving Nell sweets after I had said no. He had made a unilateral decision about her childhood and about her future and to hell with my opinion, to hell with how the changes in Nell's life might affect the whole family.

We had been through too much to unbalance us now.

In the corner shop, Matthew was unpacking magazines from two large boxes.

'Hi, Anna,' he said, standing up and smiling at my slippers.

Matthew was tall, with strawberry-blond hair. He wore black-rimmed glasses that were always wonky due to his uneven ears, and had a line in rock-logo T-shirts. He hadn't been at the village school with Bay and Nell, but the three of them had been great friends when they were little because of all the time I spent with his mother. While Viv and I had put the world to rights over hundreds of cups of tea, alternating whose garden or kitchen we'd chat in, the kids had spent hours biking and camp-building in the woods, or watching DVDs on a loop above Viv's garage, or eating the sweets that were meant for the shop's shelves. Nell was still great friends with Matthew. Bay less so. Ten-year-old Matthew had given Bay a Valentine's card telling her he loved her. She had given him one back saying *I think I love you too (but I'm not really sure)*. Whenever I came into the shop with her, he would turn a strawberry tone to match his hair.

I placed the milk on the counter and then added a bar of chocolate and a bottle of red wine.

'Home from uni already?' I asked.

He nodded and smiled. Small talk wasn't a strength of Matthew's.

'Your mum cracking the whip, is she?'

'You want to see the scars?' he said with a shy smile.

I was glad that Viv was my best friend rather than my mother. She was tough on Matthew, and there had been times when I had wondered whether he might rebel against her or fall apart under the pressure. He had done neither and her pushiness had paid off. Right now, his brain was probably swirling with cell formations and biological equations. His future would involve a high-paid job in a laboratory somewhere, top secret maybe. He was the kind of person who was likely to go through life being underestimated by everyone except his mother and his colleagues.

'Is she about?' I asked, hoping to have a chat, or a rant.

'They've gone to the cash and carry.'

'Remind her I'm coming over next Tuesday with half a bottle of gin,' I said as I left, wishing I could fast-forward to our evening together. Ever since we had met, on the doorstep of 20 Lower Road, while I hugged the welcome basket of food she'd just thrust into my arms, we hadn't stopped talking.

'Only half a bottle?' Matthew enquired.

'Cheeky,' I said, slotting the chocolate and the wine – oh, and the milk! – into my bag-for-life. 'Bye, love. See you when this runs out.'

I waved goodbye and headed back across the green. As I walked, I broke off a piece of chocolate.

Modelling would force Nell to grow up before she was ready, and I was keen to persuade Dom of this. Surely it was sensible for us to consider together the industry's reputation for anorexia and drugs, and whether the vanity and the superficiality of chasing fame would change Nell, distract her from her studies. Or whether the inevitable rejections I'd heard about might eat into her confidence. Did she need all that in her young life?

The chocolate was disappearing into my mouth too quickly.

Every moment of the girls' childhoods was precious. I wished I could freeze time and keep them in the embrace of family life forever. I knew all about growing up too fast. As did Bay.

As much as Dom might not want to think about Bay in this decision, we had to include her in the equation. Her stress levels were always in the balance and her upcoming A levels were another burden. Although there had been a wariness and worldliness in her advice to Nell earlier, a protective big-sisterly instinct, I suspected there was more to it. If we scratched Bay, just a little, turmoil was never far below her thin, pale skin.

Had Dom really not considered this?

Before I reached home, I had eaten the whole chocolate bar and stuffed the evidence of the empty wrapper into our wheelie bin. At least I had resisted cracking open the bottle of wine. I needed my wits about me to undo Dom's promise to take Nell to London.

CHAPTER FOUR

2012

Nell had wolfed down her lunch of chicken nuggets, rice and peas, but Bay was still eating. She skewered one pea with her fork, then put it into her mouth and chewed on it for so long Nell wanted to scream. There were at least a thousand more peas left.

'Come on,' she whispered, jiggling her knee under the table, 'hurry up, just stuff them in or Matthew might leave.'

Nell was keen to go outside and mess about on their bikes in the woods. They'd built the best den ever with Matthew and he had promised to bring his dad's tarpaulin over. Apparently he had learned from his dad how to fix it to trees.

'Bay can take as long as she likes,' Anna said.

Did mums have supersonic hearing? Nell wondered.

'It's just Matthew said to meet him there at twelve, and it's half past now. Look!' Nell pointed to the wall clock and then frowned at Bay, who she knew was slow-eating on purpose. Bay had told Anna that she loved playing outside, but it was a big fat lie. She always sat about and shivered and complained about getting dirty and then painted stupid pink lipstick on her cheeks to make it look like she'd been running about.

'If Matthew's not there, you can knock on Viv's door and get him, I'm sure she won't mind,' Anna said.

Nell knew this would be okay with Viv because Viv was her mum's best friend and she was like an auntie to Nell and Iris (and, she guessed, to Bay now too). For the record, Nell's actual auntie – Auntie Karen – was crackers and way too skinny.

As Nell began to relax about the time, Bay picked up her dessert spoon, scooped up at least a hundred peas and shovelled them all into her mouth at once. Mashed-up peas oozed out with her spit, and Nell watched on in horror, thinking how gross it was. Then Bay gagged and sicked up her whole lunch onto her plate. Even grosser. She wiped her mouth on the back of her hand and blinked at Nell, looking as green as the peas.

'Oh, Bay! Oh darling heart!' Anna said, rushing over with a napkin, shooting Nell a disapproving look as she mopped up Bay's face. 'Let's get you into some clean clothes.'

Before following Bay upstairs, she turned to Nell and said, under her breath, 'That was very naughty of you, rushing her like that.'

Nell had been holding her hand over her nose because of the smell, but she let it drop to defend herself. 'But Mum…'

The sick pong rushed up into her head, making her want to vomit too.

Anna spoke in her quick, angry mum voice. 'She'd do *anything* to impress you and you know it.'

Nell had never asked for that. Since Bay had come to live with them, life had become extremely complicated. All she wanted was to go camp-building with Matthew. She wouldn't be able to go now, which made her feel hot and cross.

While Anna saw to Bay, Nell sat on the step outside the back door with her arms folded tight over her chest and scowled.

Much to her amazement, her mum came outside and kissed her on the forehead and said, 'Sorry for getting angry.'

Nell felt a tiny bit less cross. 'I'm sorry I made Bay be sick,' she said, trying her best to sound completely un-cross.

'Don't worry, darling. Now off you go, you don't want to miss Matthew. But say goodbye to Bay first.'

Nell couldn't believe her luck. 'Will she be okay?'

'She'll be fine.'

But when Nell saw her tiny big sister lying on the sofa in front of the telly, pasty and sweaty after being sick, she felt sorry for her. When Bay looked up at her, her swollen eyelids hung down in the corners, as though pulled by mini weights, and Nell knew she hadn't meant to spoil her day with Matthew.

Being sick was probably worse than missing out on camp-building.

So Nell found a blanket and snuggled in next to her. They watched *Beauty and the Beast*, and at the end of the film, Nell cried because it made her so happy. And Bay laughed at her for being such a big soppy-pants.

CHAPTER FIVE

Anna

A few hours after my angry walk to get chocolate and wine – oh, and milk! – I was finally alone with Dom. The family movie, starring talking chihuahuas wearing bling, followed by a fraught hour cajoling the three girls into their rooms had done nothing to mellow my mood.

'I'm going to crash,' Dom said.

My tongue itched with undeniable gospel truths that I wanted to preach at him, passionately. I was determined to change his mind about Nell modelling, keen to talk to him about Bay; remind him how this decision could affect the family dynamic as a whole. But I knew I had to go in gently. How I handled our relationship was a strange inversion of how we had fallen in love. We had met soon after he had separated from Suki, Bay's mother. Wanting to show him that love didn't need to be so full of torment, I had immersed myself in what he needed, studying every nuance of his mood, giving my whole self to him, and there had been romance in that. Now, I was reading him carefully and prioritising his feelings to save an argument, which was like a quiet, internal mediation, a way of holding myself back, but I believed it was more important and steadying than romance and its headiness. This was how our marriage worked. This was how well I knew him, how we had grown together to function better.

'What? No nookie?' I grinned, hoping it concealed my real mood.

He gave me one of those smiles that reminded me of when we'd first met: vulnerable and cheeky. 'I'm cutting my toenails.'

'Nice.' I laughed, a little forced, waggling an empty mug at him. 'Second best, then?'

'I'm bloody knackered,' he said.

'We need to talk, Dom.'

He sighed. 'Okay. Put the kettle on.'

'The whole thing is really worrying me,' I said, taking out another mug. So far today I had drunk six cups of tea. I should cut down, but it went so well with a crisis.

'Are you overthinking it?' he said.

'Maybe, but I know a bit about that world, remember. The models we used for our end-of-year shows were messed up, and they all took lines of coke before they went on.'

I wasn't sure *all* of them had, but I remember one girl who did. The other girls had been more interested in the champagne.

He guffawed. 'Your university fashion show makes you the authority on modelling?'

'No, course not. But some of my friends did end up in the fashion business.'

He yawned. 'And what did they say about it?'

'How bitchy everyone was. I've told you about Katy,' I said, reminding him of my St Martin's friend who had gone on to work for a major fashion house, where the head designer had projected gay porn onto the walls of their offices. And someone else came to mind, but I couldn't bring him up with Dom. 'But also, anorexia is a major problem,' I added.

'Nell likes chocolate brownies too much.'

'Dom, seriously, that really is something to think about. The superficiality of the whole business is just the worst. I mean, those models are so thin. Nell is absolutely gorgeous, but she isn't all skin and bone, and we don't want her to be, do we?'

'That scout guy didn't mention it, did he?'

'He made it clear that the bookers make the ultimate decision.'

'Well, let's let them make it then.'

'And you're not worried at all?'

'You just don't want her to grow up. That's what this is about.'

'I *do* want her to grow up, but in her own time. Not with this big thing thrust at her all of a sudden.'

I had mentioned every single potential pitfall I could think of except Bay. Why couldn't I mention her fragility? The thought tapped at the back of my mind, bothering me more than any of my misgivings about a world I actually knew very little about.

'I get that there are risks,' Dom said irritably, as though they were too obvious to talk about. 'But what about the money she could earn?'

'The *money*?'

He pulled his hair back. 'Let's face it, if she wants to go to university, she'll have debts up to her eyeballs before she's even turned twenty-one. And without a leg-up, she might never get on the property ladder like we did. I dunno, why shouldn't she use her looks? They're an asset, like being born brainy, or sporty, or with a bloody trust fund. I don't really understand why you'd want to stop her from getting a head start. Just think, she could save up for university, or buy a car, or put down a deposit on a flat. We don't have the money to give her any of that stuff. At the end of the day, her beauty is a gift, right?'

My own impassioned views receded a little. It seemed he had been thinking of Nell's future just as much as I had been. I mulled over his reasoning. If I went on about the dangers of the industry now, it would seem churlish, like I was catastrophising in the light of Dom's ambition for her.

It was true enough that we were strapped for cash. I thought of the four maxed-out credit cards and the overdraft that would get filled up to zero on Dom's payday, and the penny-by-penny calculations in the supermarket. What toiletries I would sacrifice for a bottle of cheap wine on Friday nights; how low I could go on the quality of meat; how many tinned basics we could buy without losing out on nutrition. The money I made on my hats went into paying for the girls' after-school clubs, and petrol. We made ends meet and we got by quite well – we even managed a week at good-quality campsites in France every year – but there was never any spare change. Money coming into the family rather than haemorrhaging out would not be unwelcome.

'I hadn't thought of it like that,' I said, holding back my scratchy fear about Bay and her delicate emotional state.

He took his mug of tea from me. 'Nell's a good girl. She won't get into trouble. And she'll have you to look after her.' We sat down next to each other on the sofa, with our legs stretched out and our heads resting on the cushions behind us.

'She *is* a good girl,' I agreed.

'Better than *you* were at school.'

'I was very good!'

'Not when you were snogging me behind the sports hall.'

We laughed, and then fell into a companionable silence.

Most nights, we drank tea together on the sofa before bed and talked about the day. We didn't talk an awful lot about our own problems; it was all about the kids. Everything that bonded us and everything that threatened us centred around the three girls. Other couples liked to plot and plan their breaks for freedom – their evenings and weekends and holidays away without their children – but Dom and I didn't crave that separation from them.

I guessed he was thinking about Nell now. Equally, he could have been thinking about his golf handicap or a town-planning blueprint at work – he had more separation than I did.

For certain he was not clocking through every single vomit-soaked top of Bay's that I had washed, every wet patch on my shoulder made by her tears, or every night of stroking her head

after one of her violent dreams. How desperately I did not want to
go back to those days when Bay had not known that she deserved
to be loved unconditionally, whatever she did. Those days when
she had brought her challenging behaviour into our family unit
and unsettled us, when none of us had anticipated how her past
would tear at our hearts.

I remembered standing at the bathroom mirror with her as
she pulled at her face, disfiguring it, telling me how ugly she was
and how much she hated herself. Helping her to build up her
self-worth from nothing had been hard going. Today's events
would have pushed some of those entrenched insecurities right
to the surface. Nell's beauty had been starkly acknowledged by an
outsider, like a public stamp of approval on her forehead, setting
her apart. It would be tricky for any teenage sister to process, but
they were close in age, only eighteen months apart, and Bay was
sensitive, and I couldn't help feeling that our mismanagement of
this situation could be as disastrous for her as it would be for Nell.

Turning that damaged little girl's life around was one of our
proudest achievements as a family. We couldn't undo our hard
work now. I couldn't go back to how it was before. I had to bring
it up with Dom.

'What about Bay?' I said quietly, turning my head.

He looked at me. 'What about her?'

'She's so sensitive, and she's struggled so much. I'm worried
she'll get jealous and feel like the ugly sister again. You know? And
slide backwards. She won't, will she?'

Dom rubbed his boyish cheek and ruffled his hair into a quiff.
'She'll be fine. She's going to be seventeen in a few weeks. She's
not a little kid any more.'

I couldn't deny that technically she was a beautiful young
woman now, but in my heart, she would always be the little chick
I'd nursed back to health. Yet I had blinked, and she had grown
up. It seemed like yesterday when the rumours of Dom's battle to

keep her had reached me through a mutual school friend. At the time, I had just turned thirty and was bookkeeping in the cramped basement of a small Notting Hill milliner, feeling lost about my future. I had sent Dom a direct message on Facebook to check on him and had been surprised when he suggested we hook up. I had been worried it was too soon after his separation from Suki, conscious of our history as boyfriend and girlfriend at school, but he had needed a friend. We'd met in a pub in Crouch End. He had nursed a pint and shown me the photographs on his phone of his pale-faced, dark-haired baby girl, alone with her mother, whom I had learned was neglectful and unpredictable and cruel. That pale face had haunted my dreams. Not only had I wanted to save Dom, I had wanted to save Bay too.

'Seventeen, my God, I know. It's hard to believe,' I said, breathing out. 'How did she grow up so quickly?'

'She's more grown up than the rest of us sometimes,' he said. Then he delivered his most persuasive argument. 'And come on, Anna, it's not fair to hold Nell back because of how Bay may or may not feel, is it?'

I knew he was right. 'I would never want to hold her back,' I conceded.

I endeavoured to treat the girls equally, but if I was honest with myself, perhaps I sometimes overcompensated when it came to Bay, to make up for what she had lost in those early years with Suki. And this tendency wasn't always fair on Nell.

The words 'Let's take Nell up to London then' came out of my mouth, and I tried to believe it was the right thing to do.

Dom sat up straight and massaged his knees. 'After all this, she might not even get in.'

CHAPTER SIX

Bay

'Like the 'fit?' Nell said, cocking her hip, showing me the skirt that she wanted to wear to the modelling agency today. It was too short, but I tried to smile.

'You look amazing,' I said.

'Not too slutty?'

For a second, Nell's smile had the power to hold me up and make me believe that everything was going to be okay. But then it passed, and my certain knowledge that it wasn't going to be okay came flooding back in. My heartbeat fluttered, agitated. I was angry with Dad for railroading Anna and allowing Nell to go to this appointment. It was typical of him. Anna was right to worry about Nell's schoolwork, and it was sensible of her to consider the troubles of the modelling industry, which was rife with drugs and anorexia.

'Not one bit. It looks really cool,' I said, filming her.

'Oh my God. I'm so nervous,' she said, texting as she spoke. 'Jade's just posted this on her status.'

I stopped filming. She showed me a selfie of Jade and Mint, her best friends, who were girl-next-door pretty but always too heavily made-up. 'FOMO?' I said.

'It's the first inset day I've not gone shopping with them.'

She posted a sad face underneath the photograph of Jade and Mint at the train station. Most teenage girls would have posted a happy face or a thumbs-up, but Nell could never hide her true feelings. There wasn't a side to Nell.

'You don't have to go today, you know. It's not too late,' I said.

Her arms flopped by her sides. 'The whole thing is probably a total waste of time.'

She wasn't fishing. She didn't see herself as others saw her. It was like a blindness to her own beauty; an innocence that charmed everyone she met, yet a danger to her.

'You think?'

She slumped on the bed and looked shyly up at me. 'After all the fuss I made, I'm not sure I even want to do it now.'

I had once seen a YouTube clip of models before and after make-up and lighting. Before, they were pale and bony and spotty. After, they were goddesses. On the bed, even in a slouch, Nell looked like a goddess. Being her sister was hard. Next to her, I was small and uptight, somehow lesser and insignificant. I thumbed the Take One flyer that she had left on her desk. 'They're all so beautiful, aren't they.'

'I could bail. Mum would be happy.'

'You could.'

She shot up to standing. 'Can I see that photo you took?'

'It's a video,' I said. The lighting was poor. She looked fleshy in ways she wasn't.

'Oh my GOD!' she cried. 'I look fat and horrible!'

'No you don't,' I lied.

She ripped off the skirt and replaced it with a mid-calf floral one with a slit up one leg, teaming it with a black logo T-shirt. It was better on her and I suddenly knew that the agency would take her on. I didn't want it to happen. It would unsettle all of us. And I had grown to rely heavily on feeling settled.

'Will you do my eyes, *please?*'

'They said you have to go with a clean face,' I reminded her.

'Just a little bit won't hurt. Come on. It'll make a big difference.'

It took a lot of concentration to steady my hand as I painted on a sharp eyeliner flick above her baby-blue eyes. I hated the eternal shake of my hands. When I had finished, she said, 'So cool! I love it, sis. Take a pic, will you? Dad wanted one of me all dressed up.'

'I'll film you in the garden.'

Nell twirled in her skirt and the sunlight turned her hair gold. When I showed her the clip, she said, 'I look *so* much better! Thanks, Bay. You're the best sister ever. What would I do without you?'

I felt paralysed by the thought of being without Nell or Anna or Dad or even Iris one day; that they might stop being my safe place. I didn't want it to be an inevitability, like death. Nell threw her long arms around me and I tensed. Hugs were difficult for me, but it didn't mean I didn't appreciate them. In spite of being the oldest, I felt protected in her arms. Perhaps I needed this, like some people needed food.

Over her shoulder, I could see Anna through the kitchen window. The similarities between Anna and Nell lay in their eyes, which were open and engaging and trustworthy. Anna's face was squarer than Nell's, and her features, framed by her flyaway blonde hair, were uniform and sweet and pretty rather than exaggerated and beautiful like Nell's. I would have chosen to have Anna's looks over Nell's. I had always wanted to look like Anna's daughter. She gave me a big blue-eyed wink behind Nell's back, probably thinking I had somehow influenced the skirt choice.

'You're welcome,' I said, even though I hadn't done a thing to help.

I reminded myself that everyone knew they would die one day and that most people lived life as though they might not. Why not live life as though I would forever be nestled under the sheltering wing of my family, burrowed and snug? My heart slowed.

Nell let go of me. 'It's funny, because I thought you were on Mum's side on this.'

'I'm always looking out for you, sis,' I said.

Iris came up to us then and showed us a YouTube clip of a cat trying to catch a butterfly. She laughed her head off when the cat got spooked and the butterfly began chasing the cat. It looked that way, at least. Obviously, butterflies never chased cats.

CHAPTER SEVEN

Anna

Nell and I were sitting very close together on a long purple sofa in a white reception area. I squeezed her hand. Our palms were clammy.

'Bay's funny. Look what she sent me,' Nell said, showing me a meme on her phone of a little American actress from an eighties TV show saying, 'You got this, dude!'

'You *have* got this,' I said, trying to sound casual and confident, ever so relieved that Bay seemed to be coping with the notion of Nell becoming a model. I had made time for a chat with her before bed, away from Nell and Dom. Her qualms had been similar to my own, but we'd decided to be level-headed and keep an open mind. This morning she had been very supportive – the floral skirt had been her choice. 'We're here to check *them* out, remember, not the other way around,' I added to Nell.

Nell began typing something back to Bay. 'God, Mum. You've told me that about a million times.'

Repeating it about a million times had obviously undone the casual air I was trying so hard to create. I wished I could feel casual for her, but I was too nervous. There had been many tests in Nell's past that had been disappointing for her – Year 6 SATs, basketball team try-outs, Grade 1 guitar and others – but this test was not about how hard she had worked or how much she had to offer; it was about what she looked like: the lucky genetic mix. A rejection might mean she was less upset because she'd had no input in how her genes had come together; or more upset because they would be rejecting the very *fact* of her. I felt a lurch of anxiety and checked my watch. Being here didn't feel right. Behind Nell's cool make-up and clothes, I could only see the child in her; the Nell who had been flat-chested and four inches smaller the year before last. Over the past eighteen months, she had started her periods, started dating boys and started going out at the weekends to parties. And now this. There had been too much starting in too little time, and I couldn't keep up. *Slow down, Nell, slow down.*

The receptionist caught my eye. She took a pencil out of the doughnut bun on top of her head and pressed the buttons of the phone with the rubber end.

'Sorry about the wait. I'm just trying Ian again,' she said, picking up the receiver and tapping the edge of the desk with her two-inch acrylic nails.

I squeezed Nell's knee. 'You okay?' I whispered.

'Fine, yeah,' she said, applying another layer of lip gloss. Her knee jiggled up and down.

She clicked her phone on again and I stared up at the floor-to-ceiling poster of a supermodel whose name I couldn't remember. Her thick, shiny hair was lovely, and I thought of the creatives behind the scenes who would have been responsible for the image. The photographer, the make-up artist, the stylist, the hairdresser. Mostly I thought about the hairdresser. A hairdresser like Billy Young. Someone I had once known. Through a mutual friend, I'd heard that he came to London often, and travelled all over Europe as a session stylist. It wasn't impossible to imagine he was in the city somewhere right now.

Nell caught my eye and smiled nervously at me. I put thoughts of Billy aside. Billy had existed before marriage and children and country living, and he had stopped existing after marriage and children and country living.

After twenty minutes more of waiting, the receptionist got up to see what was happening. Warped shapes wobbled over the mirrored glass of the buildings on the opposite side of the road. Fear that we had come on the wrong day prompted me to recheck my email from Ian. It confirmed today's date and mentioned how lovely it had been to chat and how much he was looking forward to meeting us. He had been easy to talk to, making me feel I would be popping in for an informal chat. It felt less like that now.

'I wish Dad was here,' Nell said.

'He's really sorry he couldn't make it.' This was true. He had been called to an emergency meeting with a residents' association and a local councillor about the alarming number of trees that were being felled on a development in a protected woodland area adjacent to a new site. If he had not shown up, the fate of a majestic hundred-year-old oak tree might rest on his conscience.

Nell jerked her head closer to her phone screen and scrolled manically. 'I can't believe it!' she said, agog.

'What's happened?'

She shoved the screen into my face. 'Look!'

I tried to decipher the long thread of Snapchat posts from her best friends, Jade and Mint. They had sent her a mirror selfie in some public toilets somewhere, with a good luck message scrawled in pink across the image. It seemed friendly enough.

'That's not good?' I asked tentatively.

I was never sure. The endless monitoring of her social media posts and the upsets after a nasty message from a so-called friend ruled her moods. It was ironic that only last week, she and I had been discussing the vanity of mirror selfies, and yet here we were in a modelling agency, where surely vanity was vital.

'No, it's so not good! I told Jade to literally swear she wouldn't tell Mint where I was.'

'Why do you not want her to know?'

'Mum! You don't get it!'

'Explain, then.' I had always tried to 'get it', and even when I did, I had learned not to criticise her best friends. In spite of how competitive they were, and how they played with Nell's feelings on a daily basis, she was fiercely loyal to them even when she was annoyed with them. I had never understood why she gravitated towards girls who were so manipulative.

'She's such a B-word, and she'll totally take the piss out of me if I don't get taken on. It'll be *so* embarrassing.'

'If she does, then she's not a very good friend,' I said.

A small man stepped out of the lift. I wasn't sure why, but I hoped he wasn't Ian. There was nothing overtly unpleasant about his appearance. He was average-looking and youngish. He walked with a quick and light step, like he might dart off to the side, changing his mind about meeting us. His hair was cropped close to his head, and his black glasses were too heavy, distracting almost, as though his face was less important than the style of the frames. His small, piercing, slightly mean eyes scanned Nell's face with unnerving speed as he shook her hand.

'Hi, Nell. Hi, Anna,' he said, smiling. His top two incisors pointed inwards. 'I'm so sorry I'm late.' Freshly smoked cigarettes and the outdoors were on his breath.

He held my hand with both of his, like we were firm friends and about to embark on a long journey together. His eyes darted back to Nell's face, and up and down her body. I could tell he was used to working fast, making a big decision in a limited amount of time. A fierce protectiveness leapt up inside me.

'Step into the madhouse!' Ian said, with a sharp little hand movement.

As he walked in front of us, leading us past two units of desks divided by a partition wall to a glass box of a room stacked with actual boxes, I noticed a packet of cigarettes sticking out of the top of his back pocket. The pink, slimy bulge of a cancerous tumour showed on the warning label.

He offered us tea or coffee. I chose black coffee, which was delivered in a colourful mug by a woman of roughly my age with a thick dark fringe and wide denim jeans that I wished I owned. She smiled warmly at me and held Nell's eyes for a split second too long when she gave her her cup of tea.

'So, how are you feeling, Nell?' Ian grinned, leaning on his elbows.

Nell laughed. 'Nervous.' Her wide smile lit up her face, but I noticed her knee starting up its jig.

'Nothing to be nervous about. We're like a big family here. Tell me all about yourself.'

I felt my limbs stiffen and I wished I could answer for her. I wanted him to look past her looks to see how much more there was to offer. But it wasn't relevant to Ian that she loved mountain-biking; that she was in the basketball team; that she had won her school election as a minority candidate and inspired a record voting turnout; that her enthusiasm for life could turn the laziest soul into a zealot; that she still cried at the end of *Beauty and the Beast*; that she had a heart of gold. He didn't need to know those things. His job was to judge her on the least interesting, most superficial facet of her.

'I'm at school, I guess. Not right now, obviously. It's an inset day. And I'm here.' She laughed again, making up for her haphazard reply.

He smiled. 'And your mum tells me you're taking your GCSEs next year. Is that right?'

'Yes. I'm kind of worried about that. And this. Going together. If you know what I mean.'

'I do know what you mean. I think it's really important you take your studies seriously. I have two nephews around your age, and I totally get it. But honestly, you have nothing to worry about. Although some of my girls do give a small amount of school time to modelling, it's totally up to you and how you want to do it.'

My eyes kept darting up to the poster on the wall of girls' faces. Beautiful faces. Everywhere you turned there were photographs of skinny, line-free, high-cheekboned, wide-eyed beautiful young women. Staring back at me from stacks of cards or from torn-out magazine pages. Through the window of the office, I could see a bank of ten desks and flat-screen computers. More beautiful faces on the screen savers. Behind the desks, there were rows and rows of Perspex shelves displaying cards of more beautiful girls. I guessed Nell would have one of those cards if she joined. The sophisticated images were incongruous under the banner of 'New Faces'. I found it hard to believe they were under eighteen, but I had read on the Take One website that all girls on the New Faces desk were under eighteen.

I became hyper-aware of my own appearance, and it wasn't faring well. In this environment, where everyone seemed to make an effort to look good, I wanted to wear a hat to hide behind. But I had changed over the years, so much so, I realised, that wearing a hat would feel like walking around with an upturned saucepan on my head: heavy on my head and drawing attention to me for all the wrong reasons. The consolation was that I wasn't being looked at in the way that Nell was. I was being seen but not taken in. Like a background crowd in a film, I was essential to the process but not very interesting. That suited me just fine.

Ian's long speech about girls who achieved Oxford degrees while modelling was coming to an end. He had taken it a bit far, but I was pleased that education was important to him – as long as he wasn't spinning us a line.

'And if we were to take her on, you'd be her chaperone, Anna?'

'I'm not sure exactly how much time it would take up.'

'There'd probably be one or two castings a week, roughly, sometimes none, but I can't tell you yet how often she'll work. Hopefully loads! All round the world, maybe!'

I nodded slowly, both eyebrows a little stretched, thinking how much simpler it would be to continue hiding away in the countryside, being a mum with saggy knees and flyaway hair, making my funeral hats for old ladies and quite contented with all of that. To settle the rising panic about how this schedule might affect the whole family, I reminded myself of why we had allowed Nell to come along here today.

Dom's argument in favour of it had tapped into a deeper regret of my own. Thinking back now to those days when all my dreams of being a milliner with my own label – *Anna B.*, in swirling writing with a large full stop – had been ahead of me, I looked to Nell, young and excitable, and realised that I should allow her to have her own dreams. Modelling wasn't what I had wanted for her, but I should be open-minded. She was her own person and she had her own journey, and I didn't want that journey to be interrupted by my fears.

'Yes, I think I can be her chaperone,' I said, and I smiled at Nell, wondering how I would make it work logistically, deciding to think about it later. Nell rewarded me with a large smile. Her eyes were saying *Thank you, Mummy!* and I wanted to counter her rising excitement with a reality check: Ian might not take you on.

Ian said, 'Great. If it's okay with you, Collette will take some measurements, and a few Polaroid shots, and then I'll have a little discussion with my team and let you know. Does that sound okay?'

Nell was placed in front of a white wall in the open-plan office while the young Collette took some digital photos of her with a small pink camera. Then she took us to a room and closed the blinds.

She waved a tape measure at us. 'Okay, sorry about this. Just lift your arms, we'll do your waist first.'

Gingerly Nell raised her arms.

There was no need for her to worry about her measurements in the way that I myself would have legitimately needed to worry. Her figure was beautiful. Womanly hips and a tiny waist. But she had always been self-conscious about her body. On holiday, she never wore bikinis. Even before puberty, she had started having baths on her own. To this day, I still missed sitting on the loo next to her making pretend frothy coffees with the bubbles.

Thinking further back, I guess I had taken for granted my own youthful body, fretting about my best friend's figure, which I had thought was better than mine. I wondered whether, when I turned seventy, I would look back at my forty-five-year-old body and envy it. Not one of my favourite thoughts.

Collette held her tape measure around Nell's breasts, and Nell flinched as though she had been touched inappropriately. My diversionary conversation ran dry.

'Almost done!' Collette said.

There was another poster on the wall in here. The model was ridiculously long and skinny, stretched out alongside a pool in a metallic swimsuit. Nell looked up at her and wrapped her arms around her own waist. A quick glance over her shoulder at me told me she didn't think she had a hope next to that girl on the wall. Topics from a Year 9 talk on mental health awareness sprang to mind: eating disorders, anxiety and depression, self-harm. Words that I had hoped I would never have to think about in relation to Nell.

As Collette marked down Nell's hip size on a form, I was becoming weary of their scrutiny and their questioning of her beauty. I had an urge to jump onto the table and strip naked in solidarity and shout about negative female body image and how advertising campaigns were criminal for feeding young girls' minds with the myth that skin-on-bone was the only way to be beautiful.

'Got any scars, hon?'

'Um, sort of,' she said, almost under her breath, and my heart dropped a few inches in my chest. I didn't know of any scars.

'Whereabouts, hon?' Collette asked.

Nell turned her back on me and I thought she pulled her T-shirt down at the front. 'These, and they go under here, too.'

Collette squinted, getting close to Nell's chest. 'Oh, right, I'm not sure I can even see them.'

'What scars are you talking about?' I asked. Collette glanced up at me, mid-scribble, and I detected a trace of embarrassment.

'They're from ages ago,' Nell said.

'Eye colour?' Collette said.

'Blue,' Nell replied, looking instantly relieved at the change of subject. But I wanted to pull down her top and inspect the marks she had shown Collette.

Collette went through the list of questions about shoe size and piercings and birthmarks and tattoos while I went through the backlist of Nell's falls and scrapes. Most of them had been mountain-bike-related. None that I could remember had caused any scars on her chest.

'Do you have an Instagram account?' Collette asked.

Nell's cheeks coloured. 'I don't really post much.'

'Don't worry. That's fine. What's your username, hon?'

'Bayandnelly – and then a heart emoji.'

'Any hobbies?'

'Mountain-biking and basketball. And I play the electric guitar. Sort of.'

'Cool,' Collette said.

She continued. Allergies. *None.* Dietary requirements? *None.* Parent/guardian name and number. Me! Me! Me! Her mum, who was meant to know everything about her. And yet she had been scarred and I didn't know how. My thoughts froze. Had she harmed herself? Was that why Collette had looked embarrassed?

With last-minute jitters, I let the pen hover over the blank space where I was supposed to write my name and email address. We were not bound to this. She hadn't been asked to join the agency yet. Perhaps I could refuse to fill out the rest of the form and walk Nell right on out of there. I was still in control of her life. She was still a child.

'Is everything okay?' Collette asked me.

'Could you give us a few minutes?' I asked.

'Yeah, sure, hon. Take as long as you like,' she replied, gently closing the door behind her.

'*Seriously*, Mum?' Nell said. Her whole face was contorted in disbelief and exasperation.

'Is this definitely a good idea, Nell?'

She whispered aggressively, 'Yes!'

'I don't know. I'm suddenly worried.'

'Uh! Mum! It's *my life*. I really want this. You can't stop me.'

I didn't want to start anything here, but the fact was, I *could* stop her.

'Can I see those scars, Nell?' I asked quietly.

She flicked her eyes to the ceiling and blew out a loud groan. 'Jesus, Mum. Sometimes I just need some bloody space without you worrying about me all the frickin' time.'

'But what are they? Can't I see them?'

If I were to finish this form, I needed her to tell me that she was safe, that she was in one piece, that she was strong enough for this.

'No! You can't! They're nothing!'

'If they're nothing, why are you being so weird about it?'

'Oh MY GOD.' She grimaced, covered her face and spoke through her fingers. 'Last year, Max dropped hot wax on my boobs during, you know... for fun... and it burned me and left a tiny bit of scarring. That's all. Okay? Happy now?'

I was so shocked and embarrassed, I spluttered through a guffaw. 'Oh!'

Her apple cheekbones were bright. 'I can't believe I had to tell you that.'

'Definitely not something I needed to know,' I said, going a little red myself.

Collette knocked and came back into the room. 'Everything okay?' she asked.

I looked down at the form in front of me and then up at Nell. She nodded, as though coaxing me to finish filling it in. 'Sorry, just having a last-minute panic,' I said to Collette, laughing.

'That's totally understandable,' she said.

My little girl was not little any more. She looked beautiful and nervous and grown up, and I had to admire how brave she was for putting herself out there like this.

My days of being all-powerful, in control of everything she did and wherever she went and whatever she ate, were on their way out. She was fifteen and I had to loosen my grip and allow her the freedom to choose who she wanted to be, albeit with some parental guidance and watchfulness. She was not me, Anna Bissett-Lee – born with a name too glamorous for the person I would become – she was Nell. Nell Hart. Nell Heart-on-Her-Sleeve. Hart by name and by nature. And I wanted that beautiful, passionate heart of hers to lead her towards her dreams. Any ambivalence I had felt about coming here today would have to be shelved. I would continue to monitor the situation, but for now, I wanted her to pass Ian's scrutiny more than I had ever wanted her to pass any music exam or win any sports day race.

I took a deep breath and put my name to the form, endorsing her decision. My own heart fluttered as though a cage had been opened in its cavity, letting a flurry of feelings out into the fresh air.

The simple, cosseted life I had worked so hard to create for my girls, unchallenged and hidden away and safe, seemed to be slipping from me. As though Nell was stepping into the light and dragging me with her.

CHAPTER EIGHT

Nell

Mum and I are waiting in the first room again. Ian comes back in.

'Sorry for the wait,' he says, sitting down. 'I wanted to talk to my colleagues first.'

He pauses and looks at me and I feel more self-conscious than I have all day, and that is saying something.

'We all agree that you're a stunning girl, Nell. But it's a super-competitive business, hon. And…'

Oh no, no, no, no, no, no, no! My stomach twists like a red liquorice twirl. This is the worst. This morning Bay suggested I change my mind, so why didn't I listen to her? Instead of having a laugh with my friends in JD Sports, or biking through the woods with Matthew, I am here in this weird place with an icky, awkward feeling inside, like someone has seen me naked.

Ian! *Stop right now!* In my head, I sing the rest of the words to the Spice Girls' track. Mum sings it in the shower a lot. The Spice Girls started Girl Power, and right now I need Sporty Spice to karate-chop Ian in the gonads to stop him from making his rejection speech.

I pull out my best happy face, refusing to cry and worry Mum and make Ian feel worse about rejecting me. Maybe I should tell him that I don't like the idea of being a model anyway. Or is that rude? Like I'm dissing his business or some shit. When I think about it, *really* think about it, modelling only makes sense to me if it works out easy like Sunday morning (why all the oldie songs, Nell?).

Today has *not* been easy. It has been stressful. All the bookers around the table gave me that bitchy, check-you-out stare, from head to toe and back up again, like teenage girls do, making me feel not good enough. At least Collette was chill. She wasn't judgemental about my waist-to-hip ratio, or whatever. I guess I was like a can of baked beans to her. Mentioning my scars was embarrassing, though. Funny that she could barely see them. All my life I've worried they're really obvious, but maybe not. To be safe, I keep them hidden. Mum hasn't seen me nudie for years. At home, she always knocks before coming into my room. On holiday, I wear a one-piece, telling her it's 'on trend' and that bikinis are *so* last century. Just now, I'm pretty sure she bought the whole Max-wax story. Clever, right?

'I'm not saying we don't want to take you on…' Ian says, knocking his pencil against his lip.

Stop right now. Wait. Hold up. Scroll back. Did I just hear that right? Does that mean he is still considering me? I am all ears.

'It's just, most our girls are on average size 8, which we know is small, but sample sizes are still tiny and clients expect that.'

I think my face literally just caught fire. Jesus. Is he telling me I'm too *fat*? This day is getting worse by the minute.

Mum says, 'She is a perfectly healthy weight.'

She has that voice on, the voice that is a warning to all around her that she might get up and bop someone on the nose if they are not careful. She doesn't get cross much, but when she does, boy, it's hell. I'm not sure what is more embarrassing: my mum talking to Ian in her cross voice or Ian telling me I am too fat to join their agency.

'It's fine. Seriously, I totally understand,' I reply, to stop Mum from saying anything else.

'Oh, hon!' Ian says. 'We don't mean you have to lose weight! No, no, no, no. For some girls it's appropriate, but we think we can market you differently. A kind of antidote to the too-thin girls – who we are super-vigilant about on New Faces, by the way,' he adds quickly. 'If we think a girl isn't a healthy weight, we talk to Mum and make sure they get the help they need. We're like your parents and your therapist wrapped into one!'

I don't laugh, because I am holding my breath. Does this mean he is going to take me on? Jesus, this guy talks a lot. Cut to the chase, boy!

He drops his smile and gets serious again.

'We want to take you on. But you're a risk. I don't want to pretend you're not. It'll either blow up – in a good way – or nothing will happen. We certainly do *not* want you to lose those beautiful curves.'

'So you think I can be a model?' I say.

'I *do* think you can be a model, sweetie. Is that a good thing?'

'Yes. A really good thing. Thank you so much,' I say. I nod a few too many times, feeling happy, and then suddenly I worry about Bay's reaction. I'll probably go on to her about how fat they think I am, to play it down, to make her feel better.

Ian says, 'That's awesome. All of us think you're gorgeous. But – and there is a but – the girls and I have talked about one change we think could work for you. Don't worry, it's nothing too radical.'

Mum and I wait for him to go on.

'We think a fringe would look *a-maz-ing* on you. And if you're up for it, we'll send you to Barrie's for a makeover at his Bond Street salon. How does that sound?'

'A-maz-ing,' I say.

'Mum, you happy?' Ian asks.

'Yes, I'm happy,' she says.

I look at her, and she's smiling – a little weirdly, but hey, I'll take it. I beam one back at her.

'I'll show you around,' Ian says.

As he takes us round, he talks about castings and go-sees and headshots and charts and options and tear sheets and portfolios and composite cards and brands and social media profiles and so much I don't really understand. It is overwhelming, and his words are beginning to wash over my head, even though I know I need to concentrate. At least Mum is. But her smile has become fixed and I recognise it as her mega-stressed-out smile. If Bay was here, she would ask all the right questions, in her cool-as-a-cat way. Bay. Shit. Joining this agency is going to cause some trouble.

Mum and I sit down in a cosy place in Covent Garden where there are old tables and hundreds of cakes. The worry about telling Bay is coming into my head more strongly now that the excitement has died down.

After we order a chocolate eclair and a hot chocolate for me and a cappuccino and an iced bun for Mum, I get a Snapchat text from Bay.

Did you get taken on, sis?

I snap her back.

Yeah! Can you believe it?

She takes ages to reply. I've had time to peel off the chocolate strip on my eclair and spoon out all the cream, ready to eat the choux pastry on its own – don't judge me, it's how I've always eaten them – before she texts back.

You're going to be famous and forget all about me and I wouldn't blame you.

My next bite of the eclair tastes a bit sickly. She sends me another text straight afterwards of a crying-with-laughter emoji face.

I'm so happy for you, sis.

I know it doesn't sound like much, but her texts ruin my journey home. I can't shake off the guilt that has settled over me.

Guilt that she needs me more than I need her. Guilt that I am happy and she is not.

Mum keeps on asking me why I look so worried and I keep telling her I am fine. In the end, I bite her head off and she stops talking, looking at me with that hurt face on. I can't tell her that I have this dragging feeling inside me about Bay.

There is more to my relationship with Bay than anyone else knows. When we fight, it is different to how I fight with other people. For example, if I have a fight with Iris, we shout and hit each other. When I fight with Jade, we get down and dirty with our feelings and it blows up and is over by the following week. It's not like that with Bay. We don't have actual fights. It is probably why Mum thinks we get on so well these days. But what we have is worse than a fight, and I will have to stay vigilant.

When we get home, Iris is asleep and Dad has just come in from work. Bay is watching a film on the kitchen flat screen. She presses pause, gets up from her curled position on the sofa and gives me a hug, leaving her cheek turned into my shoulder.

'I'm *so*, *so* proud of you,' she says, very seriously, squeezing me tightly for ages.

It is a bit OTT. I haven't saved a dog from drowning or some shit like that, and I'm wary of it. In front of Mum and Dad, she is different.

'Thanks, sis,' I say, waiting for her to let me go.

Then Dad says, 'Wow. My Airfix model. You're not going to forget about us when you're rich and famous, are you?' He laughs, really goofily.

Bay laughs along too, but her eyes are cautious, as though she is expecting everyone to burst into tears at any minute.

*

Later, she creeps into my room, just as I am drifting off to sleep.

The habit of coming into my room after lights-out started years ago. The first time was when a bully at school spread the rumour that Bay's real family were travellers. Mum never knew that she cried in my bed every night that week.

'Move over,' she says now.

I put on one of those pretend-groggy voices and say, 'I'm asleep.' Thinking, *Here we go*.

'But I'm so excited for you, I can't sleep.'

'Can we talk in the morning?' I say, turning my back on her to face the wall.

She digs five fingernails into my back and whispers, 'Please, sis. I get lonely upstairs. It's so far away from everyone.'

It annoys me when she complains about her loft room. It is in the eaves, but it has a skylight and cool wooden beams and a built-in bed with a vintage curtain. Dad converted it himself in the evenings after work and at the weekends, and Mum hand-sewed the curtain to her exact requirements. It took six months and cost loads of money they didn't have. I would kill for it.

'I've told you everything already,' I say. Earlier, I told her every detail of what had happened at Take One.

She lies there for a minute and I hope she will give up.

'I'm not sure a fringe is a good idea.'

I sigh inside. 'You don't think?'

'It'll squash your face.'

'They know what they're doing, I guess.'

'It's *your* hair, Nell, not theirs.'

'A change might be fun.'

'You shouldn't let people push you about.'

'I'm not that bothered either way.'

'I really don't think you should change it.'

'It's just hair!' I say, wriggling about, feeling hot. 'I'm knackered, Bay, and I'm getting up early to go out for a ride with Matthew.'

She jumps up. 'Fine. Night, then,' she says huffily.

After she has gone, I am wide awake. I wonder if I should creep upstairs and say sorry. But my eyes close. I'm imagining shredding through the woods on my bike. Some people need whale music or the sound of waves crashing to calm them down, but I like to think about the bounce in my ribs when I hit a jump, or the power in my core when I master a wheelie. Tomorrow I will apologise to Bay for being cranky.

The next morning, I wake up late, having had the worst sleep ever worrying about Bay.

The shed is musty, and I inhale with a big breath, loving that smell. It is the smell of freedom.

But when I look for my bike, which is usually leant up against Dad's foldaway, I can't see it. Iris's purple bike is there, and Bay and Mum's girlie bikes with the baskets, but not mine.

'Mum! Dad!' I yell, running back in, rattling the combination lock at them. 'Did you move my bike?'

'No,' both of them say, looking confused.

'But it's not there. It's gone from the shed!'

'Are you sure you left it there?' Mum says.

'Yes! Absolutely one hundred per cent.'

Dad says, 'You think someone broke in?'

'Maybe. Come and look.'

We run to the shed together. Dad checks the latch, 'There's no sign of damage.' He goes straight over to the power tools, which are still there, and then to his golf clubs, which he actually hugs. 'Oh, thank God.'

'But Dad, what about my bike?'

'Why would someone take your bike and nothing else?' he says, rubbing his chin. He is less stressed now that he knows his stuff is safe, which is mega-annoying. Mum is looking around like my bike might be hiding under the workbench or hanging from the ceiling.

'Are you sure you didn't leave it somewhere?' she says.

'Of course I didn't!' I cry.

They know it is my pride and joy. They know it is like a friend to me. They know I am more careful with it than with any other possession I own.

Bay turns up at the shed door. Her dressing gown tie is neatly done up in a bow at her tiny waist. 'What's happened?' she says, pushing her black hair back from her forehead, making a quiff.

'My bike's gone,' I say.

'Oh no, really?' Mostly her big sad eyes are greyish, but they have changed colour this morning. They do that in different lights or moods, like Dad's. We always argue over what colour eyes they have. Sometimes we say green, sometimes light grey-green-brown, sometimes grey. Now they look yellow under the bulb in the shed and I know instantly that she has taken my bike.

I stop whining at Mum and Dad. 'Don't worry, I'll borrow Matthew's spare.'

'Maybe you left it at his?' Mum says.

'Yeah, probably,' I say, looking at Bay.

Her small red lips are pushed into a fake sad pout. She rubs her hand up the shaved bit at the back of her head. 'I'm sure it'll be there.'

'It'll turn up,' Dad says, patting my back.

Mum and Dad can't help me now. I know when I am beaten.

CHAPTER NINE

Anna

Ava was sitting forward on the kitchen chair with her knees parted, like a man might sit. Her wheezing was worse than usual. She patted her chest, clanging her wedding ring against her pearls. Her oversized red jumper covered a distended stomach, but her pink corduroys were baggy around her legs.

'Are you all right, Ava? Would you like some water?' I asked.

'That'd be terrific,' she croaked good-humouredly, and coughed some more, pulling out a brown envelope and a small circular hatbox from her shopper and putting both on the table. Her hand rested on the box, steady, meaning business.

As I turned on the tap, I surreptitiously checked my phone for messages. Ian had said he would call to tell us if Nell had got the job. I was desperate to hear. Bay had been asking me whether I could attend her drama showcase at school tomorrow evening. The clash was a nightmare. I didn't want to miss Bay's play, but equally I wanted Nell to get the job. After a month of castings, she was beginning to feel despondent about the rejections, in spite of Ian's reminders that making a breakthrough with an empty portfolio was tough for every new model.

Her first casting had been for an Italian spot cream commercial. Getting there had been like an assault course. Following a cancelled train, a bus replacement service, an armpit-packed Tube ride and a station closure at Oxford Circus, we had hotfooted it from Piccadilly, hand in hand, bustling and darting through the thick streams of people that spilled over the pavements. All the reasons I had moved out of London came flooding back to me. Nell, who hated crowds and hated being late, had almost been in tears by the time we reached the stuffy basement studio – late. The casting director had been brusque and overtly irritated as she talked her through what she wanted. Nell had mimed the actions of washing her face for the camera and apologised for her sweaty nose. The woman had sighed and handed her a tissue and then stopped her halfway through the third take, thanking her for coming. Two hours of travel and we were there all of six minutes.

In week two of our new after-school schedule, we had shouted at each other in the middle of Kentish Town Tube station, arguing about which way was quickest to Malden Road, where the casting for an M&S eComm lookbook was taking place. Flustered and cross with each other, we had arrived on the tenth floor of a shabby office block and then waited for an hour and a half in a strip-lit room alongside dozens of super-tall, skinny-legged, clumpy-shoed, AirPod-wearing models. When grouped together, they were almost alien to look at, like a species of human that should be studied. I wanted to stand close and touch them to see if their beauty was real. I had never felt so unattractive and washed up in all my life. When we finally met the client, a blonde woman called Moira, whose forehead was suspiciously smooth, and the photographer, Stanley, who wore a beanie and a leather jacket indoors, Moira had flicked through the empty pages of Nell's book, saying, 'We'll need more pictures, I'm afraid.' We left, and I realised I wasn't even sure what a lookbook was.

Each night, homework had been completed on the train into London and a burger had been eaten on the way back. Then Nell and I had both flopped into bed, wrung out but too wired to sleep.

Long gone was my cosy evening routine in front of the telly with a glass of wine and an episode of *Doctors*.

The glass I was filling for Ava was overflowing.

Her hands shook as she drank it. I sat down next to her and waited, quietly worrying about her. I liked Ava and I was honoured that she had commissioned a hat from me for her sister's funeral. Ava was the poster girl for old age.

When I set down our cups of tea on the table, she shifted around on her chair, wincing. 'I haven't seen your mum about,' she said. Until recently, she and Mum had been friends. I wasn't sure what had happened between them.

'I know. It's her hips. They're giving her gyp.'

'At our age, if you don't wake up in pain, you've probably died in the night.' She winked and laughed, adding, 'You're a long time dead!' through another coughing fit.

The thought of Mum being a long time dead any time soon sent a darting panic through me. When Ava stopped coughing, her eyes were loose and weepy, but they displayed a youthful alertness that Mum's had always lacked.

'So, I've got some ideas for the hat I want,' she said.

'Fire away.'

We were interrupted by the rattle of the front door and what sounded like a boot against the wooden panels.

Nell shouted from the hallway. 'Oh my God, Mum, all the DOORS in this house! You have to fix them!'

'Excuse me for a sec, Ava. That's my charming teenager.' I checked my watch. Nell was home an hour early.

'Hi, darling. Did you just kick the door?' I asked, checking it for damage.

'It's so stiff, I had to.'

'Don't do that, please, unless you want to pay for another one. No textiles club today?'

'It was cancelled. Have you heard from Ian yet?' she asked. She blinked into her new blonde fringe, blowing it away to show me her blue eyes, so full of hope.

'No. He hasn't called, I'm afraid. Why was textiles cancelled?' I asked.

'Dunno.'

'Really? That's strange.'

I detected guilt in the sideways slide of her eyes, but I didn't have time to challenge it. 'I'm in the middle of a consultation with Ava about a hat.'

'But we've got to go to London for the Zara casting!'

'It's okay. We're catching the 17.35. We have plenty of time. Now that you're home, though, could you maybe do me a massive favour and nip over to the green in about an hour to collect Iris from football?'

Before Nell had joined Take One, I had not believed that life could get any busier. Managing the schedules of three children and looking after Mum, trying to make enough money to make ends meet and maybe having a social life too had been hard enough. Casting in London on top of everything else had taken things to a whole new level of exhausting.

'But I've got to get ready!' She dropped her school bag, and her pencil case fell out. She ignored it and grabbed her black rucksack. The corners of her Take One portfolio – or 'book', as she now called it – stuck out of the top flap. The plastic pages inside were empty except for two small Polaroids on the first page. Last weekend, a test shoot for a headshot had been booked in on her chart, but the dates kept changing.

I picked up her pencil case and put it back in her school bag. 'Please, darling, you'd be doing me a big favour, and it'd give me more time with Ava.'

I had wanted to see Ava earlier in the day, but I'd had to delay our meeting when the delivery of trimmings for two commissions had been late. One hat was for a client who had a wedding at the weekend, and one was for a woman who wanted a wide-brimmed sunhat for a holiday, flying tomorrow night. If Nell was booked on the job tomorrow, I wasn't sure how I would get the hats to them on time. Tomorrow's school runs would have to be sorted out on the way into London this evening. Knowing either way about this job was becoming urgent. I had already called Ian twice today.

Nell tightened her jaw. 'Fine.' She stomped upstairs.

I returned to the kitchen, a haven from Nell's teenage strops, which were becoming alarmingly frequent. Modelling had created a hype in her that I found quite difficult to keep up with. 'Sorry about that,' I said.

'I'll never forget the hellishness of those teenage years.' Ava chuckled, pulling out some photographs from the envelope. 'Here. Have a look at these. That's me and Ellen, with Mum and Dad.'

There were two identical babies in the photograph. Ellen was being held by their mother, who wore a tweed skirt and a felt hat on a slant. Ava was lying in the long arms of their father, who wore a brown double-breasted suit. The next photograph was of a woman who looked like a young version of Ava, in a white hat with a broad rim. 'You see Ellen's wedding hat here? I'd like that kind of style, if possible. With these on the top.' She opened the box and I was astounded to see it packed with shimmering iridescent feathers in yellows and pinks and greens and blues. 'I'll be wearing a green dress. I don't want to wear black.'

I sank my hand in the soft plumes.

'They're real, I'm afraid,' she said. 'Bird of Paradise. Great-Aunt Maud was a milliner in the thirties.'

I pulled my hands out, guilty about enjoying them, knowing the bird must have been slaughtered by plume hunters to satiate the millinery fad at the turn of the century. They were so beautiful on the outside, distractingly appealing, and it would be easy to forget how they'd come to us. I hoped they wouldn't bring bad luck.

Ava added quickly, 'I wouldn't have them in *my* house. But Ellen didn't mind. She loved them. She said there was no way to bring the birds back to life, so why not keep them.' Tears filled the creases around her eyes. 'Sorry, it comes at me in waves, all this.'

I touched her arm lightly. 'I'm so sorry. You obviously loved her very much.'

She brought out a hankie from her sleeve, sniffing and sitting up straight. 'I miss her every minute of every day.'

There was an exclamation from Nell upstairs, followed by stamping and the sound of drawers being dragged open – and probably left open – then a slammed door. I wished again that Ian would get back to us about this job.

'What was she like?' I asked Ava, trying to draw attention away from the whirlwind of selfishness that Nell had become, knowing I had a bit of time while she got ready for the casting.

Ava's stories about the ups and downs of her twin sister's life took me away for a bit. Then Ian's name flashed up on my phone. My stomach somersaulted.

'Excuse me, Ava. I'm terribly sorry, I've got to get this.'

She smiled and nodded.

'Hello?' I said.

'*Chloe Does* confirmed, hon!' Ian said without preamble. 'Shooting in Shoreditch tomorrow for a five-page story about teenage girls' bedwear. I'll ping you the deets on email. Well done to Nell! This is just the start.'

I heard Nell thunder down the stairs. She stood in the doorway in her towel, biting her lip and staring at me with her eyebrows raised. She mouthed, 'Did I get it?'

I nodded. She squealed, making Ava jump. 'Sorry, Ava!' she said, kissing her on the cheek before running upstairs again.

I exhaled, thoroughly relieved about the job but worried about her missing a day of school. I clocked through the numerous last-minute calls I would have to make to ensure Iris was picked up from school tomorrow and taken to Brownies, then brought home and fed. I needed to break the news to Bay and make sure Dom got off work early to go to her showcase in my place; organise Bay's lifts to and from the stage their school was using at a boarding school miles away; and cancel the appointment I had scheduled with another client.

'Sorry about that. She just got her first job.'

'Marvellous!' Ava said.

I settled down again, checking my watch, aware that Bay was due back in half an hour.

'Can I see the other photographs?' I asked. We still had a little time before we had to leave.

More than willing to share, Ava began to tell me the tales behind the photographs. I was gripped by her life, its joys and its excitements. It had been well lived and I hoped that I would feel the same about my own life when it was time for me to look back more than forward.

I couldn't wait to get started on her hat and imbue it with her dignity and optimism, and her memories of her beloved twin. The shoot tomorrow would delay it. Usually, when commissioned with an ambitious brief from a client, I would be awake at night thinking about it, feeling the design come to life in my head. Tonight, I would be awake worrying about the shoot. Although I was happy for Nell, a studio in Shoreditch filled with fashion people was the literal antithesis to sitting in my draughty conservatory making a hat, and I was apprehensive.

When Bay arrived home, I braced myself for her disappointment, feeling awful about letting her down.

'Good day at school?' I asked.

'Hello, Mrs Grant,' she said. 'Wow. Look at those.'

She peered into the box of feathers and then politely listened to Ava tell her about their history.

'I'm so sorry to hear about your sister,' she said. 'Can I take some photos of the feathers?'

Nell loped into the kitchen. She was dressed in long, flared jeans and a pink crop top. Her hair was blow-dried and her gold eye make-up was subtle. These days, I was bowled over by how well she put herself together and how impactful her beauty had become.

'Hi, Ava. Sorry about before. I was a bit stressed out about that job,' she said.

'I don't mind a bit,' Ava said with a grin.

'Did you get it?' Bay asked.

'Yes, I did.'

I looked at Bay sheepishly. 'I'm so sorry about the play,' I whispered, hugging her small frame, fragile like a bird's. 'But Dad can go for me and film it,' I added, praying that he didn't have a prior commitment at work.

Nell took an apple from the fruit bowl. She didn't apologise to Bay about the clash, which I thought was insensitive. 'Don't forget to pick Iris up,' I said to her.

'Do I *have* to, Mum?'

'Yes, darling.'

'Shame I can't take my *bike*.' She took a noisy bite of her apple and shot Bay a dirty look, as though it was Bay's fault that I had asked her to collect Iris.

Bay said, 'I would go, but I've got to go over my lines for tomorrow.'

I said, 'You're always doing me favours, Bay. Nell, just get on with it please.' I was becoming thoroughly irritated by her.

After Nell had slammed the front door, Bay said, 'I'm off upstairs. Lovely to see you, Mrs Grant. Again, I'm so sorry to hear about your sister.'

'Thanks, Bay,' she said, watching her leave the kitchen. She looked at me. 'You've got your hands full, haven't you, dear?'

I tapped a finger on my temple. 'Inside my head there's a computerised colour-coded diary.'

Ava chortled through a cough. 'Nell and Bay are very different. Just like me and Ellen.'

'Nell's not usually so stroppy,' I said apologetically.

'She's so pretty, dear.' She put the lid back on the hatbox. 'It must be hard for the others.'

I was slightly offended on Bay and Iris's behalf, but I understood what she meant. As much as I had pushed similar concerns aside, they were always close by.

'Thankfully they're all really close, so I don't think it's been much of an issue. Bay has her own thing going on too, with her films and stuff,' I said. 'Still...' Ava arched an eyebrow at me.

'I'll keep an eye out,' I said.

In spite of Nell's recent self-absorption, I was trying very hard to believe that Bay and Nell's relationship had strong enough foundations. So far, my initial worries about Bay's moods spiralling had been unfounded. I had thought a lot lately about why she was coping so well and had drawn the conclusion that she and Nell had worked through their sibling rivalry in those early years and had forged a bond that I had underestimated. Ava didn't have this insight. All the same, she was a wise person and her thoughts were discomfiting.

Dom would say I was overthinking it.

He had convinced me that it would be worse to hold Nell back, and I held onto this tightly now.

CHAPTER TEN

2012

Bay and Nell were peering into the plastic tub that Matthew had brought round to show them.

'The dark-shelled one is called Bryan and other one is Cilla,' he said, pointing to each snail in turn.

Nell giggled at the names. Matthew frowned. 'What?'

'Nothing,' she said.

'I like those names,' Bay said.

Matthew took the snails out to let them roam about on the paving stones.

'How do you know which one is a girl and which one is a boy?' Bay added.

'Snails aren't girls or boys. They're hermaphrodites,' Matthew said.

'What's a herma-fro-thingy?' Nell asked.

Behind Matthew's back, Bay would say he was a show-off for using long words all the time, but Nell loved his long words. When she was older, she wanted to use grown-up words like Matthew.

'It means they have both female and male sex organs,' Matthew explained.

Nell giggled at the rude word, even though she didn't exactly know what sex was, and then went red.

'That's really interesting, Matthew,' Bay said. She sounded very grown up.

Matthew blinked his long, colourless eyelashes at her. 'I brought this really cool book about it. It's in my rucksack. Do you want to see it?'

'Yes please,' Bay said.

When he had gone inside, Bay whispered, 'He's such a nerd.'

Nell wanted to defend Matthew. He was her best friend and he was really clever and he was two years older than Bay, but she had learned that Bay cried easily if you disagreed with her. These days Nell was finding it really hard to know how to do the right thing. Her mum always told her to be kind, but what if being kind to one person meant being mean to another? It boggled her brain. She bit her tongue and watched the snails move along. They left criss-cross trails of silver on the stone. She thought it was funny that something so yucky, like snail slime, was so beautiful in the sunshine.

'I dare you to lick one,' Bay said.

'No way!' Nell thought she was joking.

'Go on.'

'No.'

'If you don't, I'll stamp on one and say you killed it.'

Nell couldn't tell if she was serious. Bay's eyes flashed yellow like a cat's. They didn't seem frail like the rest of her. A few weeks ago she had forced Nell to write 'Mummy is a horrible poo-head' on the bathroom mirror with her mum's favourite red lipstick. She really hadn't wanted to do it, but Bay had said she would give her a Chinese burn if she didn't. When her mum had discovered the graffiti and found her ruined lipstick, she had been more upset with Nell than angry.

'What made you *do* it?' she had asked.

'I don't know,' Nell had answered tearily. She had wanted her mum to guess that she had *not* done it.

'There's been a lot of this kind of thing lately, hasn't there?'

Nell had nodded, feeling the tears roll down her cheeks, more desperate than ever to tell her mother that Bay was forcing her to do bad things. The words wouldn't come. They had been too hard to say.

'I know it's tough on you having Bay around. She's quite a handful, isn't she?' Mum had whispered the last bit and hugged Nell. 'It's a big change for everyone, but we'll get there. Okay? Hang on in there,' she said, landing a hundred kisses on her cheek.

Her mother's words had comforted her and helped her to believe that everything would return to normal soon.

While she had wiped at the greasy smears on the mirror, she could hear her mum and Bay laughing in the kitchen downstairs, making cupcakes without her. In spite of Mum forgiving her, Nell had regrets. She really wished she had said no to Bay and suffered the Chinese burn.

Now, about the snails, she would definitely say no. Anyway, she did not believe that Bay would kill a snail.

'No. I'm not going to lick a snail,' she said firmly.

'Your choice,' Bay said. And she stood up and stamped on Bryan.

Nell leapt up and let out a cry. But Bay's scream was ear-splitting. 'Nell! *Don't*!' The look in her eyes was triumphant.

Mum and Matthew ran outside. 'What in heaven's name is going on?' Mum asked.

Bay wailed, 'Nell stamped on Cilla! Look, she's dead!'

'It's not Cilla, it's Bryan! Bryan has a dark shell!' Nell cried. It didn't help her cause. She had no idea why she had said it. Perhaps to prove that she knew the snails better and would never hurt them?

Either way, it was too late now.

Matthew stared at her in utter disbelief. His face went bright pink and he stuffed his woodland bug book back into his rucksack and ran off, leaving Cilla behind. They heard the door slam. Nell couldn't speak, she was so shocked by what Bay had done.

Bay buried her head in Mum's middle, sniffing and whimpering, her delicate fingers plucking at her skirt.

'That was a horrible thing to do, Nell. Go to your room this minute,' Mum said.

Of course her mother had believed Bay. Killing a snail was the kind of thing a girl who wrote horrible graffiti with expensive lipstick did; not sweet little Bay who sicked up her food like a baby.

'But Mum…' Nell began. She caught Bay's eyes and stopped. Those powerful eyes, with the vulnerable droop, implored her not to tell, warned her not to tell. Bay would punish her, and it would be far worse than anything her mother could do to her. Because when Bay felt hurt – however unjustified it might be – she was spiteful and did things that *actually* hurt Nell.

'Don't "but Mum" me. Do as I say!' Anna said.

Nell tore off into the house, licking the tears from her top lip.

Through her open bedroom window she could hear them talking in the garden.

'I'll take the alive snail back to Matthew if you like,' Bay said.

'Thank you, Bay. But I think Nell should be the one to take it back and apologise to Matthew. Goodness me, I don't know what's got into her these days.'

Nell sobbed into her pillow at the unfairness of it all. She did not like her new sister. She was horrible and mean and she wanted her to go back to London forever.

The next morning, early, Bay knocked on Nell's bedroom door.

'Can I come in?'

'Hmm,' Nell said, waking up and realising she still hated her sister.

'I'm so, so sorry,' Bay whispered, standing in the nightie that used to be Nell's and combing her black hair. 'Can I get in with you? Please?'

Nell did not say she could, but she got in anyway. Nell refused to budge up and Bay lay along the narrow space that was left.

'I don't know why I did it,' she said. Her fingers fiddled with her comb, and they were almost as thin and blue as its plastic teeth.

'Hmm,' Nell said again.

Bay rubbed her tiny, freezing feet on Nell's leg. Nell resented giving Bay her body heat.

Then Bay began telling her some secrets about her life in London.

First there was the story she already knew, about Bay's best friend, Joss, who had been stabbed in the leg after a fight had broken out between two boys at their school. The leg-stabbing had apparently been the final straw for Bay's mother, who had always wanted to move to a yoga retreat in Mauritius anyway. Nell hadn't known that last bit.

'Mauritius is an island in the Indian Ocean. It has a population of 1.3 million people and the national emblem is the extinct animal the dodo,' Bay said, as though she'd learned the facts off by heart from an encyclopedia.

'That's interesting,' Nell said.

'They speak French Creole in the schools,' Bay said. 'That's why I came to live with Daddy.'

Bay told Nell some even more interesting facts about Suki.

Suki liked to sit on the edge of windowsills with her legs dangling out, and she liked to have sex with her boyfriends while Bay was in the house. In the *daytime*! Nell still didn't really know what sex was, but she knew it was bad and that it was definitely meant to be at night. Bay's secrets got even worse. Nell was flabbergasted to hear that she wasn't allowed to call Suki Mum or Mummy because Suki was 'not just your mother, but a woman in my own right', and that sometimes, when she was drunk, she said she was embarrassed about having a daughter like Bay, who she thought was ugly and useless, like her father.

'Dad isn't ugly! And you are so pretty!' Nell cried.

Bay started combing her fringe again, though it kept falling back because she was lying down.

'I had to go to a stupid school counsellor at Brooklands,' she said.

'Your old school?'

She sat up and slumped over her knees and mumbled into the duvet. 'She said I did mean things to the people I loved the most because Suki made me feel like a horrible person.'

Nell didn't fully understand this logic, but she felt very sorry for Bay, and very lucky that she didn't have a mother like Suki. Though she had vowed never to speak to Bay again, she just *had* to hug her and forgive her for killing the snail.

'You're not a horrible person all the time,' she said honestly.

From that day on, whenever Bay was horrible to her, she reminded herself it was because she loved her the most.

CHAPTER ELEVEN

Anna

I made my breakfast, feeling guiltier than usual about my love of buttery toast. My good jeans were too tight, but I trusted that nobody would be looking at me today.

'How much money will you get, Nell?' Iris asked.

'Five hundred and fifty quid,' Nell said, grinning through a mouthful of Marmite toast, shaking her new fringe about.

'You could buy me a Bengal kitten for my birthday with that,' Iris said.

'All the money she's earning is going into a savings account for university,' I said.

This fact justified Nell's day off school. Ian had promised us it would be worth it, and I trusted his professional opinion. She could easily catch up on the missed work. In ten years, would it matter that she had missed one day of school? It was my new favourite mantra: in ten years, would it matter that they watched too much television on Saturday mornings? In ten years, would it matter that they had forgotten to brush their teeth one day?

Bay said, 'Remember, some of it will have to go on tax. And twenty-four per cent will go to Take One.'

'And the rest you'll save,' I said.

'But I need a new bike, Mum!' Nell said.

'Actually,' I said, reconsidering, 'that would be a good use of the money.' I felt bad that we hadn't yet been able to afford to replace it. Its disappearance had been baffling, but I had given up on trying to get to the bottom of it.

'I've seen a cool Stumpjumper on eBay,' Nell said, glancing over at Bay, who was typing something into her phone.

I kissed her forehead. 'Come on then, my mountain-biking nut, we'll miss the train if we don't go now.' I called up the stairs to Dom, twice. The first time came out croaky. All morning my regular breathing had been interrupted by little flutters of excitement. As well as my nerves about Nell's first-ever shoot, there was an abstract possibility that I might see Billy Young. I knew it was highly unlikely, as unlikely as finding a needle in a haystack, but as long as I knew that the needle was in the stack, it was impossible to dismiss the possibility. 'Dom! Are you ready?' I yelled.

I knew he could hear me and that he was choosing not to reply.

He was being deliberately contrary lately, and this was usually a sign he was stewing about something. I suspected I knew its root cause.

Last month, he had wanted to go for a promotion as a senior planning officer and I had advised him against rushing it, believing he was expecting too much too soon from a relatively new job. He had ignored me and gone for it, and the job had been given to a more experienced older woman. Symbolically, my reticence about Nell's modelling career was bound to irritate him, as though it was an echo of my previous lack of faith in his potential and by extension proved my apathy towards the girls' ambitions. He probably thought I was the wrong parent for the job of chaperoning Nell, while he was designed for it but chained to his desk, nailed to the cross, missing out on all the fun.

Dom had always been the dreamer, thinking up get-rich-quick schemes and planning our emigration to Australia or Canada, where the grass was greener and the houses were bigger. I had been attracted to that side of him, knowing it balanced out my vexing tendency for extreme caution at all times, but his parents had instilled a sense of entitlement in him, and when things didn't go his way, he'd sulk about his lot in life.

'That leaves you roughly £308,' Bay said, showing the figure on her phone calculator.

Nell said, 'That's not quite enough for the bike I want.'

'I wish I could go on the train too,' Iris whined. 'It's not fair that Nell gets to miss school.'

It was hard to know what to say. 'I know, poppet, but it's just this once. And remember that time I let you have a day off to see the lambs being born?'

She nodded.

'It's the same,' I said, even though it plainly wasn't. Nothing was the same about today.

Nell said, 'Swap places with you, sis! I'm crapping myself.'

'Language, Nell,' I said.

'You'll be amazing, Nellie,' Bay said.

I kissed Bay's forehead too. Her hair always smelt clean. 'Bye, darling. You are such a star for walking Iris in. I hope you won't miss your bus.'

'It'll be fine.'

'Nell, have you got everything you need?'

'Flesh-coloured thong, strapless bra, tick, tick!' Nell said, a little hyper and pink in the cheeks, brandishing her new purchases before stuffing them back inside her rucksack, singing to a dance track on her phone about being a different person.

Nell had a song for every occasion, for every big feeling.

'I don't want to go in,' Nell whispered.

'You're going to be brilliant,' I said, but my lips stuck to my teeth when I tried to offer her an encouraging smile.

'Don't do anything embarrassing, will you, Mum?'

'What? You mean I can't break into my best running man when some cool tunes come on?' I said, grinning at her, arms bent and poised for busting a move.

Nell pressed my arms straight and chuckled. 'Don't even joke about that.'

Only half the lights were on in the studio. We walked across the concrete floor, over criss-crossed wires, towards the brightest corner. There was a dressing room where a woman was laying out make-up. She was dressed in baggy black clothes, topped off with fierce red hair and lipstick.

'Hi. I'm Sinead. Hair and make-up.'

I smiled as best I could and hid the prick of disappointment. She seemed lovely, but she was not Billy Young.

'Hi. I'm Anna, and this is my daughter, Nell.'

Nell shook Sinead's hand. 'Nice to meet you.'

There was a fleck of red on Sinead's top front tooth. 'Lovely to meet you too, Nell. Sit. You can be my first victim.'

Nell sat down on a canvas chair. Sinead stroked a cleansing wipe across her face and they began chatting like old friends.

Two more models arrived. One had a short afro, doleful eyes and endless legs. The other had cheekbones that pulled the curtains of her chestnut mane wide of her face. They looked older than Nell, about Bay's age, but they could have been twenty-five. They sat next to each other on a sofa and began whispering over their phones, like any self-respecting Gen Z. I could see Nell eyeing them in the mirror.

Next to the sofa there was a rail of clothes. Feathers and satin on every hanger. Ian had told me it was teen bedwear, but I had imagined flannel jammies and sheepskin slippers.

The photographer appeared around the corner, introducing himself as Asif. He had a fleshy bearded jawline that he squished around as he inspected Nell in the mirror. He said to Sinead, over

Nell's head, 'Hmm. Make sure you play her lips down so they're less sexy, yeah?'

Asif and Sinead both stared at Nell. Sinead said, 'Yes, I thought the same. Her fringe is super-heavy when it's down.' She removed Nell's black headband and ruffled her fringe over her eyes. Leaving her hand on Nell's forehead, she said, 'We could do dark smoky eyes?'

'Yeah. That'll help. Great. Okay. I'll let you get on.'

Nuala the stylist arrived next. She was nervy and thin and had bouncy hair. Her sweatshirt was ironed down the sleeves and tucked into her matching tracksuit pants, and I guessed that she never slobbed about in them at home. She dumped two large bags at her feet. Asif greeted her, and together they rummaged through the rail of clothes and the bags.

When Nell's make-up was done, Nuala asked her to try on some outfits.

'No,' she said. 'It's not hanging right.' She tugged at the material on Nell's hips and chest, pulling faces, sighing, shaking her head, before flicking angrily through the rail again.

'It's not your fault, hon. It's just I wasn't warned.'

She went over to Asif to talk to him out of earshot. They stared at Nell in the tight nightie, and I stood up, ready to intervene. Nell shot me a look that sat me straight down again. Nuala returned and pulled out a knee-length silk dressing gown for her. 'You're so womanly, hon, we have to play it down a bit for the teen market. Ha!' She turned to me and smiled a skull-like smile.

It was a bittersweet experience for me to watch Nell's transformation from an innocent fifteen-year-old into a sex bomb in silk bedwear. In spite of the team's attempts to downplay her curves, they had added ten years to her age. I wanted to wipe her face clean and dress her in an old sack. Instead, powerless to intervene, I sat in a chair in the corner, trying to read my book.

Bay texted regularly, checking on Nell. Her phone seemed to be attached to her hand.

How's she getting on? She's not texting me back.

I hope you're not texting from lessons.

Study period.

Then study, young lady. She's fine.

Okay. Love you.

Love you too. STUDY.

Just one more thing. Can you send a video? I just want to get an idea of what it's like.

As long as you promise to study.

Promise.

I filmed Nell and the other two models acting out a play fight with a black satin pillow and was warned by Nuala that I couldn't use it on social media without permission.

Little feathers blew and twirled around long bare limbs, peppered by peals of fake laughter. Asif's direction as he clicked his camera boomed over the dance tracks. 'Nell, could you watch how the other two do it and loosen up a bit? Okay? You really need to look like you're having a good time.' Now and then Nuala would jump into shot and tug at a pink nightie, add or remove a sleep mask, adjust a bulldog clip, slip on different shoes, and the fun between the three girls would be halted as though it had never begun. Asif said, 'Nell, mouth closed, that's right, less of the teeth, please!… Leah, do that again, yeah, just like that… *Mouth closed*, Nell!'

I filmed with my shoulders high, reminiscing about the real pillow fights at home, when Bay would pin Nell down and whack her in the face repeatedly, when Iris would come in with her *Beano*-print pillow, laughing hysterically one minute and ending up in tears the next. I never thought I would pine for those kinds of fights.

I sent the film to Bay and she texted right back.

That photographer is a B-word.

True, I texted back, feeling useless, like a teenager who wasn't sticking up for her friend in a fight.

*

At lunchtime, we sat down next to Tally and Leah. Asif and Sinead and Nuala sat at the other end of the table and talked among themselves.

Leah and Tally chatted about a gathering at their flat tonight. They called it 'the model flat', which I gathered was where agencies housed models whose parents lived outside London. It was like a boarding house full of beautiful people.

Under her breath, Nell said, 'Mum, what did you send Bay? She just texted me about some film.'

'It was just a clip of you on set. Want to see?' I sent it to her phone and she watched it.

'I wish you hadn't.'

Before I had a chance to ask why, Leah said, 'Wanna come over tonight to our little gathering, Nell? A few girls from New Faces will be there.'

Tally picked up a sandwich as big as her head and took a minuscule bite of the corner before putting it down again. 'Yeah, come!'

Nell switched off her phone, which was odd, and said, 'Sounds really fun,' with extra oomph. I wondered what had happened with Bay.

'We have to get the train home, unfortunately,' I cut in, knowing that Nell would hate me for it. I dared to look at her. Her pretty heart-shaped mouth had dropped open and her big blue eyes pleaded with me.

'Oh, right. You don't live in London?' Leah asked.

Nell shook her head. 'No, I wish,' she said, taking up her own sandwich, staring intently at it.

'My mum used to be my chaperone,' Tally said, smiling kindly at Nell. 'We used to come down from Preston.' It was a relief to locate her accent, which I had wrongly guessed was Mancunian.

'I started when I was seventeen, thank God. Mum would have been the worst. No offence to mums, though,' Leah said, smiling.

'None taken,' I laughed.

'When do you turn sixteen, Nell?' Leah asked. I noticed she had a bit of rocket on her very white teeth, and I wanted to say something, but Nell jumped in first.

'Leah, you've got a bit of...' She motioned to her left tooth.

Leah laughed. 'Now that's a good friend,' she said.

'My birthday's New Year's Day,' Nell replied.

'Cool, babe. Capricorn.'

Tally said, 'Only six months to go until you're free!'

Nell laughed, but covered her mouth. My chest tightened. Was it worth pointing this out to Asif later? His directions on set had planted a negative seed in her mind about one of her most valuable assets: her smile.

As the second half of the day wore on, I felt more and more useless and smiled less and less genuinely myself, counting down the minutes until we were finally allowed to leave.

I hoped that Nell would never want to model again. The fantasy of calling Ian up to tell him it was over before it had even begun grew in my head until it was a definite plan that I couldn't wait to act out on her behalf.

She would have so much more fun in other jobs, but she wouldn't know this yet. When I thought back through my own career history, being a model definitely seemed worse than a fair few of the jobs I'd had over the years. I couldn't imagine what Nell would get back from today, except perhaps the feel of expensive clothes on her skin – lovely, but not quite enough. Her body and mind had been at the mercy of Asif, to be commented on and criticised and controlled.

By the end of the day, not once had anyone on the team asked Nell or the other models' opinions, and the girls had not offered them up. It hadn't been their place, and they knew it. They had been beautiful polished-up shells, admired and yet talked over as though they were hollow inside and not part of the team.

As soon as we hit the street and were free, I said to Nell, 'So, how did you find that? Are you okay?'

'It was so much fun,' she said, pulling out her phone. Over her shoulder I watched her click through a long list of Snapchats from various people.

'Oh,' I said, taken aback. 'I'm glad you had a good day.'

I couldn't say, *But Nuala was catty about your weight and Asif told you not to smile and your opinions were irrelevant.*

Nell chattered at me while she texted. 'It went so well, don't you think, Mum? They seemed really pleased with me. Do you think we should call Ian to tell him how well it went? I can't wait to see the pictures.'

My plans to call Ian and tell him to stick the modelling up his jumper – not that he probably wore anything as frumpy as a jumper – wavered in my mind. Was I thinking too deeply about the effects of modelling on Nell's young mind? If it had been me in front of that camera, being talked about like an object, I would have crumbled, but it seemed Nell was more confident and resilient. Perhaps I could credit myself for her inner strength, which wasn't shaken by outside criticism. On her behalf, my internal world had been rattled, thundering with fury at the smallest judgement. That was me. Typical me. Porous old me.

'I just got a text from Tally,' she said.

'The model?'

'Yeah! She's sent me the address for the party. It's near here and loads of other girls from the agency will be going.'

'It's a school night, Nell.'

'You let me go to Misha's party on Thursday.'

'That was different.'

She stopped at the top of the flight of stairs down to Old Street Tube. 'Why?'

'Guildford is much closer.'

'It's the same train, only twenty minutes longer.'

'Come on, let's go home, Nell. We can talk about parties in London when you're sixteen.'

She bit her bottom lip. I could usually persuade her to back down, unlike Iris, who was as stubborn as my mother. Her phone pinged. She read the message, and her expression clouded enough for me to wonder who had sent it. The next time she spoke, it was with new determination.

'I want to go to the party.'

We were blocking the commuting stampede. I pulled her to the side. We stood in front of a boarded-up shopfront. 'No, darling, you're too young.'

'I'd be home by eleven and I've done all my homework. Please, Mum.'

I couldn't believe she thought she had a hope in hell of going to this party.

'And where would I be while you're partying?'

'You don't have to wait! I'll get an Uber to Waterloo and then the train home.'

'You think I'd leave you here?'

'I'm fifteen!'

'Exactly. You're only fifteen. I mean, I don't even know who will be at this party. They're bound to be much older than you. And the last train is full of drunk people.'

'What? That's totally illogical. The train from Guildford is full of drunk people too, and you never mind about that. And I mean, we've been jumping on trains back from London, like, twice a week, sometimes more, for, like, the last two months. It is totally normal to me now! It's just an hour later than usual, that's all.'

Her phone pinged again, giving me time to think of a better argument. I was struggling. If I pinned her to the pavement and physically stopped her, I'd be had up for child abuse.

She said, 'Look, Ian has emailed back. He says he's represented Tally since she was thirteen and that it might be good to meet some other people from the agency.'

'You asked Ian about this?'

'I wanted to check that Tally was legit.'

I didn't know whether I should be impressed by how sensible she was or outraged that she had gone behind my back. 'What is Ian doing emailing you without letting me know?'

'You're cc'd in, Mum.'

I was running out of excuses that went beyond 'no'. So that was what I said. 'No, Nell. It's out of the question. No.'

'Do you even know how stupid you're being?'

'Don't call me stupid, please.'

'You *are* being stupid, though. I can't actually believe you. You'll know exactly where I'm going to be and what train I'll be getting. And I won't drink. You know you can trust me to get the ten o'clock from Waterloo if I've promised you I will. And Dad can pick me up from the station.'

'Dad would never let you go to this party,' I said, hoping this was true. 'Come on, let's go.'

I took her hand and tried to pull her gently towards the Tube station entrance. She stood, rigid, on the spot. 'No. You can't stop me.'

I stared at her. At her eyes under her thick blonde fringe, almost wiped clear of the heavy liner; at her parted mouth with its stain of pink. Fresh-faced, yet marked by the shoot, as though the make-up that was left on her skin had sunk into her and changed her forever.

'Yes, I certainly *can* stop you,' I said. 'I can cut off your phone, for starters.'

'Sure. Do it.'

'I'll freeze your pocket money, then. How do you feel about that?'

'Ian can advance me the money I'm getting paid for this job. Tally does it all the time, apparently.'

Tears of frustration were filling my throat. What else could I threaten? To lock her out of home? She'd know I'd never go through with it. To talk to her teachers? She'd laugh in my face. I was reminded of a book I used to read to her when she was little, about a girl telling her mum she doesn't like peas. In the end, after some appalling bribing, the mother accepts that her daughter will never put a pea into her mouth. 'Okay,' I said. 'If you're determined to go, I'll wait outside for you. In a pub or something.'

'I don't need a babysitter. I'm fifteen!' she said, turning her back and walking away, staring down at Google Maps on her phone. She spoke over her shoulder. 'I'll see you or Dad at ten fifty at Witley station. Or I'll pay for a cab to take me home.'

I ran after her. 'Nell! Wait!'

She jogged ahead.

Before I knew it, the crowd had gobbled her up.

I pelted back and forth, up and down side streets, crying into strangers' faces, asking if they'd seen a tall blonde girl. The email exchange between Ian and Nell did not mention the address and he had not responded to my message. The Take One office phone rang and rang. Finally a girl picked up.

'Take One Model Management,' she said.

'Hello, can I speak to Ian, please? It's Anna, Nell Hart's mum.'

'Ian's gone home, I'm afraid.'

I checked my watch. It was 6.35.

'Would it be possible to have his mobile number? It's urgent.'

'I'm afraid I can't give out that information.'

'But he's my daughter's booker!'

'I'm really sorry.'

'Would you be able to give me the address of the model flat in Shoreditch?'

There was a pause, and I imagined the girl on the other end of the line rolling her eyes. Then she said, 'I'm afraid I can't share that information.'

I was about to tell her the whole story, but I knew it was pointless. If she was a sensible and professional employee, she was never going to give me Ian's number, however heartfelt my pleas were. Nor was she going to reveal where their teenage models lived, and if she had, I think I would have taken Nell to another agency.

'Of course. I'm so sorry.'

'Have a nice evening,' she said.

Having a nice evening was so out of my reach, I could have burst into tears. A nice evening would have entailed riding home on the train with my daughter unpicking every detail of the shoot, then eating a cheese toastie at the kitchen bar while we told Dom, Bay and possibly Iris – if she was up – all about it. A nice evening would have ended with me flopping into bed next to Dom and revealing to him the other side of the story. Instead, Nell was gone, and I was frantic and regretful, wishing I had been less dogmatic with my refusals.

I called her mobile over and over. There was no answer. I couldn't believe this was happening, that she was being so rebellious, that she was somewhere in London with people I hardly knew, and that I couldn't do a damn thing about it.

CHAPTER TWELVE

Nell

I walk away from Mum, shaking all over, so angry I can hardly concentrate on following the blue dot on my phone map. Then Bay texts me asking me if I've read her group Snap. It went:

I never thought you'd stop caring about people's feelings. I never thought you would be unkind. I never thought you could be superficial. I never thought you could be selfish. I never thought you'd leave the people who love you behind. I never thought that you would change.

I thought you were different. I was wrong.

I had first read it when I was arguing with Mum before. If there had been a titchy part of me willing to go home with Mum, Bay's message killed it. All because I hadn't had time to reply to her needy texts. A whole day of them!

How's the shoot going?

Why aren't you responding?

Are you okay?

Please get back to me.

Tell me why you're ignoring me.

Stop airing me.

Seriously, Nell, this isn't funny.

Hello?

Hello?

Are you there?

Wow. You're really not going to text back?
Please text me back.

I want to block Bay forever and hurl my phone into the gutter. My *bike* was probably in the gutter. Last week, when I accused her of taking it, she squeezed tears into her eyes and said, 'How could you think I'd do that?'

She's not going to kill my vibes today. I'm not going to turn back. Not for anybody. I know I'll have to deal with her at some point, but not yet. I feel bad about how worried Mum will be. She has no idea what's going on between me and Bay, about her taking my bike, or about the past, or about her mean text just now. That isn't Mum's fault, considering I never tell her anything any more.

I text her.

Hi Mum, sorry. Pls don't worry about me. C u later. Promise to catch the 10pm. Love u. Nellie Noos ☺

The sun is sending these cool shafts of light through the buildings, and all the London people around me are on the pavements outside cafés and restaurants, laughing and chatting, having fun on a Wednesday evening. I'm going to have fun too, with Tally and Leah. A brand-new me with brand-new friends, free for a few hours, free of that grubby, guilty feeling permanently inside me at home.

Google Maps is telling me I have arrived at their address. It's a wide metal door next to a pub. I ring the bell, looking over my shoulder, suddenly nervous of being in London on my own, as though a stranger might pounce. Nobody on the street is giving me a second glance, apart from a group of suited men with smeared pint glasses. But I'm used to that. Old dudes ogling teenagers! Nothing new there.

'Hello?' A voice speaks from the intercom.

'Hi. It's Nell. From the shoot today?'

'Nell! You came! Come on up!' From the northern accent, I guess it's Tally.

The stairs are like the stairs at school, with metal handrails painted blue.

When Tally opens the door, a whole new world opens up to me.

They live in a massive loft-style apartment with low white module sofas and parquet floors. Sitting around the square coffee table, with a goldfish bowl at its centre, are tall, thin, beautiful people. Boys and girls. Not sure why I didn't expect boys.

Tally makes me a cup of tea and Leah opens a packet of digestives.

There is a guy bent over a bowl of cereal staring at the football. When he looks up, I think my heart will pack up on me – that's what Granny Berry says when she's watching Chris Hemsworth in *Thor*. His eyes slope up at the corners, with eyelashes that are longer than mine. He is literally the fittest man alive. Fitter than Thor. Fitter than Chris Evans. Fitter than Johnny Flynn. Fitter than Ryan Gosling. Fitter than any human being on earth.

'Hi,' he says.

I say, 'Hi!' really very loudly, and the other guy next to him looks up from his phone. He is fit too – Jade would die for him – but he isn't as cute as this blond dude. The blond dude has just stopped my heart. In a medical way. My cheeks burn. In fact, I'm surprised my face hasn't burned off today. Every time Asif went on about my teeth, I blushed and felt angry with Mum for not letting me fix them in Year 7. Note to self: must remember to keep my mouth closed as much as possible.

'Everyone, this is Nell. Nell, this is Lee,' she says, pointing at the hot dude. 'And this is Dave. And these girls are Lill, Nat and Amber.'

'Hi,' I say.

Amber takes out a packet of cigarettes and says, 'Smoke?'

'No thanks,' I say, with a flutter in my tummy, wondering if it is a test.

'Amber, dude! Fuck that. Go outside,' Lee says in a South African accent.

Amber shrugs and goes out onto the balcony.

I sip my tea and watch the black goldfish swim round and round the bowl.

'He's called Bryan,' Lee says. I can't believe it. Bryan was the name of Matthew's pet snail when we were kids! Matthew was the only one to believe me when I told him that Bay was Bryan's real killer. His faith in me has been defining, moving us on from being just family friends who were likely to drift apart as we grew older to something else much more important.

'Bryan what?' I ask, deadpan.

Lee's beautiful mouth smiles. 'He's like Prince. He doesn't have a second name.'

'Cool,' I say. I love Prince! He is one of my favourite dead artists. When he died, Mum played 'Purple Rain' back-to-back all day and she often sings his songs in the shower.

I put my tea on the table to cool myself down. This guy is so hot, the roof might blow off. I'm glad I came. Today is turning out to be the best day I've ever had in my life.

While I try not to stare at Lee, there is some general chat about a new fashion magazine start-up, and then some debate about whether eComm M&S underwear is paid well enough and worth doing.

'Have you guys ever worked with V&L?' Lee asks.

'The German catalogue?' Amber asks, returning from the balcony. 'My German agency is crap. I never get any work there.'

'I worked with them last week and there was this dick of a stylist who shouted at me, like, "*Scheisse!* Your legs are vay too short!" What's up with that?' Lee snorts.

'Rude!' Leah says.

'I was, like, "Your trousers are too long, dude",' Lee says, grinning.

I look at his muscly legs clad in his manly track pants and wonder how anyone could criticise such perfection.

Amber laughs. 'I know, right?' And I worry she has read my mind.

'But I'm not dissing Germany. I love Berlin, man. That city is dope,' Lee says. He winks at me. Like, actually, *winks* at *me*.

I laugh along with their chat, but I don't really know what to say, so I stay pretty silent. Not pretty silent. Totally silent. I try to think of ways to join in, but it's impossible. I'm new to this and, to be honest, I still feel wound up. Mum has stopped calling, finally, which should make me feel better but for some reason makes me feel worse. Then I receive another text from Bay.

What the hell are you playing at? Anna's just got home. She's in floods of tears.

I turn off my phone.

Amber opens a beer and offers me one. I take it. The words of Bay's Snap begin to melt away and I replace them with what I believe about myself. *I do care about people's feelings, SO much. I always try to be kind. I'm not superficial at all. I always say what I feel. I try not to be selfish. I'll never leave the people I love behind. I'll never change.*

Tally and Leah crack open some more bottles and offer them around, before kneeling down to talk to me and bring me into the chat.

'Today's pictures should be cool, I think,' Tally says. Her northern accent is lovely.

'Asif was a total dick to you,' Leah says to me.

'It doesn't bother me,' I say.

I think they are both awesome, and so beautiful.

Tally is tall and super-thin, like a beanpole. Mum would say she needs a good meal inside her. But her eyes set her apart from mere mortals, as though she's above eating. One is blue and one is green, and they are so bright in contrast to her velvet, dark skin, it's like they're lit up from inside. Once you see them, you'll never forget them. She looked out of this world in Asif's screenshots today. I think she's probably the most beautiful girl I've ever seen in real life.

Leah is not quite as thin as Tally, in a good way. She has massive cheekbones and thick chestnut hair and huge hazel eyes – like the actual Princess Leia. Her skin is so smooth it's almost buttery. On the shoot, I caught a flash of her body half-naked when we were changing. Not one weird mole or stretch mark or popped vein in sight. I never thought bodies came that perfect.

I'm guessing that Lee, sipping sexily at his beer, fancies one of them. But right now he is looking at me, and I can hardly dare believe it. In the general chit-chat, he mentions his mum, and I get the impression she lives abroad, maybe South Africa, and that Lee moved to London to model when he was eighteen, two years ago.

Tall Tally and Princess Leia then bring up that Mum was my chaperone today, revealing that I'm under sixteen, which has probably killed any possibility of anything happening between me and Lee. But they are kind about it, like big sisters. Kind big sisters with no agenda and none of the needy crap that I get from Bay. It is a major relief to be free of everyone else's shit for one night only. I sing a ballad in my head, joyfully – and a bit dramatically – about having one night only to hook up with my lover. It isn't quite my story, but almost.

Mum and Bay and school tomorrow are far, far, far away.

I take my second beer.

After my third beer, I realise I have missed the ten o'clock train home.

CHAPTER THIRTEEN

Bay

Again I listened to Anna replay the argument she'd had with Nell in London. I felt sympathetic, but Anna's fretting was infectious. Panic was now bubbling up inside me, too.

I opened up my laptop and clicked into the film I was editing.

'She'll be fine, Anna. Honestly. In her text she said she was getting the 10.03. Don't worry about her so much.'

I wanted it to be true, but I understood why she was worrying. Nell was prone to a quick flash of indignation or a stomp around her room, but nothing like this. If I told Anna about Nell ignoring my texts, and about my Snapchat message, she would freak. She might even blame me for her disappearance, which would be totally unfair. Nell was the one who had upset *me*.

She hadn't responded to any of my messages. Not since lunch. She had never aired me before, and I couldn't understand why she was being so cruel. All she had to do was send me one quick text back and I would leave her be, reassured that she was safe. It was why I had sent that Snapchat to the group, in anger admittedly, but sometimes the truth needed to be told. My friends had responded to it with sad-face emojis, or commented: *I hope u r ok?* or *Call, KK?* or *Ikr*. But from Nell – to whom it had been directed – nothing. No defence or apology. Just toxic air.

I returned my thoughts to my film. The footage I was working on was a vox pop: a young girl sitting on a picnic blanket on the beach saying to camera that she had been picking up plastic every morning before school to save the universe from a climate emergency. My shot widened to show her holding a sandwich wrapped in cellophane. Before the sandwich, I cut the clip. For Anna's sake, I muted the sound. The footage was familiar enough for me to be able to work on the rough cut lightly, mindlessly, for now. Though it failed to block out my mind's looping concern about Nell.

I was reminded of Nell's mountain bike. It had looked sad lying there on its side in the water. Its handlebar was like an outstretched arm, begging to be rescued. At the time, I had imagined telling Nell where it was, but when Sunday morning arrived, I hadn't dared admit to it. I presumed the bike was still there in the stream, its metal rusting and rotting down to nothing.

'Can I see the text?' Anna asked me, sitting down next to me on the sofa.

I must have looked puzzled.

'Nell's text? About getting on the train?'

I unplugged one earphone. 'It was on Snapchat. It's gone.'

'Bloody Snapchat,' Anna shot back.

'Sorry. I should have screenshotted it.'

'No, sorry for being crabby, darling.'

'I totally understand why,' I said.

'You're the best. Love you.' She kissed my forehead, leaving a cool, damp imprint.

Anna peddled unconditional love, which was ironic. She hadn't noticed that I worked overtime to be loved by her. As a younger child, I had been a nightmare, but over the years I had figured out how to be the dream stepdaughter. It took effort: helping out whenever I knew Anna was frazzled, keeping my awkward feelings hidden, getting excellent grades at school, being a good sister. If I had continued to be the handful I had arrived as, I wonder if her love and dedication would have hardened and become dutiful rather than loving. Perhaps she had convinced herself that she loved us the same, her three girls – not two – whom she kissed and hugged and cared for fairly and equally. I suspected she was in denial, in a good-natured and unrealistic way, about how partisan her love had the potential to be. Being a super-stepmum was a lovely idea in theory, but I could not trust in it.

'I'll call Dom again.' She got up and prowled the kitchen with the handset pressed into her ear. As she waited for him to pick up, she mumbled, 'I should never have listened to him and come home. Never. What was I thinking? I'm such an idiot.'

'What difference would it have made if you'd waited at Waterloo?' I said, but she didn't hear me, because Dad picked up.

'Hasn't it arrived?' she said. 'Oh, right, sorry. My watch must be fast… Yes… Yes… It should be in any minute, though… Okay… Yeah, speak then.'

She hung up and sat down next to me again. 'All of this is so unlike her.'

Was it? When I had first met Nell, before I lived with them, I remembered the easy-going, mischievous way she had cheated in those games of Monopoly. It was obvious she hadn't been scared of being naughty, hadn't been scared of being told off. I had been in awe of that lightness of spirit, of her innocence.

'It's classic teen behaviour,' I said.

Anna smiled at me. 'You never did anything like this.' Her eyelashes were curled and clumped with black mascara. The application was rushed, always – and smudged now – but the spidery make-up flared around the warm blue of her eyes. She added, 'I know Nell's been a bit stressed lately, getting used to modelling and everything, but I never thought she would defy me like she did today.' She paused. 'It was like she hated me.'

I saved my edits and closed my laptop. 'All teenage girls hate their mothers,' I said.

Anna tossed her phone into the corner of the sofa. 'I told your dad this modelling thing wasn't a good idea.'

'She might have rebelled anyway.'

'You think?'

'Oh my God, Anna, some day soon, Jade would've taken her to Ritzy's in Guildford and forced tequila shots into her, or something. Seriously, a cosy gathering of supermodels in a flat in Shoreditch might not be so bad.'

Anna laughed. 'I hope you're right.'

Since the beginning, I had benefited from Anna's kind parenting, but I had always feared blood ties would win out in a real crisis. Was this our first proper crisis? The moment I had dreaded, when the falsities of the Hart family would spurt out? Was this the moment when Anna would display more love for the baby she had given birth to than for her husband's child?

As Suki's daughter, I had grown up to be circumspect.

Most days, she had force-fed me meals I hadn't liked, like mushroom omelette or tofu stir-fry, telling me that children should eat what was put in front of them. I had tried to be good and swallow each mouthful down before she shovelled in the next, but my body had rejected the food, unconsciously rejecting Suki herself. Consciously, I had believed that if I ate the food, she would love me. Conditions had been part of the deal if Suki were to love you – and she had not loved me – and I had a hunch that Anna was the same, underneath the picture of equality that she liked to display. Perhaps it was why she liked hats, to hide away, figuratively – I loved that word – under the brim of a cloche or behind the netted veil of a pillbox.

Was she warning me? 'I hope you're right', or else? Or else I would be in trouble? Did she know more about our argument than she was letting on? The fear of being blamed became more like a sound in my head than a feeling; the sound of a scream that was getting louder and louder. I recalled a nightmare when

I had clutched at a machine gun, shooting everyone around me while screaming at them to get away from me. My fright had motivated me to pull the trigger over and over at an unknown threat, leaving dead bodies everywhere I walked. It felt a bit like that when it came to Nell, as though I might be responsible for something happening to her, even if I had no desire to harm her. I loved Nell. I needed her to love me.

A text came through on Anna's phone. I braced myself.

'It's from Dom,' Anna said. 'The train is delayed by five minutes.'

'She *will* be on that train, Anna. Keep the faith.'

She exhaled and slumped back. 'I'm glad Iris is asleep through all this.'

'She'd be freaking out,' I said.

I put the back of my hand briefly on my forehead, wondering if the stress was giving me a temperature. I used to get temperatures all the time when I lived with Suki.

'There's nothing bad going on at school, is there?' Anna asked.

I clicked into another clip and said, 'I mean, it's near the end of term. Everyone gets a bit sick of each other.'

'But nothing out of the ordinary?' she asked, twisting to face me.

'Nothing that I know of.'

There was a deathly space between one beat of my heart and the next, and it was clogged with guilt.

'Hmm. She'd usually tell me,' she murmured.

'Absolutely,' I said.

Another text arrived. As she read it, she rested her head on the heels of her hands. 'Oh my God, Bay. She wasn't on the train.'

I stared at the screen of my laptop, unable to focus on the images, poleaxed. A brief, terrible opening in a recess of my mind allowed me to consider how it would feel to lose Nell.

Nell was the perfect child; the child more beautiful and more likeable and more lovable than me. The child Suki might have loved more. The child Anna loved more. The fact of her had been a burden from the moment I had set eyes on her lovely, happy smile. My pretty little sister had flagged up everything that I wasn't and could never be. If she didn't come home again, I would not have that impossible standard to live up to; and I realised with one ghastly whoosh of relief that I would be liberated from a secret we shared between us. Until now, I hadn't realised quite how much it weighed on me.

CHAPTER FOURTEEN

Anna

Dom had waited at Witley station for the arrival of the 10.03 train from Waterloo. But Nell had not been on that train. The next one was due in thirty-two minutes, at 11.34, and he was nipping home to go to the loo. I was keen to see him. It would bring comfort and distraction from the agony of worrying about her.

Earlier on, when I had called him from Waterloo to update him on the situation, he had said there was no point in me hanging about for another two hours, doing nothing except worry.

'What's the point? You'll just end up sitting on the train opposite her, staring at her moody gob all the way home,' he'd said. I was standing in the throng, being jostled by people rushing for their trains.

'I guess.' I had been reassured by his light-heartedness and had felt slightly less hysterical.

'Let's show her we trust her, yeah?' he had said. 'Reverse psychology.'

As I had stared up at the departures board, the orange letters and numbers had jumbled and my neck had ached.

'I suppose,' I had said, walking mindlessly towards my platform, the phone clamped to my ear.

'Better she comes home with her tail between her legs, then you'll be able to take the moral high ground and make up properly over a cup of hot chocolate or something.'

Dom was always the one to downgrade a catastrophe. Always the one to tell me to stop fussing so much. Always the one to tell me it was all going to be fine. But he had sounded less blasé on the phone just now after her no-show, and I was beginning to regret my decision to leave London. If I had stayed at Waterloo, I would have been nearer to her, consoled by the pretence that I was helping in some way. There was nothing worse than this sense of powerlessness.

Countless times we had tried to reach her on her phone, calling from my mobile, from Dom's, from Bay's, even FaceTiming her from Iris's iPad, but each time it had gone straight to voicemail or had not been picked up. I was refusing to picture the murdering, raping, mugging, gun-toting, knife-wielding, drug-addled criminals driving cabs or lurking in doorways waiting for her; waiting for Nell, fresh from the country, on London's mean streets at night. No, I was not thinking about any of that.

Bay clicked away at the touchpad of her laptop.

She didn't often irritate me, but she was now. I didn't say anything. I understood that editing her films was her way of de-stressing. In the early years of her life in our family, on the days when she became particularly uncommunicative and threw up her food regularly, I would sit her down with colouring pens or a notebook or a box of Lego to redirect her feelings and stave off one of her terrifying meltdowns, which were infrequent but ferocious. The first one we'd experienced was four months after she'd first stepped over the threshold. It had been provoked by an argument with Nell. They'd been playing some kind of make-believe game in the Wendy house and Nell had run into the kitchen while I was feeding Iris, screaming, holding her little finger out.

'She stamped on my finger on purpose and I can't move it!' she had cried.

'What?' I had taken her finger in my hand and asked her to move it, which she could, but it had been red and swollen.

Bay had come in next, shaking and crying, and I had said to her firmly, 'Bay. That's not a very nice thing to do, is it?' I had hugged Nell.

'I'm sorry!' Bay had screamed, high and thin. 'I'm sorry, but she was mean!'

'I wasn't mean,' Nell said, quieter and with more conviction.

'*She* said,' Bay shouted, pointing at Nell, 'that I wasn't her real sister and that you were only *pretending* to be my mum!'

'Oh Nell! You didn't say that, did you?' Blindsided, I pulled away from her a little.

'No! I didn't say that! I didn't! I swear on my life!'

'You did too!' Bay screamed. Her little bones had seemed to rattle with rage.

I hadn't known whom to believe, but it had not sounded like something Nell would say.

I was careful, trying to be even-handed. 'Even if Nell says something mean, you mustn't ever hurt her, okay?'

Bay had screamed over and over, '*She's lying! She's lying! She's lying!*' She had begun to lose sense of what she was screaming about. Standing there convulsing, incandescent, her pale face pink and blotchy. Maybe Nell *had* been lying, I had thought, but I had no time to work it out before Bay exploded into a full-blown tantrum. I had tried holding her, just as I had held Nell during her terrible twos phase, but at eight, Bay had been less easy to control. Her elbows had dug and twisted, and she had wriggled free, knocking a mug off the table, screaming about not wanting to be in this family and how much she hated us, thrashing about, kicking doors and hitting pictures off walls. My jaw had clenched shut to physically hold back my own anger. After four months of day-in, day-out, minute-by-minute management of her delicate moods, I had a lot of it stored up, but I had not been able to let loose like she had, and I had been awakened to the fact that this was only the beginning of an uphill struggle. It had hit me hard that day.

Bitterly I had longed for our family as it had been before, when I hadn't had to care for this strange child and be mindful of every single damn thing I said and did, just in case it upset her. My sympathy had come a few hours later, when her outburst had passed. I had stroked her too-long fringe off her forehead and she had listened to old music on her vinyl record player, conking out before the first song on the A-side had finished. Then I had kissed her cheek and told her I loved her.

Now, there was a burst of noise from her laptop. A child's voice. The mic being scuffed by the wind.

'Whoops. Sorry,' Bay said.

I almost snapped at her, but that wouldn't be fair. Bay was not the child I should be annoyed with. It was clear-cut this time. But my fear for Nell's safety had overridden any anger I'd held about her defiant behaviour. I simply wanted her out of harm's way. And in return, I vowed, with a heart full of love, that I would never raise my voice to her again, as long as I could see her back home in one piece tonight.

When Dom's key rattled in the lock, I leapt up, half hoping that he had brought Nell with him, that he might have concealed her to surprise me. The door opened. Even though my rational brain knew he would be alone, the disappointment of not seeing her arrived like a kick.

'No text yet?' I asked him.

'Nope. One second.' He jogged to the loo, undoing his flies as he went. A waft of cigarette smoke lingered in the hall.

He emerged with his hair pushed back, damp from the rain. 'That's a relief,' he said.

'Are you sure you don't want me to take over?'

'It's fine.' He checked his phone and pocketed it. 'And Bay's definitely heard nothing from her?'

I shook my head. 'Maybe her phone ran out of battery,' I said.

'You think?' He picked up Iris's sunhat from the floor and swung it around and around his forefinger. I had seen it there earlier and had failed to tidy it up, as though that one tiny task could have sent me over the edge.

'Or she's having the time of her life and can't be bothered,' I said, trying to smile.

He bunched his lips up tight, like a point, and looked me right in the eye. 'Let's hope so.'

There was a dulling of colour in his eyes, like a black cloud moving over fresh green grass. That stale, loaded look of his jogged a memory of my own father. Never before had I consciously made a connection between the two men. I was startled by it, catapulted back to the house I'd grown up in and how I had felt as a child during my father's heavy, accusatory silences. The silences of unutterable unhappiness, for which I had somehow felt to blame.

Dom hung up Iris's hat and slammed the door behind him as he left.

Bay came up behind me. 'You okay?'

'Yes,' I said, jumping slightly.

I started cleaning the kitchen, just for something to do, and my thoughts returned to Dom. I pushed that reproachful look of his away and my mind drifted back over our marriage, over our steady and functioning relationship, to our first few months together, before I knew I was pregnant, when sex had been less important than the snug, dependable chats afterwards. We had talked of our future together, of securing a nice life in a nice house outside of London. We had both needed nice. Nice had been an antidote to his toxic marriage to Suki and a comfort for me after years of not moving on from my separation from Billy Young. We had become best friends who had sex, and it had been very nice indeed.

*

After the most drawn-out, not-nice twenty minutes of my life, car lights streamed through the glass panels of the front door.

'Is that them? Why didn't he text?' I cried.

With Bay close behind me, I ran to the door and flung it open, feeling a lurch in my stomach, fearing that Nell would not be sitting beside Dom in the passenger seat.

But she was there.

Warm, sharp relief spread through me. Light rain cooled my face.

'Do you think she'll be drunk?' Bay asked over my shoulder.

'I hope not,' I said, not really caring if she was.

Through the flare from the street lamp, I couldn't see her expression clearly in the passenger window.

The car door opened.

Taking me by surprise, Nell darted out, pushing past me and Bay. Bay tried to touch her arm. 'Nell! Er. Hi?' Nell flinched, actively avoiding her touch.

'Excuse me, young lady,' I said. 'A hello is the least we deserve.'

'I'm going to bed,' she said.

'Okay then,' Bay said, moving closer to me, shivery and fragile.

My heart contracted. In recent years, rarely had I seen Nell so angry with Bay, and I wondered whether Bay had told me the whole story. Dom came into the house behind us.

'She's just tired,' he said. He threw his boots into the shoe basket.

I followed him into the kitchen. 'Did she say anything to you in the car?'

'No, not really.'

'What do you mean, not really?'

'She didn't say anything, Anna. I'm going to bed too. I've got an early meeting.'

'Night then,' I said. Now that I had seen my father's look in Dom, I couldn't unsee it. Would there be any point in convincing

Dom that I was not to blame for Nell running off? *Had* I really been to blame?

Out in the hall, I watched him climb the stairs, back straight, hands like small white balls. I heard him say goodnight to Bay, and the click of our bedroom door closing.

I stood there with mixed emotions: misjudged and at fault, and suddenly very tired.

There was the sound of Bay knocking on Nell's door. 'Nell?'

Then I heard Nell scream at the top of her lungs, 'JUST FUCK OFF, BAY!'

I ran up the stairs, two at a time, and found Bay with her arms limp by her sides and the colour drained from her already pale skin. 'I only wanted to see how she was,' she whispered.

Anger rose inside me. I shook my head at Bay. 'All this over a bloody party.' I was furious. I rattled the door handle. It wouldn't open. It seemed Nell had pushed something under it.

'Nell. *Nell*, open this door!' I hissed, not wanting to shout in case I woke Iris.

How dare she treat us like this? Had she no concept of how we might have been feeling while she had been partying in London? All evening we had been waiting for her and worrying about her. Was she really not sorry? I tried the door again. It was not budging. I gave up. For now. Tomorrow morning she would have some explaining to do.

'Come on, let's get you into bed,' I said to Bay.

'Uh-huh,' she yawned, plodding upstairs. I followed her up.

She climbed into bed with her tracksuit on and I sat down on the top step. The beams above our heads were covered in Polaroids and fake flowers and I felt comforted by the pretty homeliness that she had created. The charge of anger began to subside, and my hands stopped trembling so much.

'Won't you be hot in your trackies, darling?'

She reached for her Kindle. 'No. I'm freezing.'

'Okay, I'll leave you to it. Don't read for too long, will you? It's been a long day.'

'It really has.'

'Oh darling, I'm so sorry about all this.'

She closed the Kindle and picked at the fraying corner of its cloth cover with her delicate, fluttery little fingers. 'It's not your fault.'

Dom thought it had been.

'Hmm,' I said now. 'I probably could have handled it better.'

'You know, Ty's mum grounded him for a month once.'

'What had he done?'

'He went to a pub with his mates and got drunk. He was only fourteen.'

'Did he stop going to pubs after he was grounded?'

'Yes. Totally.'

Grounding Nell seemed harsh, but perhaps it would be the only way to protect her from too much too soon.

'Look. Don't worry about it. Your dad and I will sort her out. She'll be feeling awful about it tomorrow.'

'I guess so. Night, Anna.'

'Night-night, sweetheart. Love you.'

'Love you too,' she said.

As I slipped into bed next to Dom, I decided that grounding Nell might help us to claw back some sense of control. I turned on my side with an exaggerated tug of the duvet, hoping an icy draught would shoot down his back. I was always the one to fret after an emotional drama with the girls, and he was always the one to go to bed and have sweet dreams, unperturbed somehow.

It had been the same when Bay had arrived. She was his daughter, but he had been disengaged, telling me to stop worrying about her so much. He had shut me down, as though he were a fifties husband who considered his wife a silly bubblehead for thinking of girlie things like emotions. 'Stop worrying your pretty little head about it, dear!' A proper man didn't have time to bother himself with the domestic strife of his own children. But Dom would vociferously deny thinking like that, insisting he was a very modern man.

What rankled me now was how heavily involved in the drama he became when it suited him, when there was a big, 'manly' decision to make – usually when money came into it, like Nell modelling – but because he never paid attention to the nuances of the girls' emotional hinterlands, he had read the situation all wrong. Encouraging Nell to model had been his mistake; mine had been listening to him.

CHAPTER FIFTEEN

2012

Bay snuck into Nell's bed after lights-out when she heard Dom and Anna fighting in the garden. Iris was fast asleep in her cot. Bay and Nell listened to them shouting about Granny Berry, shouting about Dom's job, shouting about getting married.

'For *Mum*? What the hell are you talking about? I don't want to get married for *Mum*, I want to do it for us and for the girls!' Anna shouted.

'For them or for *you*?' Dom shouted back.

'Us, them, me, you. It's all the same thing, isn't it?'

Their voices went quieter. The two girls couldn't hear what they said next. They tiptoed to the windowsill, straining to listen, shoulder to shoulder. More mumbling. There was a scrape of the outdoor chairs on the patio.

Then Anna yelled again. 'You don't ever listen to anything I'm saying!'

'I spend my whole bloody life bloody listening!'

'But you don't ever *hear* me! I'm like white noise!'

'Jesus. You're so fucking neurotic!' Dom shouted back.

There was another silence. The girls looked at each other.

The conservatory door slammed, and they scurried back to bed.

'Dad's a big meanie,' Nell said, sniffing. 'I don't like him swearing.'

Secretly Bay agreed, but she couldn't say anything bad about their dad to Nell. She thought carefully about him marrying Anna. If they got married, Anna would officially be her stepmum, and she wanted this very much.

'I'm going to write him a letter,' Bay whispered to Nell. 'Can I borrow your pink notepaper?'

Nell said she could, and Bay laid out her feelings on the matter.

Dear Daddy,

Me and Nell herd you fight with Anna in the garden last nite. Nell cried. I think it is herrific that you don't want to marry her. Here are ten things why I think you shoud:

1) she is really, <u>really</u> pretty when she puts her hair up
2) she likes boring things like walks just like you
3) she never shouts like you even when I am horrible and naughty
4) she always remembers to pick me up from school
5) she sings really loudly in the shower and it sounds like happyness and makes the hole house feel happy
6) her hats are weird but she works esstreemly hard on them (I'm happy she doesn't wear them outside though)
7) her hair smells of perfume every day even when she looks very tired
8) she is so fun when she drives too fast in our yellow car and you tell her off (but I know you secrotly love it)
9) she makes the most delishuss chocalit cake ever

10) I want her to be my reel mummy because she's
    really special

I bet you will change your mind now.

Yours sincereley,
Bay xoxoxoxoxoxoxoxoxoxo

PS your the best daddy ever

She sealed it into a matching pink envelope and wrote his full
name, 'Mr Dom Hart', on the front. In the morning, Bay and Nell
together pushed it under their parents' bedroom door and waited.

Suddenly the door opened and Dom was standing above them.

'Can I help you?' he said, holding the pink letter in his hand.

'Come here, you two,' Anna said from the bed.

The girls weren't sure whether they were in trouble or not.
They scrabbled under the duvet either side of Anna. Close up,
Bay could see tears on her face.

'I think you're really special too, my darling Bay,' she said into
her ear in a whispery voice. And then, louder, 'How do you girls
feel about being bridesmaids?'

Bay and Nell burst into giggles and jumped up and down on
the bed. Dom tickled them both until they screamed for mercy.
Bay had never thought it was possible to feel this happy. Anna
was going to be her other mummy and she was going to love her
just as much as she loved Nell and Iris.

CHAPTER SIXTEEN

Anna

I hung up the phone, stunned.

'Everything okay?' Mum called out from the kitchen. A picture of poppies in a field came into focus. The print on the wall in Mum's hallway was the only colour in her beige flat, and I realised I had been staring at it for the whole conversation with Ian. I straightened the frame.

'Sorry, that was Ian,' I said, returning to Mum, putting the last few items of food into her fridge.

'Who's Ian again?' Mum said, licking her finger and turning a page of the local newspaper.

'Nell's booker,' I reminded her.

She turned another page. 'This is a very good newspaper, you know,' she said.

Her lack of curiosity suited me. I needed time to process Ian's news, uncertain how I felt about it.

'There. That's all done,' I said, wiping off a dried stain of something from the counter. 'I'd better get going. I've got frozen peas and ice cream in the car.'

'Oh. You're not staying for coffee?'

I noted how much older she looked today and felt bad about rushing off. Her white fringe was a little dirty and there were deep hollows under her cheekbones. She was still beautiful. There was no doubt that Nell had got her looks from Mum.

I sat down at the table next to her and held her long, cold fingers. 'Did you call the WI?'

Her tone of voice sharpened. 'I don't want to make *jam*.'

'They're really much more modern these days. They have dances and feminist speakers and loads of fun events. It would get you out a bit. I'll join with you, if you like.'

We had had this conversation before. I didn't know why I thought it would make a difference today. She lived only ten minutes' walk away from the town's high street, yet she hadn't been out in months. Persuading her to join a club had been a fond hope.

'You don't have to worry about me,' she said, sounding irritated, and then she smiled to herself. 'Nell is so like me, you know,' she said, repeating what she had said before Ian had called, when I had been telling her about Nell's rebellious episode in London last week.

'You look so alike,' I said. They were polar opposites in personality, though. Nell was a sunny day and Mum was a rainy one.

'I mean in spirit, you know. I've told you, haven't I? About when Maman...' And off she went, reminiscing about her upbringing in France, retelling a story I knew so well. I folded her bags-for-life and put them into my handbag, and listened patiently, imagining the ice cream in the boot of my car melting into milkshake.

'...and then Didier and I found Maman snoring under the olive tree with a bottle of absinthe lying against her stocking – they wore them in those days – so we tickled her hairy chin and still she didn't wake up! And then Papa threw the bottle at her head and she woke up and ducked and it smashed on the tree trunk instead! Can you imagine? Oh, it was so funny!' She cackled.

I laughed along, but I found her *petits contes amusants* – as she called her stories – uncomfortable to listen to, knowing they were horribly romanticised. The absinthe had probably been bog-standard gin, and the olive tree had probably been a toilet cistern. When we had visited our grandmother in Roussillon as children, my brother and I had laughed at her crazy dancing and enjoyed her sentimental hugs, but had been a little bit scared of her cirrhotic yellow eyes and her late-night outbursts at Dad – *le rosbif!*

'Papa was such a kind man. You never met such a kind man in your life before,' Mum said now.

Sentimental talk of my *grandpère* was my cue to leave. 'Okay, Mum. I'd better get back to give Nell the news.'

'What news is that, dear?' she asked, and I realised my mistake. I hadn't wanted to tell her yet. I knew it would unsettle her.

'Oh, nothing, just something about a job,' I said, which wasn't a complete lie. 'I'll be back with your Gaviscon in a bit. Tesco didn't have the sachets you like.'

At home, I hesitated at the kitchen door. The volume was too high on the television. I could hear two Australian child actors talking about a secret note they had found in a drawer. It was the detective series that Iris loved watching after school every day.

I walked in and put the shopping bags down by the fridge. Iris was sitting close to the TV, chin tipped up. Bay and Nell were at opposite ends of the sofa. Over the past week, since Nell had told Bay to fuck off, they had barely spoken to one another.

'Hi, girls.' None of them reacted. 'Sorry I took so long.'

It seemed I was talking to myself. I wondered if they had noticed that I had been out at all.

I projected my voice. 'Can you turn your screens off, please, girls?' The news I was going to share warranted a temporary media blackout.

I had debated telling Nell first, alone, and then the other two, but had decided against it. I didn't like secrets. In my own childhood I'd had the sense that there was always a secret being kept; feelings trapped behind my parents' faces and inside their voices, often before something shocking happened. Suddenly. Without warning. Like Dad leaving when I was fifteen.

In this case, the news was not shocking so much as thrilling. For Nell, at least. 'Nell?'

'Yeah?' Still she didn't look up from her phone.

'I've just had a call from Ian,' I said.

She shot up. 'And?'

Iris said, 'Can I just watch—'

Nell grabbed the remote and switched the television off. 'No, Iris. Go on, Mum.'

I could tell she had guessed what the news might be, but I had asked Ian to hold off from sending the confirmation email until I had told her myself.

'You got the job in New York. Flying on the twenty-eighth of July,' I said, trying to get the tone right, balancing enthusiasm for Nell with sensitivity towards Bay and Iris.

'But what about being grounded?' Nell said, as though holding her breath before she reacted properly.

'You're off the hook. This time,' I said sternly.

'Oh my God! I love you so much, Mum. You won't regret it!' she squealed before throwing her arms around me.

For a split second, Bay was frozen as she stared over at us, dumbfounded, but then she leapt up and jigged about nervily, flapping her hands, hugging Nell, saying 'oh my God' over and over. While they jumped up and down, they seemed to have forgotten they were cross with each other. Iris tried to get in on the dancing and hugging, but her two big sisters were ignoring her. Her little smile faded.

I beckoned her over. 'Exciting news for Nell, isn't it?'

'Yeah! Will you be going too?' Iris said.

'Yes.' My stomach somersaulted.

'But who will look after us?'

'Daddy.'

'Cool,' she said quietly.

When I had told Dom about New York on the phone earlier, he had sounded excited for Nell and unfazed by the childcare he would now have to juggle with his job for five days of the summer holiday.

In theory, he had always been a working dad. He was a dad. And he did work. But he was one of those working dads who was of the generation that didn't know what 'woke' meant and was still learning about equality. Even the road cycling phase had passed him by; he'd stuck instead with his dad's hobby of golf. Dom was a traditionalist, not a feminist, which I hadn't much minded about until now. Under these circumstances, I would have liked him to be a working *mum* so that I could feel confident about legging it to New York at such short notice.

As it stood, he didn't know much about how I ran the girls' lives. He didn't know that Bay and Iris never ate the same foods. He didn't know that unless you asked Iris ten times, she wouldn't brush her teeth. He didn't know that he would need to wash her favourite, and now faded, *MEOW* T-shirt most nights because of hot chocolate or ketchup drips. He didn't know the addresses of Iris's friends for play dates or have the contact details of the activity clubs that could occupy her while he was at work. He didn't know how finely balanced the coordination of the pick-ups and drop-offs of Bay's social life were, which unfairly took precedence over Iris's. He wouldn't be mentally on call to take time off work to nurse the girls if they were sick. He wouldn't want to stay up way past his own bedtime, dog-tired after a day in the office, to soothe them back to sleep or talk to them about friendship issues. He didn't know that Mum's repeat prescription was due for collection next week or that her plumber was popping by for his cash.

'I want to go to New York too,' Iris said.

'We'll go as a family some day soon. Promise. I can check out the cool places to visit.'

On top of worrying about Dom in charge at home, I worried about getting Ava's hat finished before I left. I checked my watch.

Bay came over to me and said, 'I'm so excited for her!' but her pale face said otherwise. It was a flashback to the way she'd looked as a little girl before she was sick.

'I wish I could pack you in my suitcase,' I told her, tucking a pointy chunk of hair behind her ear.

'I'm small enough,' she said, pushing out her bottom lip sweetly, like a baby.

I laughed and pulled her into a hug. 'I promise to send you lots of photos.'

'I'd love that.' And she went off upstairs, reasonably sanguine. I hoped.

'Right, you two. I have to pop back to Granny's with her medicine. I'll be back in half an hour.'

'Can I come too?' Nell asked.

'Have you done your homework?'

'I don't have any. It's the last week of term.'

'I'm only nipping in and out.'

'But I want to tell her my news!'

'Okay, come on then. Don't faff around, though. I want to leave now.'

'I'm just getting my socks,' she said, running upstairs.

As I was putting my shoes on, I heard Nell and Bay whispering on the landing above. Feeling nosy, I hovered in the stairwell to listen.

'I just don't buy all that "I'm so happy for you" crap when I know you're not,' Nell hissed.

'I am really happy for you, Nellie. I was a total dick to you last week. I was jealous. I love you so much.'

'That group Snap really hurt my feelings. You know for a *fact* I'd never leave you behind! You *know* I'd never be unkind!'

'Of course I know. I'm so sorry.'

There was a pause and some mumbling from Nell about something being taken from her. They must have moved into her bedroom. I heard a drawer being opened and closed.

'I swear to God I didn't take it,' Bay said, louder. 'You have to believe me. It must have been kids or something. You can't keep going on about it. Seriously, it's so insulting. I don't do that kind of stupid shit any more.'

There was a long pause and I considered Nell's accusation, which must have been about her bike, wondering why on earth she'd think Bay had taken it.

'I probably wanted someone to blame,' Nell replied finally.

'Your socks don't match,' Bay said.

Nell laughed.

'Hug it out?' Bay said. 'We should've talked about this sooner.'

There was another pause, when I guessed they were hugging, and my heart settled.

'I wish you could come to New York,' Nell said.

'Why don't you ask Anna if I can?' Bay shot back. 'She did say she wanted to pack me in her suitcase.'

Nell said something I couldn't hear, and I hoped she was shutting it down. We could not afford to take Bay to New York.

'Don't, then. It's okay,' Bay said.

'No! I will ask her. I promise.'

'What are you doing, Mummy?' Iris appeared behind me.

'Nothing,' I said, caught out. 'Come on, Nell, if you're coming!' I called up.

'Stay for a drink,' Mum said, sitting down heavily on her sofa with a grunt. I could sense she was in low spirits, which would not make Nell's news easy to share. I expected her to be as put out as Bay was about me going to New York, though for different reasons. She would think I was abandoning her to spite her. She was capable of turning nasty if she was upset, and I didn't want Nell to witness her viciousness, or worse, be on the receiving end of it. Or maybe I was worried she would jinx the trip, somehow stop it from happening. But this was silliness on my part, an echo of trouble from the past. Mum had changed since then.

'What would you like, Mum?' I said, loudly.

'There's some red on the side. But I won't have anything.'

'You sure?'

'You two go ahead, though. I'll be okay.' She smoothed her long fingers across her brow. 'The migraines are back.'

'Oh dear, Granny, I'm so sorry,' Nell said, looking suitably grave, as though she hadn't heard her grandmother say this every single time we visited.

It was almost as if Mum's life had stopped when Dad had left her, thirty-odd years ago, whereas Dad's had flourished. A photograph of him in his new life existed somewhere. It had come tucked in the folded page of a letter, sent all the way from Sydney. In the picture, his big arm had secured his new wife around her waist and the smile through his blond beard had been carefree and blissed out. My brother Martin had been sent the same photo and an identically worded letter announcing their marriage. Bitterly, he had remarked that our father was only happy because he had taken all of my mother's happiness with him. It had not sounded like an exaggeration. We had agreed that we would not write back, like a sibling survivors' pact.

'Oh Nellie dear, I'm just getting old, that's all,' Mum said.

'Are you sure you won't have a little drop, Mum?' I asked, knowing that she drank most evenings.

She dropped the gentleness of her tone. 'No. Thank you.'

I sat down next to her. 'I've put your Gaviscon by the fridge.'

'Sorry to interrupt your evening again. I know you're all so busy.' She sighed, tugging her cotton skirt over her long thighs.

'Don't be silly. You can interrupt our evening any time,' Nell said.

Mum leant towards her. 'It's so lovely of you to come,' she said. 'My beautiful granddaughter!'

Nell grinned. 'I've got something to tell you, Granny.'

My mother looked at me and wrinkled her brow. 'Oh?'

'I've got a modelling job in New York, and Mum's coming with me!'

'New York, you say? Really?' Mum looked at me for confirmation, as though she might have misheard.

'Yes, it's true, for a teen clothing catalogue.'

I waited for questions about who would make her pharmacy run and get the cash for John the plumber.

'New York, eh? Well, well, well,' she said, eyeing me. '"Those people in New York are not going to change me none",' she sang.

I moved on quickly, with an inkling that she had remembered who lived out there. 'It's an advertising job for the young adult range at Focus, the supermarket.'

Her mouth straightened. 'A supermarket, you say?'

'It's really nice, Granny, honestly,' Nell said. 'I've seen it online. Ian said I'll be on billboards in America and get paid loads of money!'

This seemed to cheer Mum up. 'Billboards?'

'Yes, definitely.'

'Well. Maybe I will have a little glass of the red after all.'

I smiled. 'Sure. I'll get it.'

'And one for Nellie too.'

'I don't think that's a good idea on a school night.'

My mother said, 'At Nell's age, I used to drink a little wine at supper every evening.'

I nipped into the kitchenette to pour her a glass of wine, relieved to miss the rest of her speech about her French upbringing and their superior drinking traditions, happy that she hadn't been morose or unpleasant about our trip away. For Nell, it seemed, Mum had been capable of thinking of someone else's feelings before her own.

'…and we'd meet boys. Under the trees. Where the old men played boules in the dust,' she was saying to Nell when I returned.

Nell knew to ask questions about the French village boys and what they went on to become – surgeons and lawyers and dentists and teachers, any job my mother could think of that was better than my father's job as a plumber. The chat about the boys she should have married and the sunnier life she should have had in Le Sud lit her up in ways most other subjects could not. She became poetic and wet-eyed at the flourishes and embellishments of her stories, and followed them with a sigh and a passing comment about her drab, damp, disappointing adult life on the outskirts of nowhere in the UK. My father's name was never mentioned, but the hatred she had for him underpinned every memory. Nell wasn't old enough to understand the subtext. She loved the romance and naughtiness of Granny Berry's stories.

'Good times!' Mum said. She waved her wine glass around, gesticulating as she talked. Worried that the red droplets would splatter her sofa, I gently took it from her.

It seemed to decompress her. She sat back and sighed. 'Up and down, life is. You can never rest on your laurels.'

'We'd better get going,' I said, looking at Nell. 'I said I'd pick Dad up from the driving range.'

Mum stood up, still so tall even when stooped, and shuffled behind us to the front door. Her hand rested on the frame for steadiness.

'Come over and tell me all about New York when you're back.'

'We will,' Nell said, kissing her on the cheek.

'I'll call you with the arrangements for when I'm away, Mum,' I said.

Just as we started down the stairs, she called after us. 'You should look him up while you're out there, Anna.'

Distractedly I said, 'Look who up…?' then stopped.

Nell swivelled round on the step below mine. 'You know someone in New York, Mum?'

'No! I don't know anyone in New York! Come on. Let's go.'

I couldn't believe my mother had brought him up in front of Nell. 'Bye, Mum!' I did not turn around for her to enjoy my flushed cheeks.

'Bye, darlings!' she trilled.

The door closed and we descended the two flights of stairs to the foyer. Nell said, 'Who do you know out there? Is it an old boyfriend? I won't tell Dad, promise.'

'Nell! Stop it! Granny Berry's losing her marbles.'

'Why are you bright red then?'

'It was hot in there.'

A text bipped on her phone, and her focus shifted, giving me time to try to slow my galloping heartbeat.

When we got into the car, Nell said, 'Mum?' in that tone that suggested she was going to ask a difficult question. I braced myself for more questions about my mystery friend in New York, glaring up at Mum's window. It wasn't a pretty building. The red bricks were too red, and the door was utility, almost institutional. I imagined Mum inside, grinning, pleased with herself for mentioning him. She and Billy had a history too.

'Mum?' Nell said again.

'Yes, darling?' I said, pushing at the handbrake.

'Can I pay for Bay to come to New York with us?'

My heart burst. I put the handbrake on again, soaking up the sight of my kind-hearted, wilful child by my side. 'Oh darling, you are a love. Bay will be okay.'

Her chin wobbled and she dropped her head, letting all that blonde hair fall over her face like a mop. 'She really wants to come, and it'll be the summer holidays by then. And she's just texted me again saying she's happy to sleep on the floor in the hotel.'

'But that money was going to buy you a new mountain bike.'

'I can buy a mountain bike with money from the next job I get.'

'That might be months away. And you love your bike.'

'Can I borrow it from you and Dad? I'll pay you back, promise.'

A sense of inadequacy sank through me. 'I wish I could give you the money, Nell. I hate that we can't afford it for you. But we just don't have it at the moment.' Finding a few hundred pounds to buy a bike or a plane ticket right now was beyond our means.

'Bay's going to be so angry.'

I was confused. 'Angry?'

'Disappointed, you know. We were convinced you'd let her.'

'Is that what you two were whispering about upstairs?'

'She said you'd suggested it.'

I wished I had never made the joke about packing her in my suitcase. 'I'm so sorry if I gave that impression. It's not appropriate for her to come. You'll be working, remember?'

'It'll be fine!'

'And did you think about Iris in this plan of yours? If both of you went and she was the only one left behind, imagine how she'd feel.'

'I guess so.'

'It'll be fun, just us two, won't it?'

'Yes, of course,' she said.

'Come on. Show me some love and high-five it, Nellie Noos!'

She laughed and slapped my palm. 'You're so uncool, Mum,' she chuckled, and went back to texting on her phone.

The point was, I didn't want Bay to come. I loved Bay and I would gladly go away somewhere with her some day, but this trip was about Nell.

CHAPTER SEVENTEEN

Bay

Nell came up the stairs into my bedroom and flopped down on the bed next to me.

'So?' I said, bracing myself for bad news about New York. Lately, I had been trying my best to manage my envy about Nell's modelling career. Going with them to the States and being part of it in some way was a middle ground, a bit of give and take.

'She said no,' she sighed, and then propped herself up on one elbow to face me, with her hand lost in her mane of beautiful golden hair. 'I'm so sorry.'

I clenched my teeth together and tried not to cry, but I had to turn my head away from her. When I turned back, she was lying on her back. Her profile was edged by neon pink from the fairy lights and her fringe had fallen back off her forehead. She looked younger than fifteen. She had lived a small life up until now. But modelling was not small. New York was not small. Billboards across America was not small. Nell's future was big, and I wondered where it left me.

'No worries,' I said. I stayed quiet for a few moments while I processed the deadening disappointment. Keeping it inside was hard, but I was not going to make the same mistake as I had last week by allowing my gremlin feelings to get out. I would try to be a better sister than that.

I held my camera phone up to Nell's face, close up, and pressed record.

'Miss Hart, in a statement made earlier today in response to your recent release from your twenty-eight-day grounding at Lower Road Prison, after contravening the 2021 No Partying in London Act last week, you told Mrs Hart…' I paused, cleared my throat and said in a deadpan tone, '"I love you, Mum. You won't regret it". In the light of your upcoming success in New York, do you have anything to add to your statement?'

She sat up. 'Yeah. It was a miscarriage of justice.'

'Do you deny running away from Mrs Anna Hart on the evening of Thursday the fifteenth of July to an unknown address in the capital city of London where strangers lured you into underage drinking?'

'I was innocent! And I only had a couple of beers! That lot are squarer than Jade and Mint!'

'Jade and Mint aren't square at all.'

'True. Anyway, stop filming,' she said, chucking an old sock at the camera. 'I've got a secret to tell you.'

There was a knock on the door. 'It's me, Iris.'

I wanted to tell her to go away. 'What secret?' I whispered.

'It's about Mum. I'll tell you in a minute,' Nell said. Then, to Iris, 'Come in!'

There was a smear of chocolate in the corner of Iris's mouth. She was never clean, even after a bath. She snuggled up to Nell on the bed. They looked alike. Entangled sweetness and blondeness. I raised my phone and began to film again.

'Will you buy me a present in New York?' Iris asked.

'Yes. What would you like?'

'Something with a cat on it.'

Nell laughed. 'What a surprise.'

'Is Dad back?' I asked Iris.

'Yes. He told me to go away because he needed to talk to Mummy.'

Nell and I glanced at one another. 'They've been having a lot of talks,' Nell said, biting her lip. I wondered if their talks were related to the secret that Nell was about to reveal.

'Did you know that married couples don't have sex?' Iris said.

Nell and I both spluttered. 'Iris! Where did you hear that from?'

'Megan at school told me.'

'Married couples *do* have sex,' I said.

Iris screwed up her face. 'Eugh. Gross.'

Nell said, 'Let's not think about it.'

'Iris, will you go get us some snacks?' I said.

'Okay. What do you want?'

'Salt and vinegar crisps.'

'Sure,' she said, trotting out.

I called after her. 'See if you can hear what they're saying!'

Nell let her head drop back onto the pillow next to me. A strand of her hair fell over my face, and I hesitated, taking in its Nell scent, before pushing it off.

'So tell me this secret,' I whispered.

'Well, I think Mum knows some guy out in New York.'

I raised my head. 'What guy?'

'I don't know for sure if it is a guy, but she acted so weird when Granny Berry brought it up and went really bright red.'

'She's never mentioned knowing anyone there.'

Anna was the sort of woman whose independence had been worn away by years of motherhood. She was the sort of woman people in the village called 'lovely', in spite of the unfashionable clothes and boring haircuts. She was the sort of woman everyone waved at enthusiastically when she bopped past in her sunshine-yellow car. Anna was *not* the sort of woman who knew strange men in New York.

Then I remembered her drunk at Dad's fortieth. Her hair had been swept into a chignon, showing off her wide jaw and pretty features. Her tight dress had accentuated her curves. Her eyes had darted around with flirtatious energy, as though they had once looked further afield than her cosy life in Grayswood. Anna had not always been a down-home mum of three.

'I think it might be an old boyfriend,' Nell said. Then she guffawed.

A finger of irritation jabbed my ribs. She wouldn't laugh if she knew what could happen to a family when a third party came into a marriage. 'She's a dark horse,' I said.

She nudged me. 'It's not something to worry about, Bay. I just thought it was funny.'

'I'm not worried about it,' I said, but I felt uneasy, as though the solidity of our family life had wobbled a little. 'I'm just a bit sad about not going with you guys, that's all.'

'I know, it's so crap, but I'll take loads of pictures when we're out there and send them to you,' Nell said. It was plain that she had liked the drama about the mystery man in New York, but that she was not, at her core, concerned. She trusted her mother. I wondered if I, too, might be able to trust Anna.

Distractedly I replied, 'Yeah, loads of photos and FaceTimes, then I can live vicariously.'

'What's "vicariously" mean, again?'

In a spooky voice, I said, 'It means I can live through you.'

'Don't be weird.'

'It's not weird when you want to be an award-winning film-maker.'

'What's your next film going to be about?' Nell asked.

I dragged my thoughts away from the man in New York and tried to focus on creative thinking, just as Anna had taught me, which usually helped me with my anxiety. 'Did you know that twenty per cent of Year 6 children in the UK are obese?' I said, but my mind immediately filled up with bad thoughts again, this time with unwanted projections of Anna leaving Dad.

'That's insane,' Nell said.

'I looked it up on my phone when I was standing in the queue at Sainsbury's.'

Nell grinned. 'What, when you were buying supersized M&Ms and crisps?'

'What?'

'You were buying junk food while worrying about obesity?' Nell said. My expression remained serious. 'Never mind,' she said.

'The whole queue was kids from our school, and they were all fat.'

'Bay! You can't say that.'

'Sorry, I meant they were big-boned or curvy.'

'Like me, you mean.'

'Bloody hell, Nell. Don't be an idiot.'

'Try working with girls like Tally.'

'Seriously, you need to read up on body dysmorphia and female disempowerment.'

'Do I need to watch a Bay Hart film about it?' Nell said, grinning.

I considered it. 'That's not a bad idea.' Thinking aloud, I murmured, 'Female body image in advertising and its impossible standards.'

'I could be in it! Size 12 is the new 2!'

'Quite a good title.'

Nell laughed, as though it was all one big jokey idea, but my mood was starting to improve. 'You could shoot some stuff for me out in New York. Those famous billboards in Times Square, maybe? And you could interview other models about their experiences.'

Nell sat up and hooked her hair behind her ears. 'You're serious about it?'

'Why not?'

'I guess I could be like one of those supermodels who speaks out about a cause close to her heart.' She pressed her hand across her chest and looked up into the eaves with an earnest frown.

'Without the "super" bit,' I said.

'Rude!' Nell cried.

'The job in New York might make you into a supermodel,' I said, flattering her to keep her on side.

'Imagine.' Nell leapt up, singing the song from *On the Town*: '"New York, New York…"'

I continued the song by speaking the lyrics, deadpan, about people riding in a hole in the ground. In truth, I felt more optimistic than I sounded. Now that I had a film to make with top-drawer access, I felt engaged in the changes in Nell's life, rather than excluded.

Nell went on singing the jollier lines, louder than me. We both knew all the words, having watched the film many times in the room above Matthew's parents' garage on rainy days. By the time Nell had reached the second chorus, I had joined in. Together we screamed the lyrics at the tops of our lungs, and I felt part of Nell's excitement for the first time since Anna had announced news of the trip. For now, the worry about the man Anna knew was pushed away. I was going to go against my instincts and make a conscious decision not to doubt her loyalty.

CHAPTER EIGHTEEN

Anna

'I'm great,' Dom said, lining up his club with the ball. 'Why?'

The noise of the thwack reverberated through my head.

'Monday evening at the driving range?'

'I just fancied it.'

He looked across the range, swept a chunk of hair back, and leant down to position another ball.

'Nell wanted to buy Bay a ticket to New York.'

'Really?'

'I said no.'

'Yes.' His swing was too fast. The ball went off course. 'Shit.'

'Supper's on,' I said, keen to get home.

He placed another ball down on the tee. 'How was your mum about you leaving her?'

'She seemed okay, actually.'

I checked my watch. The chicken would be ready in fifteen minutes. I had asked Bay to baste it while I was out collecting Dom. As reliable as she normally was, I imagined the kitchen filling with smoke and the alarm going off and a charcoaled carcass crisp in the oven.

'Was she pleased for Nell?'

'Very. Can we talk about this in the car?'

He pocketed three balls and rested his club on his shoulder, like a cowboy with a broken shotgun. He stood with his legs wide apart. 'What time is your flight on Wednesday?'

Every time I thought of getting on a plane to New York, my heart beat hard and fast. It was such a thrilling and nerve-jangling prospect, I could hardly think straight. 'Eleven fifty,' I replied, hurrying to the car.

'How are you getting to the airport?'

'Ian said we can claim back for a taxi.'

When he unlocked his foldaway bike from the rack, the handlebars got tangled with another bike and he swore. Then he said, 'That's great, Anna.'

I felt guilty about going. Thinking back to the *Chloe Does* shoot, I knew it would not be much of a break exactly, but it was going to be hands down more fun than Dom's job: assessing planning applications and building warrants and writing long, boring reports about regulation.

Poor Dom hated his job. Over the years, it had dragged him down and changed him. Only our camping holiday in France every year would transform him back to how he used to be – for ten blessed days. Lounging by the pool, biking through the countryside and drinking cold beers in beach bars, he became less uptight and more himself. But as soon as his foot touched British soil and the light changed to grey, so would he.

'It's a shame we can't go together,' I said.

'I'll have to give you a list of good restaurants.'

'Thanks,' I said, grinning, kissing him, grateful and surprised that he was being gracious about not going himself. For the first time since I had heard the news, I began to relax a little about leaving everyone.

I headed to the car, stuck my head in the boot and tried to push the back seats down flat. 'These things are so stiff.'

'I'll do it.'

'It's okay, I've got it.' I shoved it, but it wouldn't go. 'Jesus! This thing drives me mad!'

Then, out of nowhere, Dom yelled at the top of his lungs, 'Anna, for fuck's sake! I'll do it! I'LL DO IT! Why do you have to make everything so fucking complicated all the fucking time?!'

It knocked me sideways. Dom was more likely to sulk than to shout like that. I backed out of the car, gaping at him. He refused to meet my eye. 'I could've cycled home,' he hissed.

'I just thought it would be nice to have a chat about everything without the girls' ears flapping, that's all,' I said petulantly, sitting in the driver's seat, arms folded, listening to him swear at the bike some more as he wrestled it into the back. He slammed the boot. Our tiny car shuddered.

As we puttered along the sun-dappled lanes, both of us silent and cross, my mind snapped backwards in time, to Suki and Dom's divorce. She had accused him of being aggressive and had stated that she was scared he would hit her. Because Suki was mad, nobody had taken her seriously, but sometimes I knew what she meant. Not about being hit – Dom would never hit anyone – but there was a quiet, simmering rage in him that you couldn't pinpoint until it surfaced, when it was slightly scary, revealing how much he was holding in. Third wave of feminism aside, men's anger in general was quite an intimidating phenomenon for me still, like an atavistic reminder of their physicality, and I had an urge to remind him of that now. To make him feel bad, to redress the balance. Or maybe I was being feeble and wanted a fight for the sake of it. He so rarely lost his temper, I wasn't sure what point it would serve to get at him, so I focused instead on what I should pack for New York, finally allowing my excitement to flood in.

To hell with Dom! To hell with childcare schedules! To hell with my mother! I was going to take full advantage of a once-in-a-lifetime opportunity and throw myself into the experience.

*

In the bottom of my sewing drawer, I found the box where I had hidden the postcards that Billy Young had sent me from New York years ago. Lying on top of it was a small tissue-paper package tied with pink string. At first I couldn't remember what was inside.

I undid the tissue paper to find hatpins sparkling in the light from the window. I smiled. My eye caught the ruby-red pin in the pile. I picked it out and twirled it in my fingertips. It had been a present from my boss, who had cried when I left my job at his Notting Hill hat shop to go on maternity leave. We had both known in our heart of hearts that I would never go back to that eccentric, energetic workshop in his basement.

I had worn the ruby pin on my wedding day, and it had given me strength to hold my head up high. There had been some clucking old dears in the village who had been judgemental of our request to marry in the local church on the green. They disapproved of Dom's divorce, and of our children born out of wedlock, and of the 'strange' little girl living in our house: 'Where's that child's mother?' they had whispered of Bay.

Helen, the vicar, had ignored them, and the day itself had been magical. Though my plan to keep it low-key – church, pub, knees-up – had gone awry.

A huge gathering of villagers had congregated outside our house and clapped and cheered when I emerged, shyly, onto the doorstep in my white knee-length dress, with Nell and Bay holding the veil that my old boss at the hat shop had sent me as a wedding present. The ruby pin had fixed the veil to my low bun and given me courage, even though my knees had been knocking together. The girls were sweet in their coral bridesmaids' dresses, and Viv – who had agreed to be my maid of honour on the proviso she wouldn't have to wear a pink puffball dress – was by my side, as ever. She had chosen a non-matching purple linen calf-length dress and flats – so she could dance – and had dressed Matthew in a waistcoat.

Everyone had followed us, in a jolly, chit-chattering procession, all the way to the church.

My mother had carried Iris, who had only been two. We had dressed her in ridiculous pink pantaloons and little white trainers. She had cried when she saw me stop at the altar, and wriggled in my mother's lap, holding out her chubby arms for a cuddle. My mother had soothed her, singing 'Incy Wincy Spider' over and over into her ear. If I hear that nursery rhyme sung now, I whizz back in time, feeling the butterflies in my tummy, tasting the dust in the air of the church, seeing Dom's eyes mist over.

When Helen had allowed Dom to kiss me, Bay and Nell had giggled, setting the rest of us off. My heart could have burst with all the love blooming inside me. I had never been so proud of the three girls, fidgeting, pigeon-toed, in the folds of my veil or crawling under the pews at my feet.

As I walked back down the aisle with Dom, the naughty side of me had wanted to blow a raspberry at Mrs Teal, whom I had spotted in the pews at the back of the congregation. She had been the worst of the doom-mongers, telling Viv that she thought we'd never last. I had wanted to call out, 'Check us out now, *lady*!' Because there we were, a perfectly imperfect blended family, shiny ribbons tangled in our hair and smiling eyes, brimming with love for each other.

Thinking about my happy wedding day was possibly not the most appropriate moment to open up the box and take out the five postcards from Billy Young.

The top one was of the famous New York skyline, with the Twin Towers standing tall. It was the last postcard he had ever sent me, over twenty years ago. I hadn't read any of them through for almost as long. The last time, I remembered, had been after the 9/11 attacks. Pointlessly I'd looked for him in the running crowds of sooty faces on the news. I hadn't slept until I heard from a mutual friend at St Martin's confirming that he was alive and well. Every year since, on September 11th, I revisited the horror of that day, remembering how terrified I had been for Billy. But Dom didn't know any of this. I had barely mentioned Billy. Dom knew I had dated some guy – Bill? Barry? Ben? – back at art college, but he had never known the fully story.

As I turned the card over, I was overcome by fear. I closed my eyes, momentarily, bracing myself before looking.

As I knew it would, his handwriting dragged me back to him. The unique, spontaneous artistic form of each letter, many of which weren't joined up, reminded me of his creative heart and his anxious energy. The essence of him was in that writing, even before I had read a word. On the surface, his news round-up seemed unexceptional. He talked of visiting the Museum of Modern Art every week, of takeout coffees from Dean & DeLuca, and the remodelling of his hair salon premises in the Meatpacking District. Of a driving holiday to the Big Sur and a chance meeting with a student we had known at St Martin's. He had fulfilled his promise to keep in touch, as though on a yearly Christmas card list. Yet I read between the lines. Visiting MoMA had been on my bucket list; the salon had been my idea; the Big Sur destination had been the holiday we had booked together and then cancelled because my mother had fallen ill. The St Martin's student, Katy, had been the mutual friend I had called after 9/11. Katy and her boyfriend, Stewart, had been close friends of ours during the period when we had been very much in love.

The next postcard in the pile was a promotional one: a charcoal cartoon of the salon. *Billy's Hair* was dashed across the signage in black italic lettering, and underneath was printed its address and opening hours. This was what I had been looking for. I typed the address into my phone before putting the cards away.

Then I set about steaming a felt hood for Ava's hat, imagining it perched at an angle, low on her broad forehead, the plume of feathers fixed by a hatpin. It would take me all day, and well into the night to finish it, interrupted only by packing for New York, dropping in to check on Mum, and feeding the children.

Dom promised he would deliver the hat to Ava while I was away. The funeral was on Saturday at the church on the green. I really wished I wasn't going to miss it.

'How's your mum been about you going away?' Viv asked, holding up a pair of baggy jeans that I never wore. 'These are nice.'

I pulled in my stomach. 'She's called me three times today to remind me to book seats in the middle of the plane in case it crashes.'

'At least she cares,' Viv said, grinning, folding the jeans into my holdall.

I had delegated my packing to Viv. She was throwing in what she thought I would need. Actively helping was what she did, and it was why I had asked her to come over.

My stress levels about flying to New York tomorrow had blown up inside me like an inflated balloon. All day I had felt like I was permanently holding my breath, fearing that if I relaxed for a second, I would whizz about in the air like I'd been let go of without being tied up.

'Dom's *promised* to drop in every day.'

'I can too, if you like.'

'Thanks, Viv. That's really kind. I think she'll be okay if Dom goes.'

'And Bay's not too jealous about New York?' She tucked my suede heels into the bag. I hadn't worn them since Christmas.

'She has been fine actually.' Viv had never fully warmed to Bay, and I was never quite sure why. I changed the subject. 'Dom's been to New York before and he's given me some places to go.'

Viv picked up a pair of green tracksuit bottoms with a hole in the bum. 'Imagine if you bumped into Billy wearing these.'

And there it was. Out there in a way that only Viv could put it.

'Viv, shh,' I said, pointing at the closed bedroom door. 'I'm not going to bump into him,' I whispered.

'They say Manhattan is like a village. Everyone knows everyone, apparently.'

'Who says that?'

'The magazines!'

'Grayswood is a village. New York is a massive metropolis.'

'What if he's the hairdresser on Nell's job! Just *imagine*!'

I *had* imagined. Many times. The thought bumped my heart up my throat. 'He won't be.'

'Shame.'

'I'm scared of seeing him.'

'Really?'

'Not *scared*, exactly. Just, you know… I mean, it was so long ago… I can't really even remember what he looks like properly,' I rambled, with a crystal-clear vision of his animated eyebrows, twitching constantly with mischief or anxiety, like a cat's ears, sensitive and aware. He used to scratch his big beard when he was thinking – so much careful thinking – and he had large, dinner-plate hands, which had always given me a safe feeling and had worked so delicately through his clients' hair.

Viv said, 'I still talk to Oliver on Facebook sometimes.'

'*Do* you?'

'Yup,' she chuckled. 'But it's not like I want to run off with him or anything. Or even see him, for that matter.' She made a face. 'He's a tub of lard now. And bald as a coot.'

I thought of Viv's husband, Greg, who was also large and bald, and still attractive. He had a quiet nature, seemingly distant, which drove Viv bananas, yet when you spoke to him, he was in tune with life, acutely so, and he cared about humanity, and was

endlessly sensitive to its destructive ways. Matthew was more like
Greg in temperament, but his sharp, practical brain came from
Viv. There was no way I was going to be able to lie to Viv and
get away with it.

'Okay. I admit it. I dug out the address of Billy's salon and put
it in my phone.' I sat on the bed, puffing out my cheeks.

'I knew it!'

'I'm not going to go in and see him, though, seriously. I just
want to walk past, maybe.'

'In shades and a hat?' She chuckled.

'He'd never recognise me anyway.'

'Why not?'

'I'm not sure I've still got it, Viv.' I laughed, weakly.

'*What*? You're a total babe.'

'I love you for saying that.'

'Greg says you're the best-looking woman in the village.'

I grinned. 'I'd be flattered if the average age wasn't, like, one
hundred and ten.'

'Come on, Anna, Mavis Teal is a serious hottie.'

I chuckled. Mavis Teal was eighty-five years old with a face as
sour as lemons. 'What about you, Viv? Where were you placed in
Greg's Hottest Woman in the Village awards? Number 3? After
Mavis and me?'

'I didn't even get a look-in!'

We laughed, and then Viv looked serious. 'You're gorgeous,
Anna, inside and out. I never know why you can't see it.'

'Dom doesn't see me that way.' Even as I said it, I questioned
where it had come from. Was it true? I explored it now. Certainly
Dom had stopped holding my hand, had stopped saying I looked
lovely, had stopped instigating sex.

'Even if you were a total hound, it's Dom's job to make you
feel like the most beautiful woman in the world.'

I smiled. 'Or in the village, at least.'

'Seriously, though.'

'Actually, he was a bit of an arse the other day when we were at the driving range. He totally lost his temper about his bike, and he's been moody ever since. I mean, he's not *saying* it's about New York, but I think it is.'

'That's a bit rubbish.'

'Don't tell anyone, will you.'

'Who would I tell?' she exclaimed.

'I don't know.' I laughed sheepishly. 'I just don't want Greg thinking badly of him.'

'Don't worry, Greg knows what he's like.'

I looked at Viv, seeing in her eyes a hint of something I didn't want to question further. Greg and Dom were good friends. Greg was one of Dom's only friends. They played golf together, bonding over the fact that they were the only two middle-aged men in Surrey who had not bought mountain bikes.

I said, 'Billy and I used to talk all the time about the salon he wanted to own one day, and how we'd both design it. I suppose I just want to see it with my own eyes, to know he made it happen. Does that make sense?'

'Perfect sense,' Viv said, squeezing my knee.

'I've been feeling really bad about it.'

'Anna! Blimey, you're so good at beating yourself up! It's completely normal to be curious about an old boyfriend.'

'He was more than just an old boyfriend,' I said, exhaling, feeling the muscles across the whole of my body release. Out of nowhere, tears sprang to my eyes.

She hugged me. 'Looks like there's some unfinished business there.'

I gulped away more tears. 'No, seriously. I can't see him. It would be too much,' I said decisively.

Nell would be the priority in New York. Nell and Bay and Iris were always my priority. They were more important than anything else in my life. It was absurd to think that my need to feel attractive could cloud what was right for them.

It was truthful to say that the girls were the glue between Dom and me. They were our shared achievements. Not least Bay. When Suki had called Dom to tell us that she was making a new hippy-dippy life for herself in Mauritius, he had resisted the dawning new reality for our family of four, soon to be five, but I'd known he either had to step up and do the right thing, or he would never sleep easy again. Bay had taught us how to give more than we thought possible.

Dom and I had probably lost sight of each other in the midst of bringing the three of them up. Admittedly, there had been times over the years when I had turned to agony aunt columns or articles by psychologists to look for reassurance. They had confirmed that love changed over the course of a marriage and often lost its passion, that stamina was needed and effort should be made to reignite sex and intimacy. If a therapist or marriage guidance counsellor had listened to Dom and me talk, I hoped they'd think, *Oh yes, childhood sweethearts, sixteen years together, eight years married, a stepchild – a challenge they battled through admirably – good, tick, tick, archetypal, unremarkable, nothing of any interest here, I might nod off.*

It was okay. It was good enough.

I would never threaten Bay's sense of security for a second time, nor would I shatter Nell and Iris's for the first time. Bay had assimilated and adapted and worked hard to become part of the family. She didn't deserve any more disruption, especially not in the last crucial year of her school life. Her turnaround from the nervy, sickly child to the poised young woman she was today was awe-inspiring. Her happiness and the girls' hard-won sisterhood were paramount. Always had been, always would be.

CHAPTER NINETEEN

2012

There was rain outside. Bay and Nell were stuck indoors.

'Let's pretend I'm the doctor and you're the patient,' Bay said. She opened up Nell's medical case and brought out the pretend stethoscope. It was made of rubber and metal and Nell thought it was terribly realistic.

'Can't I be the doctor?' Nell asked.

'No. I'm the doctor.'

'Can I be the nurse?' She liked clipping the safety-pin watch onto her jumper and taking people's pulses.

'But who would be the patient?'

'Big Ted?'

'That's stupid.'

'What about Iris?' Iris was with Anna downstairs eating Cheerios from her high-chair table.

'That's even stupider.'

Nell really didn't want to be the patient. 'Okay. But can I be the doctor after you?'

'Maybe.'

She accepted her role. 'Let's pretend I have a broken leg.'

'No. Let's pretend you're paralysed from a terrible car accident.'

'What's paralysed again? I forgot.'

'It means you can't move at all.'

Nell was stricken, as though confronting the prospect of real paralysis.

'Okay then, let's pretend you come through the door and say, "Oh no! I can't move my legs and arms".'

'But how can I walk in if I can't move my legs?'

'Oh yeah! Let's pretend you're lying down on the floor saying, "I can't move my legs and arms".'

Nell did as she was told, getting into character. She began to groan in pain, with a small smile on her face. It was quite fun.

Bay said in a serious voice, 'Come on, patient, let's get you on the bed. Patient, stop whining, please, because it will only hurt more.' She held Nell under the arms to pull her up, but Nell giggled.

'Don't giggle! It spoils the game!' Bay cried, holding tighter, dragging Nell.

'Ow! I'll do it by myself!'

'That's stupid. You're not supposed to move.'

'Let's pretend I got better for a minute because of the medicine.'

'Okay. Let's pretend I give you an injection that makes you better for a little while.'

'Okay,' Nell agreed, lying down on the floor again.

Bay scrabbled in the medical case and brought out a large plastic syringe. 'Let's pretend you start to cry and try to get away from me because you're scared of needles,' she said.

'But I can't move.'

'Let's pretend you can move your arms.'

So Nell cried and tried to move her arm away.

'Stop being so naughty, patient. You're being so bad, I'm going to have to put these on you to stop you from moving.' Bay pulled out an old pair of tights and tied Nell's wrists together.

'That's too tight.'

'Stop talking, patient. I have to give you the injection.'

Nell wriggled her wrists. 'I don't want to play any more.'

Bay put her hand over Nell's mouth. 'Stop talking, patient, or you'll be in trouble.'

Nell was shocked by the ferocity of Bay's acting. It was very convincing and scared her much more than a real doctor might. She stopped talking.

'Now, you'll just feel a little pinch,' Bay said, holding Nell's upper arm.

The large plastic syringe was still on the floor. Just as Nell noticed this, she felt a very real sharp pain in her upper arm. She yelped. Bay's hand clamped to her face again.

Anna called up from downstairs. 'Is everything okay, you two?'

'Just playing!' Bay called out.

Tears sprang to Nell's eyes. She tried to turn her head to see what had caused the pain. The opened safety pin from the pretend nurse's watch was fully embedded in her arm. When Bay pulled it out, the tip was wet with blood.

'Stay still or I'll tell Anna you stole her earrings.'

'But I didn't!' Nell said.

'So?'

Bay's face above her loomed large. Her glasses reflected light from the window. Nell couldn't see her eyes, and felt fear gather in her throat.

'Are you ready for your second injection, patient?'

Nell shook her head and gulped. Fat tears plopped out and ran into her ears as she endured another long, slow puncture into her arm. Instinctively she knew that if she stayed still and did as Bay said, she would be safer.

'Don't look so frightened,' Bay said. Her scary doctor voice was gone suddenly.

'Can you untie my hands?' Nell asked, grabbing the opportunity.

But instead of freeing her, Bay began tickling her. Nell cried for mercy. It was almost worse than the safety pin. She wanted

Bay to stop. She began screaming at her. Screaming and screaming and screaming. But Bay wouldn't stop, and so Nell bit her on the shoulder. Bay's eyes popped out. Nell expected her to scream too. Instead, she untied Nell's hands and then let out an almighty wail.

Anna came rushing in. 'What the hell is going on?'

'She bit me!' Bay cried. 'She bit me! Look! And we were just playing!'

Anna pulled back Bay's T-shirt to reveal the horrible teeth marks Nell had made. Angry and mean-looking.

'Nell, biting is unacceptable and you know it! Totally unacceptable!' Anna was livid.

'But Muuum! She stuck a pin in me!'

'I did not!' Bay countered.

When Nell showed her mum where Bay had stuck the pin, it looked only a little bit red, and there was just a tiny pinprick of blood, even though Nell tried to squeeze more out.

'How did that happen?' Anna said, holding Nell's arm and looking at Bay.

'I did it by mistake!' Bay cried. 'She wriggled and it pricked her! It wasn't my fault!'

Nell and Bay both began crying and shouting accusations at each other.

'You two, both of you, calm down, right now. Sometimes I don't know who to believe. I think you're as bad as each other.'

Nell knew she was not as bad as Bay. Bay had started it. Like always. But it was impossible to make her mum see it. A shrinking feeling began inside her. She burrowed under the duvet and lay there in the hot space, finding it hard to breathe.

'Okay, Nell, you stay here and think about what you did. Bay, come with me and let's have a closer look at…' Her voice faded as she led Bay downstairs.

Nell lay there distraught. She might have slept for a bit, she wasn't sure.

A while later, Anna came in and sat down on the bed. She pulled the duvet down off Nell's head.

'I want to talk to you about what happened.'

'I don't want to talk,' Nell said, pulling the duvet back. What was the point? She had told her mum what had happened and she hadn't believed her.

'I know having Bay living here is a hard adjustment for you to make, darling. I do understand that. But you're going to have to find a way of being kinder to her. Okay?'

'But I *am* kind!' Nell yelled through the duvet. 'She stabbed a pin in me!'

'And she's very upset about that. But she did it by accident, Nell. It was a mistake and for you to then bite her because of it was really not nice at all.'

'I didn't mean to,' Nell said.

'I think you are a kind girl, Nell, and that's why it's disappointing when you behave like this.' Anna poked Nell's chest gently. Nell was impressed that her mother knew where her chest was from the outside of the duvet.

'I *am* kind,' Nell agreed, sniffing.

'But Bay thinks you hate her.'

Sitting up and flinging the duvet off, Nell said, 'That's a lie! *She's* the one who hates *me*!'

Anna sighed. 'You know that's not true. She loves you so much. Bay is a very vulnerable little girl and you need to think about that instead of all this "me, me, me" feeling-sorry-for-yourself stuff. It's not like you at all.'

Nell remembered a time when her mummy had understood absolutely everything about her. *Special mummy vision*, she had called it. When Nell was sad, Mummy would know why. When she was naughty, she would know how. She had believed absolutely everything Nell said if it was true, and had seen a lie behind her eyes if it was there. Now, everything was the opposite way round.

She didn't understand a thing. Mummy had lost her mummy vision, which felt quite disastrous.

'Nell? Can you say something, please?'

'What?'

'You're not sorry?'

Nell thought: maybe she hasn't lost her mummy vision after all.

Anna continued, in her best stern voice. 'Okay. Listen up. Imagine, just imagine, if I chucked you out of the house right now for being naughty, and went off to live halfway round the world because I thought you were too difficult to live with.'

Nell's heart stopped. 'You would never do that!'

'No. Exactly. I would never, ever do that. And you know it right to your heart that I wouldn't. You are lucky enough to take it for granted. But it would feel pretty awful if I did leave, wouldn't it?'

'It would be the worst thing ever. Ever.'

'Well, that's what Bay's mummy did to her. She told her she didn't want to live with her any more.'

Even though Nell had heard the stories about Suki from Bay, hearing it from her mother made it real and less like a fairy tale. Bay's life was almost as bad as Tracy Beaker's in the Jacqueline Wilson series, and those books had made her both laugh and cry. A bit like Bay did.

'Is her arm all right?' she asked.

'It's fine. You didn't break the skin, thank goodness.'

'I'm sorry, Mummy.'

'Bay is the one you need to say sorry to. And I've told her not to play with safety pins in your games. Okay?'

After hugging Anna and saying another genuine sorry, Nell found Bay in the garden in the smelly Wendy house. She gave her a big cuddle.

'Sorry, Bay.'

'That's okay,' Bay said, combing her fringe with a toy brush. 'You can be the doctor next time, if you like.'

'Okay.'

'When I'm the patient, I won't be a baby about it.'

'I wasn't a baby!' Nell remonstrated, feeling the frustration surface again.

'You were. Babies cry and always tell.'

'You told on me too!'

'Only because you cried your head off. Like a big *baby*.'

'I'm *not* a baby!'

'You can't tell on me then, ever again.'

'I won't tell on you again.'

'Promise?'

'I promise. On. My. Life.' Fiercely Nell made a cross over her heart. Telling didn't work anyway. Grown-ups didn't like the truth, even though they said they did.

CHAPTER TWENTY

Nell

We're at the airport in the queue for check-in and Mum gets a call from Ian. She comes off the phone looking bloody pale.

'Ian just told me we're going in on a tourist visa,' she says.

'That's okay, isn't it?'

'To be honest, I'm not sure. I just assumed he'd sorted it all out. I didn't know that you're supposed to have a stamp in your passport.'

'We can still go, can't we?' I say in a panic.

She holds her temples and whispers, 'We'll have to lie at Immigration. Say we're going on holiday.'

'It's kinda true,' I say. 'A girlie city break in New York?'

'Apparently models do it all the time.'

'If Ian says it's okay, then I guess it is.'

'Not much choice now,' she mumbles angrily. 'You haven't packed anything that gives the game away, like a composite card or portfolio or something, have you?'

'Flesh-coloured thong?'

She laughs, sort of, and pushes our trolley forward in the queue with a frown on her face.

But when the air stewardess asks us the reason for our trip, she becomes extra jolly and acts like a pro.

*

We are millions of miles above the Atlantic Ocean and I order tomato juice. Mum puts a mini bottle of vodka in hers. At home, I wouldn't touch tomato juice with a bargepole, but I want to be sophis on the plane. I feel so unbelievably lucky to be flying to America, it is unreal.

'Cheers to you, sweetheart. This is fun,' Mum says, exhaling with her first sip, then dropping her voice. 'But I might need a few more of these to get us through US Immigration.'

'Mum, chill. Leah does it all the time.' I know this because I texted her at the airport, secretly worried.

I press record on my phone and film Mum. 'Did Ian say anything about the hotel?'

'No, he didn't. And no more filming!' Mum says, putting her in-flight magazine over her face.

'It's for Bay,' I say.

Bay told me to film everything, even stuff that isn't obviously related to her documentary idea. She said she needed to craft a story and wasn't sure how that would go until she had some material, and she pinky-promised me she wouldn't use any of it in the final edit unless I gave her permission.

Mum peered over the front cover. 'Was everything okay between you guys in the end?'

'Yeah, totally, we made up,' I say, grabbing the magazine from her. 'What perfumes would we buy if we were rich?'

Mum goes for Chanel Chance and I go for Celeste Paris. For Bay we choose Marc Jacobs Daisy and for Dad Mont Blanc Night. And for Iris, a teddy dressed as a pilot. There are no cats.

Being with Mum like this, on our first trip to America, gives me a fuzzy feeling in my tummy, like a post-wheelie high. I put my head on her shoulder, feeling close to her, and not because we are literally sitting crammed next to each other, but because I have her all to myself. For the first time in years, she is not making sure Bay is okay before me. I was secretly pleased when she said Bay couldn't come with us. I also felt like a brat just for thinking it, but it's true that Mum worries about Bay too much. Nobody else's feelings are as important. I'm sure that's why Mum didn't want me to be a model, because she was worried about Bay being jealous.

I try a question out in my head: *Do you know what she used to do to me, Mummy?*

Once, I actually dreamt that I told Mum what Bay used to do to me as a kid. In the dream, Mum didn't believe me. Okay. Correction. It wasn't that she didn't believe me, it was more that she wasn't bothered by it, as though I had told her the most normal thing in the world. That was tough for the me in the dream to take. When Dream Mum shrugged and said, 'Don't worry, poppet, I'm sure she's sorry,' and then asked me what I wanted for tea, I felt this terrible alone feeling. Like nobody in the whole world understood how I felt. Literally, genuinely nobody. And that feeling was dark, and it was a drag the next day when everyone kept asking me why I was in such a shitty mood. Mum kept telling me off for being on my phone too much and I said I had a migraine and told her to shut up, which blew up into a massive row. Nobody understood how bad that dream was.

The plane is chilly and the blowy air sends sharpish tingles across the skin on my chest. I shudder, turning the nozzle off and getting rid of the feeling. It is strange to live with a secret that is so big in my head but so far away from ever being talked about.

'You okay, darling?' Mum asks, stroking my hair.

Is her special mummy vision back? I think, laughing inside. I believed in that shit as a kid!

'I'm freezing,' I say.

Mum takes her blanket off and tucks it around my knees. 'Here you go.'

'But you need it!'

'I'm not cold.'

Obviously a lie. It's, like, minus degrees on this plane. She is such a good mum. I feel awful for having ungrateful thoughts about her just now. She loves me so much. She cares for us three sisters equally. And that is the real truth. I do that a lot, think one thing and then think the total opposite two seconds later. Everyone does that, right?

Mum drops off to sleep with her blow-up pillow around her neck.

I listen to some music on my phone and do some filming of the clouds for Bay and of Mum asleep with that dorky pillow. To make Dad and Iris laugh.

Later, when I film the opening of the foil on my meal – a weird slab of something with some mushy sauce – Mum tells me off.

'Next you'll be filming yourself going for a wee,' she says. 'Put it down and experience life without that thing in front of your face, and then store the memories in your noodle. It's what it's for.'

'You don't get Gen Z, Mum. We film stuff. That's what we do,' I say.

And I promised Bay. If I don't send her footage, she'll get in a mood when I get home. Then again, I doubt Bay will need film of my lunch for her documentary. Already I'm losing sight of what she wants me to film versus what I want to film for my own memories. My head is a mess about it.

The immigration guy at JFK is super-fake nice and asks us way too many questions, and at one point I think he sees right into our lying eyes. I act mega-casual and smile a lot. Then he waves us through and says, 'Have a nice trip!' As we walk away, Mum squeezes my hand so tightly my eyes water. 'Phew,' she says.

Arrivals at JFK is a bit manic. Ian said there'd be a car to meet us, but it hasn't shown up. We wait in line for a yellow cab. I can't believe we are getting inside one exactly like in the movies.

It is stinky and cramped in the back, and the driver drives badly and swears a lot, and now I know where the clichés come from.

Dramatic music plays in my head when I see the New York skyline for the first time from the Brooklyn Bridge. I could be in a movie as I film it on my phone. It is totally meta.

When I get out of the cab on W23 between Seventh and Eighth Avenues, the air is thick and smells like hot, filthy sidewalks. If there is an absolute polar opposite of Grayswood, this city is it. It is the smelliest, noisiest place I have ever been to in my life. The sirens sound alien, honking instead of whining. When I look up at the hotel and see the stripy awning and the long metal sign that says *Hotel Chelsea* – Ian called it the Chelsea Hotel – I think my head will explode.

People are cutting across us, super-fast, and I dodge through them to get to the front doors. Mum stands in the middle of the stream of people and looks around her, mouth open, and says, 'Land of the free and home of the brave!'

The room is freezing cold because of the air con. It is really posh and stylish, like a hotel in a magazine. We get excited about all the free bottles of stuff, obviously, and I film Mum smelling each one, acting dumb and swoony like she's never smelt anything more delish in her life. It's really funny.

Then Mum lies on the bed and reads the information booklet.

'This is interesting. It's not always been so posh here,' she says.

I film her reading the history of the hotel and who lived here in the seventies, before the big refurbishment. It was where Nancy, the girlfriend of Sid Vicious from the Sex Pistols, was stabbed to death. They were drug addicts. In the photos, they look like nutters. Mum goes on to tell me that Dylan Thomas also died here, of pneumonia. When I hear that there is a hotel black cat called Dylan – I saw him sitting in a pot plant by the lift – I can't wait to tell Iris. Lots of other famous people, like Janis Joplin and Leonard Cohen and Grace Jones, lived here back then, when it was cheap. Mum sang some of their songs to me before I knew who they were. I have to say, though, there is a creepy edge to all the stories, and I hope that none of the bad stuff happened in this room.

'Mum, what time is it at home?'

'It's four thirty here, so it'll be nine thirty at night there.'

'Bay wanted us to FaceTime when we got here.'

'Good plan. She'll still be up.'

Bay picks up quickly.

'Hi, darling!' Mum says, crowding me out on the screen.

Bay is eating, her hair pulled back by my pink spotty towelling hairband.

'Liking the look, Bay.'

'Camera-ready.' Her smile is brief and fake.

'You're eating supper?'

'Chicken nuggets.' She films her bowl.

'So late?'

'I forgot earlier.'

'Where's Dad?'

'Downstairs, I think. Show me your hotel room, then!'

Mum ignores her request. 'But is that all you've had, darling? Chicken nuggets? No peas or veggies?'

'I'm not that hungry.'

'Did Dad make peas for Iris?'

'Mum!' I cry. 'They'll survive without peas for a couple of days!'

I zoom around the room, showing Bay. 'Cool, right?'

Mum butts in again. 'Is Dad there? Can I have a word?'

'No, Mum! You're being mental.'

I go into the bathroom and lock the door, showing Bay the line of mini bottles and doing a silly mirror selfie. Bay's smile for Mum is gone.

'How's it going?' I say, sitting on the bog.

'Yeah, good.'

'I've filmed loads of stuff for you.'

'Thanks.'

'Are you okay?'

'Yeah, sure, I'm really great, watching you in some posh hotel room while I'm eating nuggets in my shitty bedroom. Hashtag rub it in my face,' she hisses, under her breath so that Mum won't hear her.

She asked me to FaceTime her and now she's pissed off that I did. I wish I hadn't bothered. Always when I think we're okay, when I relax a little, she catches me off guard. 'Sorry, I thought you wanted me to—'

'I've got to go. I'm editing. Just send me the footage. Especially stuff from the shoot.'

The screen goes dead.

After an early supper of burger and chips in the hotel bar, Mum and I get into bed, exhausted. I want to talk to her about how crazy Bay can be, the pressure she's putting on me to film everything and all the guilt trips. And maybe other stuff? As Mum said herself, America is the land of the free and the home of the brave, right?

The light from her Kindle shines into the dark. I am just plucking up the courage when she closes it, sticks in her earplugs and settles down under her duvet. It is too late now.

I try to sleep, but the air conditioning is too loud and the noises of New York outside the window sound weird and creepy, keeping me awake, churning up deeper thoughts about Bay. Sometimes I wonder if she can help erupting like that. I don't reckon she intends to be mean and I know she regrets it straight away. When she was little, before she came to live with us, her counsellor explained that she was often horrible to the people she loved the most. I think that's about right. She feels secure with me, I guess, and knows I'll forgive her. And I'm not, like, totally blameless. It was actually stupid of me to show off about the room like that. I should have known better, read between the lines. I regret it now and I wonder if I'll be able to get some really awesome footage of tomorrow's shoot to make up for it.

Night-night, Bay. Sorry, I think, drifting off to sleep in a fug of guilt.

CHAPTER TWENTY-ONE

Anna

Being out on the sunny New York streets thrilled me to my bones. I felt I knew the city somehow before I had even arrived, as though it was someone I had loved in a past life and could fall in love with all over again.

I felt cool from my shower still. The pummelling water had been as good as any massage. At home, the flow was so weak it would dry up completely if anyone turned on a tap downstairs. Hotel showers were a luxury Dom and I had not had the pleasure of enjoying since our honeymoon. We had stayed in a place just outside Palma. There had been a cocktail bar with stools in the pool so you could sip a gin and tonic while paddling your legs. Every evening, there had been a live band. Dom and I had danced together, sunburned cheek to sunburned cheek, drunk with sunshine and all-day drinking. We'd gone to bed singing love ballads to each other in silly Spanish accents. The memory seemed to belong to someone else.

On the call sheet Ian had sent us was the address of a diner on 33 Leonard Street on West Broadway in Tribeca, where we would find the crew and the location bus. It was a forty-minute walk from the Chelsea, further downtown.

The morning heat was building. The smell, the noise, the people, the promise of a future I had never dared even dream of was thrumming through me. My mother had been wrong all those years ago: my twenty-year-old self would have loved this. For a second, I was stung by resentment, and a yearning for something lost. I shrugged it off. It was too long ago to mope over. It was Nell's future that mattered now.

Arm in arm with her, I felt lighter, unburdened and excited. This was her big break. But Nell seemed subdued and obsessed with filming everything.

'Please put your phone away now, Nell,' I said.

'But I don't want to miss anything.'

'I'm serious. Stop filming or I'll wrestle it off you.'

Nell put it away and was quiet for a bit. I wondered if she was more nervous than she was letting on, and using her phone to hide behind, as Bay did. At home, I let Bay get away with it. Filming helped her to process her problems. I was tougher on Nell, whose problems had not involved an abusive mother.

'You're going to be great today,' I said, kissing her on the side of her head.

The grid system was easy to navigate. In my mind, there was an imaginary cross at the address of Billy's salon, only a few streets away from the location of the shoot. It was close enough to walk there, if I was able to nip away.

'There it is,' Nell whispered, pulling out her phone again and pointing at a silver bullet diner. It stood alone on a scrap of pavement in the midst of the tall uniform buildings of the city, as though it had been airlifted onto a film set. Next to it was parked a long white and black Winnebago.

I snatched her phone and stuffed it back into her rucksack. 'Seriously.'

A tall, lanky young man with a shaved head and cartoon-like chisels for cheekbones was leaning into the open door of the Winnebago talking to another man sitting in the passenger seat. They turned their heads towards us as we approached.

'Hi,' they said.

'We're here for the shoot.'

'Uh-huh. Bonnie's in there,' the guy with the cheekbones said.

'I'm Nell,' Nell said. She stuck her hand out to shake his. Her confidence astounded me.

He laughed and took her hand. 'Nice to meet you, Nell. I'm Alexander.'

Inside the van, the brown glass skylight cast a dull shadow over the spacious interior. Bonnie wore an oversized black hoodie with the sleeves pushed up to the elbow, showing lean, tanned forearms. I couldn't understand how she could wear black in this heat, but there wasn't a bead of sweat on her freckled, oblong face. She had her head down, sipping coffee from a black thermos cup, sifting through pages of A4 sheets with small photos of garments printed next to the type.

When she saw us, she smiled, so quickly it was almost not a smile at all.

'Good to meet you,' she said, looking Nell up and down, ruffling her hand through her yellow-blonde straggles, rattling the chunky silver rings on every finger and thumb. 'We'll get you to try some stuff on, okay? Before Grace starts make-up.' She glanced over at another woman, who continued rearranging her make-up suitcase. She had a large, round head and her hair was shiny black, like a Lego figure helmet.

While Bonnie scanned her sheet, she asked us about our flight and our hotel and how we liked New York. The questions came out by rote, with little eye contact. I let Nell answer for us. Her charm was lost on these two women. They were hard work, unpleasant even.

Bonnie pressed a finger on one of the photographs and went to the rail at the back of the van. She pulled out a pair of shorts and a gingham corset top with laces.

'Try these on in there,' she said, pointing to the bedroom at the back of the van.

Nell took the clothes and avoided my eye. I knew what she was thinking: the clothes were too small by about five sizes.

CHAPTER TWENTY-TWO

Nell

Bonnie hands me a minuscule top and pink denim shorts. It's obvious I'm not going to fit into them, and I pray that she has some other sizes.

She says, 'Kirk wants you to act all goofy in these at the diner counter, swinging around on the stools like you're a kid again. Okay?' She raises one eyebrow at me.

I *am* a kid, I think. But I say, 'No probs,' to keep things running smoothly.

I guess I should be chuffed she's not treating me like a kid, but I'm not warming to her. Her blink-and-you-miss-them smiles remind me of my passive-aggressive Spanish teacher. Weirdly, I long to be in Miss Richer's class right now, sneaking fried-egg gummies from my blazer pocket.

As I turn my back and pull my jeans down, giving her a lovely view of my backside in the ugly flesh-coloured thong, I take my phone out of my back pocket and press record, then leave it on its side as though it has been discarded, though actually it is slightly propped up in the folds of the duvet.

I squeeze the shorts over my hips. The top two buttons won't do up and the material digs into my thighs, leaving bulges. Then I put on the hideous gingham corset and tug at the laces.

'Let me try.' Bonnie physically twists me around to face her. I didn't care so much about my bum being on show before, but I don't like the thought of her seeing my scars and asking about them. I'm getting flustered. The room is tiny and hot and the bed takes up most of the space. It reminds me of a posher version of a caravan we stayed in in Wales once. Thankfully the brownish light in the room is terrible and she doesn't seem to notice the marks on my skin.

As she pulls the laces, my boobs bunch up. My ribs prickle and tingle. The scars are still sensitive, even after all this time. Sometimes one swells up and seeps, but mostly they're hardly noticeable.

'Jesus, this is not gonna fit,' she says, pressing my boobs down like they are her own. Her freckly face crinkles as she pushes up her sleeves and tries to tie it tighter. I can hardly breathe. 'Your fat is spilling out all over the place,' she says.

I stay quiet, thinking about my phone on record.

'Your portfolio on the website says that you're 84-62-86, but you're not, are you?' She says it as though I have lied to her.

'I'm a 12 in UK size,' I say, unsure of my exact measurements.

'That's a 10 in the US.'

'I guess so.'

'Can you change out of it, please?' she snaps, leaving the room. Through the door I can hear her talking to Grace. She comes back in with a red version of the top. I try again, but it won't do up.

'You're too big.'

'Oh,' I say. I think back to Lee's story about the German stylist who thought his legs were too short. *Or maybe your trousers are too long?*

Bonnie looks up to the ceiling as though she's going to cry, and I feel bad for her. Then she looks right at me. 'I'm guessing your sizing is more plus-size than regular, honey. Have you considered joining a plus-sized agency?'

'Not really,' I say. *Remember I'm just a kid, FFS, and this is being recorded for my sister's film, you B-word.* I'm trying hard not to cry too.

'I'm gonna have to make some calls,' she says.

I'm guessing she's going to have to find more clothes from somewhere.

While I wait, I sit on the bed and immediately plug my earphones in and watch what has been caught on film. The images are blurry, and only catch the tops of our heads, but our voices are as clear as a bell, full of all Bonnie's sighs and bitchy comments. Bay is going to be scandalised and thrilled. It'll make up for my stupid FaceTime room tour.

CHAPTER TWENTY-THREE

Anna

While I hung around on the sidewalk, waiting, I watched through the window of the silver bullet diner as the photographer and his assistant set up. The photographer was stocky and tattooed, fiddling with a large SLR camera in his tiny hands. His assistant was tall, in a scruffy T-shirt. He was pulling up a light reflector and angling it down to face the stools at the bar. They looked too busy to disturb, even though Bonnie had said I could go in and say hi. I pretended to scroll through my messages on my phone.

Bonnie came out of the Winnebago with her phone pressed to her ear. She ignored me and crossed the street, gesticulating with her free hand. Sensing that something wasn't right, I popped my head into the van to see how Nell was getting on.

Grace looked up and shot me half a smile. 'Go in if you like.'

I knocked on the door of the bedroom. 'Nell?'

'Come in.'

She was half dressed and on her phone. I closed the door. 'None of the clothes fit me,' she whispered.

'Is she ordering more sizes?'

'I guess so. She was horrible to me, Mum. Really horrible.'

'Oh darling!' I reached out to her, but my phone rang. 'Oh. It's Ian. I'll call him back.'

'No! Get it!'

'Hello?'

'Anna, I've got some bad news. Bonnie from Focus has been on the phone and they're pulling Nell from the shoot.'

'What?'

'I'm so sorry, hon. I've tried to talk her round, but…'

In utter disbelief, I walked away from Nell and out of the van, shielding her from what I was hearing, asking Ian to repeat what he had just said. As I listened, I stared through the diner window to see Bonnie standing with the photographer, talking closely. Their grave faces said it all.

'But *why*?'

'She says the clothes don't fit her.'

'But that's *their* fault.'

'I know, right? At least we can insist they pay a percentage of her day rate.'

Not being paid hadn't even occurred to me until then. 'She won't get paid?'

'They're saying they were told the wrong measurements, which they so were not, I can tell you. I mean, check the website, right?' Ian snorts.

Suddenly suspicious, I ask him, 'And you're sure her details are correct on there?'

'Of course!'

I sighed. 'Nell is going to be totally gutted.'

'It sucks for her, really. Do you want me to call her myself?'

'No. Thank you,' I said, baffled by the idea that I'd let him call my own daughter, who was a few feet away from me.

'Bonnie felt it would be cleaner if I spoke to you first.'

'She chickened out, you mean.'

There was a pause and his tone changed. 'She's got a rep for being a total bitch. But hear it from me, they'll regret this shitshow when Nell's a big star. You tell Nellie that. In fact, I'll call her myself to make sure she knows.'

'She'll appreciate hearing that. Thank you,' I said.

'Do you want me to book a car to JFK for you tomorrow?'

'Tomorrow? Our flights are booked for Saturday evening.'

'Oh. You wanna stay anyway? Happy to keep the Chelsea Hotel booking for you guys. But it will be at your own expense.'

'Focus won't be paying for the extra nights?'

'I've tried. They're not moving on that either.'

'Wow. Okay. It's going to be fun breaking this to Nell.'

'Real crappy. I feel for her. Call me if you need anything. Anything at all.'

'Thanks, Ian.'

'Speak later, honey.'

I was trembling all over. Without looking at Bonnie, who was still hiding out in the diner, I stormed into the van, ignoring Grace.

In the bedroom, with the door closed, I whispered urgently to Nell. 'Have you got all your stuff together?'

'No, why?'

I threw her flesh-coloured bra into her rucksack. 'We're leaving now.'

'What? We can't do that!'

'I'll explain in a minute. Just get your stuff.'

'Not until you tell me what's going on!'

'Please, just trust me, okay?'

'What have you said?'

'I haven't said anything.'

'I'm not going anywhere until you tell me what's going on.'

Realising that she wasn't budging until she knew, I told her what Ian had told me.

A flush of heat crossed her face. She pushed her fingers into her eye sockets. 'Oh my God.'

Gently, I said, 'Follow my lead, darling. Let's get out of here.'

With our heads down, we flew past Grace and stepped out of the van. Bonnie was still inside the diner. She began making her way to the door, looking grim, possibly emerging to say goodbye and sorry. I didn't give her the chance. We stormed along the sidewalk, almost running.

Nell held it together for as long as possible. When we turned the corner, out of sight, she burst into tears. 'I've never been so humiliated in my life!' she sobbed.

'Oh sweetheart. I'm so sorry.' I wrapped her in my arms, feeling murderous towards Bonnie.

She sniffed. 'You don't think Ian gave them the wrong measurements, do you?'

'I don't think so. He sounded genuinely upset about the whole thing.' I cupped her forlorn face in my hands and wiped her cheeks. 'He said they'd regret it when you're a big star.'

She guffawed snottily. 'Not likely.'

I planted a kiss on her nose, like she was little again. 'How about some thrift shopping to take your mind off everything?'

'I'm not sure I'm in the mood now.'

'What? Are you the Nell Hart I know and love? Or has she been lobotomised?'

'I'm still here, I think,' she sniffed.

'Come on then,' I cajoled, trying to lift her spirits. 'Pancakes first, at the place Dad suggested, and then shopping for stinky old-lady clothes.'

'Pancakes and old-lady clothes sounds good,' she said, offering up half a smile. We linked arms and fell into step. My eyes felt suddenly scratchy from the jet lag I hadn't had time to notice until now. The reality of taking her home so soon, back to normal life, saddled with such a negative experience, sank through me. The only upside would be that she'd see her sisters, who would build her up again.

The breakfast diner that Dom had recommended was empty and sunless. Nell was puffy-eyed. The waitress slapped down the menus and spilled water as she poured it from the jug into our tall, smeared glasses. As we ordered, she impersonated our British accents. We were like unwanted guests here. Imposters.

I was reminded of everything my mother had said to me, years ago, when I had discussed the idea of moving out to New York with Billy. 'You'll always feel like an outsider. That's what I went through moving here from France as a child. I've never felt at home. Ever,' she had warned. 'It'll be the biggest mistake of your life.'

I didn't want Nell to feel like an outsider, or any more rejected than she already did.

There were other diners.

I whispered to her, 'We are not wasting our one New York breakfast in here. Come on. Let's leg it and find that coffee shop I read about. It's nearby, and Insta heaven, apparently.'

We made our way there with the help of Google Maps.

I made her try my lavender-infused hot chocolate and we admired the decor of pot plants and string lights. I bought her a floral branded coffee-cup-to-go, then we browsed the boutiques in SoHo before heading to the thrift stores in the East Village. My dream of visiting MoMA was put aside. I didn't mind, as long as Nell remained upbeat. Reminding her of who she was and what she loved, and how much I loved her, was a way to build up her self-worth and undo the damage of this morning. One knock-back would not change her, but as I looked into the future, I couldn't help wondering how many more of these she could take before her confidence disappeared completely.

As the afternoon wore on, and my legs wore out, I knew the chance to see Billy's salon was slipping away. I didn't want to interrupt Nell's shopping flow, but as the minutes ticked towards evening, I realised that another opportunity might never come along in my lifetime.

While she tried on the fiftieth pair of old jeans, I searched the internet on my phone, identifying a small dim sum restaurant nearish Billy's called RedFarm. Nell loved dim sum as much as I did. If we went there for supper, I would be able to pass the salon without drawing her attention to the detour. It was win–win.

'Fancy an early-evening dim sum?' I asked her, peering around the changing room curtain with my breath high in my chest.

The thought of seeing Billy again sent a whoosh of stars across my eyes.

CHAPTER TWENTY-FOUR

Nell

Flying to New York to go shopping for one day is a pretty insane thing to do, and I want to feel good about that, but I'm not there yet.

I'm standing in the changing room of a thrift store trying on yet another pair of second-hand jeans. Thrift stores are an awesome consolation prize for my crap morning, but I don't seem to like anything I try. All the clothes look bad on me. I can't shake off Bonnie's comments about my body, and I cringe every time I think about being chucked off the job.

I need to talk to Bay, who hasn't responded to my texts yet. I can't believe she's still airing me because of the room tour. If only she'd open my messages and see that the news is big. Maybe she stayed at Ty's, where the reception is terrible. I know she'll be happy that Mum and I are coming home early, and as enraged as we are about what Bonnie said. Her anger on my behalf and on behalf of the sisterhood will cheer me up. Her feminist talk will give it all meaning. It's weird, but it will be easier between us because of what happened this morning, and that is almost a comfort.

I Snap her again:

Did u get my message? Nx

Then I take a mirror selfie of me in my bra and jeans and ping it off to her.

Wadda u think? These ones or…

I change into another pair. The TikTok influencers make thrift store shopping seem super-easy, but finding the perfect jeans takes staying power I'm not sure I have.

Mum pops her head around the curtain. 'Fancy an early-evening dim sum?'

I quickly text Bay the second mirror selfie.

Or these?

She texts straight back:

Second pair x

Mum says, 'Nell? Dim sum?'

'Sure,' I say. 'Bay thinks these ones. They're only fifteen dollars.'

'They look great.'

As I change back into my own clothes, I wonder why Bay managed to reply to my text about the jeans, but not to my text and film about the huge thing that happened to me this morning.

While I wait in the queue to buy the jeans – which I am still not sure about – I text her again:

Did u see my text about the shoot? And get the clip?

She airs me again! For ages! When we are almost at the dim sum place, she texts:

Watched it. EPIC FAIL Angle n light are shit. What's that bulge in the way? A DUVET??? Could've put it higher maybe?

I stare at my phone in shock. WTAF? I expected solidarity, not some frigging critique on the filming. She is unbelievable. If this is payback for the hotel room tour, call it even. I'm over it. Over her. Earlier, when Bonnie was being nasty to me, I was more concerned about recording it for Bay than I was about how I was being treated. That's how guilty she makes me feel. And now she's dissing the footage and hasn't even tried to find out if I'm all right – evidence in the vid, sister! If she really cared, she would have FaceTimed me or sent me a kind text.

I don't know why I expect her to react normally. The truth is, my 'epic fail' today is going to make her super-happy. Because she's jealous. She always was and she always will be. I am sick of stepping on eggshells and the constant flip-flopping of her moods. I can't keep up any more, I can't do anything right. As soon as I start to feel that things are okay between us, she does something vicious to ruin it.

'You all right?' Mum asks me.

'Yes. Why?'

'You've gone so quiet.'

If I tell her about the video and about Bay's text, everything will come spilling out of me in one long, angry overshare.

'I'm fine,' I say. I check my phone map for the route to the restaurant.

Mum turns left down a side street.

'That's the wrong way,' I say.

'This is a shortcut,' she says.

'Oh, right.' I know she is wrong, but I can't be bothered to fight with her about it.

We walk past a fancy jewellery shop and a small coffee shop and I check my phone again to reread Bay's text, wondering if I have overreacted. Mum yanks my arm out of its socket and pulls me along really fast, like a nutter. She says, 'Don't stop here!'

I look around me, wondering what I'm missing. There is a hair salon and a lorry being unloaded just ahead of us by an old muscly dude with torn-off shirtsleeves.

Once we are past the lorry, she begins breathing really fast. 'Sorry, I'm not feeling too good.'

The old dude presses a button on the back of his lorry and it sets off a loud beeping noise. Mum squeezes her head. The ramp thingy, loaded with crates, moves upwards. Mum suddenly sits down on the edge of the sidewalk and puts her head between her knees. I'm getting worried. She's not the type to faint.

'You okay, Mum?'

Before she can reply, the old dude says, 'You doin' all right, ma'am?'

Mum says weakly, 'Fine, thank you!'

He disappears into his lorry. Loud crashing and banging come from inside.

'I think I've got low blood sugar,' Mum says.

'No wonder. We've been walking for hours. You need some dim sum.'

'Yup,' she says. 'Dim sum makes everything better.' And she smiles in a weird way and stands up.

'I'm in charge now, Mum. My phone says this way and it has never let me down before.'

I link arms with her, relieved that I haven't burdened her with my whingeing about Bay, and we walk back down the street. On the way past the hair salon, she speeds up. I tell her to slow down.

We find the dim sum place without her collapsing again. The waitress, Jun, gives us a table in the corner.

I want everything on the menu, even though I'm obviously too fat to be a model. But I love food too much to be super-thin. I feel for the girls who count calories, like Tally. She misses out on so much yumminess. Not that models are the only people with eating disorders. Most of my friends at school watch their weight and go on all sorts of unhealthy fad diets. Even some of the boys.

Mum laughs at how much I order. 'I'm glad you're hungry,' she says, and I guess she is relieved that Bonnie hasn't turned me anorexic.

As soon as the food arrives, I ask Mum to hold open the basket lids so that I can film my chopsticks picking out a shrimp and snow pea leaf parcel, which is all steamy and perfect for an Insta video post. For the first time, I am filming for fun rather than for Bay.

But then Mum drops the bamboo lid on the floor, and when I look up at her, she has gone as white as the rice dumplings and is staring at the door like she has seen a ghost.

CHAPTER TWENTY-FIVE

Anna

'Anna?' he said.

I froze, thrown by his voice. His face. His presence in front of me – was it real? – filled every nook and crevice of my being. Those expressive eyebrows and the curly hair, too long below his ears, now shot with grey. Time had not worn him out, had not lessened him.

'Billy!' I said, leaping up. 'Billy! Wow.' It was all I could manage for now.

Our hands clasped together in a handshake that sent a wave of pleasure through me. Having fretted about my appearance, I found I didn't care now. Billy and I were beyond appearances.

'I thought it was you, going past the salon,' he said.

'You saw us?'

He didn't immediately reply. I knew he was weighing his thoughts.

Softly, openly embarrassed, he said, 'I followed you here. Then I was a coward and I went back to the salon. But then I turned back. I had to say hello.'

'I'm glad you did,' I said.

To others he would seem cool and calm, but I saw the slight tremor in his big hands. He jammed them into his pockets and said, 'So, what brings you to New York?'

'Hi, I'm Nell, by the way,' Nell said, standing up.

With a start, I remembered we weren't alone. 'Oh my God. Sorry, Nell. Billy, this is my daughter, Nell. Nell, this is Billy, an old friend from St Martin's.'

He looked at her with his light grey eyes, deep-set and thoughtful.

'So grown up and beautiful,' he said, taking a hand from his pocket to shake hers.

I beamed at her. 'And we've got your sisters Bay and Iris at home, haven't we?'

'They didn't get to come?' he asked.

I was about to reply, but Nell said, 'I wish. I was supposed to be on a modelling job, but I got chucked off and so we're going home tomorrow.' Her level of frankness matched Billy's.

'Who were you working for?'

'Focus superstores,' I said.

'Oh dear. Bonnie Steiner.' He nodded knowingly.

'Do you know her?'

'I've worked with her once. But everyone knows Bonnie. She's famous for making models cry.'

'Really? It wasn't fun, was it, love?'

Nell shook her head. 'She was a proper B-word.'

He grinned. 'Dim sum will make it all better.'

'That's what I said.' Deep in his eyes, could I see the feelings he'd once had for me, still there, dancing about like a reflection?

He said, 'How's your mum these days?'

Briefly I glanced at Nell. She didn't know the full story about Mum, and I hoped that Billy wouldn't say too much. It was strange to think that he had been there at one of the most intimate and terrible moments in Mum's past, and yet here we were, near strangers. I felt mortified that he might now be thinking of her naked in the shower with a clump of wet hair in her fist; seeing again that bald patch above her right ear; hearing her wail as more hair came away in her fingers; smelling the antiseptic of the psychiatric hospital in Woking; feeling my sweaty hand in his after we'd left her there.

Unless he had forgotten. After all, she was not his mother. But I suspected he would still remember. It had happened a month before his departure for New York and it had decided both our futures.

'She lives down the road from us,' I said.

'Does she?' He said it with strained surprise.

I bristled. 'She's pretty self-sufficient now.'

Mum had only called me once today. And I had been very disciplined and had not called her back. Instead I had texted Dom and then Viv as backup, asking them to call her for me, worrying about her alone in her flat without me there.

'It really is great to see you,' he said.

'You too.' I tried to think of something to say that would not drag us back to the past.

'I'd better leave you two to it,' he said.

But I couldn't let him go. Not yet. I blurted out, 'Do you have kids?'

'I have a daughter,' he said. 'Dixie.'

'Oh, how wonderful.' All at once, I was both thrilled for him and possessive. Dixie must have a mother who had shared a life with Billy.

'She's five, but she lives in London with her mum,' he said. His brow hung low, casting a shadow over his face.

'London? Wow,' I said. I'd heard from Katy that he often travelled to London, and Europe, for work, but I'd had no idea his daughter was living there.

The waitress came up to him. 'The usual?' she asked.

'Not today, Jun. Just saying hello to an old friend.'

'You're a regular?' I asked when the waitress had gone. I had landed on a restaurant that he knew well, and I couldn't help feeling there had been serendipity in that choice – putting aside

my deliberate stalking of him at his salon and the fact that I knew
he loved dim sum as much as I did.

'The best dim sum in New York,' he said.

'We're starved of it in the country.' I smiled.

'Where are you staying while you're here?' he asked.

I didn't want him to know. If he knew, he might contact me there.

'The Chelsea Hotel,' Nell said.

'The Chelsea! Cool. I have a friend who lived there before its
refurb. I hung out with Grace Jones in the lift once.'

'I love her music,' Nell said.

'One of your mum's favourite shower songs.'

Nell burst out laughing. 'That's how I know it!'

'I'm glad my talent is appreciated,' I said.

'And your hats?' he asked.

I shrugged. 'Pillboxes for funerals mostly.'

'That's not true!' Nell said. 'She's started making them for
weddings and for Goodwood last year.'

Embarrassed about my small accomplishments, I changed the
subject back to him. 'You have your own salon now?'

Walking past in my dizzied state, I'd been able to see the
impressive space, the modern decor of Moroccan tiles and cacti
and mirrors and retro barber seats, and the gold star award stickers
lining one side of the glass window.

'It's taken me four tough years to turn a profit, but I love it,' he
said, one eyebrow and one corner of his mouth twitching. 'And
I've just launched a new hair product line.'

'That's amazing, Billy. I'm so impressed.'

'It's the dream,' he said, smiling.

I laughed. It was what he used to say about every tiny enjoy-
ment in his life. A cup of black coffee in a sunlit loft: 'It's the
dream!' An illicit kiss in an empty lift: 'It's the dream!' A supper
of beans on toast in front of the telly: 'It's the dream!' Simple
pleasures were never lost on Billy.

He looked at me now, right into me. I glanced away, unable to bear the intensity. But he was like a magnet. My gaze moved back to him, over him, taking in every single vein and sinew, scar and mole, mapping the touch of my fingertips from the past.

There was a tattoo on his forearm that hadn't been there when we'd been together. It sent a second shock wave through me. It was of a woman in a bathing suit, wearing a large hat that covered her face. I had drawn that very picture in art college. It had been a poor self-portrait, from a snap on holiday, but the composition had been nice.

His hand brushed over it and I saw the goosebumps rise. 'I'd better get back. My client has foils in.'

'Good to see you,' I said. 'The salon looks amazing.'

'You look amazing, too,' he said, and I flushed, glancing at Nell. Then to Nell, 'Your mum never appreciated how beautiful she was.'

Nell's eyes widened at his indiscretion, but she nodded. 'Still true.'

He winked at her. 'Look after her for me.'

'Yes, I will,' Nell said sincerely and politely.

'Bye, Billy,' I said.

He turned away, and I felt a physical wrench as he closed the restaurant door behind him.

'Billy was my first proper boyfriend,' I told Nell. I couldn't be wholly truthful with her, knowing her loyalty to her dad would be fierce, naturally, but I had to say something. Billy and I, blindsided by seeing each other after all these years, had not hidden what had been between us.

'I think he's still got it bad,' she said, shoving a dumpling into her mouth.

'Don't be daft.' My dumpling kept slipping out of my chopsticks.

'"Your mum never appreciated how beautiful she was",' she said, grinning, splashing soy sauce out of the saucer.

'He always was a charmer,' I lied. Billy was the opposite of a charmer. He was indeed charming, but he was self-contained. Flirting wasn't something he did. When he complimented someone, he meant it, right from the heart. I glowed at the thought. When we had been together, he would look at me as though I were the most beautiful woman in the room. Even in my best years, I had not been beautiful, by any stretch, and I'd never cared either way, but I had loved how fervently he had believed it. He had taught me that love is blind.

'Dad would have knocked him out.'

'Dad's not the jealous type,' I said. I laughed inside at the thought of slight Dom fronting up to Billy, who was broad and sturdy. Dom was more likely to sulk and bitch than knock anyone out.

'I can't wait to see him tomorrow,' she said. Her shoulders rounded and she played with one chopstick, drawing squiggles through the chilli sauce she had poured onto her plate.

'It's disappointing to be going home, isn't it?'

'Yeah, kind of,' she admitted. 'It's going to be embarrassing explaining to my friends why I'm back early.'

'I know. But if they're good friends, they'll be sympathetic.'

'I guess.' She shrugged, plainly unconvinced.

'At least you can show off your cool new jeans.'

'I've gone off them.'

I was taken aback. 'Really?'

'I only got them because Bay said I should.' She held eye contact with me for a second before continuing her doodling. All of a sudden, it seemed her mood had changed.

'You'll probably live in them when you get home.'

'You didn't even see them properly. You were too busy on your phone.'

'Do you want to go back to the shop?' I checked my watch, wondering if the thrift stores would still be open.

'It'll be closed now,' she said.

'You had fun looking, at least.'

'Yeah.'

I wished she had bought something she was happy with. I might have worked out what was going on if I hadn't been glued to my phone, searching for restaurants near Billy's salon.

'Maybe we can pick up something at duty-free for you,' I said, thinking I could buy her the perfume she had wanted with the contingency money I had put aside. It would be a superficial fix. I knew that the high of shopping and presents could only last so long.

'It's not that. Honestly, Mum. I'm fine.'

Every inch of me knew that she was not fine. But it was very hard to contradict her and unpick what the problem was.

'Better out than in, Nellie,' I coaxed.

'That's not true,' she said. She put her chopsticks down and focused on lining them up centrally on her plate.

'Oh?'

'Sometimes when it's out, it makes it ten million times worse.'

I worried that this was about Billy, that our meeting had unsettled her somehow, rattled her sense of security. I felt selfish for seeking out the salon and behaving so oddly around her. It had been irresponsible and childish, and ultimately futile, stirring up feelings inside me that might have been better kept under wraps, just as Nell was suggesting.

'Give me an example,' I said, hoping I wasn't in for it.

'Well, like, when a woman's been sexually assaulted at work by some pervy boss and she tells the police about it, and then she goes on trial and she has to tell everyone what happened to her, with everyone staring at her while she relives the worst, most shameful thing possible, and then the lawyer tells her she's making it all up and that she's a liar, and then, after all that, after all that *heartache*, the pervy boss gets away with it.'

I was a little startled by the force of her reply. 'Oh darling, nothing like that's ever happened to you, has it?'

There was a pause so momentary I wondered if I had imagined it. Then she said, 'No! Course not! But you see why women don't tell, right?'

'But maybe telling people *does* help that woman, even if the boss gets away with it. Maybe getting it off her chest helps her to move on with her life.'

'Or she's not believed at all, and she's so humiliated she just kills herself.'

I was deeply perturbed to hear her talk like this, and unused to her sounding so angry. Rewinding, I thought about the shoot with *Chloe Does*, wondering if she had spent any time alone with Asif. Had something happened at the party in Shoreditch? I'd heard her talk about a model called Lee. Had he touched her inappropriately, or worse? More grim scenarios tripped through my mind. Forcing myself to ask her a question that terrified me, I said, 'Is there anything that you're keeping to yourself, Nell?'

'Nooo, Mum,' she sighed. 'I always tell you everything.'

Still, fear spread through me. Had that split-second pause been a contemplation of a confession before deciding against it? 'Are you sure? Nothing is too big to tell me.'

'Don't be mad, Mum. I was just using it as an example.'

Her jolliness had snapped back with as much suddenness as the opposite mood had come on, and I felt suspicious of it.

'It's always better to talk about it, Nell,' I said firmly. '*Always.*'

And then I realised what a hypocrite I was. Although I had not experienced a trauma like a sexual assault, I had lived with a different kind of secret in my heart throughout the entirety of my marriage. A buried feeling that was definitely best not talked about.

When we got back to the hotel, there were two messages for me at the desk. One from my mother – no surprise there – and one from Billy.

'What's that about?' Nell asked.

'Granny Berry and Dad called. I'd better call them back,' I said, folding the two slips into my wallet.

'Why didn't Dad call your mobile?'

'My battery ran out.'

Little lies, like baby spiders crawling out of their mother. Lies on top of lies on top of lies.

If I threw away Billy's number, I wouldn't have to lie again. But I could not throw it away. It would be like throwing *him* away. And that was impossible now.

CHAPTER TWENTY-SIX

Bay

The New York trip had messed with my head. *Literally*, as Nell would say. Over text, I had apologised to her for being crabby, and her reply had been fine, but there had been fewer emojis than usual and long delays before she had reacted to my subsequent memes.

They were due home later today. I was impatient for their return, desperate to apologise face to face and to hear them both swear to me they'd never leave me again.

'Iris, get your shoes on, Willow will be here any minute.'

'But I haven't had any breakfast!'

'Didn't Dad make you toast?'

Yesterday, before Dad went to work, he had toasted frozen waffles and served them with chocolate spread. They had been soggy. He had chatted more than was usual in the mornings and hadn't noticed that Iris had left hers. And it had struck me that he was jollier without Anna around. Not that Anna was dictatorial or difficult to live with. Quite the reverse. Perhaps Dad felt inadequate around her. Anna would have happily made pancakes from scratch and served them with fresh fruit and honey and hand-whipped cream. The effort was always worth it for her. Dad was lazier. And in the end, he was too lazy even for frozen waffles this morning. The fun had already worn off.

'I don't like toast,' Iris said now. Her disappointment about her father's poor efforts over the last couple of days would be stored up for later – I knew that much. When I'd been little, Suki had told me many times over that Dad got bored easily, which was why he had left us. 'Babies are boring to men,' she had said, not caring that I had been the baby in question. Dad leaving us meant I had few expectations of him now. While Anna and Nell were in New York, I had accepted the novelty of existing side by side with him, testing it out, seeing how it felt to be his sole focus – or almost – for the first time in my life.

'You could have got yourself a bowl of cereal,' I said to Iris, who was attempting to tie her trainer shoelaces on the bottom stair.

'I forgot.'

'What about a handful of dry Shreddies?'

'Okay,' she said.

If Anna had been here, she would have stepped in to tie Iris's laces by now. It seemed that it might be better to leave her to it and see what happened. When Willow's mum's car was outside, I would do it for her then.

'Can you help me?' Iris asked, looking up. Poor Iris. She wasn't as pretty as Nell. Her ears stuck out at odd angles and her blonde hair was always wispy and static.

'You're ten. You should be able to do it yourself.'

I left her and went into the kitchen to dig out a handful of cereal.

'But my fingers are tired!' she yelled.

I returned and watched. The cereal was getting soggy in my hand. I found some foil, again leaving Iris struggling. There was a loud thud.

'I want Mummy!' Iris screamed.

Her trainer was lying by the kitchen door.

She hurled the other one at me and missed. I could have reminded her that Mummy and Nell were coming back tonight, but I didn't feel like it.

'Well, you can't have Mummy,' I said, contemplating throwing the trainers back at her and deciding I couldn't be bothered do to that either.

I wanted Willow's mum to take her away to their football club because I was eager to get on with editing down Nell's footage from New York. When I had first watched the clip of the woman from Focus telling Nell she was fat, my fingertips had become sweaty on the touchpad. I had clicked to rewatch it several times. The picture was partly obscured by a duvet, which had propped the phone up, but it was clear what was going on. I had not been able to believe what I was watching. Those five minutes of footage were documentary gold dust. I could hang my whole film on them.

Later, the house was quiet, and I lay on my bed and downloaded more of Nell's video clips onto my laptop.

I viewed shots of thrift shops and coffee mugs and sunny New York streets and began to get bored and hungry. Most of it was unusable, except the clip of the woman from Focus.

Thinking I had found the only nugget worth keeping, I watched the rest lazily as I ate crisps and drank Coke, skimming through most of it, laughing at Nell's silly poses in the changing rooms, almost nodding off.

Then suddenly there was a clip that woke me up. It started as a boring shot of chopsticks and dumplings, which trailed off to a black screen, but the video continued to record sound for three minutes and twenty-one seconds more. Rewinding it twice, I listened to the voice of a man with a British accent. A man Anna had known. A man she had called Billy.

It seemed my hunch had been right.

*

That evening, I sat down next to Dad on the sofa to watch television, pent up with questions about the man called Billy.

In the advert break, he read out a text from Anna to say their plane was delayed.

'She says not to wait up,' he said, yawning.

My phone had the same message from Nell, and I clicked into Instagram to see if she had posted any photographs in the airport.

Dad peered over my shoulder. 'How's the blogging going?' he asked.

I cringed at his mistake but didn't correct him. 'Yeah, cool.'

My thumb stopped scrolling at my best friend Ty's post of his Boston terrier, Badger, who was dressed in a wig of a lion's mane. I guffawed.

What would I do without Ty and Badger making me smile? I would be forever thankful that his parents had divorced and his father had refused to pay the fees at his private school, and that Ty had ended up in my year at Guildford Comp. Initially he had been bullied for being rich and overweight and bad at football, but I had worked on his image, and by Year 9 he had come out as gay and arty and had lost all the weight. The bullies had moved on, leaving us be.

'What's so funny?' Dad asked.

I showed him, and he squinted at the image. Now might be the time to ask about Billy, while I had his attention.

'Whose dog is that?' he said, instead of laughing.

'That's Badger. Ty's dog.' It shouldn't have bothered me that Dad hadn't remembered Badger, but it did. In the comments section underneath Ty's post I wrote:

I'll report you to the RSPCA for ruining his street cred.

'How's Ty? Still in love with you?'

'Dad, Ty came out years ago.' I showed him a photograph of Ty linking arms with his mum at the Gay Pride march in Brighton.

'I can't keep up with all the pan, bi, gay, trans kids in your year,' he said.

The sports quiz programme started again. He turned the volume up.

I was relieved he had dropped it. His questions had brought to light the distance between us, but I was disinclined to catch him up. There were too many lost years. Too many years of Anna stepping in to fill the gaps. It was why I could not broach the subject of Billy. As angry as I was with Anna for not taking me to New York, my loyalties lay with her more than anyone. She cared about my feelings, and I had learned to value that.

The house felt empty without her and Nell, as though Dad and I were dazed and shipwrecked, marooned on an island with Iris, the orphaned child. Anna and Nell were the heart and soul of the family. Mentioning the strange man in New York would be counter-intuitive, wouldn't it? It risked cutting out the heart that beat for all of us.

Before bed, Dad and I cleared our plates into the dishwasher. He said, 'We should probably get thinking about your UCAS personal statement soon.'

Applications were in October. I had two months to write one page. He was finding solid ground, covering over the stickiness of earlier. Safer to stay on the subject of my education. Messier to delve into my personal life, my desires, my passions, my friendships, my love life, my *feelings*. In that he was like most fathers, I guessed. School chats had boundaries, like business meetings.

'I've written a rough draft already.'

'First choice is still Norwich? Or London Film School this week?' he said.

We dissected the pros and cons of each course. During our discussion, I changed my mind and changed it back again, more muddled than before.

'We don't have to decide now,' he said.

It was clear he wanted me to put Norwich down as my first choice, and I became suspicious of the reasons for his bias.

'If I go to the London Film School, I could stay at home,' I said.

'We'd love you to stay at home,' he said. The use of 'we' sounded formal, and I sensed a 'but' hanging at the end of the sentence. He switched the dishwasher on. It made a whirring sound. The dishes clinked. I wanted to look inside, to see how the jets cleaned the dirt away.

I said, 'I guess Norwich would be a bit more of a change of scene. It might be good fun, if I was on campus with other students.' Then I added, 'If I'm not having a gap year.'

I tried to look sadder than I felt. My wish to travel around the world on a gap year and take photographs for a project on neocolonialism had caused a huge family argument. Dad had wanted to borrow the money to make it happen and Anna had said we couldn't afford it. I might have been able to spend six months earning and saving the money myself, but I would not have accrued enough to go to all the necessary countries, so I had decided to postpone it until after college and do it properly.

Dad rubbed his leather-soled slipper on a pea and mashed it into the linoleum. 'I really thought I'd get that bonus last year,' he said. It was his self-pitying voice. He was sad – not about my gap year, but about his own life.

'Honestly, it's okay.'

'If I get that promotion this year, we'll be able to help you with your rent in Norwich.'

I took a cloth and wiped up the green smear near his foot. Dad wanted me gone, I just knew it.

'Thanks, Dad,' I said, and pecked him on the cheek. 'I'm off to bed.'

The voice of Billy in New York filled my mind.

'Night, darling,' he said. He looked relieved, as though he had got away with something.

At the door, I turned back. With sudden spitefulness, I wanted to hurt Dad more than I cared about my loyalty to Anna right now. Billy was ammunition.

'By the way,' I said. 'Who's Billy?'

He was plugging his phone into his charger. 'Billy?'

'Anna's friend in New York?'

He looked up from his phone. 'She doesn't have a friend in New York.'

'Oh, that's funny. I must've got it wrong. It's just Nell said something about having dim sum with some guy called Billy.'

Dad stared right into my eyes. I felt connected to him in a way I had never felt before. Our alikeness had never been clearer to me: our changing eyes and soft jaws, our thick ebony hair, our discontented – some might say sullen – natures.

'You must have got that wrong,' he said. He sounded firm about that.

And I went to bed conscience-stricken, already regretting my vicious outburst, and apprehensive about Anna's return home.

CHAPTER TWENTY-SEVEN

Anna

There was an unreal quality to being home. To the sun diffused through the smoke of the barbecue; to the sight of Bay and Nell lying next to each other on beanbags on the grass, whispering out of earshot; to Iris's face, obscured by an old pair of my sunglasses as she read a sixties *Beano*; to the low volume of Dom's mood, turned down, while my vision of Billy was switched up in my head. New York should have been the unreal bit, but it felt solid in my mind, like I was still there. Everything around me now felt like the perfect image of family life projected onto a wall on a bright day.

A remnant of our trip was folded into my wallet. I had no intention of calling the number on the slip of paper, but I loved to take it out and look at it; at the humbling, conciliatory piece of evidence of a wrong righted. The fragment of a wall, perhaps, erected long ago, separating one part of my brain from another.

I sliced the tomatoes for the burgers, trying to connect to the fruit under my fingers.

'How long until they're ready, do you reckon?' I asked Dom, whose back was rounded over the grill as he poked at the meat with his prongs.

He didn't answer. He was probably punishing me for berating him about failing to drop in on my mother. I had been livid about it, and our argument had spoiled my return home. Golf, this morning with Greg, had not broken his mood as I had hoped it would. As usual, I would probably end up apologising, even though he had been in the wrong.

'Dom? How long will the burgers take, roughly?' I asked again, only wondering about when to cut open the avocados.

I waited for him to answer.

'Five minutes,' he said at last.

The table needed laying. I rallied the girls. Nell loped over and milled about unhelpfully.

'Could you get the chair cushions from the Wendy house, Nell?' I said. She looked at me as though I had asked her to put her hand in a cadaver.

'Do I have to? I'm so jet-lagged,' she groaned.

'I'll get them,' Bay said, brushing a finger across her alabaster forehead, gently pushing a piece of her hair away from her eyes, making a pretty side parting.

'No, Bay. Nell can get them.'

Nell grunted and stormed to the Wendy house.

'Shall I cut the avocados?' Bay said.

I found a chopping board for her and twisted the salad spinner.

'How are you getting on with your films?' I said, aware that the focus had been skewed towards Nell lately.

'I want my next documentary to be about female body image in advertising,' she said over the whirr of the spinner.

'Oh yes?' It explained all the questions she had fired off at Nell about the disastrous shoot.

'Nell's okay with it,' she said, tapping the avocado stone with the knife.

'She's not going to be in it, is she?'

'Why not?'

Off the top of my head, I said, 'The exposure would be too much.'

'It would only get a few thousand viewers.'

A few thousand viewers sounded huge to me. 'The subject matter is quite controversial, and she's only just started out.'

'So you're saying she should just stay quiet about the body shaming of children for the sake of her career?'

Put like that, I felt ashamed of my hypocrisy. 'I suppose you're right.' I took a slice of tomato and ate it, still thinking about why I did not want Nell to be in a documentary about body shaming.

We sat down to eat. The cushion on my chair was still damp from a downpour last week. Nothing ever dried out in the Wendy house. Later, I planned to talk to Bay some more about her documentary. My mother would say that making a film about the ills of modelling would be like biting off the hand that fed you. But Nell's career didn't feed her. We did. Then I got confused about why we had allowed her to be a model in the first place. After Bonnie's meanness, I was regretting it more than ever. I reminded myself of Nell's university fund. Whereas Bay would go through college without a spare penny. I still felt upset that we hadn't been able to fund her gap year photography project.

Iris squeezed a dollop of ketchup onto her patty. 'Top Cat lived in New York,' she said.

'Yes,' I laughed.

'And *The Secret Life of Pets* is set in New York,' she added.

'There was a hotel cat where we stayed,' Nell said, clicking into her phone and showing Iris the photograph of Dylan curled up in the pot plant by the lift.

'Cute!' Iris cried.

All weekend, Nell had chatted about New York, detailing everything from the food we ate to the colour of the hotel linen, analysing the incident with Bonnie many times over, but neither of us had brought up Billy. Yet.

I would never have told Nell *not* to mention him. It would have been wrong to ask her to keep secrets from her own father. If she did mention it, I would ride it out, be casual, say how funny it was to have bumped into him after all these years; double down on my message that he was of no consequence. There was some truth in that.

'Have you heard about Bay's new film idea?' I asked Dom.

'A new blog, darling?' Dom said to Bay.

'Vlog!' Nell cried. 'Dad. A blog is written stuff, like a diary or a website. Vlogs are videos. Bay does vlogs.'

Bay smiled. 'It's going to be a long-form documentary this time, I think.'

'You could get it on Netflix,' Nell said.

'Why the hell not?' Dom nodded. 'What's it going to be about?'

'The exploitation of children in the fashion business,' Bay said.

I put my burger down. Dom stopped chewing and wiped his mouth with his napkin, looking at me as though it was my fault. 'Really?' he said.

'Isn't it about female body image in advertising?' I said, trying to mitigate the shock value.

'It's evolving,' Bay said. 'The industry's abuse of power includes the insidious fostering of eating disorders.'

If Nell or Iris had been pompous like that, I would have told them off.

'No fear of that with Nellie,' Dom said, pointing to Nell, whose mouth was stuffed with burger.

'How do you feel about it, Nell?' I asked.

It took her a long time to swallow. 'I'm cool with it. I'm only modelling to make a bit of extra cash. It's not like I want it to be my real job when I leave school or anything.' She picked up her plate and licked the ketchup off.

'Nell!' I cried.

Iris followed suit. Dom shoved in his last mouthful and did the same. Bay and I laughed. 'Who brought you lot up?' I asked, grinning.

Three plates came down to reveal goofy smiles and ketchup smears. For a moment Dom had forgotten how moody he was, and I was reminded of where I belonged. New York and Billy were a long way away.

The tinkling tune of the ice-cream van started up.

Iris shot up. 'Ice cream!'

'Off you go. There's some cash in my wallet,' I said.

'Go and eat them on the swings,' Dom said.

All three girls left the table and hurried out of the house, leaving Dom and me sitting alone. The musty smell of their chair cushions was left behind.

I poured more wine. He took a sip and pulled out his roll-ups. Sometimes I preferred this defiant smoking of his, when he was inviting disapproval from me, unapologetic about his habit. It was better than the secrecy.

This was my opportunity to bring up Billy, casually, but I just couldn't face it. I looked at Dom, assessing the timing, the setting and his mood, building up to it. Now that the girls had gone, he looked glum again. His top-heavy head of hair had flopped and flattened, his boyish chin was bunched up and his black eyelashes fluttered down over his eyes. He dangled a wrinkled cigarette between his lips. His expression reminded me of a photograph I had seen of him as a boy, standing pigeon-toed, two fingers flopping in his open mouth, eyes downcast. Before his mother died, she told us she had taken the photograph because she thought he looked sweet when he cried.

I needed to care more about Dom and stop thinking about Billy. How was Billy relevant to us now?

'You got the Sunday-night blues?' I said gently.

His gaze flicked up to mine before he lit his cigarette. Inhaling deeply, he said, 'Who's Billy?'

Heat rushed through me and up into my head. I flapped at the smoke to divert attention from my reddening face, and put enormous effort into looking relaxed. 'Yeah! So weird. Billy Young. Did Nell mention we bumped into him?'

He shook his head slowly, giving me a sidelong glance as he blew smoke out. 'I don't *care*. I'd just never heard you talk about him.'

'I've mentioned him before, haven't I? He was a mate from St Martin's. We went out with each other for a bit. He lives in New York now.'

'And you got in touch and had supper together?'

'What? No! I did not get in touch or have supper with him!'

'No?' He let out a small laugh. Making fun of me.

'No! Nell didn't say that, did she?'

'I must've got the wrong end of the stick then.' He raised both eyebrows at me.

I gathered myself and stated coolly, 'Nell and I were having dim sum and Billy happened to come into the restaurant. His salon was around the corner.'

'Salon?'

'He owns a hair salon.'

Dom smirked. 'He's a *hairdresser*?'

Irritation shot through me. Why did he always have to be so childish? Sixteen-year-olds were less petulant than Dom at forty-nine.

'Yes, he's a hairdresser,' I said lightly, finishing the last few sips of my wine in one gulp. Dom didn't know that hairdressing had been Billy's way out, that he had grown up in rural poverty in Cornwall, that his mother had never taken him or any of his five siblings to the beach three miles away, that four of his siblings had never found jobs of any description. *Actually*, Dom, it's incredible that Billy's now an award-winning stylist and a session hairdresser working on worldwide advertising campaigns. *And* he has a tattoo of me on his arm! *If* we're being childish about this.

'Bloody weird coincidence, seeing him like that,' Dom said, pouring us both more wine.

'Yes,' I said. Manhattan was indeed a village.

As he rolled another cigarette, I got up and wandered inside. I found a scented candle and put it between us on the table, then struck a match and watched the feverish explosion of heat. I wondered if it was possible to carry on plodding through with Dom after seeing Billy again.

I blew out the match, shocked that I could even think like that, and poured another glass of wine.

To shut out the doubt and the terrible disloyalty, I forced myself to think about something else. Hat designs. And I resolved to stop procrastinating and call Viv's friend about designing a website. I would work harder on my hats. I would work harder with Dom. Hard work was what sustained lifelong marriages. All the experts said so.

'I'm glad you're home,' Dom said, touching my thigh.

I guess it was nice to be touched. It had been a long time since he had shown me affection.

The effort would pay off, I told myself.

CHAPTER TWENTY-EIGHT

Nell

'I'll be leaving home next year, so if they split up it won't affect me so much,' Bay says.

Iris is on the swing when she says it and I'm glad she's out of earshot. She would be really upset. I lick the drip from the bottom of my ice lolly. Stupidly, I joked to Bay – a little meanly – that Mum might run off with Billy, and she's taking it way too seriously. For a start, there is the little issue of him living in New York, which ends the idea before it has begun. I'm annoyed with Dad, though, who was really crap and forgot to visit Granny Berry while we were away. I heard Mum 'having words' with him about it. But I know they love each other. Married couples aren't supposed to *like* each other very much, are they?

'But you won't be leaving home if you go to the London Film School,' I say, trying to move away from the subject of Billy. Since Mum and I got back, Bay has been especially melodramatic and clingy, even though I totally let her off the hook about her unsympathetic, crappy texts. As per usual, I rose above it, so high I was practically in the clouds, but underneath it all, I am whacked out by her jealousy. Seriously, I could be a homeless person with fleas, a crack habit and one leg, and she'd still think I'm the lucky one.

'Dad wants me to go to Norwich.'

'Even so, you'd be back in the holidays, wouldn't you?'

'If they got divorced, they'd have to sell the house.'

'Can we not talk about it?' I say, getting the hump.

Just because Dad and Suki split up, she thinks she knows everything on the topic of divorce. But I know Mum better than her, and I know that she would never, ever split up our family. I'm not so sure about Dad. But Suki was a nutjob. No surprise he decided Mum was a better bet. Not that he had an affair with Mum. It had been over with Suki. When Dad was drunk at a party once, he gave a speech about how much he loved Mum, and how he had called her after he and Suki had split up, knowing that Mum would be the best person to talk to about everything, remembering from school that she had been really kind and understanding, and wise beyond her years. Imagine marrying someone you knew at school. Literally, like, yuck.

'There's Matthew,' I say, pleased to see him. Matthew used to have a big crush on Bay. 'Matthew!' I say, waving him over.

Bay says, right into my ear, 'Did you have to?'

Iris jumps off the swing and runs over to Matthew, taking his hand. 'Hi, Matthew Michaels,' she says. She always says his full name.

'Hi, Iris Hart,' Matthew says.

'How's it going?' I say. I shield my eyes to look at him. The sun is setting behind him.

'Lovely evening,' he says, sounding like a grandad.

Iris runs off back to the swings.

'It *was*,' Bay says.

I try to laugh off her rudeness and budge up on the bench so that Matthew can sit down.

'I can't. I'm just dropping these off for someone.' He has a bunch of newspapers in his hands.

'Who are they for?' I ask.

'Mrs Cole. She likes reading three different newspapers every day.'

'She's asked for a *personal* delivery, has she?' Bay says. Then she hums the tune of 'Mrs Robinson'.

'Yes. I find her very desirable,' Matthew says, pushing up his wonky glasses. 'I find her the most attractive of all my parents' friends.'

I laugh and Bay clicks her tongue. He's taking the piss, adapting lines from *The Graduate*. It's one of the films the three of us watched together millions of times above his parents' garage on their ancient DVD machine. We thought it was naughty and exciting, and I remember, after one viewing, whispering to Matthew that I wanted to kiss him.

'Is Mrs Cole okay?' I ask.

'She's fine. She had a knee operation and can't get down to the shop.'

Matthew Michaels is such a dude, I think.

'Bye then,' Bay says, in a rude voice, waving at him like she's shooing away an annoying dog.

He saunters off, reading the front page of one of the newspapers.

'Can I go with you?' Iris calls out, scuttling after him.

Matthew stops and takes her hand. 'I'll take her home, if you like?'

'Cool, thanks!' As they walk away, I say to Bay, 'You're so mean to him.'

'He doesn't care,' she says.

It's probably true.

I eye up his butt in his jeans.

'I quite fancy him,' I say.

'Nell, that's just wrong. And he's got a girlfriend.'

'I know. I'd never do anything with him. It's just, he's funny.'

'You'd actually *do* Matthew Michaels?'

'You *did* Josh Humphreys and he's as nerdy as they come.'

'At least Josh talks. Matthew's on the spectrum.'

I want to hit her. Matthew has been nothing but kind to her from the moment they met. 'He is not on the spectrum,' I say hotly.

She laughs at me. 'Doing Matthew would be like doing your own brother.'

When Bay and I get home, it is almost dark. Mum and Dad are still at the table, chatting together. They have lit a candle. It's a bit embarrassing because Dad has his hand on Mum's thigh, but it is good to see them being romantic. I hug Mum and then I hug Dad, really tightly. Bay's scare stories about divorce don't seem so scary any more.

'Aw, you two are so sweet,' Bay says to them. 'Night, guys.'

'Night, girls,' they say in unison, smiling at each other.

In the kitchen, I whisper angrily to Bay, 'They seem fine.'

'Oh Nellie, I *do* love you,' she says, patronising me.

Bad feelings towards her crowd in. I can't seem to snap back to the way we were before New York, when I would be able to think around her bitchiness and her annoying texts and forgive her more easily.

I really miss my bike. I've been borrowing Matthew's spare, now and again, but I don't keep it here, knowing his mum uses it. Now I want to spin the pedals and fly off into the woods and feel the air under my wheels and find Matthew Michaels and maybe kiss him, to take my mind off everything. I have never before wanted to actually kiss him. He is hopelessly in love with Belinda at uni and everything, and he would literally never cheat on her.

If we snogged just once, would it count? I've been around so long I'm practically family. Eugh. Put like that, it sounds gross. Snogging family is wrong, obvs.

Maybe if I catch him now walking back from Mrs Cole's, we could sit on the bench in the playground. Maybe I could snuggle up to him and talk to him about everything, like in the movies.

Catching up with him this evening, secretly, like we're having a grown-up affair, is such a thrilling idea, I decide to make it happen.

Of course I don't want Bay to know, so I sneak out through the side gate. On my two feet. Without my bike. Easy as pie.

The birds are tweeting and there are no cars on the road. The village is as pretty as a picture. As I look for Matthew, I think about everything we'll talk about: New York and Mum and Dad's marriage and the film I don't want Bay to make, and about what she used to do to me when we were little, and he will hold me in a loving embrace and tell me that everything is going to be okay.

PART TWO: SWEET SIXTEEN

Five Months Later

CHAPTER TWENTY-NINE

Anna

Wrapping up Nell's present had been a challenge, involving a whole roll of dotty paper. A pointless exercise, considering that its shape would give it away. I couldn't wait for her to open it this morning. The first of January. Her sixteenth birthday. For all the trouble we'd been having with her lately, I couldn't help feeling terribly soppy about her. The moment I had set eyes on her for the first time, in my ravaged post-birth state, I had been instantly fascinated by her and who she would turn out to be. There had been a distinct personality there, in her face, in her aura, that I couldn't wait to get to know. We'd had another name lined up, a more traditional name, but I had known that it would not suit her.

The house was quiet. There was frost on the window, but the kitchen was warm. I loved this time before everyone else woke up, when I could drink a cup of coffee and listen to what was being said on the radio without telling someone to shush. I found flour and milk and sugar and eggs and vanilla essence to make waffles. I chopped strawberries and bananas and mixed them in a bowl with blueberries. The cream could be whipped last minute. While the bacon sizzled in the pan, I set the table for five, putting out the other essentials: Nutella and maple syrup. It had been Nell's favourite breakfast ever since she was five years old, when I had first served it up on Dom's fortieth birthday.

Everyone had told me that Nell's childhood would whizz by. In those early weeks of her life, sixteen years ago, I hadn't believed them. Every day had felt like a lifetime. The learning curve had been steep; so steep that the line on a graph would have been vertical, sometimes tipping backwards into an alternate universe, where nothing was manageable, where nothing was as it should be, when it would become unrecordably hard.

Though Nell had been a good baby, I had wanted to be the perfect mother to her. I had been confused that breastfeeding hadn't come easily to me, and I had monitored her bowel movements with such obsession I could have written a PhD on the subject of the regularity and consistency of her poo. If she went for more than two days without a soiled nappy, I was off to the GP. The baby books I had read had scuppered my chances of instinctive mothering and had ensured that I felt a failure every day.

Dom, who had done it all before with Bay, had accused me of overthinking it, and – considering he *had* done it all before – had been remarkably useless at empathising. His day at work had always been harder than mine. 'I'd kill to potter about with Nell at home!' he had yelled at me during one of the many arguments we'd had about who was more exhausted. Trying to communicate how hard it was to look after a baby 24/7 was impossible. It was one of those 'you had to be there' situations. He had never done it, and he would never know the emotionally desperate extremes a main carer went through. I had called him pig-headed and selfish, but I had blamed myself for getting pregnant too soon, only months after he had split from Suki. The pink cross on the stick had been a shock. Neither of us had been ready.

I pressed the lumps of flour out of the batter and continued stirring long after it needed it. Stirring and thinking; jumping when I felt Nell's arms come around my waist.

'Morning, Mum,' she said.

It was the first unsolicited hug I had received from her in weeks.

'Darling heart! Happy Birthday! I didn't hear you come down,' I said, enveloping her in my arms, squeezing extra tight to make up for the recent absence of this closeness. I could smell cigarette smoke and perfume in her thick, shiny fringe.

'Is everyone else still asleep?' she asked.

'Yup,' I said, offering her a strawberry. 'Birthday strawberry?'

She took it. 'I might go back to bed for a while then.'

'Okay,' I said, a little disappointed. I had hoped to make her a milky cup of tea and sit with her, without the others, to tell her again all about the day she had been born. How the Nigerian midwife had said in pidgin, 'God dun butter your bread,' when looking down at Nell in my arms, minutes after the hell of childbirth, and I had replied, 'Oh my goodness, thank you, yes please,' thinking she had asked me if I wanted some actual bread and butter. Nell always laughed as hard as the midwife had when I told her that bit. And I would bring out the pink certificate confirming that she was the first new baby of 2005 at Hammersmith Hospital, which proved, without bias, in official print, how special she was.

'Would you like a birthday cuppa?' I asked her now, wanting to eke out some time with her.

She yawned and rubbed her eyes, smearing last night's eyeliner flicks. 'No thanks.'

'Birthday lie-in,' I said, reminding myself she could do anything she wanted today.

I watched her go, slouchy and sleepy in her oversized hoodie and tracksuit pants, yawning some more, coughing, whispering under her breath into the speaker of her phone, verbally texting, too tired even to use her fingers to type. She would be communicating with her friends about last night, or sorting out Drama, with a capital D, between Jade and Mint, whom she had offended by going to a New Year's Eve party at a club in London with Tally and Leah instead.

Short of tying her to her bed, there had been nothing I could do to stop her, however many times I reminded her she was underage. I imagined it wasn't the first time in the last few months that she had slipped past bouncers undetected, and it wouldn't be the last. It was the third time since Christmas Day that she had been out to celebrate her birthday in London. At least she had come home last night, at the decent hour of 3 a.m. As a birthday present, Tally and Leah and two other girls from the model flat had clubbed together to pay for a car to bring her home so that she could have birthday breakfast with us. It had cost them fifty quid each, and I was grudgingly grateful to them. We'd been less lucky on Tuesday night, when she had texted me at 11 p.m. to say she had missed the last train from Waterloo and that she would be staying at the model flat. Whether she had or not was a different story, and one she would never tell.

Last night, as Dom and I had stumbled in at 1 a.m., tiddly from Viv and Greg's New Year's Eve party, with Iris bumbling sleepily along with us, I had wondered whether Nell would turn up for her birthday breakfast at all. Dom had joked that she would never miss out on presents, but judging by the hug she gave me just now, I suspected it was more than presents she was after; that she wanted a bit of family love, too. It gave me a spark of hope about the year ahead. Maybe turning sixteen would mellow her and still those raging hormones.

Slowly, everyone sloped downstairs. Dom kissed me on the forehead and said, 'I don't feel old enough to have two such grownup daughters.'

'I do,' I said. I felt ancient, hung-over and worn out by the last six months.

Bay was the last down. She had been finishing off her little birthday film for Nell, which was going to be a surprise for her after cake and tea this afternoon with Mum and my brother and his family. She had come home earlier than all of us last night, just after midnight, slipping away from Ty's silent disco at his pool house. She had never liked big parties.

The five of us were together at last, sitting at the tiny breakfast bar crammed with food, elbow to elbow, gobbling and chatting about the funny things that had happened at our various parties.

'Ty was dancing so hard to grime, he fell into the pool by accident,' Bay said. 'And Badger jumped in to save him!'

There were lots of coos about Badger, who was a lovable rogue of a dog who used to pad around our house eating anything and everything he could find, just like Ty had when he was younger. Unlike Badger, Ty had since lost his puppy fat and grown tall and lean, dyed his hair tips peroxide blond and taken to wearing skinnies and Breton striped tops every day. Somehow I doubted that he had fallen into the pool by accident. By design was more likely. Ty was an interesting boy. He had manufactured himself brilliantly to survive secondary school. But his downturned mouth would always be the same; he was soppy-faced and soft-hearted like Badger, and it reminded me of how damaged he had been before the zaniness and the new image had come along.

'Matthew Michaels made me a special cocktail, called the Iris Cocktail,' Iris said.

'Did you get drunk, sis?' Nell chuckled.

'Mummy and Daddy did!' Iris cried.

Dom rubbed his head and croaked, 'He made strawberry daiquiris.'

'Lethal,' I admitted.

'Didn't Matthew go out with his mates?' Nell asked.

'He told me he wanted to spend New Year's Eve with his parents this year,' Dom told her.

'He's so sweet,' Bay said.

Nell, who was cradling a cup of tea like her life depended on it, shot a distinctly dirty look at Bay and I wasn't sure why. Both of them had history with Matthew, but I rarely understood the ins and outs of their triumvirate.

'But he always goes out on New Year,' Nell continued.

'I think he might have split up with his girlfriend,' I said, knowing that he definitely had. Viv had been more devastated than Matthew. Belinda had been the one he had rejected Cambridge for. She had got a place studying architecture at Sheffield and he had followed her there – perhaps that was the rebellion I had always expected of him! Viv had only tolerated his decision because she thought the two of them might settle down after their studies and give her grandchildren sooner rather than later.

'Really? They've actually split up, properly?' Nell said.

'That news has perked you up,' Dom said, winking at her.

'Shut up,' Nell said.

'Nell,' I chided gently, sick of her rudeness but not wanting to tell her off on her birthday.

Her cheeks coloured, brightening her ashen, hung-over face.

'I read somewhere that you're supposed to meet your soulmate before you're twenty-one, like Mum and me,' Dom said, continuing to tease her, not reading her cues.

'Matthew is not my soulmate!' she cried.

'The lady doth protest too much.' He laughed, and I chuckled, but the three girls did not. Moodily Nell tore off a bit of dry waffle and nibbled on it. Bay picked up her phone and began scrolling. And Iris, who had a crush on Matthew Michaels, looked hangdog. The birthday mood was dissipating, but I was desperate to keep us upbeat.

'So, Nell, is it present time?'

Iris leapt up. 'Yay! Presents! I want to get them! Can I get them, Mummy?'

'They're in the cupboard under the stairs. Be careful!'

Iris ran off and I began clearing the plates. Nell snuggled on the sofa under a blanket, cross-legged. 'I love presents,' she announced.

Iris came through carrying two smaller gifts on top of the guitar-shaped main present. According to Bay, Nell wanted her own electric guitar more than she wanted a new bike, which had surprised me. She had begged me to keep it a secret, promising it was going to be the best surprise ever. Bay loved to surprise people and knew that Nell would never ask for an electric guitar or a bike, knowing either present would be out of our price range. I was thrilled about giving her the guitar. Since Year 7, she had been borrowing the school instrument, and she had never asked for one of her own. She'd showed half-hearted interest in her practice, but I hadn't let her give up, believing that learning a musical instrument of some sort was important.

Iris placed the presents on Nell's lap.

This new guitar symbolised hope. A renewed hobby. A new start.

Mum had helped us out financially to buy it for Nell, who had frittered away her own money on partying in London and train fares. She had not worked since New York, and had not been paid by Focus, and Ian had become distinctly less attentive, sometimes taking days to call her back. Part of me wished he would chuck her out of the agency and be done with it.

She began opening the small ones, much more slowly than was traditional, with no exclamation about the shape of the main present. First the fluffy socks from Iris, then the AirPod case from Bay, customised by Ty with an elaborate flame design, then the guitar.

I couldn't see her face under her hair as she opened it, but I detected strain in her voice when she said, 'Thank you so much.'

'Granny Berry contributed,' I said. 'But she was happy for you to open it before this afternoon.'

'It's amazing. Thanks so much, honestly, it's really generous.'

There were no squeals of delight or hugs of gratitude; it was awful. She was disappointed. I couldn't bear it. The build-up and secrecy surrounding this present had been going on for months.

Dom and I glanced at each other. He shrugged, looking as perplexed as I was. I caught Bay's eye. She was biting her lip, staring at Nell as though waiting for her to react as we had expected her to, which she did, finally. Gathering herself, she brought down her amp and played a faltering rock version of 'Happy Birthday'. We clapped and laughed, breaking the awkward atmosphere.

Later, after a walk and some mooching around, I flung the table-cloth over the fold out garden table in the conservatory, preparing for Nell's birthday tea. It was going to be a squash and a squeeze when everyone arrived. I couldn't wait to see Martin and my nieces and nephews, Tessa, Toby, Tina and Thea – the Ts were Karen's idea – and I was even looking forward to seeing the frighteningly thin Karen, who had been unusually open and frank on the phone recently about the problems she'd been having with Tessa, who was the same age as Nell.

Martin had his hands full with his four near-feral children and Karen, but we had always been close. Every school holiday, we visited them in Somerset and stayed in their draughty house. It sat in a field that flooded every winter. We always wore two jumpers and secreted hand-warmers and crackers in our pockets – heating and eating didn't come high on their list of priorities – and on the way home, we would vow to stay in a hotel next time. We never did. Martin's different life choices, his wicked sense of humour and the privations of our visits enhanced our lives. I loved him dearly. And I hoped the girls would feel the same about each other when they became adults, in spite of how different they were.

Today we would be together here, which was going to be interesting. My second-attempt rainbow cake and Bay's *Sweet*

Sixteen film, which she had been very secretive about, were the two main events. I had a feeling the film would make us all cry, and I hoped that the cake wouldn't. Cakes weren't my forte. Hats were my forte. They had been my only sanity over the past few months. Already I had six new commissions to get started on in January and, finally, I had set up a meeting with a designer about a website. For the first time ever, I couldn't wait for the girls to go back to school.

Martin and Karen and the kids arrived while Dom was collecting Mum from her flat. The bustle and fuss of their arrival was heart-warming. The girls and their cousins took up where they had left off, hugging and chatting and collecting into a gang in the sitting room. The blood tie was strong for Nell and Iris, and Bay took her role as the oldest cousin seriously, becoming maternal, a little superior and full of worldly advice, lapped up by the younger teens.

When Mum arrived, she became the second focal point, other than the birthday girl. I made sure she was not left alone on the sofa, where she had settled, and provided her with a steady flow of tea.

Martin launched into his hilarious and tragicomic story about the day his roof collapsed, and I laughed my head off. My brother was sandy-haired and gentle and thoughtful, and different to Dom in almost all respects. During his story, I had one eye on my mother, who listened haughtily, with only a slight upturn of one corner of her mouth. She was pretending she couldn't hear him. This act was part of her ongoing campaign to punish Martin for daring to move away to a different county with his wife – of all people! – whom she believed was the devil incarnate. I was jealous of how he had broken free of Mum. Once, he had begged me to do the same, insisting I go to New York with Billy, promising me he would look after Mum while she recovered in hospital. But he had been newly married to Karen at the time and already living miles away, and I had decided the responsibility to care for Mum after her breakdown was mine.

When I looked at her now, in battleaxe, martyrdom mode, I wondered if I had helped her at all by staying. Perhaps I had indulged her, fostered her dependent tendencies, prevented her from making a real go of things.

Though I was grateful to have her here in my life, in the girls' lives.

And the birthday tea was making up for the disaster of the guitar. Nell seemed to be enjoying herself and appeared less hungover than she had at breakfast. Her beauty hid a multitude of sins.

The secret cavern of Smarties in the middle of the cake delighted all the children, even Nell. In spite of huge plates of sandwiches and pizza slices, everyone finished their cake, and some of them asked for seconds, which was a good sign, and I was relieved I had put in the effort to make it all over again after my first leaden disaster.

Empty plates were the cue for Bay to play her film.

I helped her to pull the blinds and pin the sheet up where the film was to be projected, and everyone found their seats.

Martin shouted, 'Bravo!' before it had even started.

The film began with the title: 'Before Me'.

Clownish music was the soundtrack to sped-up clips of Nell as a cute toddler running about in various crazy guises, with sunglasses on upside down, or sauce-covered grins, or bare-bottom mooning, or dressing up with shoes that were too big. The whole family was giggling and guffawing, and already, through my laughter, I felt my throat tightening with emotion. The tears began sliding down my face when the second half began, kicked off by the title slide 'After Me'. The clown music segued into a Beethoven piano concerto. The clips were of Bay showing Nell how to do various tasks: build dens, draw pictures, bake cakes, tie her shoelaces, and many more, demonstrating the amazing bond they shared. There wasn't a dry eye in the room. The third section was titled 'Without Me', and she had used Albinoni's Adagio as the final piece of music. Stills and video clips of Nell dressed up on a shoot, or with her new friends in short skirts looking precociously beautiful, partying and posing, composed and grown up, were spliced with sad, unflattering shots of Bay, whose self-deprecation made everyone laugh. Without me, Bay was saying, Nell had branched out and blossomed into a beautiful and sophisticated woman.

Everyone else in the family was oohing and aahing at the flattering shots of Nell, enjoying the satisfying, seemingly magnanimous narrative that Bay had crafted.

'So gorgeous. Oh my goodness, just stunning,' Karen said as she watched. 'And so funny, too, Bay. You are so talented. You'll be the star of Norwich.'

But as it played on, my grin had become fixed. I caught Nell change position and hug her knees defensively. I guessed she was reading the subtext behind the montage, just as I was; recognising it as typical Bay truth-telling, designed exclusively for those in the know. Even Dom wouldn't have clocked the message it was sending out about the rift that had grown between the two girls lately, how self-sufficient Nell had become and how left behind Bay felt.

Only last week, Bay had come to me in tears, telling me how much she missed feeling close to Nell. Making a film about it had apparently been a desperate attempt to communicate the message to her. I sympathised, but Nell's sixteenth birthday party wasn't the appropriate forum to say how she really felt. To give her the benefit of the doubt, I tried to imagine that the messages in the edit were unconscious, and that no offence was intended. If I hadn't noticed Nell's discomfort, I might have been able to dismiss this cynical reading of it. I wanted to.

At the end of the film, everyone clapped and hoorahed. I saw my mum wipe a tear from her eye. 'Nell reminds me of me when I was that age.'

Dom stood up, clapping the loudest. 'That was absolutely fantastic! Oscar-worthy. Well done, Bay! I think this calls for more bubbly!' he said.

When the lights came on, nobody but me noticed that Nell had slipped away.

I nipped upstairs and knocked on her bedroom door. 'Can I come in?' Cautiously I peered around the door, staring in horror as she threw her nightie and make-up bag into a holdall.

'I'm going out,' she said.

'What do you mean? Where?' I stammered.

'Just out.'

'But it's your birthday!'

'Exactly. It's my birthday and I can do what the hell I like,' she hissed, pushing past me and jogging downstairs.

'Nell!' I said, flying down after her, 'What about the others? You can't just leave.'

'Whatever.'

I intercepted her and put my hand flat on the front door, whispering urgently. 'No. Not today, Nell. Please.'

'Fine. I'll go round the back.'

'Nell! Let's talk about this.' I darted in front of her.

She cocked her hip and hoisted her bag onto her shoulder, staring at me defiantly.

'Okay, Mum, let's talk. That film was fucked up. And FYI, I never wanted that guitar, I wanted a new mountain bike, but I didn't want to say because I thought you couldn't afford it! And Bay bloody well knew it, too!'

She was so beautiful and so full of fire, I was suddenly scared of her. Scared of my own daughter.

'I didn't know, honestly,' I said, losing my voice halfway through the sentence.

'*Exactly,*' she spat, shunting past me towards the kitchen. I was relieved she was going to say goodbye to everyone at least. But she switched back on her herself and stormed past me out of the front door. Helplessly I ran out to the pavement and watched her go.

Tears filled my eyes. Today had started so well.

The cold air penetrated my bones, and I imagined her waiting at the bus stop. I contemplated swinging by in the car and taking her to the station. Then I decided that it would only endorse her enraging decision to leave.

Inside, the house was warm, too warm. I found Martin in the conservatory, pouring Prosecco. Through the glass door that separated us from the kitchen, I watched the others milling around.

'Nell's just left,' I said, swallowing.

'Left? What do you mean, left?' he said, crinkling his bushy blond brow. I imagined grabbing his big arms imploringly, asking him to run after her, to *do* something about it, to save the situation, but I knew it was no use.

'She's gone to London probably. I'm not really sure.' Hot, thick embarrassment rolled through me like nausea, as though Nell's behaviour was my fault.

'Gone for good?'

I laughed. 'No. Not for good, you clot. To a party. In London. It's all she cares about these days.'

'Oh, phew. Partying is okay.'

'Is it? *I* don't think it's okay at all.'

'Tessa does this,' he explained. 'She just decides to go out. "I'm going out!" It's become a catchphrase in the family.'

'She didn't do it on her sixteenth birthday, though. She was a delight that day.'

'Yeah, lovely in front of you lot, but a total horror behind the scenes. She and Karen have terrible rows.'

'It's so hard to believe,' I said, watching Tessa, who was listening politely to something Mum was telling her. I found it impossible to imagine that my gorgeous niece, who had loved magic tricks and Cluedo only a few years ago, ever behaved like Nell.

'I'm not kidding you, overnight she turned from my sweet little Tessa into a bloody monster, just like Kevin in that Harry Enfield sketch.'

I laughed. 'Nell is a reincarnation of Kevin.'

After New York, like Kevin, like Tessa, Nell had changed. She had complained about jet lag for days, then weeks, and then months. So-called jet lag had become a permanent state of grumpiness. Whether the change in her was down to the rejection from Focus or whether her eyes had been opened by the energy of New York, I didn't know.

Under his breath, glancing at Tessa, Martin said, 'These days, I'm not sure I even like her very much.' There was a conspiratorial twinkle in his blue eyes. He and Tessa were as close as any father and daughter could be.

'I know what you mean,' I agreed guiltily.

The last six months had rivalled those early baby months. The same desperation had returned. The same anxiety levels. The same feelings of being completely out of control. The same sense that my patience was being tested and tested and tested, over and over, that I was being pushed and pushed, and pushed some more, that my frustration was accumulating into a mountain of pent-up rage.

'The only way we get through it,' Martin said, 'is to not sweat the small stuff. Karen even lets it go when Tessa tells her to fuck off. And I never thought I'd see that day. Imagine if we'd ever said fuck off to Mum. Jesus, she would have fallen into a coma.'

I looked over at Mum, more fragile than ever. Holding her head up looked like an effort. For all of her faults, she had never had the energy to hover over us and control us.

'Pick your battles, you mean,' I said vaguely, repeating what Dom had said to me. How impossible I found it, when each battle felt like a war that needed to be won in order to keep her safe. How tempted I was to blame Dom for everything. If we had not allowed her to join Take One, she might never have started partying.

Martin sighed heavily. 'It's their hormones. It's all normal.'

'I guess I expected another Bay. She wasn't anything like this.'

'Bay's less outgoing. And maybe she got her difficult phase over and done with when she was younger.'

It negated the theory about hormones, but I liked it. 'Yes, maybe.'

'They leave home in the end, remember,' he said.

'On days like these, I can't bloody wait,' I said, finding an empty flute and shoving it in his direction.

He poured me some fizz, dropped his arm around me heavily and laughed. 'I don't believe that for a second.'

Side by side we sipped our Prosecco and watched our family chattering away in the kitchen, oblivious to the birthday girl's abscondment.

I groaned. 'Everyone is going to be so offended.'

'My lot'll love the drama. Come on. I'll go and tell Dom, and you tell Mum that Nell's got a migraine. Then I'll gather my troops and get them back to the B&B, and Dom can get Mum home.'

I remembered Bay and the film and had a further slump when I thought about having to talk to her about it. It was my turn to sigh. 'Thanks, Martin.'

'Nell will be fine. Don't worry about her,' he added, before going through to the kitchen.

I decided to believe him. Partying at sixteen wasn't abnormal, even though I'd have preferred it to be local partying. But would it make any difference whether she was in Guildford or on the Grayswood green? Drugs, alcohol and sex were readily available anywhere if she wanted them. I had to let it go and accept it, or I would go mad.

CHAPTER THIRTY

Nell

I'm out-out, again. Since my birthday and Bay's stupid-arse film, I take every opportunity to be out-out and out some more. Being at home means being around Bay, and I can hardly look at her without wanting to tell her how I really feel about everything. And obvs I can't do that. It is obvs-obvs she regrets it, though. Last week she tried to say sorry and I told her I didn't want to talk about it. Not talking about it is turning out to be quite a challenge.

'Ian's here,' Tally says. She holds out her lighter for me and Leah.

'Is he?' Leah says, jumpily.

We are squashed and shivering in the courtyard smoking area under heaters that don't work. Through the floor-to-ceiling windows, there is a packed bar. Mini cans of a new whisky and Coke brand are everywhere, stacked on the shelves and being circulated on silver trays, free to drink. My eye is on Lee, who is over by the bar talking to two other guys. He is the main reason I'm here tonight (apart from getting away from Bay). I want him to take my virginity. I'm sixteen and legal and ready. And tonight is the night. Not that Lee knows it yet.

'And here are my favourite girrrls,' Ian says in a pretend American accent. His tiny blue eyes flash at us from behind his big eyewear. I get nervous and excited when Ian is out. He is like a VIP boss and a friend. Or maybe he is more like a dad: someone you have to behave well around and someone you kind of love. Not *love*, exactly. Need something from. Oh, I don't know. Ian is confusing. Whatever he means to me, his presence at this party means it is the place to be tonight.

'Hi, babe,' Tally says, and she gives him an elegant kiss on each cheek, and then one more, like the French. I guess they don't kiss like that in her home town of Preston.

'Hi, Ian,' Leah says, giving him a hug. He blows smoke over her shoulder.

He turns to me. 'Nell. Princessa. Have you lost weight? I think you've lost weight. You look S-T-U-N-N-I-N-G.' I keep my mouth closed when I smile but I feel my cheeks go red.

'I've been going to the gym,' I say, which is true. After school, I've been getting off the bus one stop before Grayswood and using the cheap gym in town where all the muscly local dudes work out. It is stinky but I quite like it. Nobody bothers me. I tell Mum I'm staying behind to practise a tune on my new guitar with a friend who sings. I hate playing guitar. I've thought about selling it and buying a second-hand mountain bike on eBay – the one I told Bay I wanted for my birthday – but it would kill Mum. She loves me playing the guitar, even though I am shite at it.

These days, I keep a lot of things from Mum. Get this, Tally told me that overseas models aren't even allowed to work in America if they're under eighteen. Everyone knows that they do anyway and get away with it, especially for the shows. It means Ian lied to Focus about my age (and size maybe!). I'd never dare tell Mum that, right?

'Smoking is very bad for your skin,' Ian says, clicking his tongue and flicking his ash into the tall ashtray. 'Come on, you three, I want you to meet Francis Ray. He's got a massive Celeste fragrance campaign coming up.'

Francis Ray is a big-name photographer in the business and Celeste Paris is my favourite scent ever. I swipe another little can of whisky and Coke from a tray and we follow Ian through the crowds to a corner table. Francis is small, with dark grey hair that is ruffled back and a large nose with a bump on it and narrow, mean eyes. Still, I'm star-struck. He is so famous even Mum would have heard of him.

'This is Tally. And Leah. And this is Nell, my New Faces girl,' Ian says.

'I know Tally,' Francis says, sliding his hand down her long bare back, which looks like a shot of black silk, beautifully exposed by her jumpsuit. Next to her, I look plain in my T-shirt and black denim skirt. 'John Lewis advertising, wasn't it? How's it going?'

His accent is so posh, I'm sure he's putting it on.

'The shots were awesome,' Tally says, cool as ice.

'That's terribly kind of you to say, Tally. And good to meet you, Leah.' She is wearing a short, sequinned dress that would have looked disco-hideous on anyone else. Her warm honey-brown hair frames her cheekbones and her smile is white, like in a commercial. But Francis barely even glances at her because he is staring straight at me, as though I am the only girl in the room suddenly.

'Wow. This is the Nell you were telling me about. Hi, Nell,' he says.

He is a hundred years older than Dad and he is acting like he fancies me. Super-gross. I'm polite, and smile and say hi like Mum would expect me to, but I'm squirming inside.

Then something wonderful, and perfectly timed, happens. Smooth, muscular arms are around my waist, pulling me away.

'Come dance with me,' Lee says into my ear.

My tummy flips about all over the place.

Lee and I have been flirting with each other for a while now. Every time I go over to see Tally and Leah at the Shoreditch flat, he is there, hanging out. One night we chatted for hours. He told me he loved horse riding back in South Africa, and I told him about mountain biking, and we related to each other about growing up in the countryside. I thought he was sexy when he talked angrily about the politics in his country, and even sexier when he mentioned that he raised loads of money for charities by taking part in swimathons.

Holding onto his fingertips, I follow him down the stairs of the nightclub. The music gets louder as we descend, until we are in the basement, where it is dark and heaving with sweaty people. I grab another whisky and Coke from the bar and dance with Lee.

He shouts something at me.

'What did you say?' I ask.

'Francis Ray is a creep.'

'You jealous?' I say. (It's the whisky talking.)

'Nah,' he says, a bit too seriously.

'Why is he a creep?'

He replies but I can't hear what he says. Anyway, I don't really care about Francis Ray. I am dancing with Lee, who is still, without doubt, super-hot. His slanting blue eyes and blond buzz cut and broad shoulders do something funny to me.

The whisky and Cokes are getting a bit sickly, but I need to be even drunker if I'm going to lose my virginity tonight.

I already decided, weeks ago, that I wanted to sleep with him. Being a virgin sucks, especially when Leah and Tally talk about sex all the time. I haven't outright told them that I'm a virgin, but I imagine they have guessed. Not that Tally is having sex with anyone these days, not since splitting up with her boyfriend. But Leah has a new boyfriend every few weeks and falls madly in love each and every time, and has lots of sex with them. It's all about sex for Leah, and I secretly wish I could be more like her.

When the club closes, I stuff two cans of whisky and Coke into my handbag and we pile back to the Shoreditch flat, where we drink and smoke some more.

Lee and I are sitting next to each other on the sofa, and his thigh is muscular next to mine.

He says, 'Come with me.'

He leads me into the bathroom, locks the door and just starts kissing me, like he literally could not wait for one second longer. It happens really fast. Suddenly he puts a condom on and pulls my knickers to the side and actually pushes it right in! Oh my God, I am actually losing my virginity. Bloody hell, it hurts. Mother of GOD. But I like it too. I like how forceful and desperate he is to do it. It is cool to be wanted that much. Towards the end, I begin to quite enjoy it. At one point, someone knocks on the door. Lee tells them to piss off. We laugh, and he carries on.

'That was nice,' he says afterwards, pushing my hair back, kissing me really gently, saying, 'You go out first.'

'You go. I need the loo,' I say. Feeling a bit woozy and sore, I lock the door and lean against it, grinning madly, full of butterflies, taking stock of what just happened. Then I rummage around in the cupboards for some sanitary towels. All my friends say they bled after the first time. It's why I'm wearing black.

Before I flush the loo, I see the condom in the water. The tip is plastered to the side of the bowl and I think it looks misshapen, as though it has torn. I consider fishing it out to check, but there is old wee in there and so I leave it, deciding to double-check with Lee.

He swears it didn't break, and for the rest of the evening we pretend that nothing happened between us, which makes it all the more exciting. Even when I am talking to someone else, we flirt with each other across the room.

When we kiss goodbye, he says he will call me.

'You'd better get some revision done today, Nell,' Mum says to me the next morning.

'I will,' I say, knowing I won't.

'Your mocks are only two weeks away!'

I shove a hung-over leg into my track pants. 'Obviously I know that.' Then the other leg.

'Seriously, Nell, I'll be talking to your teachers tomorrow if you don't get your head down today.'

The nagging is getting to me. I scream at her, '*Shut up*! I *am* going to revise, okay? Seriously, get off my back!'

She goes silent. Finally. And leaves.

The words on my revision cards are blurry. Nothing is going to go into my head today. There is too much of last night still dancing about there. Whisky is cruel.

There is a knock on my door. I hide my phone under my files quickly, thinking it's Mum again.

'Do you want some help?' Bay says.

'Nah, it's okay,' I say, taking out my phone again.

'Was last night fun?' she asks.

The image of Lee and me in the bathroom comes back to me in vivid aquamarine – the colour of the shower curtain.

'Yeah, wicked.'

Bay sits down on my bed and begins neatening the books on my bedside table.

'Where did you go?'

'A party in South Ken,' I say.

In my heart of hearts, I want to tell her everything about last night, but I'm still annoyed with her. Losing my virginity was huge. Maybe I am a new person today. I do feel *womanly*.

Bay has talked to me before about her first time and what to expect. She lost hers when she was fourteen to her first and only boyfriend, Sean, who was Ty's other best friend. They did it at Sean's house when his parents were out at the pub. She and Sean split up last year because she accused him of cheating on her. Ty stopped talking to Sean after that, even though Sean vowed he hadn't kissed the other girl.

'Did you see Lee again?' Bay asks.

'Yeah, he was there.'

I want to ask her about split condoms and the morning-after pill. Instead I carry on texting Leah, who wants the gossip about Lee.

Think condom split but Lee said it didn't. Whadda u think?

Play it safe babe. Get Ellaone. Love u gtg xxxx

Bay says, in a sad voice, 'Okay, just shout if you need any help with your work.'

Tomorrow I'll ask Jade to come with me to the chemist after school. I'll skip my workout at the gym, just this once.

'Yeah, thanks,' I say.

I feel bad about shutting Bay out, and I almost give in and tell her everything, but there is also something thrilling about holding it back. It is the first big thing I haven't told her.

I'm becoming an expert at keeping secrets.

CHAPTER THIRTY-ONE

Anna

I was driving Nell to Guildford to buy her some tights and pants. She needed them tonight. Not this weekend, not tomorrow, but today. The rising hysteria that had filled her voice on the phone – at lunchtime from school! – had been effective emotional blackmail, and I had agreed to make the trip for an easier life. Small stuff mattered to teenagers, I told myself. I had called Mum to explain I would check in on her later than planned.

The car journey should have been a good time to catch up with Nell. So far she had been coughing a lot and talking very little, offering one-word answers, glued to her phone. Ping, ping, ping-bloody-ping it went.

'That cough is really chesty,' I said.

No response.

'It might be worth getting some cough medicine in Guildford while we're there.'

No response.

Ten minutes into the journey, she came to life and exclaimed, 'Oh my God! Oh. My. God.'

'What?' I asked, panicking. I couldn't tell whether it was a good 'Oh my God' or a bad one.

'Ian's just emailed. I've been put on hold for the Celeste perfume campaign!'

I glanced over and caught her grinning at me. It was nice to know she could still smile at me, I thought petulantly.

'What are the dates?' I was thinking about her upcoming mocks.

'Dunno. He didn't say.'

'Did you go to a casting for it?' I asked, thinking back to the emails I'd read from Ian, who still copied me in even though I was no longer needed as a chaperone.

'No,' she said, returning to her texting.

'They're optioning you for a commercial based on your portfolio?' I asked, sceptically.

Still texting, she said, 'I met the photographer already. Francis Ray?'

'So you *did* go to a casting?'

'No,' she groaned. 'Look. Don't worry about it.'

'Go on, explain, please.'

'I met him at that party.'

'On Saturday night?'

'*Yes!*' she yelled.

I breathed in and put on my calm voice. 'There's no need to be so rude, Nell.'

'I met him at the party, okay?' she repeated, more politely.

'Fine, but surely you need to go to a proper casting for a job like that.'

'I'm going to a request casting this week. He wants me on film.'

And there was the information I wanted. Why it had to be such a battle to get it out of her, I didn't know. 'Right. Okay. That sounds exciting then.'

'Yes! Thanks for finally, *actually* being happy for me,' she said sarcastically, pulling her hood up, still texting, slumped into the car door.

I had more questions about the Celeste job, but I chose to leave it, knowing there was little point in forcing answers out of her when she was being uncommunicative. I drove the rest of the way in silence, deciding I would email Ian about it.

As I pulled into a space in the multistorey car park, she said, 'Don't worry about coming with me. I won't be long.'

'Really?' I asked. Another thwarted plan. Our Guildford routine should have included a gingerbread latte and a gossip.

'Yeah, it'll only take a minute.'

A minute was optimistic. Sifting through the Wall of a Thousand Tights to find the magic combination of denier, size and colour, on the overheated second floor of M&S, was a tiresome task that she would usually happily delegate to me. I was suspicious, and I wondered whether she had a secret agenda and a more dubious shopping list than tights. Was she buying something she hadn't wanted me to know about? I went through the various seedy options. Condoms? I shuddered at the thought. At sixteen, she was old enough legally to have sex, and I had talked to her about birth control, as per the PSHE teacher's advice, but there was a chemist near her school and one in town.

'I'll come. I don't mind,' I said.

'What? You don't even trust me to get my own underwear now?' she snapped, and clambered out of the car with her wallet in her hand, slamming the door behind her.

I watched her lope off on her long, gangly legs. There was a hole in her tights on the back of her thigh, and her school skirt was rolled ten inches too high. She disappeared down the stairwell.

'No, actually, I don't trust you much at all these days,' I mumbled to myself, gloomily.

If she was having sex with the South African model, Lee, who was nineteen, she would need condoms. Another shiver. It was impossible to contemplate. Perhaps I was jumping to conclusions. She might simply want to choose some lacy knickers without her mother hovering about.

After I had emailed Ian to ask him about the dates holding on Nell's chart for the Celeste campaign, I scanned my podcasts for something to listen to while I waited. I chose an interview between a child psychoanalyst and a psychologist-turned-author who had written a book called *Taking Back Control*. As I listened to the experts talk about the differences between more permissive, child-led parenting versus the more intransigent, boundaried style, I clung to the idea of the latter. Safeguarding Nell's future by having rules at home was important. At the same time, I had to admit there was a dwindling sense of family harmony. The fighting about revision for her mocks, or lack thereof, and her new love of partying was causing a terrible atmosphere at home, for everyone.

Towards the end of the podcast, Ian's return email pinged up on my phone.

Hi, Anna. No probs. Dates holding on 1/2/3 Feb tbc. Might change to following week. Speak soon, Ian.

That was that, then. The dates clashed with the first three days of her mock GCSEs. Under no circumstances would I allow her to miss the exams.

It took Nell forty-five minutes to return, during which time I finished listening to the podcast, ordered *Taking Back Control* on Amazon, called Mum to say I would be late, and texted a client about the preferred colour of trim for the inside of her straw trilby. It had been a productive forty-five minutes, but this did not prevent me from communicating my irritation about the delay.

'That was a long minute,' I said pointedly, fully expecting a counter-attack.

She chucked her very small, very light M&S bag into the back seat and strapped herself in. 'Sorry,' she said.

'Granny Berry will be waiting.' I harrumphed and started the car.

'Sorry, Mum. And sorry for being so pissy before,' she added.

The 'I-hate-you-Mum' edge to her voice was gone and her expression was free of its scowl. Love swirled back into my heart. 'That's okay, darling. You're allowed to be pissy sometimes.' I smiled.

In stark contrast to the journey out, the return ride was fun. She chatted non-stop about Jade and Mint, who were apparently still cross about her going to the New Year's Eve party in London, and told me more about Lee, and how kind and lovely Leah and Tally were, and how exciting it would be to get the Celeste job. I listened avidly, keeping to myself my knowledge about the clash of dates, relieved that she hadn't checked with Ian yet. I didn't want her to be distracted by it.

When we reached the High Street, I checked my watch and said, 'Would you mind coming with me to Granny Berry's? She'd love to see you. She's been a bit low lately.'

I waited for the sigh and the excuse about being too tired or not in the mood. She coughed, and I thought, here it comes. But she said, 'Yeah, cool. Why is she feeling down?'

'It's her birthday soon,' I said.

'Only Granny Berry would be sad about a birthday!'

'I think it's because her mum died at seventy – it's a bit of a milestone.'

'We can organise a party!'

'She hates parties.'

'Not a big party, but a really lovely family party, with just us lot, to cheer her up.'

'That is a wonderful idea, Nell.'

'Maybe we can make it special and have it in the evening, with candles and stuff, and we can all dress up and make French food. I mean, it is her *seventieth*.'

'Let's suggest it to her now,' I said, pleased.

It seemed that Nell's excursion to buy new tights – or condoms – had been a miracle cure for teenage stropdom. Perhaps I didn't

care what she got up to when she was away from home, as long
as she was nice to me.

Even so, I would be calling Ian tomorrow to make it clear to
him that, sadly, we would have to turn the Celeste job down if it
clashed with Nell's mocks. Nell would be more than a bit pissy
about it, but that couldn't be helped. In spite of the psychoanalyst's
compelling case on the podcast, I would have to put her feelings
and rights aside, favouring instead the bigger picture of her long-
term well-being. Until she turned eighteen, I was determined to
maintain that she was still a child who would continue to need
guidance from me, Dom *and* Ian, in a united front. The podcast
had helped me to recognise that I feared the downwards-sliding
scale towards all-out permissiveness. Permissiveness, I decided, was
a fancy name for giving up; and I was a long way off from giving up
on Nell, however hard she pushed back. She would thank us in the
end when she passed her GCSEs. Big perfume campaigns would be
there for her when she was ready, and when there was less to lose.

As soon as the Take One offices opened for business, I called Ian
and waited as the receptionist put me on hold, fully expecting
her to tell me he would call me back. Much to my surprise, he
took my call straight away. After some light chit-chat, I told him
about the decision that Dom and I had made together last night
to turn down the Celeste perfume campaign on Nell's behalf if it
clashed with her mocks. I stated clearly that it was a decision we
were both immovable on and that we were very sorry about. And
then he had told me how much Celeste would pay.

'Sorry, Ian, could you say that again, I think I misheard you,' I said.

I put my cup of coffee down too hard, and Dom looked up at
me. He mouthed, '*What?*'

'Forty thousand pounds with a buy-out option next year,' Ian
said slowly. I pictured his smile, with the prominent incisors and

flat front teeth. He would be wearing his headset and his tight belt, with his close-cropped hair and those tiny crystal-blue eyes bright through the lenses, ready for business, gleefully delivering his punchy offer.

'Forty thousand pounds? For one day's work?' I said.

Dom's eyes popped open and he brushed his hair tightly back from his head. We locked eyes while I listened to Ian continue.

'And if it's rebought next year, they'll pay another forty, and so on, each year, until they drop the campaign. But she could be looking at three years minimum.'

My hands were clammy. 'My God. I had no idea it would be that much. I thought we were turning down a couple of thousand, which was hard enough.'

'Anna,' Ian said softly, 'this is big. Nell's so young and this is a huge campaign. The timing sucks, I get that, and I would absolutely respect whatever you decide. You have to get this shit right as a parent, yeah? If you decide no, we'll go with that. One hundred per cent.'

I remembered his small hands and I imagined them fiddling with his packet of cigarettes on his desk, or clicking into emails.

'But that's life-changing money, Ian,' I said.

'It is, hon, yes. And I have to say, for Nell, if she gets this, it'll kick-start her career. I see big things for her. She's awesome. I love her look, and there's a buzz about her in the business right now, but if I'm honest with you, you kinda have to roll with that, 'cos it ain't coming around again.' He snorted.

I knew all about things not coming around again. The memory of a busy airport and Billy's disappearing figure came charging back into my mind.

'She hasn't got the job yet,' I said.

'True, hon.'

'How likely is it, do you think?' I said, hating the keenness in my voice, the U-turn, my principles floating away.

'They've only got one other girl on hold from this agency, but it's likely they've optioned others. Worldwide. The request casting with Francis Ray this Friday is key. Which is a problem, I know, because it's in school hours.'

'Is it?'

''Fraid so, hon. I'll send through the deets now.'

'Okay, thanks, Ian. I'm grateful to you for being so understanding. I must sound overprotective and neurotic.'

'No! Anna, I get it, I totally do. You know I have a nephew the same age, and if it was him, I'd be freaking out just like you guys. Let's not make any decisions about anything until we know.'

'Yes. After all this, she might not even get it.'

'Right,' he said. 'Okay. Great to talk. I'll keep you posted. Bye, Anna.'

He was gone, and Dom and I stared at each other.

'Forty thousand pounds!' I said.

Dom guffawed. 'Christ. That's almost as much as I earn in a year. For one day's work.'

'I mean, she'd only miss one or two exams. Maybe she could take them early or something.'

'I'm sure the school could work something out.'

'I never thought I would ever consider it.'

Dom nodded. 'What did Groucho Marx say? "Those are my principles, and if you don't like them… well, I have others".'

I grimaced guiltily. 'Now I understand why A-listers do those cheesy adverts for stuff like potatoes or naff cars.'

'Because they've been offered too much money to turn them down.' Dom stated it seriously, and it felt serious. Forty thousand pounds was serious. It was definitely too much money to turn down. But we had to keep our heads. She had not got the job yet. It all came down to whether Francis Ray liked her on film this week.

CHAPTER THIRTY-TWO

Bay

The toast popped up and I jumped. That's how strung out I was. Nell and Anna were arguing. It was making me feel anxious, making me feel as though I wanted to run at them both, hold them down and put my hand over their mouths. Where was Dad? Nobody seemed to be in charge. It wasn't my place to take control of the situation, but someone had to.

'But it's a *premiere*, Mum!' Nell screamed, setting off a coughing fit.

Iris left the kitchen and I understood why.

'Oh, sorry, yes, that A-list event the premiere of *Fortress Wars* five hundred,' Anna quipped.

'Rude! Six, actually,' Nell said, between more coughing.

Fortress Wars I had been the worst film ever made, and I imagined that *Fortress Wars VI* would be dreadful.

Anna slammed shut the kitchen window, which had been opened to let out the smoke from the burned toast. She countered, 'Granny Berry's party was your idea in the first place, Nell!'

Nell's party plans had included fairy lights and French-themed red-chequered napkins, and plastic onions to dangle from the ceiling, all of which had been ordered from Amazon with great excitement.

'I know, it's the worst clash ever, but Mum, Francis Ray – *the* Francis Ray – gave Ian a ticket for me. And if I turn it down, he might not give me that Celeste job, and it's just down to me and one other girl now!'

'He can't turn you down for a job because you don't go to a party!'

'How do you know?'

'Because it's unethical.'

From a neutral perspective, I understood both sides. I understood why Nell would not want to turn down Francis Ray, and why she would be dying to dress up and go to a red-carpet event. Also, I understood why Anna was trying to teach her proper values. Better offers were only better offers if you didn't lose your loved ones by accepting them. And Anna's mother was a touchy character, who would take to heart Nell's decision to ditch her seventieth in favour of a film premiere, even if she said otherwise.

I guessed that Anna would be expecting some moral support, but I was thinking I could use this fight of theirs for my own agenda, to gain favour with Nell again. The screening of *Without Me* on her sixteenth birthday had been a mistake, though I was not sorry about making it. Sorry, not sorry – it took skill to tell a story without talking heads or narration.

'Can I say something?' I interjected. The bristly back of my head felt good under my fingertips, comforting.

'Sure. Go ahead, sweetheart,' Anna said.

'I've been worrying about the evening party idea, if I'm honest,' I said. 'I didn't want to say anything because I knew Nell was so excited about it.'

'Why were you worried about it, poppet?' Anna asked.

'Granny Berry gets tired so easily these days. She's nodding off by six most evenings, and she always hates missing *Take Me Out.*'

Nell was silent. She would be biting back her counter-argument for the evening party, knowing it did not suit her now.

Anna said, 'But she seemed quite pleased on Monday when we suggested it, didn't she, Nell?' She looked to Nell, who shrugged and coughed some more.

I continued making a case on Nell's behalf. 'But you know what your mum's like, Anna, she always says what she thinks you want to hear and then acts all sad when it's too late.'

Anna sighed and pushed her hand up her forehead, as though wiping sweat away. 'Hmm.'

Fearful that I had said too much, I winced. 'Sorry, but it is true, isn't it?'

'I suppose it is,' she agreed.

'So maybe we could change it to a lunch party the following day, on the Sunday? And then not mention the premiere to Granny Berry, just say we had a rethink and thought the daytime would suit her better. Then she can't be offended.'

'It's not such a bad idea,' Anna said.

'It's a great idea!' Nell said.

'I wonder if she might be quite relieved,' Anna added, pressing one lip under the other.

I could rest my case, and I glanced over at Nell, who was smiling broadly at me.

Later that evening, I knocked on Nell's door. She called, 'Yes?'

When I went in, she put her pen down and grinned at me.

'You're welcome,' I said, making a neat bow.

She swivelled in her chair. 'Come and talk to me.'

I took a step forward, thrilled that I was being invited over the threshold after weeks in the cold.

'I was thinking, why don't you come to the after-party with me?' Nell said.

'What about Leah and Tally?'

'Leah's away working and Tally's going back home.'

Accepting how low down the list I came, I said, 'Only if you want me to come.'

'I've got a plus-one and Lee isn't texting me back.'

'Bastard.'

'Prick.'

'Man-whore.'

'Dickwad.'

Iris called out from her bedroom, 'I can hear you, you know, guys!'

'POO-HEAD!' Nell yelled. She fell back on her bed and hugged her teddy and said, quietly, 'Lee isn't texting me back because I gave him what he was after and now he doesn't want me any more.'

'What? A goldfish?' I asked.

Nell laughed. 'No!'

'A hand-job?'

'NO!' Nell sat up and whispered, 'Shut the door.'

I shut the door and leant my back against it. 'What?'

'I had *sex* with him!'

My heart stopped. 'You lost your virginity?'

'Yup.'

I felt wild. How could she have kept it from me? I held back the hurt, knowing it could derail us again. 'Wow! That's big. What happened?'

She scooted over on the bed and I sat down next to her and listened to the story. I tried not to react to how sordid it had been. My little sister had lost her virginity in a loo with a boy who didn't mention that the condom had split. Every girl's dream!

'It definitely split?' I asked.

'I'm not sure. I took the morning-after pill just in case.'

'Seriously?' I could not believe I had been kept out of this.

'I wanted to go to the chemist near school, but Jade said that the teachers went there. That's why I forced Mum to take me to Guildford.'

'You told Anna?'

'No! My God. No way. I said I needed tights and made her stay in the car. The trouble is, the tights I got were navy. I'll have to buy another pair online, but I don't want Mum to get the package.'

'I don't think she's worrying about tights right now, you're giving her too much else to worry about.'

'I don't want her to worry about me at all!'

'I know. It's not your fault. She can be a bit overprotective, let's face it.'

'It's been so *awful* not being able to talk to you about all this.'

'Why didn't you?'

Nell chucked her teddy at my head. 'You know why.'

'Just because of my film?'

'It seriously pissed me off.'

My smile was wry. 'I thought it was quite good.'

'Bay! You drive me frigging crazy.' She flung her arms around me. 'But I love you so much. Let's never fight again. I hate it.'

'Never,' I said, realising how close I had come to losing my sister's trust, and how much more precarious family life might have become if I had.

Over the last few weeks I had felt insecure around Anna, and guilty; not just about Nell's birthday film, but about the past, which seemed to be bobbing up to the surface in my mind. While Nell was cross with me, our secret did not feel safe.

'Let's plan what to wear so we can Insta the hell out of Saturday night,' I said.

Nell nodded, childlike. 'Yeah. So Lee the poo-head knows he's made a big mistake. A huge mistake.'

'Ty's mum has some amazing vintage dresses,' I said, in control once more.

CHAPTER THIRTY-THREE

Nell

Getting out of the black cab and walking down a real red carpet
– nylon, by the way – is giving me the shakes. Behind a cordon,
a group of photographers with large lenses are snapping away at
one of the *Fortress Wars* actresses. When Bay and I come along,
they put their cameras down. Rude! Don't they know how long
it took us to get ready?

We mill about in the foyer, celebrity-spotting, before being
allowed into the auditorium. We sit and listen to the director talk
about what a long journey it has been and how grateful he is to all
those people who believed in him. My throat tickles with a cough,
even though I've taken the medicine Mum bought me. She left
it on my desk with a printout about lung cancer and smoking.

I wish this dude would hurry up with his speech. You'd think
he'd won an Oscar.

There are four empty seats next to us. When Francis Ray and
Ian scoot past the rest of the row to take up two of those seats, I
pinch myself, literally pinch myself. We are actually sitting next to
Francis Ray. Ian waves and shimmies his hands at us, mouthing,
'You look freaking shit-hot, girls.' Or I hope that's what he says.
He could have said, 'You look friggin' shit, hop it, girls.' But I
take the first option.

Finally the director stops droning on. We clap and I cough madly, getting it out before the film starts.

Francis leans forward, 'Great you guys could come. Is this your sister?'

'This is Bay.'

Bay holds out her hand and Francis takes it. I am proud of her. She looks very cool in Ty's mum's tuxedo with red heels and red lips. I'm wearing Ty's mum's white silk pantaloon all-in-one, which sounds weird, but it is super-classy. It is vintage Furstenberg (*c*.1990) and has a tiny stain under the armpit. Ty's mum said I could keep it because it's too long on her. The bones of the bodice dig into my stomach, but Bay said I looked like a Bond girl.

After her introduction, Bay whispers, 'Francis is kind of sexy.'

'Are you kidding me?'

'You know, in that posh way.'

'Gross,' I say. Francis Ray has grey nose hair. No more needs to be said on the subject.

The curtains open and the screen shows the BBFC 'Suitable only for persons of 18 years and over' warning. Ian leans forward and winks at me.

The big dramatic music starts up and Francis says into my ear, 'You looked incredible on camera yesterday.' He smells of mints and garlic and girls' perfume.

'Cool. I was a bit nervous,' I say.

'It worked. I love that vulnerability.'

I want to ask him whether I've got the job, but that would be rude and a bit desperate, so I say nothing.

'Is it okay to say that?' he adds.

'Sure! Course.'

I snort, in a weird way. Bay nudges me, as if to say 'shut up'. It was a nervous snort because I'm not sure what he meant. I guess I am okay about him saying I looked great on film, aren't I? But am I okay about the vulnerability bit? I was until he asked me.

Maybe I shouldn't be okay with it. Maybe showing vulnerability is bad. My drama teacher always says it's good, so I guess I'll stick with that. And if it gets me a job that pays forty thousand quid, I'm all for it. One hundred per cent.

As the credits roll, I don't know what to say. The film was the worst film I have ever seen in my life, and that is saying something. It made those teen Netflix originals about princesses in made-up countries who fall for normal folk look like art-house films.

I mumble something like, 'That was so good' in a vague way, and Francis laughs.

We troop outside to get a cab to the after-party together. Francis puts his hand in the small of my back as I get in.

'How does crap like that get made?' Ian says when the cab door is closed.

'It's what my mother would have called a turkey,' Francis says.

I am relieved I don't have to keep pretending I liked it. But Bay and I are still polite when we criticise it. I don't want to be ungrateful to them for giving us tickets.

'Will the director be at the after-party?' Bay asks.

'Jim. Yes. Christ knows what I'll say to him.'

'Lie,' Ian says.

'Or you could say the production values were amazing, which they were,' Bay says.

'Yeah, I'll have to wank on about the sets and the impressive dolly shots,' Francis says, chuckling. His eyes get even narrower when he laughs.

There are flames shooting up either side of the entrance to the party. I feel the heat as I walk past them. Cocktail waitresses hold trays of light pink shots with a red berry floating on top.

'Sambuca nipples,' Francis says, shotting one and rolling the cranberry across his tongue, balancing it between his front teeth, which he bares in a smile that is more Joker than gentleman.

'Fortress Wars' is written diagonally across a white backdrop, from which a photographer steps forward and ushers Francis onto the cross on the floor.

'Nell! Come in with me,' Francis says, beckoning me over.

Bay pushes me towards him. On the cross, Francis pulls me close, too close. The photographer's flash leaves purple imprints on my eyelids. Bay takes her own photos of us from behind the photographer and sticks her tongue out at me.

'You two are mischief together, I can tell,' Francis says.

Someone comes up to him, and Bay and I escape into the party. I knock back a second shot, mindful that it's Granny Berry's birthday lunch tomorrow.

'Lee's right, Francis Ray is a creep,' I say to Bay.

'Takes one to know one,' she says.

The sambuca goes straight to my head. The tunes are banging, and I dance. Bay doesn't like dancing much. She hangs about on the edge. Francis and Ian stand near the DJ box. They are talking to a young actor from the film. I try to catch his eye and dance a bit closer to him – joining some models I know from Take One – but I keep catching Francis's eye instead.

Bay looks moody and I drag her onto the dance floor and introduce her to the other models, but she looks uncomfortable and ends up going back to the side. Then a woman kisses the actor on the lips, and I think, he was a bit short anyway, and scan the room for another guy.

Francis comes up to me.

'Want a line?'

'No thanks.' I don't take drugs.

'Come with me anyway,' he says, taking my hand.

'But I love this song!' I say, even though I don't much.

'Come on, I want to show you something.'

As I walk off the dance floor, I realise that I am drunker than I thought.

I follow Francis out of the room and across the marble-floored hallway and up the wide sweep of carpeted stairs, but I wobble and have to grab onto the banister.

'You okay?' he says.

'Yeah, sorry, these heels!' I say. 'Where are we going?' I hesitate on the stairs.

'I want to talk to you about the Celeste job. Away from all the noise.'

Forty grand. Life-changing money. So I follow him. We enter a room through a pair of tall, narrow double doors. The walls are lined with floor-to-ceiling shelves of books. The books are lit up by multicoloured LEDs.

'A library in a nightclub?'

'This place used to be a private members club.'

I stand there, amazed that I am alone with this famous photographer, still a bit star-struck but pleased the door is open.

'Do you like books?'

'Yeah, sure,' I say.

He sits down, reaches behind him to pull out a book, lays it on the coffee table and taps out some cocaine from a little plastic pouch. 'Sure you don't want a line?'

'No thanks.'

He takes out a credit card, makes two perfect lines on the shiny cover and snorts them up his huge nose. A bit of white powder sticks to his nose hair. Seriously, I want to sick up in my mouth. What the frig am I doing in here?

'Come and sit here.'

'Actually, I should get back and find Bay.' I need to go. Bay will be annoyed with me for leaving her for so long.

'Sit down! Relax! I just wanna talk to you about the job.'

He pats the sofa next to him and my stomach somersaults. If I don't sit down, it will seem rude. I compromise and sit on the seat opposite him.

'Ha,' he says, staring at me, sniffing and wiping his nose. I guess he is laughing at me for sitting so far away from him.

'I'm trying to convince the Celeste lot that you're right for the campaign, but they're leaning towards the other girl.'

I try to hide my disappointment. 'Oh, right,' I say.

'But *I* want you.'

'Cool. Thanks.'

'You remind me of a young Bardot.'

His eyes slide all over me. Beads of sweat pop up in my cleavage and the little scars across my chest seem to sting and smart. How can Bay find this guy sexy? I decide that I don't care whether I get the forty grand or not, I want out of here. It's only going to rot in a bank account for ages and then be spent on boring university stuff. Maybe I don't want to go to university. It isn't worth it for this paedo. But as I stand up, he lunges forward and grabs me roughly by the arm and pulls me right up to him.

'I have to go downstairs,' I say really firmly, to make sure there is literally no way he could *not* understand that.

But he doesn't seem to get it. He puts his hand in between my legs and begins kissing my mouth. I suck back my lips and try to twist away, but his grip on my arm is too tight. He pushes me down onto the sofa and lies on top of me and puts his hand on my boob, pressing it really hard, panting like a dog, and with the other hand he tries to find a way into my jumpsuit. Struggling to get away from him physically hurts. The panic is white-hot. He is like a fucking expert at keeping me down. It is happening so fast, I can hardly think straight.

Heavy-breathing, he says, 'Jesus, this thing is like a chastity belt.'

He tries to turn me over, to get to the zip at the back. Screaming doesn't even come into my head as an idea. There isn't enough time. All his weight is on my chest. I've never felt so trapped and so scared in all my life, and at the same time I think I know how to deal with this. I've done it before. I turn my head to the side and go still and floppy and try to think about riding my bike and the wind whipping my face and Matthew in my slipstream. Better to be somewhere else with someone I love when there is literally nothing on earth that is going to prevent this horrible thing from happening.

Then I hear a voice.

'What the fuck?' Bay says.

Her voice is a real-life angel's. I want to cry with relief. But there is no time for that shit. I need to get the hell away from this old man. He looks up, startled by Bay, and I manage to roll off from under him and stumble away, twisting my ankle on my heel as I run to the door.

As I hurry down the stairs, hand in hand with my big sister, my breathing goes funny and I can't stop coughing. Neither of us speaks, not until we are in a taxi on our way to Shoreditch. I'm shaking all over. My hands won't work to push in the seat belt. Bay has to do it for me, and then she puts her arm around me and smoothes my hair. The tears fall then. I want Mum. I feel so disgusting and ashamed and so fucking stupid.

She says, 'Shh, shh, it's okay. You're safe now.'

I shiver, feeling suddenly cold. Her role as my saviour is frigging welcome, don't get me wrong, but it's kind of ironic. She's the reason I know that fighting back doesn't work and why I know how to block my mind from a harsh experience. If she hadn't turned up when she had, I would have become a machine with an off-switch. Thanks for that, Bay, I guess.

CHAPTER THIRTY-FOUR

Anna

'I thought you came back early so that you could help me get the party ready,' I said, opening Nell's bedroom curtains for the third time in an hour.

The two of them had come in at ten this morning, looking dishevelled. Nell had gobbled down a bowl of cereal and gone to bed for a nap.

'What time is it?' she groaned, coughing.

'I think we should take you to the doctor about that cough.'

'What time is it?' she asked again.

'It's eleven already. Do you want to do the table decorations or not?'

She pulled the duvet over her head. 'We've got ages.'

I was building up to being furious. Maybe I was already furious. Moving the date of Mum's seventieth celebration from last night to today had been a decision I had struggled with, for Nell's sake, and one that Mum had pretended to be happy about. Although I had not mentioned premieres or after-parties to her, she was not stupid. She had said, 'I don't really want a party, love. It's okay if we don't celebrate, if you're all too busy.' What she meant was, 'Nobody cares, nobody loves me. I'll just go right on and die, while you have fun dancing on my grave.' The whole reshuffle had felt profoundly wrong and I wondered how Nell could then behave like this, when she had been the cause of the change. I was disappointed that she was not now fully invested in making up for it by giving Mum a party that proved how much we loved her.

'We haven't got *ages*, we've got an hour and a half.'

There was no time for her teenage selfishness. The house was a tip, and I hadn't chopped the onions for the French onion soup – why had I suggested onion soup? – nor had I wrapped Mum's present, and the apples for the tarte tatin still needed to be quartered and cored.

'Nell. Get. Out. Of. Bed. NOW!' I spat, losing my patience.

She flung the duvet off and shouted, 'JUST FUCK OFF, OKAY! I'LL FUCKING DO IT! OKAY?'

I reeled back. She had never sworn at me like that. Too shocked to speak, I stormed downstairs to find Dom. He was on the sofa, still in his pyjamas, reading the newspaper.

'Did you *hear* what she just said to me?' I said.

'What?'

'She just told me to fuck off!'

Through the open door of the conservatory I saw Iris turning around and grinning at me. I didn't mind what she heard right now. I was livid.

'Sorry, Iris,' I said. 'But your sister was very rude and I'm very, very cross.'

'I'm making a cat card for Granny Berry,' she said, turning back to continue cutting up tiny triangles of multicoloured card that sprayed more mess onto the floor.

'You'd better pick all those up!' I said.

'I will,' Iris said vaguely, and I knew she wouldn't.

'Seriously, darling, Granny Berry's coming over in an hour and fifteen minutes!'

Dom had gone back to his newspaper. I said to him, 'Do you even care that Nell just told me to fuck off?'

He sighed. 'She's a teenager. That's what they do.'

'Great. Thanks,' I said, throwing my arms in the air.

'What do you want me to do about it?'

Did I have to spell it out? How about show some parental solidarity, perhaps? Maybe support me for a bloody change? But I didn't have a chance to say it. There was a wail from the conservatory. 'It's all gone wrong!' Iris screamed, tearing up pieces of cardboard and throwing them across the table. A cat ear here and a fat paw there.

I rushed over. 'Oh no, don't do that!'

It was too late. Mum's birthday card was in pieces. 'I can't do it! It's too stressful!'

'Iris, darling, look in those drawers. There are some spare ones in there.'

'I don't know where to look!'

'Dom! Could you help her, please? I've got about a thousand onions to bloody chop.' There was a whine in my voice, but I was desperate for just one person to do as I said. For someone to help me.

'Anna, just bloody well calm down,' Dom said, snapping the paper in half and throwing it onto the sofa.

I was incredulous. 'Am I the only one who wants to make it special for Mum?'

'You're the only one who wants to make it pure misery for the rest of us,' he mumbled.

Iris cried, '*I* wanted to make it special, Mummy! But it went all wrong!'

I breathed in. 'Dom, can you please help Iris find a birthday card? There'll be some in the drawer.'

'Come on, Iris,' he said, shooting me a dirty look before kneeling down with Iris in front of my drawers in the conservatory.

The onions made me cry, of course. They were not tears of anger or of joy; they were just an irritating chemical reaction. When Bay emerged, beautifully dressed in a skirt and a blouse buttoned up to the top, she said, 'Are you okay?'

'No! I'm not okay. I need some bloody help!'

She set about tidying up Iris's mess, stringing up pretend onions and laying the table with red-chequered napkins. She was being the best stepdaughter anyone could wish for.

When Dom went to collect Mum, I hugged Bay tightly. 'Thank you, darling. The house looks beautiful.'

The cassoulet had turned out well and the red wine helped our mood. Dom drank too much and talked and joked edgily, often over my half-finished sentences. I hoped he was trying to paper over Nell's rudeness. On the surface, it was a jolly French meal, and Mum seemed to enjoy the attention. But I decided it was true that a parent was only ever as happy as their unhappiest child: Nell had barely said a word throughout the meal, but she had coughed, a lot, and had even left her tarte tatin untouched. Her quietness was verging on oppressive. I cast my eye over her, scrutinising her properly for the first time that day. It was unusual to see her face bare of make-up. Her eyes were puffy and red, and her hair was a tumbled-down tangle. Worry replaced my annoyance. I would talk to her after lunch.

When I drove Mum home, she said, 'That was lovely, dear.'

'It was fun, wasn't it?' I said, thinking we had got away with it.

'Thank you so much for my smart coffee machine,' she said.

'Pleasure. It's a boomerang present, really. So I can enjoy a decent cup when I come round.'

She didn't laugh. Her instant coffee bias had never been a laughing matter between us.

I parked outside her apartment block and felt suddenly weary. I was about to get out and open the car door for her when Mum said, 'Nell was hung-over.'

We had not got away with it. 'Hmm,' I said. 'Sorry about that.'

'And Dom will be hung-over tomorrow,' she said.

'I imagine so!' I laughed.

For all Mum's vagueness and hard-of-hearing, non-sequitur contributions to conversations, she was beady about the negative undertows of family relations. I thought about Dom's behaviour at lunch and, for the first time today, wondered if his passive aggression had been directed at me.

We got out of the car and I hugged her goodbye at her door. 'Happy Birthday, Mum,' I said. 'Sorry about Nell.'

'That's okay, dear.' She pushed her chin higher, as though tipping back her head to stop the tears from falling. Her front door closed and I almost knocked on it again, but I didn't know what I could say or do to make it any better the second time.

On the way home, I wondered why I had bothered trying to make today fun. Nobody had been in the right frame of mind. Leaving Mum there alone in her flat, deflated further by the family party that had been designed to cheer her up, I felt that I had failed her. And I had failed Nell.

In trying to make it perfect, I had spoiled it. The weight of my mother's happiness came down on me, and Nell's and Bay's and Iris's and even Dom's. I needed them to be happy or the sacrifices wouldn't be worth it. The sacrifice, singular. The one big sacrifice.

Billy's number was still tucked into my wallet. I wanted to call him and tell him all about today. I knew he would laugh at me for worrying too much.

He and I had laughed a lot in the past, sometimes at the most stressful of times. Like the week I had been preparing for my final show at St Martin's, when I had torn every single page out of my drawing pad and thrown each sketch out of the window. He had snuck out, after dark, into the little London back garden – not ours, but that of the basement flat below us – and collected them up, then smoothed them out, ironed them

– with an actual iron – and given them back to me, telling me
they'd be fine, apart from the cat piss smell. I had felt so stupid,
but we had laughed until my belly ached and we'd had lots of
sex that night. He was such a calm person, not dismissive, but
understanding. He would understand now, and he would laugh
at me, kindly, for getting wound up about a small birthday lunch
for Mum. If I called him now, we'd pick up where we had left
off as though no time had passed, no heartache, no headache,
no bellyache, no loss.

Back home, I went straight to the fridge.

'Hi,' I said to Dom, who was watching television. I stared into
the fridge and exhaled, forgetting for a second why I had opened
it. Dom didn't reply. I could hear Nell coughing upstairs.

'We've got to talk to Nell,' I said. I had used the pronoun 'we',
though I knew it was me who would do the talking.

Why was I standing at the open fridge? Wine. Yes. I took the
bottle out and placed it on the worktop. I caught sight of five
postcards fanned out, writing-side up. My heart stopped. They
were Billy's, from New York.

Dom must have been waiting for me to spot them. He said,
'Iris found them.'

'Oh yeah?' I said, picking them up, shuffling through them as
though for the first time. The postcards explained Dom's excessive
drinking at lunch. 'How funny. I forgot I had them.'

The burning heat of the lie radiated through my skin.

Dom turned the television off and stood up, hands in pockets.
His lips were pursed. He scratched a hand in the thick of his quiff.
'Who is this Billy guy?' He was making an obvious effort to lighten
his tone, but I picked up uncertainty, and even nervousness.

'He was just a friend from St Martin's. I told you that already.'

'And you kept his postcards all this time?'

'I keep lots of old stuff.'

'Five postcards. That's quite a few.'

'Billy's a bit like that. You'd like him. He's nice.' My teeth ached with my glib use of the word.

'Were you in love with him?'

I thought carefully about how I should tackle this question. To continue to bluff would only get me into more trouble.

'For a bit, yeah. I did have a life before you, you know.' I laughed.

He picked the cards up and started reading the back of one.

'Did you go to that dim sum place in New York so that you could see him?'

To my utter surprise, I noted a tremor in his voice, and I looked closely at him to check that I was not misinterpreting it. There was a shallow of tears gathering in his eyes. My guts twisted.

'Sort of,' I said, knowing I couldn't lie to him any more. 'But it was only because Billy had always talked about having his own salon one day, and I just wanted to see it for myself.'

'When I saw these, I thought…' He stopped. 'I don't know what I thought.'

'I'm so sorry I wasn't honest with you about it. It was stupid of me. I don't know why I didn't tell you. I guess I didn't want you to feel…' I paused and looked at his pained, boyish expression. 'I didn't want you to feel like this when there was absolutely nothing to worry about. Just stupid sentimentality, really, that's all.'

I was embarrassed about my admission. Hankering for the past had been daft when the past was just that: the past. No amount of nostalgia or regret could change it.

It was important to remind myself of why things with Billy had ended.

Before he had left for New York, he had come with me to the psychiatric hospital every day to see Mum. When the clinician had diagnosed nervous exhaustion, Billy had joked with me – in a macabre and affectionate way – that she was exhausted by all the hours she had spent asking everyone to do things for her. It was still true that her first waking thought would be to accuse someone of not being at her bedside with a cup of coffee. Usually it was me she blamed, even though I was the one who was most likely to be standing there.

At the time, I had laughed at his joke, knowing how much he did for Mum, knowing that what he said about her was true. *Every* day was a bad day for Mum. But there had been a deeper part of me that had not found it funny. After my father had left, I had shouldered Mum's misery. I had nursed her better, made her happier, cured her – or so I had thought. At first Billy had not understood that bond between Mum and me, not really. He had not understood that I would never give up on her. And when he had finally come to terms with it, after Mum's admission to hospital and my subsequent decision to cancel my plane ticket to New York, it had been the beginning of the end for us.

Looking at Dom now, I did not have a desire to turn back time. The life I shared with him was exactly the future I had imagined for myself: a house and garden full of children, a stomping ground for them in the fields and streams of my own childhood, near my mother, near good schools and in a safe neighbourhood. These, I believed, were a solid set of criteria for a secure and happy family life.

Gallivanting off to New York back then would have meant abandoning Mum and almost everything that mattered to me. In reality, family life in New York would have equalled cramped, fume-choked apartments with noisy air-conditioning units, overcrowded green spaces and a walk to school on unsafe streets. Our kids would have known my brother and their cousins only through screens, rather than truly knowing them; and I would have deprived my mother of having her grandchildren running around at her feet. Nell and Iris, and Bay, were Mum's lifeline. I had given her that, and it was no small thing. Two successful careers – if they had turned out that way – and an edgy lifestyle would not have made up for the hole in the family that emigrating from the UK would have left.

I put my arms around Dom and hugged him. 'Sorry for being such a nightmare today,' I said. 'I just wanted it to be perfect for Mum.'

He pulled back a little, to look at me straight in the face. 'I get that you love your mum and everything – of course you do – but she's a bottomless pit,' he said. 'Nothing you do will ever get even close to perfect.'

I sighed and rubbed my face, knowing I had been falling down into that pit all my life.

'She worked out that Nell was hung-over,' I said.

'It wouldn't have taken a genius.' He reached for two wine glasses from the top shelf. They were the last remaining crystal Cabernet stems from a set of six that we had been given as a wedding present by Viv and Greg, and I wondered if he had brought them down on purpose.

'Do you think I should go up and talk to her?' I said.

'Leave her tonight. She'll be okay.'

I took a sip of wine. It was refreshingly cold, and I smiled at him, relieved that he had given me permission to avoid the confrontation with Nell. I felt supported and understood. 'Okay. I don't think I could face it now anyway. I'll talk to her tomorrow.'

If I had loved Billy enough, I could have contemplated that other life in New York; a life that was alien and uncertain and uncomfortable. If Billy had loved me enough, he could have adjusted his dream. It seemed that my love for him actually had not been enough, and that marriage was better.

CHAPTER THIRTY-FIVE

Nell

Jade texts me at breakfast.

Y u airing me, bish?

I don't need that crap today. My head is pounding and my chest is hurting from all the coughing. I feel like shit.

'Are you okay this morning?' Mum says, holding my forehead. Her touch and her voice – even though it is a bit narky – bring tears into my throat and I stop being able to swallow. For a minute I think I might tell her about Francis Ray. But how would I find the words to explain that I'd done everything she had always told me not to do, and that a disgusting old man had put his hands on my... A split second of the memory comes back to me, and even a split second of it is too much to take. I shiver it away and get up and dump my bowl in the sink, feeling sick again. I hear Mum sighing heavily as I leave the kitchen.

On the way to the bus stop, I check my phone for texts and emails from Ian. The Take One office doesn't open until 9.30, but Ian sometimes texts me when he doesn't want to talk to Mum – I guess he is sick of her fussing all the time – and today he will have news about the Celeste job. Also, I want to know if he is pissed off with me about Saturday night. It was rude of us to leave without saying thank you and goodbye. Thank you for almost raping me, Francis Ray, it was a blast!

*

'Do you get to keep the clothes?' Jade asks. She is sitting next to me on the bus and she looks insanely pretty. She always does on school days. She tones down her make-up and lets her long brown straight hair down, and it suits her better than her week-end look of hair gel and falsies and hoops.

'Nah, I wish,' I say.

Everyone asks me that. One time I walked out of a studio in a pair of white cotton socks from a shoot, forgetting I had them on, and the stylist ran down the street after me and forced me to take them off on the pavement. She made me feel like a thief.

'You revised for the biology test?' Mint asks over my shoulder. Her mass of curls gives off a hairspray smell that makes my tired eyes water.

'No,' I say, truthfully. It's a pre-mocks test on cell formation, and I haven't even glanced over the worksheets.

'You always say that,' Jade mumbles. She types into her phone and her ring makes a tapping sound on the case.

I put my earbuds in and turn my shoulder away from her. I don't have the energy for her today. Her bitchiness wears me down. I listen to my tunes and keep refreshing my emails.

All morning I refresh. At lunch break, a text finally comes through from Ian.

Good news, hon! Call me. X

A hot flush rushes up from my toes to my head and back down to my toes again. A mixture of emotions fills my chest. Is the good news that I'll be working on a job next week with the guy who almost raped me?

There is no time to call Ian back before biology.

It is the first time ever that I cannot answer any of the questions on a test, and I mean literally not one of them. Sweat is gathering under my arms and on my forehead and I can't stop coughing. I ask the teacher if I can go to the loo, and she looks disapproving and tells me to hurry up.

School loos are disgusting. They stink and there is never any soap, and the loo paper is everywhere and there is piss on the floor. But I literally can't think of anywhere else in the world I would rather be. The locked door means I can sit and think without being bothered by anyone.

Maybe I can sit here until the end of the school day.

I can't call Ian back until I have made my decision. Take the money and get raped? Or turn it down and get chucked out of the agency? Dad would never speak to me again. Or maybe I could do the job and make sure I wasn't raped. Is that possible? How would I do it? The thought of setting eyes on Francis Ray again turns my stomach. It would be like willingly taking myself into the jungle to meet a tiger.

Instead of calling Ian, I text him.

Hi Ian, soz we left on Sat nite. Bay was sick. Got science test now What good news? Nx

Hi hon, looking good for Celeste. FR loves you and said the job is yrs. Confirming with Celeste today. Should know tomoz. Love ya, princessa. Laters. X

The hideous purple doors of the loos seem to close in on me. I try to breathe in, but the smell makes me gag and sets me off coughing again. Has Francis Ray given me the job to keep me quiet? Or so that he can finish what he started? There is no way I can concentrate on a science test. My heart beats faster and faster. My chest hurts with it.

There is a bang on the cubicle door.

'Nell! Miss asked me to get you. Are you okay?'

It's Mint. Thank God it is Mint and not Jade.

'I'm not feeling too good.'

'Want me to take you to the nurse?'

'Yeah, could you?'

I know that the nurse will send me back into class if I don't have a temperature or any vomit to show her. But it will get me out of the test, at least. Mint puts an arm around me and it feels like old times. I want to go back there. Those days were so much simpler. I took them for granted.

It turns out I do have a temperature and I am sent home.

I tell Mum I'm not going to go to the doctor's, however much she hassles me. I am going to sleep. I need sleep so badly. After I have slept, I am sure I will feel better.

The duvet is like a lovely warm hug. I can't even be bothered to take off my uniform. But as I start to drop off, I have flashbacks of Francis Ray being on top of me. He is like a black mass, suffocating me.

I remember a radio show I heard in the car with Mum once. Apparently when someone commits suicide, the professionals prefer to call it 'completing suicide', rather than 'committing suicide', which sounds more like a crime. Will Francis Ray 'complete rape' on me next week?

I feel hot. I shove off the duvet and lie there on my back, trying to breathe through the coughing.

The strange thing is, the heavy mass that stops my breathing isn't new to me. I know this shadow that is on me now; a familiar old enemy.

CHAPTER THIRTY-SIX

Bay

The final confirmation call about the Celeste job had come from Ian ten minutes ago. I watched Dad hug Nell. There were tears in his eyes. He was proud of her for getting a job that paid almost as much as his annual salary. I had never seen Dad that happy before. He had never cried with joy about anything I had done. When I had passed my eleven GCSEs, he had taken me out for an ice cream, but he had been distracted. I remembered how he had rubbed at his leg angrily when a drop of his lemon meringue double scoop fell on his knee.

Watching the two of them now was physically painful. I had never experienced a hug from him like that, and I wanted to know what it would feel like.

'Okay, okay, it's not that big a deal,' Nell said, pulling away.

I wondered if Dad needed to know the real reason why it was a very big deal for Nell. If he knew about Francis Ray, I guessed he would not let her work with him.

Anna said, 'I think this calls for some Prosecco, don't you?'

For the first time in days, Nell smiled at Anna and clinked glasses with her.

I beckoned to Nell. She followed me upstairs.

'How are you feeling?' I asked her.

'Crapping myself. Did you see Dad? He was practically crying.'

'You have to tell him what happened.'

'I can't! He'll tell Mum and then I'll never be able to go out again as long as I live! Let alone carry on modelling!'

Remembering the hug between Nell and Dad, I said, 'Maybe I should tell him.'

'If you do, I'll kill you. Seriously, don't, Bay. Please. I mean it.'

'What if Francis tries it again?'

Nell pushed her fringe back and a cough rattled through her. She banged the centre of her chest with her fist. 'There'll be people everywhere on the shoot. I'll just make sure I'm not alone with him, ever.'

'Wow. Okay.'

'You don't think I should do it?' She looked imploring, and so beautiful, it hurt. I imagined her on billboards and on the sides of buses; her toothy, big-eyed siren beauty magnified.

'It's the principle, quite frankly. He tried to rape you and now you're working with him. It's fucked up.'

'But it's not fair! He's the one who molests me and then *I'm* the one who loses out on all that money?'

'Is the money really worth it?'

'It's not just about the money. I was awake all last night thinking about it, and I don't want him to win. I want to show him I'm not scared of him. It's just my way of dealing with it. Okay?'

'Fair enough.'

She wheezed and then cleared her throat. 'Don't be disappointed in me.'

'I'm not,' I said. 'I'll see you downstairs.'

'Bay!' Nell whispered. Her blonde tresses dangled over the banisters. 'Promise not to tell Dad?'

I hissed back, 'Course not.'

Downstairs, Anna was stirring the pasta and Iris was doing sums in her workbook in front of the television.

'Where's Dad?' I asked.

Anna pointed outside and then put her finger to her lips, miming smoking. Iris was the only one who didn't know Dad smoked.

'Thanks,' I said.

Outside, it was cold enough for a coat. My jaw began to judder.

'Dad?'

Plumes of smoke billowed from behind the Wendy house.

He put the cigarette behind his back when he saw me. With his thick hair and small lips, I thought he looked like a lost little boy with old-man make-up on.

'Subtle, Dad.'

He laughed and brought the roll-up back to his lips. 'Don't tell Anna.'

'Never.'

'What's up?'

Looking to the ground, I crossed my arms around my waist.

'Everything okay?' he asked.

'If I tell you something, will *you* promise not to tell Anna?'

I imagined his fatherly arms around me, thanking me. I wanted to connect with him, to remind him that I was his firstborn. The umbilical cord that had looped from me to Mum had been cut, and I wanted its loose end to be retied to my father.

'I won't tell Anna,' he said.

He *would* tell her, I knew that much. 'Promise?'

'Tell me, sweetheart.'

I felt a lightness in my stomach. Telling a grown-up was always the right thing to do, right?

'You know the party we went to on Saturday night?'

'Yes. How could I not?'

'And you know that photographer, Francis Ray? The one who's shooting the Celeste campaign?'

'Yup.'

'Well, he attacked Nell.'

'What?' He dropped his cigarette and ground it into the grass, stepping closer. His eyes glinted.

'Nell went upstairs with him to a private room and he took a line of coke then he pushed her onto the sofa and tried to rape her.'

Dad's upper body was still, too still, but his foot continued to grind at the cigarette. His expression scared me.

'I don't believe you,' he hissed, which I thought was an odd thing to say when it was obvious that he did believe me. If it came to it, I had that four minutes and twenty-one seconds on my camera roll to prove it. What I had witnessed through those doors at the club had roused in me an anger I had needed to harness and take control of, and before I could think, my phone had been my naked eye, capturing what I needed; seeing it so that I did not have to feel it. Ideally, I'd be keeping that a secret until the time was right. The moral ambiguity of watching Nell struggle while I filmed would horrify Anna.

'I saw it with my own eyes. I walked in on them just in time and she got away. She didn't want me to tell you guys, but I felt it was the right thing to do.'

White breath came out of his mouth. 'Yes. It was the right thing to do,' he said. He sounded angry rather than grateful. The proud, loving hug did not follow. His thoughts were not with me.

I said, 'She shouldn't do this Celeste job with him, should she? I mean, the money isn't worth it, is it?'

'Goddammit!' he yelled, kicking at the Wendy house. It rattled into the night. 'She gets her big break and then some fucking arsehole fucks it up for us.'

I noted the 'us'.

'I know, it's unbelievable. It's so unfair.'

The roll-ups were out of Dad's pocket again. His fingers shook. He didn't say anything for a minute or so, and when he spoke, it was through a tight jaw. 'It's really fucking unfair. Fuckers like that, who have all the privileges thrown at them all their bloody lives while the rest of us have to scrabble around making a shit living. It's funny, I looked him up earlier, and he lives in Chelsea, in one of those fuck-off town houses that must be worth millions. And there's our Nell, without a pot to piss in, and he's trying to ruin her one big chance.'

'There'll be another chance for her. She's so beautiful.'

'No. That's not how life works, Bay. Fuck him. She can't miss out on this job.'

'Anna will never allow it.'

'We're not going to tell Anna about it, okay?'

I was taken aback. 'Seriously?'

'You mustn't tell her, do you understand me, darling?'

This was not what I had expected. I had imagined – after our wonderful bonding hug – that he would storm into the kitchen and tell Anna, and Anna would be at first surprised that Dom had known something before she had. Then her anger would have kicked in, and she would have been pleased with me and she would have called Ian and told him that Nell's career as a model was over. Over and done with. Forever.

'I think she should know, Dad.'

'You don't trust me to handle this without her?'

It was an important question.

'I do trust you,' I replied.

'Good. It'll only upset her if she knows. And if Nell doesn't want her to know, we have to respect that.'

Panic set in. If I told Anna now, Dad would never trust me.

'What if he tries it again?'

'I'll go with her to the shoot and make sure he doesn't lay a finger on her.'

'Dad, that's insane. Nell would never let you.'

Why hadn't I gone straight to Anna about this? Anna would have shut it down. No question. It had been that hug he had given Nell. A stupid hug had made me angry and possessive and in need of some unobtainable, instant closeness with him. I was furious with myself for craving the attention. But how could I have predicted he would want to keep it a secret from Anna? How would I have known he would let Nell work with a man who had tried to rape her? All I had wanted was a proper bloody hug.

'I don't care what Anna thinks about it, quite frankly.'

'It'll look really weird to her if you suddenly want to go on a shoot.'

Dom nodded, and took a slow drag, and I thought about this new problem, adapting to his surprising reaction. The shoot could be an opportunity for me. Footage of Francis Ray and Nell working together would underpin the horror of the clip from Saturday night. I should have thought of this before.

'I'll do it,' I said. 'I can tell her I'm filming behind-the-scenes stuff for my documentary or something.'

'You're a genius,' he said, and hugged me. I concentrated on enjoying it, willing it to feel how it must have felt for Nell. But it didn't feel like anything. Dad was holding me, just as I had wanted him to, and I felt nothing inside at all.

CHAPTER THIRTY-SEVEN

Nell

Bay and I stand outside a large corner house in a Knightsbridge mews. The house has tall pink shutters and window boxes and elegant bars across the windows. I am shaking so much my teeth chatter. Unless I am just cold. There are big fat snowflakes melting on the cobblestones at our feet.

'Let's go,' Bay says. 'Remember what you said about showing him how strong you are?'

'Girl power?' I say.

'Girl-fucking-power, sister,' Bay says, bumping my fist.

'Yeah!'

'Let's do that again, for the camera, with the F-word,' Bay says, holding up her phone while we repeat our fist bump.

Bay has on red-orange lipstick and I have the bare face required for a shoot. I'm so grateful to her for coming with me.

'Go on, you first, so I can film you going in.'

'Shit. Shit. Shit,' I say, under my breath.

I open the door, which is on the latch, and we step into an open-plan, low-ceilinged room. I feel the heat hit me and my stomach flips.

Francis is in the corner. He and Georgina from Celeste – who I met at the casting – are sitting on a low window seat in the alcove of an emerald stained-glass window. The light on their skin is bottle green. Francis's ankles are crossed and stretched out. Relaxed, is he? Georgina's polka-dot silk trouser legs are gathered at her trainers.

They stand up when they see us and walk across the parquet floor.

Chin up, head high, I think. *Fuck him*, I think. *Forty grand*, I think. *I want Mum*, I think.

The sight of his large nose and narrow eyes sends the taste of him rushing into my head. My brain goes fizzy and messed up, like I've been shoved at high speed. Bay pinches me. Apparently he has said hello.

'Hi, sorry. Love this house, it's amazing. So kooky,' I say to Georgina. I refuse to look at Francis.

'I know. It's beautiful. I grew up walking to school past it and always wondered what it was like inside,' she says. She looks just like the kind of girl who walked to school through Knightsbridge.

'Come and see this,' Francis says. I stand still. Bay takes my hand and we follow him. 'See the floral detail on the glass? Buttercups. How great is that?'

'The fragrance is called Buttercup,' Georgina explains.

'Ah, right,' I say. 'Really cool, then.'

'I love its delicacy and fragility,' Francis says, directly to me. I want to knee him in the balls.

Bay steps a bit closer to me. She says, 'Not that fragile. It has survived for over a hundred years.'

'Indeed,' Francis says, pinching his nose and wiping his fingers on his trouser leg.

There is a tickle in my throat. I cough. It rattles through the room.

Up the green-carpeted stairs, there are ten bright yellow dresses on a rail.

Tinny music comes from a small room, where we find Molly, who is hair and make-up.

'This house is weird, right?' Molly says. She has picked up on the tension in my face as she massages in cream and hums to the radio. She is tall and pretty and rather vague.

'Really weird,' I say.

Bay hovers and films.

'This is my sister. She's shooting stuff for my Insta feed,' I explain.

Bay waves to Molly from behind her phone and Molly waves back.

The yellow dress that Georgina likes me in is short and frilly around a plunging neckline. When I change, I am conscious of how bright the sunlight from the window is and I worry about the little scars showing. Molly tucks tissues around the edge of the dress and presses foundation and bronzer over my chest. She's seen them, I guess.

On set, I sit on the window seat and do as Francis says. Behind the bright lights, Bay is just a shadow as she films. I laugh and smile and move to the music and stare into his lens. The lens is hypnotic, like some dark portal. Francis clicks his camera and fiddles around with the frills on my chest, arranging them for his dumb-ass photograph. I do not move a muscle. I tell myself he is just a shadow.

I feel nothing when he says, under his breath, 'I'm sorry if there was a misunderstanding the other night.'

An apology? The perfect gentleman. NOT!

Georgina watches us with a serious face, as though she is studying an important work of art being created. I guess this shoot *is* her work of art. It isn't for me. I am just the label on a perfume brand. I am not real. None of this is real.

*

On the train home, I have a coughing fit. People move away to different carriages and Bay brings me water. The more I cough, the less I think about Francis Ray's face.

Back at home, every time I try to get to sleep, even with my eye mask, I end up hacking my guts out. Mum brings me cough medicine and sits with me until I go to sleep. I drift off with her lovely cold hand on my forehead.

When I wake again, I am screaming.

CHAPTER THIRTY-EIGHT

2012

It always happened in the dark. In the dark of a bedroom or the dark of the Wendy house or the dark of the curtained sitting room. Bay said they were games, that it was fun. Nell knew that she had to do what Bay said.

Today they were in the Wendy house. Mummy was trying to get Iris to sleep. Daddy was at the driving range. Nell lay on the musty garden chair cushions that Bay called the stretcher. Bay said the green metal camping torch was like an operating theatre light. It was cold on Nell's tummy when Bay laid it there so that she could see better. A damp tickle of sewing thread was dangled onto Nell ribs and it made her shiver. She was glad Bay wasn't using Anna's art knife as a scalpel again. The tourniquet rubber bands weren't so bad. Bay's operating theatre was always well stocked. The other week, she had used their dad's lighter to cauterise a pretend vein, but the burn on Nell's stomach had become infected. They had told Anna that Nell had been messing around with matches. Another mistake had been the pliers. The pinch marks had left bleeding under the skin. For days they had worried, secretly fearing the 'internal bleeding' would kill her.

It took Bay a few tries to thread the needle. Nell hated the smell of the strawberry laces hand sanitiser. The disinfecting of the needle and the swabbing of the area were the last stages before it would start to hurt.

The prick of the needle was sharp and stinging, and the panic was like paralysis. The burn intensified as the tiny weapon went in and under, in and under. The thread slithered through her flesh, making her teeth ache, giving her a nasty jump in her groin and under her armpits. Her feelings separated off from her body, like a fuse in her brain had gone and was no longer able to connect to what was happening to her. She wasn't quite sure whether what was happening to her was real or whether it was a nightmare. The stiller she lay, the less real it would feel. She always kept her eyes tight shut all the way through, and imagined going out on her bike with Matthew and drinking a massive Fanta.

The needle prodded deeper than usual. Nell let out a small cry.

Bay put her hand over her mouth.

Nell's stomach cramped. She closed her eyes tightly, fearing that someone would wake up and catch them doing something so bad. The badness inside her spread and spread. She never, ever wanted anyone to see how bad she was.

The next day Nell checked her chest in the mirror. The marks were small and red and swollen.

Like a good doctor, Bay examined them every day for infection and waited for them to heal before she operated again.

CHAPTER THIRTY-NINE

Anna

'Who's that? Oh my God, someone's screaming. Is that Nell?' I shook Dom, who mumbled and put a pillow over his head.

I jumped out of bed, feeling cold and groggy and panicked.

Bay was close behind me, wrapped in her dressing gown.

Nell was bolt upright in bed.

'Sweetheart? Are you okay?' I sat on her bed and felt her forehead. She was hot.

'I had a nightmare,' she mumbled.

'Poor darling. I'll get the thermometer and some Nurofen.'

When I returned, Bay was standing in the corner, far away from Nell's bed. I took Nell's temperature, which turned out to be slightly raised.

'Here you go,' I said, handing her a glass of water and two red pills.

Nell started rambling about syringes and tourniquets and needles. It was incomprehensible. I wondered if I should call the doctor now.

Bay sneezed. I was reminded that she was there.

'You can go back to bed now, Bay,' I said. 'Don't worry about Nell. She's just got a bit of a fever. She used to get like this when she was little.'

'It's a night terror,' Bay said, stepping forward, speaking over Nell's delirious ramblings.

Nell turned to face the wall. She pulled the duvet up around her chin and closed her eyes.

'Just a night terror,' Bay repeated, quite loudly.

I put my finger to my lips and whispered, 'Is everything okay, Bay?'

'Can I talk to you outside?' she asked.

'Sure,' I said, kissing Nell on the forehead. 'You get some sleep, darling.'

I followed Bay out onto the landing and closed Nell's door behind us.

'There's something she's not told you,' Bay said.

'What has she not told me?'

'She was scared you'd be angry.'

'What is it, Bay?'

She spoke fast, with her head down. 'The photographer on the Celeste job, Francis Ray…' She paused, as though to catch her breath. 'He sexually assaulted her.'

'What?' I rasped, winded by her words, which now wound back in slow motion through my brain. 'Today, on the shoot?'

'On Saturday night. They went upstairs alone, to a room in the club, and he forced himself on her. He pushed her down onto the sofa and tried to…' She stopped and regrouped. 'He was aggressive – he was really coked up.'

'You saw all this?'

'I found them just in time and she got away.'

My thoughts ricocheted around in my skull. 'And she had to work with that fucking bastard today?'

Bay scratched her fingernails through her hair, tugging it right through to its tips. It looked like it was standing on end for a second, like a scared person in a cartoon.

'That's why Dad wanted me to go too, to look after her. But I think it was really stressful for her and now she's ill and I feel like it's all my fault.'

'Dad *knew*?'

She scrunched her lips to the side. 'He didn't want to worry you.' She began to cry.

I pulled her into a hug. The sympathy I felt for her was being drowned out by a wave of such fury, I had to be careful not to squeeze her too tight in my desire to contain it. 'Don't worry, it's not your fault, darling. None of this is your fault.'

I sent her back to bed. I would not be able to go back to bed myself. If I had gone anywhere near Dom's body, lying sleeping there, I would have pummelled him to death. It was unfathomable that he had known something this big for over two days and he hadn't told me. I could not believe it, but then I did, right to my core, know that he was capable of sending his daughter into the arms of a sexual predator. He wanted that money more than anything he had ever wanted in his life.

Another surge of rage pushed itself up from my guts and into my chest.

I charged downstairs and paced the kitchen, poured myself a glass of water. The energy inside me needed somewhere to go. The clock said 1 a.m., and I wondered if I could call Martin, but I didn't want to wake up the whole household. He would think Mum had died. If I called Mum in the middle of the night, she *would* actually die. But where could I take my feelings? Pacing the kitchen, sipping water ritualistically, as though in prayer, I felt the world coming to an end in my head. I needed to talk to someone. There was Viv, but she switched her phone off at night. I contemplated running over to the shop. It would cause such a scene, and I didn't want Matthew finding out what had happened to Nell. It was such a private, humiliating ordeal and my heart contracted at the thought. I would have done anything to put myself in her place. A scream crawled up my throat.

I counted. I breathed. I counted backwards, five hours backwards from 1 a.m. It would be 8 p.m. in New York.

The piece of paper was in my wallet. I took it out. It was luminous in the dark.

Armed with my phone, I dressed in a warm coat and boots and went out to the Wendy house.

Billy picked up after two rings.

'Hello? Is that you, Anna?' he said.

Everything inside me collapsed when I heard his voice. 'Billy, yes, it's me. I know it's crazy that I'm calling you. I'm so sorry.'

'What's happened? Is everything okay?'

'I didn't know who else to turn to, I just don't know what to do. Something's happened to Nell and I don't know how to help her and you know the fashion world and I… I…' I could barely control what came out of my mouth or speak with any coherence through the heaving of my sobs. 'I… I *hate* him, Billy. I literally *hate* him.'

Billy stopped me gently. 'Okay, Anna, start from the beginning, okay? You're all right. Let's just start from the beginning.'

And so we did. We started from the beginning again, right then and there, with me bent in the Wendy house on a tiny child's chair, with a million miles of ocean between us.

I let Nell sleep in the next morning and called the school to say she wouldn't be in. At eleven, I decided to wake her. I warmed up a chocolate croissant and made her a cup of milky tea and put them on a tray with the thermometer and some Nurofen.

She stirred, coughing a little, rubbing her eyes. 'What time is it?'

'I've called the school and told them you're not well. I've made breakfast.'

She smiled, opening her eyes enough to see the tray, propping herself up.

'Yummy. Thanks, Mum.'

I sat on the side of her bed and watched her come to and eat, relieved that she was hungry.

'Let me just quickly take your temperature.'

I stuck it in her ear. It read 37.5°C, which was normal. 'That's good.'

'Thanks for this, Mum,' she said.

She had a smear of chocolate in the corner of her mouth, which I left there, not wanting to irritate her unnecessarily before I brought up Francis Ray.

The last crumbs were in her mouth, the warm butter licked off her fingers and the tea cradled in her hands. As she sipped, I rubbed my own hand up and down her thigh, soft under her batik-print duvet, and said what I had to say.

'Bay told me what happened with Francis Ray.'

She stared me out and swallowed, though she had nothing in her mouth. 'Yeah. And?'

'Do you want to tell me what happened?'

'Er, no.' She slammed her mug down, pushed the tray off her lap and clambered out of bed, pushing me off the side. Her cough started up again as she scrabbled in her drawers. She got dressed in a tracksuit.

'Where are you going? Come on, sit down.'

'It's done now. End of.'

'What do you mean, done?'

'The Celeste job,' she said, grabbing her phone from her desk, hacking away into her sleeve as she texted.

'Nell. We really need to talk about what happened to you,' I said, keeping my voice gentle, trying not to scare her off.

'Don't make this into a bigger deal than it is, Mum.'

'This is a very big deal. You were sexually assaulted.'

'He copped a feel and Bay got there in time. Every girl on the planet has had some creep touch them up. It hasn't fucked me up or anything.'

'Last night you were screaming in your sleep.'

'It was just a bad dream. Jeez.'

'I'm going to have to tell Ian.'

'What? Seriously? No! No way! You can't!'

'I'm afraid I have to, darling. This is too serious.'

She pulled her hair into a ponytail and hissed, 'Now I know why you got me that croissant. Just to trick me.'

'*Trick* you? That is not why! I got it because you weren't feeling well and I wanted to cheer you up.'

She stood in the doorway of her bedroom and shoved both hands into the front of her sweatshirt. Her big blue eyes blinked at me through her fringe and she said, 'If you talk to Ian, I'll just tell him that Bay is a liar and that she made it up because she hates me.'

'Nell!'

But she was gone, whipping down the stairs and out of the door.

'*Nell!*' I screamed again.

I could hear her cough getting fainter as she raced off on the bike that she was borrowing from Viv. At least she might see Matthew, who was home for a couple of days to help Viv and Greg out with some accounting. He might give Nell some sensible advice. Nothing *I* said or did made any difference any more.

My God, I was a useless mother. A useless human being.

PART THREE: THE FILM

Two Months Later

CHAPTER FORTY

Anna

Nell and I were yelling at each other. Yelling so hard I wondered whether we were yelling to communicate a point or yelling for the hell of it, yelling because we just wanted to shout and shout and shout until it was all gone.

'You're not going out tonight! And that's final!' I screamed. If I screamed loud enough, scarily enough, would she finally do as I said?

'Are you listening to me, Mum? Are you actually *listening*? Ian organised a car for me and has arranged a pap photographer for me. It's *work*! I *have* to go!'

'Is this Ian's way of looking out for you? Is it? If it is, then it's a fucking useless agency!'

'Nice language, Mum! Great example you're setting!'

'Yeah, that's right, throw that stupid crap at me, just because you know you're in trouble! You know that Ian's a prize shit who doesn't give a crap about you. But hey, yeah, just give me crap about my crappy bloody language!'

'Ian gets me! More than you ever do!'

I laughed, incredulous. 'He really is such a great pal, turning a blind eye to what happened to you. Yeah, that's really, really bloody brilliant. Gold stars for Ian!'

Every time we had a row about anything – about her partying or her non-existent revision or her bad attitude in general – we would end up spiralling into an argument about Ian. Every single time. We couldn't help it. We just couldn't help it.

'He respects my privacy, that's why! I was dealing with it fine before you butted in!'

'Burying your head in the sand isn't dealing with it fine!'

'I'm not in denial, Mum, I know exactly what happened to me, to my body. Not *yours*. MINE! And I'm over it and you need to get over it too!'

'While you're still a minor, it's my job to protect your body! That's my job, as your mother!'

'Protect me? Is that what you think you're doing?' She guffawed. 'You totally broke my trust by telling Ian! Is that your idea of protecting me, is it? Really? REALLY?'

'Yes, it is, actually!'

Back in February, straight after the Celeste job and the revelation about the assault, I had arranged a meeting with Ian at the Take One offices, behind Nell's back, and told him about Francis Ray. Subsequently, Ian had fixed a meeting with Nell, alone. She had contradicted me, retracting everything, saying she had made the story up to get attention, and he had believed her. Or pretended to. It was more convenient that way. If Nell continued to deny it, he explained, he couldn't in good conscience go to the British Fashion Model Agents Association or report it to the police. There was nothing any of us could do. He had suggested she see a therapist and had given me some numbers, but Nell had refused to consider it.

With nothing to work with, I had been forced let it go, knowing she was hurting inside; feeling hurt myself that she couldn't talk to me, hoping she'd open up soon, trusting in the tired belief that we were close, that she would back down, that we would go to Ian with the truth.

But she hadn't opened up and I hadn't been capable of dropping it, and we had carried on yelling about it. In desperation and frustration and fear, I had made threats and pleaded with her and even cried, and she was impervious, doubling down on her rudeness and intransigence.

'Look, Nell,' I said, breathing deeply, trying to calm the situation down. 'You've got GCSEs in a month. It's not okay to go out partying all night and come back at God knows what hour in the morning and sleep all day instead of working.'

'I'm going to do my revision tomorrow! Okay?' she screamed.

I snapped again. 'No! It's not okay! I want you to stay in tonight!'

'You never listen to me! Never, ever listen to me!' she screeched.

'Stop shouting!' I screamed.

She clamped her hands over her ears and shouted, 'I *hate* you!'

'I hate you too!' I yelled, adding, 'Sometimes!' at the end, as though I was a fraction more grown up and in control than her, which of course I wasn't. And on and on we circled, until she stormed out.

Dom came downstairs with wet hair, having heard the familiar row from the comfort of a warm bath.

'She's going to be the death of me, Dom! She's totally and utterly impossible!' I cried.

'Well, shouting at her won't work,' he said, tying the cord of his pyjamas.

I pictured him listening from the sidelines while the floral-scented bubbles popped around his ears, making a mental list of how he might have handled it differently, storing up his pearls of wisdom for me now, when it was over.

'No kidding! I never thought of that! I do absolutely bloody love shouting. Shouting is so much bloody fun!' I yelled, wheeling about the room, throwing my arms in the air.

'Don't take it out on me.'

'Why the hell not? Can't you shoulder some of this crap with me? Isn't that what you're here for? To get involved in your own daughter's life?'

'What could I have done? Come down and started shouting too? Would that have got us anywhere?'

'I don't know, but I don't want to do this on my own!'

'She's more likely to sit down to work if you back off and stop shouting at her all the time.'

'Great, okay, good plan, Dom, let's stand by and do nothing and watch her fuck up her whole life.'

'She'll be fine,' he said. *Don't worry your pretty little head about it, dear.*

'Jesus, you're so bloody calm! It's just weird. Totally bloody weird!'

Bay appeared through the door. 'Sorry, I left my phone in here,' she said, nipping across the room lightly. I caught her eye and felt guilty, knowing I shouldn't be shouting like this. Sadly, she was probably getting used to it. It wasn't fair on her.

I counted to ten in my head, calming myself down. 'Sorry, Bay,' I said.

She smiled back vaguely. 'Can I help at all?'

'Can you knock some sense into your sister for me?'

'I could go out with her tonight?'

'No, darling, I don't want both of you tired and incapable of revising tomorrow.'

'I've done so much revision this week, I'm over it. And I could be, like, her chaperone and make sure she gets back to the Shoreditch flat earlyish. To be honest, I'd love to film her at the party. From what she said, there'll be some interesting people there.'

'You deserve some fun, love,' Dom said, going against my advice as usual. 'You could be our spy,' he added, winking at her.

I exhaled. Overcome. Crushed. Feeling that everyone was against me. 'Whatever. Fine,' I said, pressing two fingers into my forehead.

'I'll go and get ready,' she said. Before leaving the room, she gave me a little hug. 'It'll be okay, Anna.'

When she'd gone, I said to Dom, 'Why do I even bother?'

He took up his point again, angrily. 'Mum and Dad were on my case all the time and I really resented them for it.'

Dom's parents, Albie and Stella, had been quiet and straight. They were dead now, arguably worked into an early grave by bringing Dom up. They had held down two jobs each to pay for the trainers he had begged for and the school ski trips that only the posh kids could afford and the souped-up GTI that his friends envied, but in return, they had expected a good report from him each term and a sensible career of their choosing for their precious only child. I compared this approach to my own mother's lack of interest in my schooling and then her horror when I had failed all my exams. I never wanted to be like her, blaming the world when life went wrong for her, forgetting that she had agency, an ability to influence the outcome.

'And you've done well because they pushed you,' I said, oh so tired of his self-pity.

'Have I done well?' His eyes turned yellowish brown, as though they were sick. His question seemed to include me and this house and our children. The atmosphere between us shifted. He was hinting, dangerously and uncertainly, that he might be disappointed by all of it.

'You have a good job and a lovely home and three beautiful girls,' I said, reminding him that he was lucky, so bloody lucky, and that he should be happier with his life, with us.

'I want Nell to be free to live how she wants to live,' he said.

'When she leaves home, she'll have her whole life to do that.'

'Not if she's in some shit job that she hates.'

'She won't have a shit job if she gets her GCSEs.'

'I want her to get her GCSEs too, Anna.'

'Funny way of showing it.'

'Just because I handle it differently doesn't mean I don't care.'

'You care more about the money she's earning than about her safety!'

'Change the record,' he said under his breath, and walked out.

The record was stuck. The scratch on the vinyl bumped the song back to the same old line in my head: Francis Ray. My inability to forgive Dom for letting Nell work with a man who had sexually assaulted her had arguably grown into a bigger problem than the sexual assault itself. For the sake of our marriage, I had tried to contain the mountain of anger inside me, but it came out in little spurts. I would never get over how disgusted I was by his decision, how little I respected him for it, how differently I would have handled it had I known the truth.

I blamed him for Nell's unhealthy desire to keep her experience locked inside her. If he had persuaded her to talk about it and deal with her feelings, rather than suppress them and battle on – for the money – perhaps she would be less volatile now. Dom would probably say my anger was misplaced, transferred from Francis Ray, whom I could not punish, to him, whom I could.

Mostly he ignored my little digs, my little reminders, as though they were white noise, and continued with his quiet, stubborn support of Nell's modelling career: picking her up from school early so that they could share a coffee together at the airport before a job; giving her secret hand-outs for taxis for the return journey from a party I'd said she couldn't go to; calling Ian to placate him after I'd reprimanded him about sending Nell an invite to a midweek gallery event.

Nell loved him for it and hated me even more. Like tonight. I was the bad guy and Dom was her chilled-out, fun dad, who let her do whatever she wanted to do, the little dear.

After Dom had dropped the girls at the station and gone up to bed, I drank the remainder of my tea, listened to my audiobook and cleaned up the kitchen, waiting for him to be asleep before I joined him.

Whole paragraphs of the book went in one ear and out of the other, just a string of beautifully enunciated words that made no sense. Worries about Nell went round and round in my head. Dom's lack of anxiety about her trajectory enraged me. He seemed to trust in the idea that the emotional sacrifices of pursuing success could be negated, in the end, by the big house and the nice car and the satisfaction of knowing she had made it.

I couldn't have disagreed more.

It seemed that the steady walls of our marriage were weakening, and my willpower was leaking through the cracks. I was still trying to be an upstanding wife and resist running to Billy, but Dom's lack of support tonight, again, as ever, had undermined us further.

Change the record, he had said. But I couldn't and I didn't want to. I was cranking up the shouty rock track and I didn't want to swap it for easy listening. I was not the chilled-out person he wanted me to be, and I never would be.

Billy hadn't ever wanted me to change the record. Billy was the one who would dance to my alternative tune. He was the one I needed right now.

CHAPTER FORTY-ONE

Nell

The car drives us across Westminster Bridge, passing the lights of Big Ben and the Houses of Parliament.

'Thanks for coming with me tonight,' I say.

'That's okay,' Bay says.

'I think Mum would've chained me up if you hadn't. How did you even persuade her?'

'I told her I'd spy on you.' She laughs.

'Seriously, she literally doesn't get it. Ian is my *agent*, and he said I should go to this party. What am I supposed to do, say no?'

'Maybe.'

My eyes roll back into my head. Bay doesn't understand what the consequences of saying no would be. Ian would decide I wasn't taking my career seriously and favour another model and stop working so hard to get me work. End of. Literally. I can't say this to Bay because I don't like admitting to caring about modelling. It's not cool to take it seriously. As a model, you kind of have to act as though you're just really super-lucky to be working, as though there's no intelligent thought that goes into it. Not so. I feel more like a business partner with Ian. We plot and plan the next move: which jobs to take, which jobs to turn down, shaping a brand for me. It's fun and exciting. I don't want to let him down. He has a vision for me. It's why I could never make a big thing of the Francis Ray issue. If I caused a fuss, I'd be labelled forever as the girl who brought Francis Ray down, instead of a model in my own right. 'It's the way of the world, princessa,' Ian said and then he told me some horrendous stories of homophobic abuse that he and his long-term partner had endured from angry white men over the years.

Out of the cab window, the skyline is dotted with red crane lights. London is always twinkling and awake.

I can't wait until I'm old enough to live here. I will be able to have parties and stay up late and eat whatever I like. Nobody will be breathing down my neck. Mum has been on my case solidly. I could have killed Bay for telling her about Francis Ray, but I learned my lesson. She can't be trusted. I don't tell her anything secret these days, fully aware that she's Mum's spy. Now I've got Ian *and* Bay monitoring me at parties. I'm the safest sixteen-year-old in London!

The car pulls up at the club. We pass the bouncer and go through a velvet curtain and down some stairs to the basement. The corridor is covered in flock wallpaper and black-and-white photographs, like it's some old country house. There is a lady on a stool in the toilets who offers us perfume and deodorant and mints. In the main room, the tables are cramped together. The candles on the tables are the only light. The dance floor is at the end of the long room and is currently empty. Brown mirror panels cover the DJ box and old nineties club anthems are playing.

When Ian greets us and shows us to our table, I notice that almost every single guest is a white man in a tuxedo. I look around me at other tables and recognise a couple of models from the circuit dotted about like decorations. I'd guess about seventy-five per cent of the men are over fifty and a hundred per cent of the females are under twenty-five with above-average looks.

After my argument with Mum tonight, I just want to get drunk and dance.

Over dinner of salmon, Ian introduces me to a guy who works in shipping. He tells me all about his house in Saint-Tropez. Another guy on our table is in PR for a furniture company and speaks with an accent. Another is Lord Something-or-other. His hair is dyed too black.

'End of an era,' he says.

I don't know what he's talking about, but I nod. 'I know, right?'

Every time he fills up his glass, he fills mine up, too. I learn that we are at the last party to be held at the old Annabel's nightclub before it closes its doors forever. The new Annabel's is a few doors down, refurbed, with four floors, a garden terrace and a spa.

'I wish we were at the new Annabel's,' I whisper to Bay.

'It's so seedy here, it's actually funny,' she says. She brings out her new iPhone 11 Pro Max that I pay monthly for her. I've got one too, as part of a deal. They see in the dark.

The old men in tuxedos complain about being filmed at first, but when she invites them to tell her about themselves (aka how they got so rich), they are only too happy to talk.

On the dance floor later, one guy feels up my arse and another dude, who must be about seventy, asks Bay if she wants to go back to his country pad in his helicopter. If we'd wanted to get rich, this would have been the way to go about it.

There are no peng boys tonight. To be honest, I'm only after a solid hairline and some real teeth.

Ian keeps checking on us, making sure we are happy and meeting the right people. God knows what is right about any of this lot. If I am still going nightclubbing at seventy, shoot me, please. Bay basically tells him to his face that the party sucks. I can't even imagine what she'll be telling Mum. The thought annoys me.

'She's here to be papped,' Ian comes back sniffily.

For this same reason, the party invites haven't stopped since the Celeste job two months ago. The Buttercup campaign isn't out until June, but already other high-calibre jobs have been crowding out my chart. This month I've flown to a small island in the Stockholm archipelago for a Swedish catalogue, and gone on the Eurostar to Paris for a French catalogue. I've been to Düsseldorf for the day for a German sunglasses campaign and then straight over to Nice for an advertising job for Italian coffee. The advertising jobs paid good money. Editorial jobs for *Elle* and *Marie Claire* were good coverage, but paid shit money, as do shows. I have only been booked for one show so far. Ian says I'm too commercial for the catwalk. Aka too fat. But the show was good exposure and gained me loads of Insta followers.

Bay takes care of my feed, hashtagging like a pro. She posts behind-the-scenes videos and party shots of me and Leah and Tally, or memes of us doing funny little TikTok dance routines. My account helps her to build a following on her own new Instagram account, @BayShoots, which is super-slick. All the posts are flattering black-and-white pap shots of models and actors at the parties we go to. She is already at 5.5K followers.

The Easter holidays begin next week. I have promised myself I'll get serious about my revision and make up for failing my mocks. The parent-teacher evening last term was a wake-up call. I was not getting away with the juggling. All the teachers said they were disappointed and that I had been distracted and that my poor attendance was leaving gaps in my learning. It's going to be hard work to turn it around, not helped by Ian calling every day dangling jobs and parties in my face, but I know I have to get my GCSEs. After that, I can start modelling full-time. I haven't told Mum yet, but I don't see the point in A levels any more, not when I'm earning already.

Amber, one of the models at the Shoreditch flat, has gone back to the States, leaving Bay and me a room to crash in whenever we need it. Leah and Tally come to most of the parties with me, and Bay comes to a fair few when Leah and Tally are on jobs abroad. She films everything, even in the mornings, when I'm smoking outside on the balcony with my cup of coffee before breakfast. Black coffee is my new thing. It means I eat less. It is my only dieting tip. I've lost a stone without really trying. Ian is over the moon. And it helps on jobs. The clothes fit me these days. Mum worries I've lost too much weight, but I think it was just puppy fat, and I don't obsess about my body too much.

The new gym I've joined is a waste of money. I seem to get away with it by eating less chocolate and having low-sugar mixers in my drinks when we are out-out. And I dance loads. If you think about it, dancing for three hours straight, two or three nights a week, is probably a better workout than a boring old treadmill. The important thing is, I'm not anorexic. Not like Tally, who is getting thinner by the week. I worry about her, and Leah does too. Leah eats super-healthy food, like smoothies and nut butter and bone broth, and every day she goes to a Pilates or yoga class, or she swims or goes jogging. Weirdly, Tally always says she is starving hungry when we go to Five Guys, and orders the biggest burger with all the cheese and bacon and everything, and then she takes a few tiny nibbles and leaves the rest. One time we tried to talk to Ian about Tally's weight. He said he would have a word with her about it, but I'm not sure he did.

Bay taps me on the shoulder. 'I want to leave.'

It's true that this party is lame, but I don't want to go back to the flat yet. I want to drink and dance some more. Ian mentioned some after-party somewhere and I want to go to that. It is so much more fun going out with Tally and Leah. Like me, they never want to stop. All-nighters are the norm. Out-out doesn't feel out-out enough until we see that blue light of morning filter through the windows.

'Just a bit longer.'

'No,' she says. 'I'm going now.'

'You can't leave without me!'

'I'm totally over it,' she says.

'You mean you've got what you needed for your stupid film.' I point at her phone.

'Yeah, I've got what I needed. But also, this party sucks.'

'Ian said there's an after-party at the casino on the other side of the square that'll be super-fun.'

'A casino? Seriously? You're only sixteen, Nell.'

Going home is not an option. I do not want the night to end. I never want any night to end.

'Ian said there'll be people there I should meet.'

Bay rolls her shoulders back and cricks her neck to the side and says casually, 'You know, Ian's basically your pimp.'

I want to punch her in the stomach. 'Fuck off, Bay.'

'Happily,' she says. I really regret saying it when she turns on her heel and disappears through the velvet curtain, knowing she'll go back and tell Mum everything. I stand there like a wally for a minute, not sure what to do. I decide not to run after her.

Money is an issue, though. I check my purse for cash, take another glass of champagne and look for Ian. So much for being the safest teenager in London!

When I can't find him, I go up to the terrace for a fag. It's nippy. I can feel that horrible weird tingle along the bones of my ribcage, as though the games Bay played are still there inside me, like a ghost rattling chains. I look around me. There is a guy smoking a cigar. He is tanned and good-looking – for an old guy, at least. I ask him for a light.

The old guy lives in a mansion flat in Earl's Court. Everything smells expensive and my handbag looks cheap on his sofa. He tells me he is forty and I tell him I'm nineteen. We both know the other is lying.

When we do it, he snorts and groans. I just lie there. I've only done it three times before. Twice with Lee and once with a photographer's assistant on the Swedish job.

I leave before Old Guy wakes up. He would not be sad about it, believe me.

When I get back to the model flat in Shoreditch, Bay has gone home already.

I have a quick catch-up over breakfast with Leah, who is the only one awake, and then I leave.

On the train, I feel really dirty and smelly, like a wino tramp. My eyes hurt and I regret sleeping with the old guy. I have no idea why I did it. Maybe I was on a mission to have fun because I know I have months of revision ahead.

I'm dreading going home. Bay will be smug, probably making Mum a smoothie right now, and Dad will be cowering from Mum's mood. Iris, bless her heart, is the only one I can still stand. I can't wait to see her funny little face and give her a hug. I've bought her a present from Hamleys at the train station. It's a Grumpy Cat cuddly toy, and it is super-soft.

The woman opposite me is reading a book and keeps looking up at me. I check my face to see if my mascara has run or something. When I look at the black bits of old make-up in the corners of my eyes and the red scratch marks around my lips from all the kissing, I suddenly want to cry. Wow, I look like shit.

My phone flashes. There is a text from Ian and a shitty Snap from Bay. I ignore them both and scroll down to find Matthew's deets, knowing he's home for the Easter break.

Hi, M&M, fancy a Coke this afternoon after I've finished my revision? Nx

I plan to have a nap and then work hard and prove to Mum that I can go to parties *and* pass my GCSEs.

Matthew texts back straight away.

What about a ride?
Still okay to borrow your mum's bike?
Of course.
Thnx. See u by the swings.
I smile. Matthew always makes me feel like me again.

CHAPTER FORTY-TWO

Anna

Bay was making me a smoothie with avocados and bananas and spinach.

'Was Ian at this party?' I asked her, taking a sip of strong coffee, gathering as much information as I could before I called Billy.

'Yeah. His friend organised it. He's some magazine guy.'

'Also over fifty?'

'Ha. Yes.'

'Why does Ian think Nell should be going to all these parties?'

'There are pap photographers there. They take shots for the society pages in magazines.'

'And that's good, is it?'

'Ian seems to think so.'

Bay fired up the blender. 'I'm so sorry I couldn't persuade her to come home last night,' she said.

'Don't blame yourself,' I told her. 'I'm the one who should be feeling bad about all this.'

I was feeling bad about shouting at Nell yesterday and bad about arguing with Dom and bad about what I was going to do this afternoon.

'Anna, you shouldn't feel bad about anything,' Bay said, pouring out the green sludge into two tall glasses. 'Nell was being a nightmare yesterday.'

I appreciated hearing it, in a guilty sort of way. Though I couldn't absorb it with an authentic sense of self-righteousness. Everyone was right about the shouting. It didn't work. But I had another plan, a sneakier plan, that I thought might prove more effective.

I took a sip of the smoothie, which tasted sweeter than it looked.

I told Dom I was going for a walk, on my own, to sort my head out. He didn't mind. The household was relatively peaceful for a Sunday afternoon. Irritatingly, Nell had come home and knuckled down to work this morning without me nagging her, proving Dom's point. But I didn't care how it had happened, as long as she was revising.

My phone was in the pocket of my cardigan, weighing it down and bumping on my thigh. I moved it to the back pocket of my jeans, but then worried about butt-dialling someone. All they would hear would be the brush of my feet on the leaves and the coo of a wood pigeon, and they might hear my breathing. Perhaps my breathing would be more revealing than a stolen snippet of conversation. My breaths were short, pushed up high in my chest by the crowd of butterflies in my stomach.

I took my phone out of my back pocket and pressed send on WhatsApp for an audio call. It amazed me that it cost nothing to call someone in New York. It brought to mind the landline calls that my brother and I had been allowed to make to Australia three times a year – at Christmas and on our birthdays. Mum would hover over us, counting the minutes, counting the pennies, counting the cost of hearing the distant love in our father's voice.

Four rings later, I had decided it was a bad idea. Fifth ring. Too late. He was there and I was huffing up a hill. Why had I called him on the way up a hill?

'Are you running?' he said, laughing, straight in, not even a 'Hi, Anna'.

'Sorry... I'm just...' I puffed. 'I'm... walking... up a hill.'

'Are you okay?'

'I'm fine, I'm just really unfit.'

'I meant, are you okay in yourself?'

'Oh, sorry, I thought you were worried I was dying of a heart attack.'

'Should I be?'

'Possibly,' I chortled, puffing some more, stopping to catch my breath.

'Last time we spoke, you were in a terrible state. I've been worried about you.'

He had no idea how many times I had resisted calling him.

'Sorry. No need to worry. Well, you know, I'm fine. Sorry.'

'You're sorry twice.'

'Doubly sorry for worrying you.'

'I'm glad you're okay.'

'I'm fine. Sort of. I was actually calling because I wondered if you'd be able to find something out about someone.'

'That sounds shady.'

'Ha. It is, a little.'

I reached the top of the hill and gazed across the panorama. The early-evening sun topped the trees. Life felt more manageable when I was contemplating the beauty of this view.

'Who?'

'Ian. Crosbie. At Take One Model Management. He's Nell's booker.'

'I thought you said she was doing really well.'

'She is. Well, the modelling is going well, but I got the impression Nell's being put under way too much pressure to go to all these parties, and something doesn't feel right about it.'

'In what way?'

'I'm probably overthinking it.'

'Where did the overthinking lead you?'

I couldn't say my suspicions out loud, knowing they might put Nell in a bad light.

'Nowhere really. I just don't trust Ian's influence any more. I never really did, I suppose.'

'Sure, I'll do some digging for you. I know a few people who might give me some info.'

'Thanks, Billy. I'm sure it's nothing,' I added, wanting to move on quickly, feeling dirtied by my request. 'How are you?' I asked him.

He paused. Then he sighed and said, 'Actually, I'm feeling a bit shit, as you're asking.'

I imagined his large hands, like plates, turned upwards on his knees, and the tattoo of me on his thick forearm, delicate across his pulsing veins. A gentle giant.

'Oh no. Why? What's going on?' I couldn't bear hearing the sadness in his voice.

'I just spoke to my little Dixie.'

'Shouldn't that make you happy?'

'It's just, she's growing up so fast and I'm not there. It's like I'm such a shit parent and I always promised I'd never be shit like my parents were, you know?'

'Of course you're not shit,' I said, knowing he couldn't possibly be. No more than the rest of us, anyway. I wondered what had gone so wrong with Dixie's mum. To be separated from his daughter like that, something very bad must have happened.

'Joy said they were only flying to London for a few weeks. But it's been a bloody year. On and off.'

I couldn't imagine having missed out on the girls' lives at that age and for that long. 'Can't the courts do anything?'

'We weren't married. We just kinda randomly shared Dixie, week on, week off, and any evenings in between. When Joy had a film, I'd take Dixie when she was shooting, and it always used to work. But now, it's not working for sure. For me or Dixie.'

'I'm so sorry.' But I wasn't sorry he hadn't married Dixie's mother.

'I've flown over to London a few times now, to see Dixie, but also 'cos I wanna talk to Joy, to suss it out. Every time, she swears they're coming home.'

'Do you believe they will?' I wanted to know more; I wanted to know everything.

'She's kept the sublet in Brooklyn on, which is good, I reckon. And in London, they're still at her mate's house in the spare room and she hasn't yet found a flat to rent. Which I guess means she's not putting roots down yet.'

'It's awful that she's stringing you along like that. It must be very unsettling for Dixie.'

'Yeah. And then Dixie mentioned some English bell-end who took them to the park, and I'm thinking that's why Joy's dragging out her stay, because of him.'

'And if she does?' My heartbeat stopped, not for long enough to kill me, but almost.

'It'll change everything,' he sighed. 'Everything.'

I began my descent down the other side of the hill.

'You'll want to be near her.'

'Yes. I'd have to move back to London.'

My stomach turned over. London was much closer than New York. Too close.

'And give up your salon?'

'What choice is there?'

My cheeks burned. Years ago, he had chosen New York over me. But love for a daughter was different. Missing Dixie's childhood wasn't a choice.

'It's so unfair of Joy to put you in that position.'

'I understand she has to find happiness too. She's not a bad person.'

'A selfish person, maybe?' I suggested.

He laughed. 'She *is* an actress.'

'Say no more.'

He chuckled.

'What hats have you made this week?' he asked.

'Another pillbox for a funeral and a gorgeous wide-brim for a mum at school.'

'Send me pictures.'

'You don't really want to see them.'

'I do, actually.'

I was so pleased, I didn't notice a low branch and it whipped my cheek. Punishment for too keenly enjoying his interest in my hats.

'Do you have time to make any for yourself?'

'No chance.'

'You always looked great in a hat.'

I could not hear his flattery without a sense of falling. It was my ego, perhaps, that fell for his praise. I thought of Ava. Her sister's funeral had been held at Grayswood church and I had stood at the back behind the baptismal font. Seeing her wearing my creation had been the only upside to the early return from New York. She had teamed it with an ankle-length green shift dress, unlike any of the colourful clothes she wore around the village, and the hat had said everything it needed to say about her love for her sister. Its controversial history, its two fingers to convention, its lack of sentimentality, its flamboyance. None of its success had been my doing. Ava had brought me the props of her life and I had fixed them in place. If Dom had praised me for it, what would it have meant? I hadn't made it for praise; yet, I admit, it would feel nice to receive it from Billy. Each hat had some of me in its brim. I might send him a photo of Ava. Just one.

'I'd better get going, Billy. Thanks so much for helping me out on the Ian front. I'll call you.'

'You sound like an American cop show. "Don't call me, I'll call you",' he said. I smiled to myself.

'It's just easier,' I said.

'You're allowed to talk to old friends, you know.'

'Old friends,' I repeated.

'I'm not about to steal you away,' he added.

I was glad he hadn't said 'from Dom'. Saying his name out loud would have brought him into being between us, in a very sticky and guilt-inducing way. At the same time, I felt a sharp pang of disappointment. If Billy forcefully stole me away from Dom, I wouldn't then have to feel responsible for the ransacked life I left behind.

'Keep me posted about Dixie, too,' I said.

'Next time I'm in London, we should hook up.'

'Hmm. Okay. Lovely. Bye, Billy.'

'Wait. If I can't call you, how will you know when I've found out something about Ian Crosbie?'

'Text me.'

'Texting is okay?'

'Yeah, sure. Bye, Billy. Speak soon.'

'I'll text you,' he said.

'Yes, cool. Okay, bye.'

'Bye.'

'Bye,' I said, hanging up finally.

We had never been good at goodbyes. His final goodbye had torn my heart from its veins, violently and ruthlessly; detaching it from me as he walked through the departure gates, taking it with him, bloody in his hands, expecting me to stay alive without it.

I had. And here I was.

When I emerged onto the lane and passed the green, I could see Nell and Matthew sitting on the swings together drinking Coke, just as they had when they were little. It was a good sign, a small glimmer of hope that she wasn't lost to us yet. Not yet.

I still had time.

How long would it be before Billy texted me with news about Ian?

Now that I had a proper plan of action, I felt fired up, as though I had some power left and could stop Nell from getting into more trouble. And I would be waiting every minute of every day to hear.

CHAPTER FORTY-THREE

Nell

Matthew props up his bike on the railings and hands me a perfectly chilled can of Coca-Cola from his rucksack.

'Hi,' he says.

'Hi, how's it going?'

It feels majorly awks between us. We haven't seen each other in ages. The last time he came down from Sheffield, we didn't hook up. That kiss last summer changed us, even though we swore it wouldn't. Secretly, I even worried that it was the reason he broke up with Belinda over Christmas. Trouble is, I think we both knew that the kiss, and my confession about Bay, meant something big but that we weren't quite up for finding out exactly what. Correction, I wasn't.

'You know,' he opens his can, 'the usual.'

Trouble is, I never know what 'the usual' is for Matthew. He keeps his cards close to his chest.

'Mum's been on my case,' I say.

'Uh-huh.'

'She is really doing my head in.'

'Hmm.'

'She doesn't understand anything.' I begin coughing. I'm better, but my cough is lingering, to use Mum's word.

'Good night last night?' he asks.

'Brilliant.' I shiver.

'You hung-over?'

'Do I look it?'

'Kind of.'

'Thanks.'

'The hair gives it away.'

'What do you mean?'

I didn't look in the mirror before I left the house. He reaches out to my head, and I jerk back from him.

'Sorry, it's just you have a massive bird's nest,' he says, pulling back his hand.

'Attractive,' I say, coughing, tugging at it and then pulling my hood over my head.

'You get away with it,' he says. He sips his drink and watches me with that look of his. It is the look that transforms him from being a geeky strawberry-blond dude to being the sexy, all-knowing guy I want to kiss again. But I've got to stop kissing guys. Then again, Matthew is different.

'Wanna head to the dirt jumps?' I ask.

'Sure.' He hands me my helmet.

We don't talk about anything on the way. On bikes, you can just ride and not talk. The worn rubber of the grips feels like an old friend. I've missed the speed and the lightness in my chest and the lift of my tummy on the bumps.

When we get there, we prop our bikes on the fallen oak tree and sit on it as we watch two boys trying to get some air over the earth mounds and failing.

Matthew says, 'For every action, there is an equal and opposite reaction.'

'I learned that in physics.'

'Newton's third law of motion. In every interaction, there is a pair of forces acting on the two interacting objects.'

'Uh-huh.'

'Basically, you only get out what you put in.'

Somehow I get the message that we are not just talking about the kids on the bikes. 'You just have to pedal a bit faster, that's all.'

I take out my fags and light one. The nerve endings across my ribcage prickle. It's the chill of the woods. Whenever it is cold, I can feel those tiny, horrible scars.

Matthew carries on staring at the cyclists.

'I dissected the lungs of a dead smoker in a hospital mortuary once. They were completely black.'

'Good to know,' I say.

'If you stopped smoking, your cough would go.'

One of the boys falls off. We both suck in our breath, and I jump up. The boy dusts himself off and gets back on his bike, and I sit down.

'If you hadn't gone into aeronautical engineering, what would you be?' I ask Matthew, out of the blue. I'm not sure why I'm asking him. I guess I'm wondering if he is doing what he really wants to do or whether he is under pressure from Viv.

'I'm studying *biomedical* engineering, Nell.'

'Whoops. I knew that.' I laugh. 'Seriously, though, if you could have any job in the world.'

'I don't know. I've never thought about it.'

I am a bit disappointed. Where is his imagination? He can be very one-track about life. 'We're so different,' I say.

'Why is it we're friends again?'

We laugh. It is a running joke between us.

'I can be very clever too. Actually, like today, let me tell you, I drank loads of coffee and studied really hard.'

'Just today?'

I flick my cigarette away. 'Don't you frickin' start.'

'Start what?'

'Go on at me about how shit I am.'

'Okay. If you're not in the mood today.'

I hide my smile from him and swing my legs over and slide down to the other side of the log, out of sight. Matthew follows suit. The ground is cold on my bum. He pulls a woolly hat from his pocket and offers it as a cushion to sit on.

'I'm not going to fail my GCSEs, you know, I'm not an idiot.'

'You failed your mocks.'

'Ugh. Shut up, Matthew.'

I go to hit him, playfully, but he catches my arm and holds it up in the air and stares right into my eyes, and our hands slide together and interlace. He rests them on his thigh. I put my head on his shoulder.

'I'm earning loads of money,' I say, wanting to explain.

'Good to know,' he says, mimicking me, taking the piss.

'Seriously, though, Ian says the parties are like castings. You have to be seen around.'

'I literally know nothing about that.'

'Are you saying that for the first time in my life I know more than you about something?'

'You know more than me about a lot of things.'

I want to cancel out the horrible kisses in Earl's Court with the old guy, and I lean in to kiss Matthew. And then the worst happens. He turns away and my lips meet his cheek.

'Pffft! Okay, fine,' I say, pulling my hand out of his and taking out another fag.

He jumps up and brushes the leaves off his bum, missing a few that stick out from the backs of his knees.

'You asked me just now what I would be if I could have any job in the world, and I said I didn't know, but I do know. I would be a biomedical engineer. Every time. That's what I'd be. Nothing exciting like a photographer or a fashion designer or a film director,' he says, angrily. 'Just a boring old scientist.'

'Okaaay? Scientists are cool.'

'Come on, put that thing out. Let's go.'

'You go, I'm fine.'

'No, Nell, you're not fine.'

'I'm totally fine.' I throw his woolly hat at him.

He stretches it and kneads it in his hands like it is dough.

'You used to care about yourself.'

I take a long drag of my cigarette. 'I've got too many other people doing that for me right now.'

There is a squeak of bike brakes and a roar of laughter from one of the boys.

Then Matthew asks, 'How's Bay?'

I press my cigarette out into the ground and think about her leaving me at the party last night. 'She's okay most of the time, and then out of the blue she can be a total bitch.' Before he can respond, I say, 'I didn't mean that. We're just fighting a lot these days, that's all.'

'You are allowed to say bad stuff about her,' he says, picking up my fag butts and folding them into a tissue from his pocket.

Without his woolly hat, I feel the damp seep through to my pants. I put my forehead on my knees and feel like crying. 'Mum thinks she's so frickin' perfect.'

He sits on the log behind me and touches my shoulder for a second.

I tell him a few of the recent stories about Bay. The film she made that ruined my sixteenth. Telling Dad stuff she swore she wouldn't tell (I haven't told Matthew about Francis Ray). Hassling me about the parties. And last night, when she effectively told me I was a dirty-ass ho.

'You know you have to tell your mum what you told me last summer.'

My face goes hot. I wish I hadn't told him that.

'Or I could just ride it out until she leaves home?' I laugh, even though it is really unfunny.

'You think it's all going to go away because she leaves home?'

'She was just a kid. It's in the past.'

'But can't you see it, Nell? Everything you've just told me about is recent. She's still doing it to you now.'

'What can I do about it, though? Stop modelling to make her happy? I know that's what she wants.'

'It's not the modelling,' he laughs. 'It's Anna!'

This stops the breath from moving down into my chest for a minute. What he's implying shocks me, and I want to cover over his words right away.

'Bloody hell, she can have her.' And I meant it. Just looking at Mum gives me rage these days.

'Remember, Bay was rejected by her real mother.'

'But Mum loves her! So much! Just as much as she loves me!'

'That can't be true, Nell. I wish it could be, but it's not realistic,' he says, really quietly and certainly, and I don't like it.

'I'm sorry, okay? I had all the luck, did I? What am I supposed to do about that?' I yell.

Matthew gets down on his knees and holds mine.

'You have to tell Anna about what Bay did to you. It's eating you both up. It's why you're fighting all the time and it'll only get worse. Telling your mum is the only way you'll heal, and it's the only way that Bay will be able to sort herself out and deal with her feelings.'

I look up at him, suddenly furious.

'I can't do that, Matthew. Bay's a fuck-up, but she's my sister and I love her.'

He stands up and jams his hands in his coat pockets. 'Just make sure you don't become a fuck-up too.'

'Jesus Christ. I only wanted a fag and a bit of fun,' I say, mean as hell, standing up, grabbing my bike and pedalling off, the wheels wobbling over a tree root.

He calls out after me. 'You should know by now, I don't *do* fun!'

'No kidding!' I shout back.

'In fact, you should know that I don't want any fun at all, especially from you.'

I put the brakes on. 'Sorry, *what*?'

'I hate fun with you.'

I want to cry, but I bite the side of my mouth. 'Okay, dude, you've made your point,' I say.

He opens his mouth to speak, but I don't want to hear it. I cut him off before he has a chance. 'You were right before. How are we even friends? We literally have *nothing* in common.'

That stops him from saying anything else to upset me. That shows him.

I give him back his mum's stupid bike and run all the way home. My chest hurts. I slam the front door, slam my bedroom door and put my music on really loud. Nothing makes sense any more. Everything is shit.

CHAPTER FORTY-FOUR

Bay

I was filming under the table. This documentary had taken over my whole life, even over my schoolwork. Revision had become like a mechanical exercise. I got it done so that I could go back to my film. I was obsessed; obsessed with what my phone was capturing. Nell didn't always like me accompanying her to parties, but she knew it was the only way Anna would allow her out. We had fun together, too. We were like partners in crime, and I was the undercover cop.

A man's hand squeezed Nell's knee and she didn't swipe it off. It belonged to the man – not a boy, a man – to her right whom Ian had introduced her to a few months back. His name was Marco and I suspected he was after her, but I didn't like him and I wanted to find out how involved they were. He was good-looking in a greasy way. He had a square, short face, with a widow's peak and hair tucked behind his ears. His two-tone tracksuit was designer but too relaxed for the restaurant, for a birthday party, for his age. He could not take his eyes off Nell.

She looked especially beautiful tonight. The blonde of her hair had been lightened one shade for a job and her fringe was heavy on her eyelashes, tousled, the rest long and thick, tumbling around her shoulders. Her new gold chain dangled into her cleavage and her eyeliner stroke was brushed up in line with her cheekbones. Her laughter was all over the room.

I thought of her at home, cross-legged on her bed, picking old chocolate off her track pants and talking about the spot on her chin or what silly item she'd ordered from Pretty Little Thing, and I felt less jealous. These men did not know Nell in the way that I knew her. They never would.

'Nell's going to be in my book,' Marco said.

'Yeah?' I said. I looked around the restaurant, as though there might be someone else more interesting to talk to. Our long table was scattered with espresso cups and plates scraped of desserts. At the head, there was Ian, the birthday boy, neat in his tight shirt and belt. Under the downlighters, his large glasses left strange shadows playing across his face. His smile, with the pointed incisors, brought character to his characterless face – unpleasant character.

'Do you want to be in my book too, Bay?' Marco asked me.

I sipped my wine. 'What kind of book is it?'

'A coffee-table book.'

I directed my question at Nell. '*Do* I want to be in his book?'

'No, sis, you'd rather die than be in it. *I* would rather die than be in it,' Nell said.

I'm intrigued. 'Why?' I asked.

'It's basically posh porn,' Nell said.

'Harsh!' Marco said. 'I like to call it art.'

'I'd rather die than be in your book, Marco,' I said to Marco, deadpan.

'Damn, these sistahs are brutal.' He clicked his tongue at me.

'Do you want to be in my documentary film?' I asked.

He looked at Nell. '*Do* I want to be in her film, Nell?'

'Yeah, sure,' Nell said. 'She'll be famous one day.'

'Interview me now,' Marco said. He sat up straight and pulled out his gold chain – a chunkier version of Nell's – and organised it over his sweatshirt. He looked shorter sitting up than he had when slouched.

I pressed record and fired off some seemingly boring questions, catching the essential information I needed, building up to the material I wanted. 'What's your name?'

'Marco.'

'Marco what?'

'Just Marco.'

'How old are you?'

'Thirty-two.'

'Where do you live?'

'Leytonstone, born and bred.'

'What do you do, Just Marco?'

'I take photos.'

'What or who did you photograph last?'

He sucked his teeth. 'Oh man, I had the privilege of shooting Abebi.'

'Describe her in one word.'

'Fierce.'

'What did she wear?'

Just Marco hesitated and looked at Nell as he spoke, and I panned to capture both of them – a sixteen-year-old beauty and a short, greasy man twice her age. I knew in that moment that they were dating.

'She wore a leather Egyptian headdress and panties,' he said.

'Where will we see the photographs?'

'*Vogue*. August edition.'

'What was your inspiration?'

'Belly buttons,' he said, straight to camera.

I paused, processing my distaste.

'What is the worst thing that has ever happened to you?'

'My vinyls melting in a house fire.'

'What are you shooting next?'

'Nell Hart.'

My heartbeat sped up. 'For what?'

'The next Gap campaign.'

Nell's eyes widened. 'Shut up, Marco,' she said.

'I'm serious, baby,' he said.

'Thank you, Just Marco,' I said, pressing end.

'Let me know when your film is out,' he said, winking at me.

I knew he had not taken me seriously and yet I knew he would have to when he watched my film. Now that I knew he was dating Nell, I was determined to include him.

'I look forward to reading your book,' I said archly, trusting I would not be seeing my little sister on its pages.

CHAPTER FORTY-FIVE

Nell

Ian and I go outside the restaurant for a smoke.

'Marco's cool, right? He's so *cute*,' Ian says.

Ian knows most things about me now, but he doesn't know I'm sleeping with Marco. Nobody knows. Not officially. Marco doesn't want anyone to know. Because of my age.

'You know, he joked about using me for the Gap campaign,' I say.

'Oh yeah?' Ian's blue eyes flash at me through his glasses and he grins his toothy grin. I wonder if he knows about Gap already.

'He was only joking, I think,' I say carefully.

'He wouldn't joke about that.'

'Really?'

'Why is it so hard to believe?'

'Dunno.'

'I hope your sister isn't feeding you too much anti-fashion propaganda.'

'She's so embarrassing.'

'Don't be scared of success, Nell Hart.'

'Bay says success is a subjective thing.'

'Hmm.' He rests the point of his elbow into the palm of his hand and blows smoke into the night above us. 'My idea of success is fame and money.' He cackles.

I laugh too. 'That doesn't sound all bad for a small-town girl like me.'

He eyes me up, squinting at me. 'Are you and Marco dating?'

'What? No!'

'Oh my God. You're lying. You *are* dating!'

'We're not!'

'You are the worst liar ever.'

'Don't say anything to him. And don't you dare mention it to Bay.'

'I won't, hon. You can trust me. I introduced you guys at the gallery thing because I just totally knew you'd vibe on each other.'

'Really?'

'I'm going to talk to him about your career and how we can shape it together.'

'That's cringey.'

'It's my job, Nellie. I'll do anything for you, you know that.' He stubs out his cigarette.

'Bay and I have to get going. I promised Mum we'd catch the last train home,' I say.

Bay will make sure of it. This film of hers is becoming a pain in the arse.

'You have exams next week, is that right, sweetie?' Ian says.

'Thursday.'

'You must study hard, promise?'

'I will.' I've been trying to revise. It has been hard to concentrate.

'If you don't, your mum and Bay will hunt me down and pull out my guts and I'll never be able to make you famous.'

If Ian was a doll with a pull-cord on his back, he wouldn't say 'Mama! Mama!' but 'I'll make you a star! I'll make you a star!'

'Mum's so embarrassing.'

'She's just looking out for you,' he says. 'Let's talk about Marco. Have you seen his work?'

'Yeah, some of it.'

I've flicked through every single one of the contact sheets lying around at his house and I've stalked him on Insta, wanting to stab out the eyes of all the beautiful girls he shoots with. He has posted lots of photos of his supermodel ex-girlfriend. They are friends still, apparently, even though she is half-naked in all his photographs. Most of his models are half-naked. In a beautiful, arty way. I wonder which girls he'll be using for his coffee-table book. He really wants me to be in it and I have said no way. He says the images will be anonymous. I guess I'm still considering it, only because nobody will know it's me. And because, you know, I am so in love with him and everything.

'It'll be my new mission, to get you two working together,' Ian says, taking my arm and leading me back inside, adding, 'He's doing this amazing coffee-table book. Has he told you about it yet?'

CHAPTER FORTY-SIX

Anna

A May shower sprayed the panels of glass above my head. Working in the conservatory should have been a welcome distraction from the recent stresses. It wasn't. My commission bored me and my worries about Nell returned to me like a heavy sack of rubbish I'd thrown out. She'd promised me her first few GCSE exams had gone well, but I couldn't take her word for it. When I bumped into other mothers in town, they talked of their children's high anxiety levels and of their worry about the amount of time they were shut in their bedrooms. One mum talked of providing cups of sugary tea and home-made cake when her son took revision breaks. Another described how her daughter had sobbed the night before her maths exam, panicking that she hadn't done enough. I could only stand there and nod, and pretend to relate to them, quietly wishing that Nell had panicked enough to sob. I couldn't admit that she was barely at home, let alone in her room, and that I had zero control over her comings and goings.

I stared down at the gaudy fabric in front of me. I had no clue why I had said yes to making this dreadful hat for a friend-of-a-friend's daughter. It was for a school play, and the girl, who had the main part, had very specific requirements about colour and style. Last week, carried away by her bullish ambition, I had even made a special trip to Luton to buy some sinamay and some more ferrules. Now it felt like self-flagellation.

Just as I was pinning four layers of pink fabric to my hat block, my phone buzzed. A text from Billy flashed up and I pricked my finger, making it bleed.

Hi, Anna, sorry for the delay. Due diligence wasn't as simple as I'd thought. But I've got something on him. Call me. Billy

A thud of fear landed in my gut. My hunch about Ian might be right. I looked at the clock. Iris's school pick-up was in half an hour. I wasn't sure there was enough time to call Billy. There would have to be enough time. I couldn't wait a second longer.

He cut straight to it. 'Sorry it's taken so long. First I called a photographer friend and he asked around for me, but he took ages to get back to me and then all he told me was that Ian is known for being ambitious and for having a good eye for a girl who might make it big, and for getting them young. But there was no controversy to speak of.'

I fiddled with a circle of wire in front of me.

'But then I spoke to a make-up artist mate, Tracy. She's amazing and gets on really well with the models and she—'

'Make-up artists are always the loveliest on the jobs,' I said, interrupting, delaying Tracy's story, terrified of hearing it, knowing I had to. I stared at my table, littered with thread and glue and scissors and cling film and blocking pins and pliers, wishing I could get back to the spoiled girl's hat.

'You'd love Tracy. She's hilarious. And kind, which is why this Scottish girl opened up to her, I guess. It was a few years back, and apparently the girl just broke down in tears about her bad skin, and Trace took her into the loos and the poor girl went on to say she was exhausted all the time and that Ian was pressurising her to go to all these parties, saying they would make or break her career.'

'Yes. That sounds familiar.'

'Also, some guy Ian introduced her to started calling her all the time and asking her out and she kept saying no, but Ian was saying it would be a mistake if she turned him down, and the girl was desperate to work. She was only just eighteen, seriously broke and a long way away from home. But she said she didn't want to go out to dinner with him and Ian apparently dropped her from the agency. She said Ian was pimping her out like a prostitute. Exact words, apparently.'

Fear crawled through my insides. 'That's appalling.'

'I thought so too.'

Francis Ray had been an introduction through Ian. Had there been design in that meeting, beyond her modelling career advancement? If so, did it mean there were other men like him? Her new boyfriend was called Marco, but that was all we knew. Now I wanted to know how old he was.

'Is it normal for a booker to put pressure on models to go out all the time for the sake of their careers?'

'No, It's not normal. I dated an ex-model once and she was great friends with her booker. She liked the fact that Penny slept well before jobs, for obvious reasons.'

'Yes, Nell looks like shit, quite honestly.' I didn't mention her hacking cough, which worried me more.

'Her booker should be looking after her. Defending her from creeps like that photographer you told me about. Penny's booker was ferocious if someone didn't treat her right on a job.'

'When we first met Ian, he said he'd be like a second mother to Nell.'

'Ha! She shouldn't need a second mother.'

'That's what I thought,' I murmured, though I wasn't so sure any more. She might actually need a second mother, a better mother, a mother who had been more ferocious and denied her the so-called opportunity of modelling. In Billy's eyes, I must seem useless.

'I mean, this is just one girl's account. It doesn't necessarily mean he's a bad guy.'

'But her story is so similar to Nell's. Apart from the fact that Nell loves the parties.'

'Which she might have been into anyway, whether she'd started modelling or not.'

'Yes,' I said. He was trying to make me feel better for making a decision that both of us knew had been the wrong one. 'What do I do now?' I literally had no idea.

'Maybe she could switch agencies?'

'I'll definitely have a go, but she's so bloody attached to Ian.'

'Hmm. Especially while she's making so much money.'

I let my head hang back and saw the cobwebs worked into the corners of the conservatory frame. I never liked to break up cobwebs, knowing they were a spider's home. Or had been. The heavy grey dust that clung to each strand suggested the spider was long gone. 'I'm going to have to talk to her.'

'She may want to talk to you about it, you never know.'

'You never know,' I repeated. I would try. What else could I do?

'I'll be in London next week,' Billy said. 'We could get Tracy and Nell together.'

'That might be a bit heavy-handed at this stage,' I admitted. 'I'm going to try talking to her first.'

'Yes.'

I waited for more.

'Well, good luck with it.'

'Thanks.' I wanted him to stay on the line.

There was a pause. 'Okay then. Keep me posted.'

My heart sank. I felt so alone.

'I will.' I didn't want him to go, but I had no energy to continue the conversation. I had no reserves left beyond my concern for Nell and how I was going to handle the situation. His information about Ian had burrowed into me and was worming about, taking everything I had.

Then Billy surprised me with a question.

'Want a coffee?' he blurted out.

'What?' For a split second – a surreal split second – I imagined him outside the door, holding a steaming mug.

'Next week,' he clarified. 'Just a coffee, while I'm in town.'

Until now, I had failed to register the news of his imminent arrival in the UK. Next week we would be separated by a few miles rather than thousands. A bridgeable gap. A gap that could be closed by one large leap of faith. I didn't have the strength for it.

'I can't. Sorry,' I said, sounding too blunt and more certain than I felt.

'No worries. I understand.'

And then he was gone, and I was late for the school run.

As I sprinted along the pavement, saying hello with big smiles to the stream of mums already holding hands with their children, the blood pumped through me. It seemed I had the energy when I needed it, for the girls, and for Mum, and for Dom, but never for myself.

I interrupted Nell's revision, bringing tea and digestives. I felt shaky and terrified of her reaction.

'Hi, Nell, can we talk?'

'I'm working.'

'Just five minutes.'

She coughed. 'You get angry with me when I don't work, and just when I settle down to it, you disturb me.'

She said it as though it happened all the time. Ignoring her, I sat on the bed, inured to her backchat, focused on what I needed to say. There was a faint whiff of smoke mingled with her sickly body spray.

'I think it's time we went to the doctor about that cough,' I said.

'Is that why you've come up here?'

I hesitated, wondering if I should try again when she was in a better mood. But then when would that be? In the next life?

'No. It's not why I've come up here. I've come to talk to you about Ian.'

She sipped her tea. 'Has he emailed you about a job?'

'No, it's not that,' I said. And I told her the story about the Scottish girl, using the exact words that the girl had used about Ian pimping her out like a prostitute.

Nell's blue eyes widened until they seemed to take up her whole face. 'I can't actually believe you,' she said in a choked-up voice. A tear rolled quickly, almost angrily, down her cheek.

'Oh darling, don't cry,' I said, reaching out to touch her knee. She swivelled away, out of my reach.

'Bay is twisting all this, you know, telling you about the parties we go to and exaggerating everything just to get me in trouble.'

'Bay didn't tell me anything, darling,' I said. Even though that was a lie. Bay had told me plenty about the party at the old Annabel's nightclub.

'Who did then?'

'Just a friend.'

'And you were talking to this "friend" about how awful your daughter was, were you?'

'No, I wasn't,' I said, thinking, *kind of.*

She sniffed, another tear rolling down her face. She wiped it away. 'Your friend is wrong. Ian looks out for me. Maybe he's the only one who does,' she said, looking me straight in the eye, knocking me out with her defiance and loathing.

I was flummoxed. I simply couldn't understand why she continued to be so unbelievably belligerent, but I finally realised there wasn't a damn thing I could do about it. If there was a breaking point, I had just reached it. Having always imagined it would come in the form of a massive hissy-fitting, losing-the-plot, tearing-the-flesh-from-my-bones kind of way, I was surprised that it felt more like a sudden release of responsibility. Like I'd been kicking and screaming to hold onto the back of a moving vehicle with precious cargo inside, and now I'd just let go.

The show of good parenting over the years had turned out to be a series of ghastly, embarrassing flops.

'Okay,' I murmured, as though breathing my last as a good mother. 'I just thought it was important you knew. But, I guess you have to make your own decisions.'

It took an effort to simply stand up, take my mug and put one foot in front of the other to make my way downstairs again.

I poured the cold, grey tea down the sink, feeling battered and hurt and utterly powerless.

I was numb in the aftermath of a catastrophic failure. The years of feeling proud of Nell's charming, spirited personality – as though my nurturing was solely responsible – seemed a distant memory. Praise from teachers, good grades, happy friendships and compliments from other mums about her behaviour at play dates had given me the satisfaction of a job well done, but it had been pride before a fall. My belief that nurture won over nature was coming back to bite me, and it exposed me as a bad parent. While Nell's friends at school were rebelling within the bounds of normal teenage development, going to pubs underage and drinking one bottle of beer too many, Nell was in London at drug- and drink-fuelled nightclubs, coming home smelling of cigarettes and men's bed sheets, and possibly failing the exams she had been destined to excel in. The mistakes I had made were clocking up in my head, one after the other, like a series of fruit machine mismatches. I was bankrupt as a mother. I had not succeeded.

*

Before climbing into bed, I went to say goodnight to Bay. She was propped up in bed with her laptop resting on top of her duvet.

'You still revising?'

'I'm having a break, editing the film for a bit.'

'Don't stay up too late,' I said. I always said this, and I always knew she would ignore my advice. At least she was being productive and dedicated and passionate about a worthwhile project.

She said, 'Don't worry, Anna. Nell will come to her senses. I'll make sure of it.'

I didn't quite know what she meant, but I was too tired to question her further.

'Night, Bay. Love you,' I said, relieved that Dom and I at least had her to remind us that our dedication as parents hadn't bombed entirely.

CHAPTER FORTY-SEVEN

Bay

Nell was kicking her trainers into the side of the bus stop shelter. We were perched on the red bench seat. Oxford Street was filling up with Saturday-afternoon shoppers.

'What's that thing Mum says? You wait half an hour for a number 22 and then four come along at once?'

'It'll be worth the wait,' I said, alert to every single photographic campaign that moved past us on the buses. The thought of seeing Nell, big and bold on the side of one, sent tingles across my skin.

'But we don't even know if we'll see it,' Nell said.

An old lady with a shopper arrived and leant heavily on the handle, sighing. Nell got up and gave the woman her seat. I stood up to join her.

'Dad said he's seen it twice this week on a number 22 and a number 88,' I said, shouting over the sounds of London.

'We could be here all day.' She puffed up her cheeks, almost comically.

'Don't you want to see it?'

Her lack of enthusiasm shouldn't have been a surprise. Anything that wasn't her new boyfriend, Marco, failed to animate her. These days I got the impression she simply tolerated me, which ate into me painfully.

'I've seen the campaign in magazines already,' she said.

'But not on an actual, *real* bus?' I was trying.

''Spose not.'

'Don't worry about it if you want to go,' I said, shrugging, turning away moodily.

'No, I don't want to go.'

'Seriously, I'm sorry if I'm getting overexcited about something that's so bloody boring for you.' I pulled the strap of my canvas bag tighter onto my shoulder and clutched at it, feeling tense and cross.

'It's not that,' she said, texting into her phone.

'I'll get the shot without you in it.'

'Bay. I'm okay about doing it!'

'Fine,' I said. If I had not wanted the shot so badly, I would have told her to piss off.

When the next bus arrived, the bench emptied again. We took up our places in silence.

I had not seen much of Nell over the past month, not since she had started dating Marco. Most weekends she stayed at his house in Stoke Newington, which maddened Anna. During the week, she said she was revising for her GCSEs, often late into the night, but I couldn't guarantee it. Anna said she could have been watching Netflix, for all she knew.

The weekends were different without Nell. Iris was self-sufficient in a way Nell never had been. Reluctant to have strange conversations about the *Beano* or cats, I avoided her. Unlike Nell, who would pore over the comics with her and laugh about the latest antics of the Bash Street Kids or Minnie the Minx.

Anna and I talked a lot over supper about Nell and about Ian and his bad influence on her. Dad ate in silence, zoned out, as though the conversations bored him. Were they repetitive? Yes, I thought, they were. Anna went around in circles, analysing and despairing. It was because she cared. 'Sorry, are we boring you?' she would spit at Dad sometimes. There was tension between them. But lately there was a resigned air to Anna, as though she had given up her attempts to rein Nell in, had given up on trying to lessen the damage, had given up reminding Dad it was all his fault. This defeatism spurred me to do the opposite, but I didn't tell her what I was planning.

'Oh my God! There it is!' Nell cried, leaping up from the bench and out of her stupor.

She beamed at me and I began filming her. The bus approached. *Buttercup* was written in loopy white lettering across the green glass backdrop. Underneath, Nell was laughing in a yellow sundress. Her tanned knees were pulled up to her chin. Red lips. White teeth. Her sparkling blue eyes, fresh and open, smiled out, casting innocence and joy on everyone in Oxford Street. I could almost smell the scent, which Nell never wore, emanating from the stinky old bus. My envy moved inside me, like a shifting animal resettling for sleep.

Nell pointed and yelped. 'There I am!' Her excitement was sweet rather than showing off. A man wearing an eyepatch and carrying a blue plastic bag looked at her with his one weepy eye. In a thick Jamaican accent he said, 'Buttercup! Oh my! Does she like butter?' He chuckled.

Nell laughed. 'Can you believe that's me?' she said, moving to stand next to the old man, as though he were a friend.

The doors to the bus wheezed open and dozens of passengers piled out onto the pavement, oblivious to Nell's face above them.

'Bye, bye, Buttercup!' the old man said as he stepped on.

The bus blundered off, emitting a cloud of fumes.

From behind the camera, I filmed Nell watching it go. Her smile faded as her bright, happy, fixed-forever image rolled off into the distance. She turned back.

'There you go. I'm famous,' she said, shrugging one shoulder up to her ear, matter-of-fact and a little bit sad.

It was the perfect closing shot for my documentary.

'I'll see you at home tomorrow,' she said, kissing my cheeks three times, like the French, and walking off with her overnight bag. I got one more shot of her melting away into the crowd. Just another body among hundreds of others. Nothing special at all.

CHAPTER FORTY-EIGHT

Nell

Marco looks as sexy as hell when he opens the door. He is wearing his vest and tracksuit pants combo. His body is tanned and smooth and hairless.

'Hi, beautiful,' he says. His voice is croaky, as though he has just woken up. His hair is greasy when he pushes it back.

I follow him across the wonky floorboards of his house. It's a Victorian villa. Cool paintings and dangling pot plants and big metal-framed windows. The terrace has a hot tub in one corner, surrounded by potted palm trees and wind chimes and woodchip beds.

He makes coffee and kisses me, putting his hand under my hair at the nape of my neck, giving me a shiver.

He whispers into my ear, even though there is nobody else there. 'I read something that reminded me of us. Come, I'll read it to you.'

The sofa is more like a bed. It has two ends but no back, and tons of cushions. We plant our heads on the bank of cushions at one end, shuffling them about to make it comfy. Marco reaches for a tatty paperback that lies next to the lamp on the side table. It is called *Delta of Venus* by Anaïs Nin. He begins to read.

'Hot, right?' he says, sounding a bit panty, and a bit like the wolf in the extract.

He then takes off my T-shirt and bra top and just stares at me naked, eating me up with his eyes. He makes me feel beautiful. In a dirty way. I want to be crushed under him, like in the book. He takes up his SLR camera and clicks. The flash goes. He scrutinises the picture he just took.

'You can really see them in this,' he says, pointing at the faint pinprick pattern of scars, brought out by the flash, kind of killing the vibe. His hand brushes between and under my breasts, over them, and I shiver, not because I am turned on but because the nerve endings are different there. He takes another photo.

'For my own collection,' he says. He is the only one who has ever touched my scars. He traces his fingers along them but doesn't ask about them. 'They're so strange, like some kind of African tribal marking. Kinda pretty.' I have never offered up an explanation. He might think they are self-harm scars. My body is littered with marks that have healed, which a flash from his fancy camera would not pick up. Only my memory has images of those.

I pull a cushion over myself.

He yanks it out of my hand and throws it across the room.

'Never hide your beauty,' he says.

He reaches for a condom on the coffee table – it's just lying there next to a packet of cigarettes – and puts it straight on, without fully taking off his track pants. Then he pulls my knickers down, slowly, his face near my body, his breath on my inner thighs. He stops and takes up the camera again and kneels back on his haunches. His massive boner is bouncing about while he puts the camera up to his face and points it between my legs. I snap my thighs shut and swing my hips to the side, hiding myself.

'No, Marco. It's not going in your book.'

In one swift move, he lies on top of me, putting the camera down.

'You have to be in it, baby. Nobody will know it's you.'

I now feel grossed out, not turned on. 'Marco, don't force me. I don't want to do it.' He starts kissing me, super-hard, and we have rough sex. It isn't always rough between us. Sometimes he takes hours on me, like I am some kind of fascinating science project, but I get cold when he does this, and I don't like it much.

Afterwards, we potter about, and I wonder if Bay is home yet. She got her shot of me in front of the bus and I did as she asked. Lately, our relationship has become transactional, as though we both need something from each other and accept that it is mutually beneficial. I need her to tag along to parties to keep Mum happy and she needs content for her documentary. There are moments of love between us, but not a lot. She basically thinks Ian is my pimp and that I'm whoring myself about. She won't dare say it again, to my face, like she did at Annabel's that night, but I sense it. I don't feel close to her, not properly. More often than not, I feel physically repelled when she's nearby. But I need her, so I play nice.

'Beer?' Marco asks. And I say yes. This is our routine. His expectations are low, and he's never disappointed in me.

It is a warm day and I stay in my bra and pants. It's liberating, wandering around half-naked, smoking, drinking bottles of beer, having sex every so often. We eat crisps and olives from Moroccan bowls, curled up under a blanket, looking through Instagram together, going through his favourite photography hashtags.

Marco has some pretty wild stories about the industry.

Then we have sex. Again.

Later that afternoon, when Marco invites friends over, we don't act like a couple. Some of them guess something is going on between us, but he never refers to me as his girlfriend, or anything like that, and he never kisses me in front of them.

Because it's a hot afternoon, he takes the cover off the hot tub. A model from another agency steps out of her mini shorts and gets in the water in her knickers. She has crazy falsies like Jade, and I suddenly miss Jade so much I want to cry. I wish there was a button I could press to transport me right now to her messy bedroom, where we could share Doritos and post funny mugshots on the group chats.

Marco persuades me to get into the hot tub with the model. By this point, I have drunk too much champagne, and so I think, why not? I leave my bra on, though. Then Marco gets in. The three of us talk for a bit, but I notice that the girl's breathing changes and I can see, through the bubbles, that the shadow of Marco's hand is between her legs.

Everything stops being fun. I sober up instantly. Without caring what Marco or the girl think, I stand up and climb out, shooting Marco a filthy look. He doesn't come after me. Sopping wet, I get back into my jeans and T-shirt, grab my bag and leave his house.

I'm so upset, I'm shaking all over and start to cry. I text Leah to give her a brief headline and ask her if she and Tally are about. They are the only people in the world I want to see right now.

What a dick! Come over to the flat. We have a surprise visitor Lx

The Tube is swarming with people. I am self-conscious about crying and feel naked in my wet T-shirt, and I'm freezing cold, even though it is a warm evening.

When I get there, I walk in and stop in my tracks. Bay is sitting on the sofa with Leah and Tally.

'What the…?'

'You forgot your train ticket,' Bay says.

'Oh, right. What a shit night.' I rub my face and Leah comes straight over and gives me a hug. Over her shoulder, Bay winks at me kindly.

I guess I'm grateful she has come over, and I'm relieved I don't have to fork out for another train ticket – I have been spending a fortune on train fares recently.

'Tell us exactly what happened with Marco, sweetie,' Leah says.

She sits down cross-legged on the sofa. She's wearing a white V-neck T-shirt tucked into high-waisted super-short shorts. When she tips her head to the side, sympathetically, it looks as though she is also taking the opportunity to stretch out the muscles in her neck.

I open a beer and sit down and tell them about Marco and the hot tub. Bay doesn't say much. She sits with her knees together and sips her beer and watches us.

'Marco is a right slag,' Tally says. Her northern twang is stronger when she is drunk or angry or hungry. She is skin and bone in her black tank and long floral skirt. She adds, 'You know, I heard some rumour that he's actually asking loads of girls if he can take pictures of their vajayjays for some photography book!'

'You'd never do that, would you, Nell?' Bay asks me.

My heart races. 'No! Course not! Like, no way would I ever do that!'

Leah says, 'Hon, Mars is in retrograde right now. It's why things are so weird this week.' She moves to the floor, kicking off her flip-flops, pushing her honey-coloured legs straight out in front of her and putting her forehead on her knees. Two curtains of hair pool around her ankles. She stretches her arms to her toes and wiggles them. 'We should all learn to love our vaginas.'

Nobody knows what to say to that. Bay raises her eyebrows at me, and we grin at each other. Tally's phone buzzes. 'Ian's just asked us to a party.'

'Cool,' I say.

'He's offering to send a car.'

'Where's it at?' Leah says.

'He doesn't say.'

'Shall we go?' Leah was asking Tally.

'Nothing else to do,' Tally says.

'I'm up for it,' I say, looking at Bay, keen to go out-out, get drunk and forget about Marco and vaginas and hot tubs, and about how raw and humiliated I felt after seeing him feel up that girl.

'Okay, sure. Do you have a phone charger here?' Bay says.

We spend the next hour getting ready, borrowing clothes and lipsticks, dancing to loud tunes. In the end, Bay warms up and starts having fun. When her phone is charged again, she films us. It is her way of being involved, and Leah tells me how cool and smart and inspiring she thinks she is.

The doorbell rings at 9.30.

The car is an actual Bentley. I take a picture for Dad. It is so big inside, we can face each other, like in a limo. There is an ice bucket in the armrest with four flutes and a gold bottle of champagne called Cristal. We talk non-stop, especially when Marco texts me, causing a flurry of advice like 'Tell that perv to take a flying leap, the old pacdo!' and other constructive stuff.

At one point, Tally asks the driver where we are.

'Kingston,' he replies. I look out of the window to read some street signs.

Before we know it, we are on a dual carriageway.

'Where the hell is this party?' I ask.

'Dmytros's house is in Chiddingfold,' the driver says.

'Chiddingfold? In Surrey?' Bay says.

He nods. 'Yes.'

'What?' we all cry in unison.

'Are you kidding me? We're going to a party in *Surrey*?' Tally shouts.

'Chiddingfold's, like, fifteen minutes from where we live!' I say.

'You won't be needing that train ticket any more,' Bay laughs.

'Is Ian even going to be there?' Leah asks.

'I'm just texting him now,' Tally says. Her fingers move fast.

We arrive at some big gates before Ian has texted back.

The long, super-straight driveway cuts through fir trees that sway above the car. Street lamps light the way. Ten or more cars are on the driveway. All of them are posh: Porsches or Mercedes or BMWs. The driver parks up next to a floodlit fountain in front of a new-build mansion with columns and too many windows to count. Goggle-eyed, we walk up to the glossy double front door.

Inside, the hallway has tacky red walls and a huge gold side table. We are led by a maid, in an actual maid's uniform, to a side door under the main staircase.

Leah and I catch each other's eye, and I can tell she is both impressed and wary, too. We carry on down a narrow flight of stairs. Bay films as we go.

We come to a basement room, like a spa. The pool is half inside and half outside. Through the open windows, the garden is brightly lit, with uplighters along pathways lined with palm trees. Inside, men in smart shirts and slicked hair mill about in small groups.

We walk past a billiard table, where two men are playing. They look up and say something in a foreign language – it could be Russian. Or Greek? There is a dance floor. Six or seven men in suits dance around two trashy-looking girls in bikinis with fake breasts and orange tans. It reminds me of a documentary I saw about the Playboy mansion.

'This place has bad vibes,' Leah says.

'But there's free champagne,' I say. Marco has emptied me of good feeling, and I need to be filled up again.

'Hey! Hi! Are you Ian's girls?' A greasy, toady man wearing a blue shirt and a gold signet ring calls out to us. He stands up at the bar and beckons us over. I slap Bay's hand down to stop her filming. He shakes our hands, introducing himself as Dmytros, the host. A waiter behind the bar pours three glasses of champagne.

'Is Ian here?' Tally asks.

'No, sorry, girls. Shame, he's a laugh, no?'

We sit at a small circular outdoor table, inlaid with gold mosaics. I wonder if the gold is real. It is the kind of house where real gold wouldn't be a surprise.

'Do you think we should leave?' Tally says, shouting over the R&B tunes that boom out of large speakers.

'Already?' I ask.

'Look at those women, they're like hookers,' Leah says.

A good tune comes on. 'I want to dance,' I say, refusing to let them drag me down again.

Leah joins me for the odd track and then floats off again.

The men are terrible dancers and too friendly. Lots of shiny shirts and shiny shoes and gold jewellery. Loud sports car engines sound out front. More men arrive. Some are with young girls in tight dresses, others come alone. The men outnumber the girls, by far.

When a bad song comes on, I go outside to find the others and light one of Tally's cigarettes.

'I'm going to kill Ian for this,' Tally says, glued to her Uber app, trying to get us a car back to London. Bay has on her serious face. Her red lipstick has bled into the corners of her lips.

'My app still isn't working,' Leah says.

'Reception's non-existent,' Bay says. 'It's ironic, considering this house must have been built to the highest spec.'

I walk away from them, thinking, you guys are killing my mood.

Another man's eyes are on me. He has an angry spray of acne on his forehead and a large gold wristwatch. Bay comes over and I try to get her to dance, but she just circles me, filming me. Two guys are pumping and grinding right up against me.

'Stop filming, will you?' I say to Bay, but I don't really care, as I long as I can get drunk and dance the night away. And forget. Forget about everything.

And I do get drunk. Quickly and suddenly. I haven't eaten a proper meal all day. At Marco's we grazed on crisps and olives. And at the Shoreditch flat, I ate a bag of Wotsits. Too late now. Maybe I could find some milk from somewhere and try to line my stomach (Mum's advice).

A man lifts my arm above my head and twirls me around. He is tall, with a receding hairline and sharp eyes that look as though kohl has been drawn around them. His jeans are pulled too high and he wears loafers with tassels and no socks. He stares me out, even when I am not looking.

'Want another drink?' he says.

'Sure.'

When he holds the bottle over my empty glass, I can't hold it still and the drink spills.

'Whoops! Sorry.'

He waves at a guy by the bar, who hurries over and clears it up. I thank the waiter a million times.

'Don't worry about him. He gets paid well,' he says.

'Sorry,' I say again, to nobody in particular.

We chat. My tongue isn't working around my words too well. His name is Ali. He guessed I was one of Ian's guests. We dance some more. My toes are pinching and my stomach is acidic after all the champagne. But Ali's attention takes me over. I'm not sure why. He must be well over forty and I don't fancy him at all. It's like dancing with one of my dad's friends at a wedding. But there is an air about him that is attractive. Something commanding and confident. I imagine he owns a Porsche and a big company with skyscraper offices and has lots of secretaries who run around booking him flights to Dubai or Moscow or Beijing for business meetings.

'I'm going for a cigarette,' I say.

'Sure.'

I try to walk in a straight line to our table, but my ankle gives way. I grab the table to steady myself.

'I've asked Dmytros to get his driver to take us home,' Tally says.

'Okay,' I say, disappointed, taking one of her cigarettes. I look over at Ali, who is talking to Dmytros by the bar.

'Just one more dance,' I say.

'I love this song!' I say to Ali, who is back by my side.

'Your friends aren't having a good time?'

'They're having a great time!'

'Are you going home with them?'

'I should, probably.' But really I'm not sure what I should want or who I should be.

'Do you live in London?'

'I live in a village a few miles away.' My village. Sentimentality grips me for a second: *my village, my stamping ground, my home; where Mum is, only a few miles away.*

'Even more reason to stay,' he says. 'I'll book you a cab later.'

I am taken by the way he is looking at me, as though he wants me more than he has ever wanted anyone before. Still, I consider what this means. I think about Marco and his fancy house and his cool friends and about the girl in the hot tub. I can't bear to think of it. I'll do anything to blank it out.

'Okay,' I say, following him.

Before we mount the carpeted section of stairs, he takes off his loafers. His feet are revolting. Wiry black hair sprouts from his long, thin, crooked toes.

He takes me along a corridor to a room with a four-poster bed and a black eiderdown.

'This is my room.'

'You live here?'

'No,' he says, like I am stupid but sweet. 'I'm just staying for the weekend.'

He begins to kiss me. His spit is cold. We get onto the bed. I decide to lie there underneath him, floppy, and let him do exactly what he wants. When his hand runs from my collarbone down, down across the spiteful little pinprick scars to my knickers, I hate myself. I hate myself so much, but I do nothing to stop him. When he guides my hand to his thin hard-on, I pull it away. I decide not to touch him. He doesn't complain. It is obvious he desires my body enough to put aside how I feel about him.

Allowing him to do what he wants reminds me of Francis Ray, and it makes me feel miserable about myself but it also feels right. The pretty smiles have been stripped away and I am left with the truth. I am feeling my truth.

Marco should be here, I think absently, to see what he's doing to me. He would get his camera out and take some pictures of me. He would get off on me being naked, being pinched and stroked and pumped by a fully clothed old man. By a wolf.

After Ali comes, he lies on his back and watches me put my clothes back on.

'I hope your friends haven't left already,' he says, and reaches his arm out to the side table and takes up his wallet. 'Here,' he says, holding out a wad of twenties.

I stare at the money, shocked.

He laughs. 'For a cab! It would be my fault if you've missed Dmytros's car.'

The money isn't for the cab. It is for my services.

I leave the money sitting in his hand and go downstairs.

'Jesus, where have you been?' Tally asks me.

'Sorry,' I say, lighting up a cigarette, feeling sticky between my legs. 'I didn't know you were waiting.'

'Dmytros keeps saying his driver is stuck in traffic,' she says. 'If one more guy hits on me, I'm going to call the police.'

'It's like we're captives,' Leah adds.

'Let's just walk out.' I down Leah's champagne.

'But we're in the middle of nowhere,' Tally says.

'Actually, we're not,' Bay tells her. 'We know this village. It would take us about an hour to walk back to our house.'

'It's not too far?' Leah asks.

'We've done it loads with Mum and Dad from the pub in Chid,' I say.

'Walk? Are you serious? I'm wearing four-inch heels!' Tally frowns.

'Have you got any other ideas, Tall?' Leah says angrily.

'It's not too far, honestly,' I insist.

'I know,' Bay says. 'I have a better idea. Nell, call Matthew. He has a car.'

'We don't need him,' I snap. The thought of seeing him after what I've just done makes me want to retch.

'You'd prefer to walk?' Bay asks.

Tally rolls her eyes. 'For the love of God, Nell, if this Matthew guy has a car, call him.'

'I don't know. We're not best buds at the moment.'

'We could kip in the room above his garage,' Bay adds. 'It would save us waking Mum and Dad up.'

'True,' I admit. It would save me from having to get into my own bed, from dirtying it.

'I can't believe we're in this situation,' Tally says.

'You go first, Nell,' Bay orders, 'and call Matthew outside so nobody hears. Wait for us in the driveway.'

'Okay.' Anything you say, I think angrily.

'We'll follow in a couple of minutes, one at a time, maybe go via the loos first or something. Go on, off you go.'

And off I go, laughing about how dramatic they are being.

I am not scared. The worst has already happened.

*

We manage to walk to the gates, but they are electric and locked tight. We have to crawl around them through the rhododendron bushes, on our hands and knees, to get to the lane where Matthew's powder-blue Renault 4 is waiting.

I get in the front with Matthew, avoiding eye contact, and move the seat forward to make room for Tally's long legs. After brief introductions, Matthew pulls the gearstick out from the dash and we lurch and bump along over the potholes. I steal glances at him. His strawberry-blond hair is tufty and his glasses keep steaming up, and we swerve every time he wipes them.

None of us are in the mood to talk.

Into the silence, Matthew says, 'You know that house belongs to a guy who is a known arms dealer? I think he's Ukrainian or Russian or something. The police are always breaking up parties there.'

'I thought Surrey was meant to be posh and full of nice people in green bloody wellies,' Tally says.

It isn't funny, but the three of them begin to really laugh, even Bay, who doesn't belly-laugh often. I guess it is nervous laughter.

I can't laugh. They're so naïve.

Matthew just drives, probably quite tired and baffled and pissed off about how un-fun this is for him. But I am so grateful that he doesn't do fun. Fun is totally overrated.

CHAPTER FORTY-NINE

Anna

The train carriage was almost empty. I watched the countryside shoot by, sipped my weak tea and worried about everything. Both Bay and Nell had exams this week, and I had no idea how prepared Nell was for hers. For a change, she had been home last weekend. Something had happened between her and Marco, but I wasn't sure what. I'd heard her crying about it over the phone with him. Dom kept telling me not to worry about her – 'It's just what teenage girls do!' – and I kept telling him he needed to worry more. We were living under the same small roof and sleeping in the same bed, yet we were miles apart.

I thought about last night. Our bedroom had been cold. Dom had opened both windows. I had climbed into bed and pulled a throw over the top of the duvet, for extra warmth, having given up arguing with him about room temperature back in the nineties. The throw had smelt of dust. I had begun reading my book but resented how cold my arms were. I imagined having cold arms for the rest of my life. It was this silly, small thought that had changed my mind about Billy.

I had got out of bed and gone downstairs, telling Dom that I was getting a banana for some potassium to help me sleep. Instead, I had gone straight to my phone and tapped out a text.

Hi Billy, are you still free tomorrow? Sorry for short notice. Anna x

I had cracked open a banana, suddenly actually wanting one, and he had texted straight back.

Meet you at Granger and Co. on Westbourne Grove at 1 p.m. Bx

Such a small, silly thought about cold arms had led to such a big decision.

Now, an announcement from the train guard made me jump. It was a garbled message and the woman diagonally across from me laughed and said, 'What the hell was that?'

If the guard had said 'Everyone off now! All trains to London cancelled!' I would have decided it was fate, a lucky escape. Guilt swelled inside me and then excitement swamped it.

My phone rang.

'Hi, Mum,' I said quietly into my cupped hand, aware of the woman opposite.

'Darling, you sound weird. Where are you?' Mum said.

'Is everything okay?' I asked, evading her question.

'Could you get me some yeast?' she said.

'Sure, I'll bring it round later.'

'I need it now.'

'I'm so sorry. I'm on a train.'

'Where are you going?' she asked, sounding incredulous.

'Luton.' It was the same lie I had told Dom.

'Luton? Why?'

She knew very well that Luton was where I bought all my millinery equipment; it was the mecca for milliners.

'I need a new hat block.'

There was a pause. The train sounded its horn.

'But I wanted to make bread today.'

'I'm so sorry, Mum.'

'I was going to make sourdough.'

It was heartening to hear she had the will to make bread and I was keen she shouldn't give up. How frustrating that this train was going in the wrong direction, that I was thwarting her attempts to bring herself out of her eternal slump.

'What about asking Jeff next door?'

'It doesn't matter,' she said.

'But Mum, it's great you're making bread. Are you sure you couldn't brave it and go to the supermarket yourself?' I was ever hopeful she might one day leave her house for something other than a doctor's appointment.

'Mum? Are you there?'

There was a clatter, as though she had opened a kitchen cupboard.

'You may as well know. I've decided to move back to France,' she said.

'*What?*' The woman across the way turned her head a fraction. I was amazed and insulted and sceptical about what I had just heard my mother say. She was unable to leave her house to go to the supermarket, but she could make it to France?

'I was speaking to Didier the other night and he suggested I move into one of the rooms in his B&B.'

'You still talk to *Didier?*'

He had been a friend of her brother's, before her brother had died. He had been in love with her and she had not been in love with him.

'He understands me in a way that nobody else does. I'm lonely here. So lonely, you have no idea. You have no idea what it's like.'

I heard the tears in her voice. My mind flickered back over the many evenings when I had sat with her, holding her hand, listening to her angry diatribes about her loneliness. My brain would always scrabble for new ways to say the same thing: 'I'm so sorry you feel like this' or 'It must be so frightening to feel that way' or 'How awful, I really sympathise'. And I did, genuinely, though every platitude I came up with sounded thin from overuse. I'd suggest that she ask her GP for some leaflets about group therapy (aka pills), join a bridge club or a sewing club – she had loved embroidery once – learn to play golf. She might agree to do at least one of these things, and she always promised to think about it overnight; but by the next day, the old fears would have settled back down again, like a film of dust over her life. I'd call to check on her, spoon-feed her some phone numbers, and she'd snap at me and say that she didn't need any of those numbers, that she hated clubs.

Today, on the way to London to meet Billy, I wasn't in the mood for all this. I couldn't face her tears. It was too much. I only had headspace for where I was going.

'I'm sorry, Mum, you're breaking up. I'll call you later, bye!' I said, hanging up, feeling bad, sensing her disappointment, disapproval and suspicion.

Whereas Dom had not been in the least suspicious. These days, he wasn't paying attention to anything I did, except when he didn't like it. His selective indifference to me did not justify lying to him, though. I had been awake half the night worrying whether I should tell him I was meeting Billy, whether I was insane for even considering meeting him, and whether I should wear jeans or a dress.

And here I was, on the train to London, having lied to Dom, wearing the high-waisted flared jeans that Nell had bought me for Mother's Day, giddy with it, knowing it was wrong on so many levels and right on so many others.

I felt good in my new clothes, different. I'd shed my wife and mother selves – those two weighty outer shells – leaving just the woman. The woman who was spontaneously meeting an ex-lover for lunch in London because she'd had cold arms.

The restaurant was as fashionable as my jeans were, and yet I still felt out of place. Judging by the way people were looking at me,

I wondered whether I had a message projected onto my forehead that read: *Surrey Mum: Seriously Uncool, Not One of Us.*

The maître d' led me to a table for two. It was squeezed in between two other couples. As I waited for Billy, I listened to a young woman telling her friend about her horrible boss. On the other side of us, an older couple shared photographs of their grandson. It was impossible not to listen to their conversations and I dreaded them hearing ours.

I wished that Billy hadn't chosen this place.

When he arrived, he fitted in. He had on a faded black T-shirt, and his salt-and-pepper hair was particularly wild, tamed only slightly by the bits tucked behind his ears. His jeans were baggy and his trainers were scruffy and his great big gentle hands, which may as well have throbbed red in tune with his big gentle heart, swung by his sides haphazardly. His knuckles grazed strangers' shoulders as he passed by, loosening their bags or unhooking their jackets from chairs, which he corrected with smiles and apologies.

'Hi, how are you?' I said, formally, awkwardly, kissing him on either cheek, sitting back down again.

'Hi, great,' he said, smiling, raising his expressive eyebrows briefly, uncertainly, as though recognising the stakes of our meeting. 'How are *you*?'

He squeezed through the tiny gap between the tables and took up the space opposite me with his larger-than-life self, making everyone next to him seem puny and irrelevant.

'Good. How are you?' I said again, so nervous my mind was blanking out.

He laughed at me. 'You look well.'

I concentrated on the menu, waiting for my cheeks to cool. 'The fritters and bacon sound yummy.'

His physical presence was utterly intoxicating, as though the cells of my body were being pulled to his with the strength of millions of tiny magnets. The wave of sexual feeling was like an awakening. I couldn't concentrate on making conversation and wondered, for a second of madness, whether the only way to cure it would be to drag him to a hotel room and get it over and done with. Probably not the best idea – being married, and all that. My motivations for wanting to see him were not completely dishonourable. Not really. It was more about memories and revisiting our old lives and checking in on him. Viv had been right. We had unfinished business that I was here to finish.

It took us until the waiter had taken our orders and our food had arrived before we began to talk. I had asked about Dixie and told him a little more about Nell. Our conversation was stilted, unlike it had been on the phone, unlike it had been back then. I was aware that we were sharing intimate details of our lives and that the couples next to us could hear every word of it. But Billy didn't seem to care.

'Strange,' he said. 'In many ways, we're going through similar experiences.'

Swallowing a mouthful before I had chewed it properly, I said, 'You think?'

'We both feel we're losing our girls and we both feel we have absolutely no power to stop it.'

The salty-sweet food became mushy and bitter in my mouth. I could not lose Nell, no, no, I could not lose her. Surely his situation was far more perilous than mine. For a start, Dixie lived in a different country. Nell lived under my roof still. It was different, I had to believe it was different.

'Well, I mean, I'm hoping Nell will come round,' I said, disingenuously. It was a meaningless statement. I suddenly wanted to leave. It had been a mistake to come here. We were worlds apart.

'I'm sorry,' he said hurriedly. 'That was insensitive of me. You're not losing Nell. I didn't mean that. What I meant was that you *feel* like you are. You've still got her at home and you've had sixteen years of such a close bond. It means everything. I'm scared of losing that with Dixie. The bond in the early years is so important. I don't want her to grow up thinking I gave up on her, which I never will. Your fights with Nell prove how close you are and that you're not giving up.'

I was reminded of difficult conversations that Billy and I had shared in the past, usually about my mother – always about my mother – when I would bristle and then capitulate, knowing that he had read me right. And he was right now. So right. I did feel like I was losing Nell, and my heart contracted, as though Billy, the messenger of this truth, was squeezing it in his large hands, stopping the blood from flowing to my head.

'Let's go,' he said. 'This is all wrong. I can see you hate it. *I* hate it.'

'But you haven't finished your…' I managed to say.

'I've got cash.'

He left two twenties on the table and stood up. I wiped my mouth and followed him, apologising to the waiter as we left. Strangely, the waiter smiled kindly at me, as though sensing that something was terribly wrong. Yes, I wanted to say, everything *was* terribly wrong. My eyes swelled with tears.

On the pavement, we stood opposite each other.

'Where shall we go?'

We were both lost. A strong and sudden gust of wind blew an escaped tear back towards my ear and tossed my hair, exposing my face to Billy, baring it, as though ripping off my clothes. A twirl of leaves danced at our feet, scratching at the paving stones, settling in a cluster. My tears receded when I looked into his brown eyes. I imagined his hands cupping my face, warming it in the way the gust of wind could not.

'The park?' I said.

'Yes.'

We walked through tree-lined avenues and crescents and mews and into Hyde Park, exchanging information about various big life events, covering the decades at speed and with no cohesion, as though they were snippets from other people's life stories. It was unsatisfying and depressing. I was taking in the information he shared and sharing my own, but I felt we knew nothing more about each other than we had when we had first said hello.

The manicured plantings and the pathways thick with people did not feel like an escape from the hot, smelly city streets. I remembered pushing Nell in the pram around Clapham Common, imagining her snuffling breaths clogged with exhaust fumes; and the relief I had felt when I had pulled her out of the car seat at 20 Lower Road for the first time. I had held her in my arms, pointed at the field opposite, saying, 'Look, a horsey,' and taken in a lungful of air, feeling like I'd come home. I guessed Billy would welcome this park air and enjoy this pretty green space: another reminder of how different we were and how much our lives had diverged.

My mobile rang. I stared at the screen.

'Who is it?' Billy asked.

'It's Mum.'

'Don't pick up.'

I looked at him, searching his face. His eyebrows were pulled down, just a little, not cross but serious. 'What if something's happened?'

'She'll be fine.'

'How do you know?'

'If she isn't, she'll text or leave a message.'

It rang and rang. My teeth clenched. I deliberated, worrying about her, knowing that her call was probably about the yeast, or something like that. Going against my instinct, hoping this wouldn't be a horrible example of cry wolf, I let the call run out. 'I hope she's okay,' I said, a little accusingly, as though he had physically restrained me. I put the phone on silent and away in my bag.

'How's she doing these days?' he asked.

'Better than she was… Not great. She doesn't really go out.' I checked my watch, thinking about train times. Iris's school run was covered, but I would need to get back a little earlier than planned if I wanted to swing by Tesco for Mum. Part of me was relieved that I wanted to get home as soon as possible, confirming that this had been a mistake. All the guilt I had been suppressing rose up. The years of not seeing Billy had created a chasm between us that was too huge to bridge.

'But physically, she's capable?'

'So the doctors say. But the GP just shoos her out mid-sentence. I mean, I do worry they might have missed something more serious. She's always so tired.'

'I had hoped she would get better.'

I bristled. I knew what he was implying. 'We have good days.'

'We?' he said, eyeing me from the side.

I stopped walking. '*She* has good days. She's really much more independent. She even said she was thinking of moving back to France.'

It was too much too soon. We were taking up where we had left off, as though twenty years had folded into nothing. However long you left something hanging, unresolved, in the atmosphere, it never seemed to go away. The bottom layers of us were still there, in spite of the years laid over the top.

'I guess it's easier, in a way, living near her. The combo of Skype and emotional blackmail would have been grim,' he said.

Yes, Billy, I did the right thing.

'She's never forgiven Martin for moving to Somerset,' I said.

'Is Martin happy? I still miss him.'

'He's very happy, actually.' I smiled, thinking of their haphazard house and their beautiful girls.

'Moving away worked for him then.'

'And staying worked for me,' I said pointedly. Adamant. Cut-and-dried about my choice to stay behind and look after

Mum. Then I remembered my desperate dead-of-night phone call to him from the Wendy house. 'I mean, Nell's a nightmare at the moment, and Dom and I have our ups and downs, but that's just marriage for you, that's just family life. Mostly I'm pretty happy.'

Was I? Even as I said it, I knew it was a lie.

'I'm glad you're happy.'

'I am,' I said. Saying it might make it true. My pulse was racing. I saw a bench and wanted to sit down, but I couldn't move from the spot. I pictured my reflection in the bathroom mirror this morning. My eyes and hair and body were a crushing disappointment, manifestations of what I had not managed to give myself: sleep, self-care, love perhaps.

We walked along in awkward silence. Kensington Palace was on our right and I wondered if the royals inside were in the middle of a family crisis, like the rest of us. I tried to imagine William and Kate making sandwiches in the kitchen and having a fraught conversation about Louis's sleeping patterns or Charlotte's eating habits or George's inability to concentrate on his phonics books; wicked thoughts came to me of Kate fantasising about her tennis coach's muscular thighs and William wishing he was nagged less. If they glanced out of the window at me and Billy now, and saw into our souls, I wondered whether they might feel connected to us, empathetic rather than regal and superior.

A gaggle of geese escaped from the Round Pond to our left and waddled across our path. There was an ice cream van painted in racing green up ahead.

'How about a Mr Whippy?' I suggested.

'Two flakes each,' he said.

We smiled at each other.

Once we had bought the ice creams, we found a bench opposite the pond.

'What's Dom's daughter like?'

'Bay? She's amazing. Damaged. Her mother was a nightmare, so she needs more reassurance than the other two.'

'You're not the wicked stepmother then?'

'Ha! At the beginning, she was hard work, but we got through it. She's been helping me, actually, with Nell. I think she worries about her as much as I do.'

'They're close?'

'So close,' I said. 'I'm lucky. It worked out, taking her in. I mean, it was a big decision.'

'Dom must have been very grateful to you.'

'He wasn't keen initially.'

'Really?'

I could have told him about the fights Dom and I had about Bay, which I hated thinking about. Dom had refused to consider taking her in. He had accused me of being a martyr and of being easily manipulated, and I had condemned him as selfish and callous. I had questioned how I could love someone who was not capable of listening to his own daughter's cries for help. Bay's stories of Suki had made me angry and had made me cry. Of Suki slapping her and pushing her and shouting at her; refusing to make her meals and leaving her alone for hours. How could I respect a man who could leave his six-year-old child in an abusive home like that? It was a question I had asked myself every day of those terrible weeks of arguing. If he had not, ultimately, agreed to offer Bay a safe home with us, I'm not sure how I would have reconciled it. I couldn't share these thoughts with Billy, as much as I wanted to. Criticising Dom risked opening up the inappropriate idea that there were opportunities to exploit, weaknesses in our marriage that might give Billy hope that shouldn't be there.

'He worried that taking her from her mother was too disruptive,' I explained. As I said it, I realised how insensitive it was, given Billy's personal situation, but it was too late to take it back.

'It's why I have never gone to court about Dixie.'

'And Dixie's mum isn't abusive, from what you say. Whereas Suki was,' I qualified. 'Honestly, it was heartbreaking. It was like taking in a chick that had fallen from its nest. She needed so much extra love. For months, she just cried about everything and anything. At night she had this horrible recurring dream about a red mist in her head that killed all the good thoughts and she couldn't get rid of it.'

He hung his head. There was a pause before he spoke. 'It must have been quite an intrusion for Nell and Iris, too.'

'Iris was too young to be that bothered, but Nell was difficult. Really jealous, and always fighting with her.'

'Maybe Nell felt more like the chick, shoved out by a cuckoo,' he said, taking a lick of his ice cream.

'She was never sidelined, believe me,' I said, irritated that he was naming something I refused to admit. 'It was good for her to learn first-hand what some children go through in abusive homes, and how lucky she was. I mean, we literally had to *teach* Bay how to be loved and how to take that love for granted. I think it helped Nell to be more empathetic. Anyway, now they're close, so it paid off.'

'It sounds like you've done an amazing job,' he said.

'No,' I said firmly. 'It was a group effort.'

'And then modelling came along.'

I chuckled, in spite of the anxiety it pulled up in me. 'Tell me about it.'

'I'm guessing she didn't go for the change of agency idea?'

'No, though I tried.' I paused. 'You said earlier that our fighting was a good sign because it meant I hadn't given up on her. Well,' I swallowed, 'the fighting has stopped.'

'You're saying you've given up?'

'Billy, I can't fight her any more.'

His hand went for my knee, but he noticed a drip of ice cream on his thumb and wiped it with a napkin. I imagined going home with a large sticky handprint on my thigh. 'You're only human, Anna. There's only so much you can take.'

I spoke as though it were a continuation of my thoughts. 'If only I'd put my foot down.'

'About the modelling?'

'I knew it was wrong, right in my gut, I just knew it. The timing was off. I wanted her to be older, more mature, to wait until she'd done her GCSEs at least. But I just gave in. It was the worst mistake of my life.'

'What did Dom think?'

'He was determined to let her follow her dreams. To be fair, the idea was that she'd be able to pay her university tuition fees with what she earned and start her working life without debts.'

'She must have earned enough to do that now, no?'

'Yes. She has. That side of it is amazing. I'm grateful for that. But I'm not sure it's worth it, you know?'

The ice cream was melting down the cone and I dumped it in the bin by the bench.

'I know,' he said.

'What would *you* do if Dixie wanted to be a model at fifteen?'

'I have no idea,' he said diplomatically.

I knew what he would do. He would say no. We would have been on the same side.

'I should have stopped her,' I gasped, pressing my fingers to my mouth. My fears about Nell's safety gripped my insides and twisted them.

Billy put his arm around my shoulders and gave them a squeeze. 'It'll be okay. She'll find her own way through. Keep the faith.'

We sat for a bit watching the model boats.

My dreams for Nell had not been the same as Dom's one-size-fits-all idea of success and happiness. I had wanted her to find authenticity, a purpose that nurtured her; something that might go against everyone else's expectations but that she was brave enough to follow regardless. I wanted this for her because it was what I had not done for myself. I had not fulfilled my ambitions as a milliner with my own label and I had not followed Billy across the ocean. Out of an obligation to Mum, I had settled into the comfy life that she had expected of me.

'You had faith in me once,' I said. I hadn't meant it to slip out.

'I still have faith in you,' he said, turning to me.

His eyes were inside mine. I remembered leaving him at Gatwick and going straight back to the hospital to see Mum. I remembered the nurses coaxing her to drink something as she lay staring up at the ceiling, balding and thin. I remembered being terrified that her depression would pull me down until I was lying in the bed next door. My stomach lurched. 'Mum needed me,' I said.

'I needed you.'

I blew out, as though expelling what he had said before it settled. 'I'm sick of being needed.'

I stood up and began marching around the pond, dodging the goose poo, not knowing where I was going. Walking in a circle, possibly about to meet him back at the same spot and feeling silly about it. My legs seemed incapable of changing course, of veering off across the grass and leaving him there, as though they were programmed to keep walking around and around, passing him every so often.

Had I hidden behind my mother's needs? Had I hidden behind Dom's? Both of them wanted me to make them happy. Both of them radiated disappointment. Both of them had unrealistic goals. Both of them played the victim. Whenever life gave them lemons, they expected other people – me! – to make the lemonade for them. Why had I never seen it so clearly before?

Billy was by my side, jogging to keep up with me.

'I don't *need* you any more,' he said.

'Right, okay, great. Thanks.'

'I mean, I was a mess back then too. I blamed you for choosing your mum over me, but I was selfish. I should have given you time.

I was so damn impatient to start a new life, I couldn't understand why you weren't.'

'You were right to leave.'

'No, I wasn't. I wanted to run to the other side of the world to escape my family, but I couldn't escape, because the bad shit was all in my head. And in my heart. But I don't have anything to prove now. What I mean is, I've worked stuff out. I understand more why I do things.'

'It's pointless to think in terms of what ifs,' I said, telling myself more than him.

'I know, and I've never believed in regrets before.'

'Before what?' It was a silly question.

'Before seeing you in New York.'

'Don't say that, Billy,' I whispered.

'Anna, I've stayed away because I never wanted to be the reason your life and your girls' lives were turned upside down.'

The idea of turning my life upside down for Billy scared me rigid, and I laughed nervously. 'Don't worry, I would never let that happen. I'd never do anything to disrupt my family. They're everything to me,' I said, still insisting this was the God-given truth.

Then he stepped in front of me, blocking my way, and took my face in his hands.

The world began turning the wrong way. The water beside us worked itself into a whirlpool. The birds flew backwards. The trees grew upside down. Everything around me was topsy-turvy. I was kissing a man who wasn't my husband and yet this kiss was the only thing that felt right in the universe. Instead of the crushing guilt that I imagined I should feel at a moment as treacherous as this, pure joy slipped through me.

CHAPTER FIFTY

Bay

All day I had been in my darkened bedroom editing my film when I should have been revising for English Paper 3 tomorrow. Dad was at work and Anna had gone to Luton and Iris was on a sleepover. And Nell, who didn't have any exams today, had gone to London to see Marco. They'd made up on the phone. Sort of. Apparently she'd misinterpreted what she'd seen in the hot tub and he had begged her to give him one more chance. She was a fool for going back to him, but she didn't listen to me about anything any more.

I texted her just now to check on her, to check she was okay, and to instruct her to keep her phone close by.

Why?

It's a surprise.

Tell me.

Wait and see.

The empty house gave me real headspace to finish off that surprise.

The first cut came in at thirty-nine minutes and thirty-one seconds.

It had evolved into an exposé piece, stylised with bold captions and edgy tracks.

Watching it back gave me a sense of real achievement and pride.

This film was for Nell. And for Iris when she grew up. For all the extended sisterhood out there. This film was to stop other girls from being used and abused by an industry that didn't care about them; to raise feminist hackles and to tap into the psyche of anyone who wished they were like Nell, whether or not they had been born with the right face. I wanted them to think before they posted their sexualised selfies, to think before they aspired to impossible ideals and idolised the fantasies of advertising. I wanted them to reassess their Instagram feeds with feminism and female power in mind. I wanted a whole generation of young girls to think more than they already did (which was already more than Anna's generation had).

My message needed no narration, only careful editing and an emotive, energising soundtrack. Throughout my story I had spliced flash cards, like subliminal messages, worded in pink and green capitals: DREAMS. EQUALITY. COURAGE. FEMININ-ITY. POWER. CONTROL. KINDNESS. INNER BEAUTY. SELF-LOVE. CREATIVITY. AMBITION. The affirmations were integrated with footage of predatory men and semi-nude teenag-ers and male subjugation and casual sexism and body shaming. Edited together, an overall picture built of an industry that was hypocritical and sophisticated and coercive and destructive. Not just for the young models like Nell who were its direct victims, but for all young girls everywhere.

Dreams. Equality. Courage. Femininity. Power. Control. Kind-ness. Inner Beauty. Self-love. Creativity. Ambition.

On my behalf, Nell had obtained Tally and Leah's written consent to appear in the film. They understood its potential content, having read the small print. Marco and Ian and Francis Ray – at the end of the Celeste shoot – had also signed my form. None of the men had read the carefully worded jargon properly; none of them had cared that it might be posted online, none of them had taken this seventeen-year-old girl's little YouTube film seriously.

One signature each, easily gained, and I owned them.

However, permissions had not been gained from the random men I had captured at the various parties they had attended. To protect myself, I had pixelated their faces or cut off their heads so that they would not be identifiable, having paid attention in my class on privacy, data protection and defamation. Even Bonnie Steiner's voice in the Winnebago in New York was distorted and unrecognisable, just to be safe.

When I posted my film later tonight on my YouTube channel, I did not want lawsuits to follow. The film didn't suffer for it. If anything, the faceless, computerised versions of my unwitting contributors enhanced my message and reinforced their own ugliness. At the time, they had thought nothing of being filmed. They had liked the camera turned on them; their vanity had allowed it.

As the evening wore on, I tweaked and rearranged, enlarged type and reduced it, switched interviews and shortened clips.

At last I had a final edit, a polished film.

It was my gift to Nell, with a tag that might say: *Be the best you can be, Nellie.*

The only thing left was the title. I lay back on my pillows, exhausted and satisfied, and thought and thought.

The title eventually came to me: *Pretty*.

My film would be called *Pretty*, as ironic as the flash cards it contained.

A film that was ever so pretty on the surface and yet ever so ugly underneath.

CHAPTER FIFTY-ONE

Nell

Marco and I are both naked in the hot tub. The sky is a dome above us, fuzzy at the edges as the sun goes down. Through the branches of the tree at the end of the garden I can see the backs of the houses opposite, which are identical to Marco's. I don't care that someone might be having a nose and getting off on our nudity. I lay my head back on the blow-up cushion feeling lazy, lazy about sex, lazy about talking, lazy about what I might do next. Lazily, I think about Bay's surprise, which I am too lazy to get excited about. Everything exists in this one second of wooziness and drunkenness, until I move into the next second of wooziness and drunkenness. The second after that is just the same as the one before. I could live like this forever. Why not? I am broken down. Enough to accept Marco's lies. I don't care how he treats me or how anyone treats me any more. I don't care about any of it. I just don't frigging care.

Can I even remember a time when I did care?

Oh yes, I can.

When I was with Matthew in the woods and I timed a jump perfectly and floated through air, *literally*; when I brought Mum a cup of tea in bed and snuggled in for one of our best-ever chats; when I let Iris watch a 12 movie on my laptop and covered her eyes for the kissing bits.

My heart shudders, jellylike in my chest, before regaining its leaden, drunken beat.

Marco is on his mobile. He is arranging some drugs for tonight. I still don't take drugs, but Marco likes them. The other night he said that everyone should try everything once and I said, 'Okay then, what about climbing El Capitan without a rope?' He laughed. 'Sure. Why not?' And I thought, you'd die doing it, dumbass, but hey, you tried, right?

About the girl in the hot tub he said, 'You know, you'll learn that all guys cheat. Stone-cold fact, baby girl. But unlike other guys, I'll always be honest with you about it, right?' Somehow that made sense. Especially given how dishonest I've been with him. The party in Chiddingfold is my secret shame. Thinking about Ali makes me to want to vomit.

The only good bit about that night was at Matthew's, lying on the futon in the room above the garage in the nook of his armpit, which smelt of Lynx. The next morning, he made coffee and croissants for everyone and we ate them in the garden. Viv and Greg – confused by their gazelle-like guests – joined us for a bit. Viv asked me if Mum knew we were there, and I lied and said she did, just so she didn't call her and ruin the morning. Matthew was chattier than usual, unfazed by my new friends' beauty. He and I told stories about some of the stuff we'd got up to when we were little, and he dropped in dry one-liners, making everyone laugh. Of course, Bay got in a mood. She didn't like it when I told the story about her love note to Matthew: *I think I love you too (but I'm not really sure)*. Everyone thought it was so funny and sweet.

'Did you say your sister was coming over, baby?' Marco says when he hangs up. He takes a sip from his tumbler of whisky and Coke.

'I don't know,' I say. 'She said something about a surprise. I thought maybe she was coming to London. But she hasn't texted back.'

'Do you want me to put her down on the list at StarBoy's?'

'Maybe,' I say. 'Just in case.'

I check my phone again to see if she has replied to my text:

What surprise u talking bout, sistah???!!! Wanna come to StarBoy's tonite? Nx

She hasn't replied. There have been no texts from her over the last few hours. It is seriously unusual. I doubt she'll want to come to StarBoy's with us. She hates that club. It is in a dark basement in Notting Hill and the music is always too loud. Even for a night-club. The low ceilings don't help. I know I will have tinnitus for a week after tonight, but I like the music. It is old-school nineties hip-hop and nobody ever bothers you when you dance. Not like in Chiddingfold! Who knew Surrey could be more dangerous than a dungeon club in London?

Soon Marco's house is filled with people. The doorbell keeps ringing. Marco's friend Si has brought his Rottweiler, which prowls around with its big head. When the dog finally settles down at Si's feet, a girl called Monet goes to pet it and Si says, 'I wouldn't.' Monet whips her hand away.

At about ten o'clock, Marco slides his arms around my waist from behind. Into my ear he says, 'Wanna get some Ubers for us, baby?'

I unplug my phone from the charger. A message from Bay is on the screen.

Be the best you can be, Nellie. www.x54s/slrub-vP23/youtube

It is her surprise! Now I know what she's been getting at. She must have finished her documentary.

After I book three cabs on my app, I click into the link.

The title card reads *PRETTY* in pink capitals across a black screen, and then *A film by Bay Hart*. I press play, just to check how long it is, wondering if I have time to watch it before the cabs come. It is almost forty minutes long, which means I won't have time. But I am excited about watching it later, maybe in bed with Marco.

Marco comes back into the kitchen. 'Come,' he whispers, taking my hand.

We go up to his bedroom and into the adjoining bathroom. It has floor-to-ceiling black tiles. He locks the door and starts kissing me and pulling up my dress and undoing his flies.

The tiles are cold to lie on. He scrabbles for his phone in the pocket of his jeans. 'I have to get a shot of you for the book now, baby. No more excuses.'

'Go on then, you pervert. As long as you don't put my name at the bottom.'

You see? I don't fucking care.

'Call me a pervert again,' he laughs, husky in my ear.

There is some barking and scratching at the door. 'Fuck off, Rover,' he says.

'He's not called Rover,' I say.

Marco is fiddling with his phone. The dog keeps barking outside the door. I want him to hurry up and get the photograph over and done with. I'm getting sick of him hassling me about it.

Then he says, 'What's this? Is this from your sister?'

I look at the text he's showing me. It is the same YouTube link Bay sent me.

'How did she get your number?' I say. It sounds like I might be jealous and suspicious.

'I don't wanna fuck your sister, believe me,' he says.

'It's just her film. You know, the one she was making about modelling?'

He clicks into it and sits back against the side of the bath, with his flies undone. 'Wow, it's had over a thousand views already. Let's watch it.'

'It's too long to watch now,' I say, pulling myself up, wriggling my dress down, sitting next to him and peering over at his screen. The dog keeps barking.

'We've got time,' he says.

Angry hip-hop music kicks it off. *PRETTY* comes up in bold pink capitals against a black screen. It is followed by cleverly edited scenes of me as a young girl in my uniform, with the school logo pixelated out, and some of me on my mountain bike in the woods. Then *DREAMS* flashes up, in pale green capitals on black, followed by shots of me half-naked on shoots, looking worried and upset. *INNER BEAUTY* in baby blue on black, followed by the undercover scene in New York of Bonnie – her voice disguised – telling me I'm fat. *EDUCATION* in lilac on black, followed by me screaming and swearing at Mum about a job I wanted to miss school for. *AMBITION* in red on black, followed by scenes of Ian telling me I'm going to be a star. *SELF-LOVE* in magenta on black, followed by parties full of old men flirting with me and other young models. *EQUALITY* in white on black, followed by a male photographer ordering me to bend down for more cleavage. *FEMININITY* in pale pink, followed by me striking naff sexy poses and twerking on set (it was a bloody joke!). *STRENGTH* in purple, followed by me slouching down a London catwalk next to a girl who looks anorexic. *CONTROL* in light grey, followed by a snippet of a conversation where Ian tells me that parties are part of the game. *POWER* in orange lettering, followed by clips of me drunk in nightclubs with leering men.

Marco keeps saying, 'What the fuck?' over and over.

All of the footage is familiar, so familiar. But I don't recognise it. I don't know myself. It isn't my life.

CREATIVITY flashes up in red on the screen, followed by Marco's face. My mouth dries. It is the interview he gave Bay in the restaurant on Ian's birthday.

'What or who did you photograph last?' Bay asks.

'Oh man, I had the privilege of shooting Abebi.'

'Describe her in one word.'

'Fierce.'

'What did she wear?'

'She wore a leather Egyptian headdress and panties.'

'Where will we see the photographs?'

'*Vogue.* August edition.'

'What was your inspiration?'

'Belly buttons,' he says, straight to camera.

The way Bay filmed his face, so close up, showing the grease of every pore, makes him look like the pervert that he is, sweating over little girls' belly buttons, like mine. 'What the fucking fuck?' Marco says.

I can hardly breathe when I see the next shot, following the word *COURAGE*.

Tall doors are in the foreground of a high-ceilinged library. Inside the room, the camera zooms in on the back of Francis Ray's head. He kisses me. His words are distorted, disguised, but Bay has put subtitles across the bottom of the screen:

Sit down! Relax! I just wanna to talk to you about the job... I'm trying to convince the Celeste lot that you're right for the campaign, but they're leaning towards the other girl... But I want you.

I'm sitting with my back to the camera in the chair opposite him. *Cool. Thanks.*

You remind me of a young Bardot.

I stand up.

Francis Ray is on top of me, but we are part hidden behind the door.

Jesus, this thing is like a chastity belt.

'You got it on with Francis Ray?' Marco says, plainly disgusted, typically hypocritical, like all men are. 'Casting couch, was it?'

I begin to wheeze. It's hard to speak, 'She's made it look... That's not how it happened...' I puff, out of breath.

The horrible film goes on playing. Both of us sit glued to it. I begin shaking.

Next is a montage of me and Leah and Tally dancing around the model flat, half-dressed, talking about how schoolwork doesn't matter.

'We were actually talking about how school doesn't define you!' I say, like it matters.

More spliced clips: shots of us boozing in the limo, legs sprawled, and then dancing in our short dresses in Dmytros's luxurious mansion. Then Ali and I are holding hands up the stairs as we slip away. The difference in our ages makes us look like a father and daughter, until he puts his hand on my arse.

'What the fuck?' Marco says again, under his breath this time.

The final flash card says *FEMINISM*, followed by a shot of me in front of the bus with the Buttercup advert plastered on its side.

'Can you believe that's me?' I'm saying.

The bus drives past.

'I'm famous,' I say to camera, then shrug and smile.

I spit bile in the loo as Marco rants at me. 'Are you fucking kidding me? What the hell was that? Is your sister fucking insane? I can fucking sue her for this. She makes me out to be some fucking paedo! Ian is going to go fucking mental! He comes across as your pimp! Jesus Christ! What the fuck?'

The dog is barking outside the door again. Growling and barking. I sit on the closed loo seat with my head in my hands, wiping my mouth.

'Si! Shut that fucking dog up!' Marco yells, flying out of the bathroom. There is a whimper as he shoves past the animal.

The dog pads in. At first, I freeze, frightened of him, still trying to suck in air, feeling like I am drowning. He trots over and nestles his wet nose into my bare legs. I stare into his dinner plate eyes. 'Hi, Snowflake,' I say, rubbing his thick neck and putting my face up to his. My breathing regulates a little. He licks my nose. He knows. This beautiful dog knows I am in really big trouble.

CHAPTER FIFTY-TWO

Anna

The last light of the evening struggled through the net curtains. The desk chair and the multicoloured stripes of the carpet were washed with grey. Billy and I lay on top of the divan, talking. The sheets were tucked tightly and chastely under the mattress. We had not done what we had both wanted to do.

'I have to get home,' I said, for the fifth time in the last hour.

'Nooo, please. I can't let you go, it's impossible,' he said.

His lips were on mine, and I wondered if we would ever be able to stop kissing long enough to live, to eat, to work. To part.

The enormity of the consequences of our desire for each other hit me. I wouldn't let it. Not yet.

'When's the last train?' Billy asked.

We faced each other.

'Eleven fifteen,' I said, knowing I had to get up.

Our noses were almost touching. His face was as familiar to me as my own. Like family, almost. His big eyebrows and his big bones and his soft eyes and his wild hair transported me back to where I felt safe and forward to where I wanted to be. He encompassed my dreams; the prospect of losing him now was a fresh nightmare.

How had we let this go? How had our timing been so appalling? Leaving each other had been destructive, then and now. The effects were far-reaching.

'What's going to happen to us?' I blurted childishly, pressing my palms into my temples, staring up at the ceiling.

'Well, you're going to hell, that's for sure,' he said, finding my hand.

'Billy, please don't make light of this,' I begged, pulling my hand away.

'Sorry,' he said.

We were silent, lying side by side. He tucked his forearm under his head, his tattoo obscured by his hair.

'I don't know what to say. It's easier for me,' he said.

'And it's totally impossible for me.'

'I could be your secret lover?'

'Billy. Stop trying to be funny.'

'I'm not. I'm serious.'

'There's the small problem of you living three and a half thousand miles away.'

'What if I moved to London? If Joy has fallen in love with someone here, I'm pissing in the wind thinking she'll come back to Brooklyn with Dixie.'

'You'd actually close your salon there?'

'I'd move it here. Why not?' I could think of any number of reasons why not.

'But wouldn't you lose money?'

'Yes, it would be like starting over. I like starting over. Life's short, right?'

'Sometimes it feels very long,' I groaned, my head about to explode with my confused feelings.

'Seriously, I've been thinking about it ever since she left with Dixie. And there is no way I'm living in a different bloody country to my own daughter. No way.'

While he was in New York, the prospect of an 'us' was hypothetical. A move would change the landscape of possibility, but I couldn't set foot there.

'It still doesn't change the fact that I have a family.' I sat up and placed my feet on the scratchy hotel carpet. I wondered how Nell was, whether our paths might cross this evening. She was in London with Marco and I hoped she was safe. These days, hoping for her safety was like a prayer. I put blind faith in a greater being, accepting that I had no actual power over anything.

'But you could have both. Me *and* them. Is that awful of me to want that?'

'Yes. You know it doesn't work like that. Iris is only ten years old. I'd have to live a lie. I couldn't do that to them, or to Dom.'

He exhaled. 'No. You couldn't.'

I was relieved. If he had put pressure on me, I would have hated him for it. Hating him would destroy me as much as loving him would.

'I need a shower,' I said.

I closed myself into the bathroom and undressed, catching sight of my body in the mirror. If Billy walked in now, I wouldn't be shy of my nakedness in front of him in the way I was with Dom. When I was naked in front of Dom, I felt middle-aged and saggy, in need of diet and exercise. My nakedness in front of Billy would be just that: nakedness. I would be just me, as I had been at twenty, and I liked the idea of that.

After showering, I brushed my teeth with his toothbrush. Wisps of hair had escaped from my shower cap and pinged up into childlike curls. When I came out, he was still in the same position, on his back on the bed. His feet were bare, his ankles crossed. I loved his feet. There was something endearing about them. I longed to lie back down next to him. But I forced myself to be disciplined.

Purposefully I swung my handbag onto my shoulder. It felt heavy. It carried my life. The bank cards embossed with Dom's name; the AirPod case that didn't have AirPods inside, which Iris had painted with blossoms for me; the lip salve I'd chosen in Boots with Nell; the notebook that Bay had given me for Christmas; the keys to the home I had bought with my husband for our children. All of it represented the life I had built with the people who loved and relied on me.

'This can never happen again,' I said to Billy, and turned away from him before he could respond.

I hurried out, and into the long, characterless corridor.

On the street, I needed to catch my breath before making my way to the Tube. I reached into my bag for my mobile, dreading switching it on and returning to my real life.

I imagined Dom on the sofa watching television. Earlier I had texted to remind him that Iris was sleeping over at Willow's and to tell him that I had decided, last minute, to go from Luton into London to meet my old boss at the hat shop for an early supper in Notting Hill, and he had texted back with a joke about having the television to himself for a change. Thinking of that exchange, of his light tone, of his trust, my denial shattered. I couldn't believe what I had done.

I waited for my phone to reboot. There was a waft of rubbish from the basement of the hotel. The pavement under my sneakers was sticky. London was dirty. I was dirty.

On the screen, I was alarmed to see three missed calls from Nell, one from Dom and a string of WhatsApp messages from Nell.

Mum. Call me back.

Have you watched it yet?

Mum. I need you.

Mum. Please. I know you're angry with me, but just call me.

I'm so sorry.

There were dozens more. None of them made any sense. They were desperate and I felt desperate. I called my voicemail to listen to her messages. A tremor started in my hands then broke out across my whole body. After hearing only a few seconds of her breathless sobs, I pressed her number and began to run.

It went straight to voicemail. I tried again. The same.

As I charged through the lamplit streets of Notting Hill, I listened to the rest of her messages. Mostly they were unintelligible, but what became clear was that she had needed me, and I feared with a gasping terror in my soul that my help might now come too late. The wave of sickening guilt felt like a blow to the backs of my knees, and I stumbled slightly as I ran.

The blue and red Tube station sign reared up above me. Hesitating at the top of the steps before descending, I scrolled frantically through my WhatsApps again to check whether Nell had mentioned where she was, whether she was at home or still in London. Lost in the dozens of texts from her, I noticed that Dom had sent one. It included a YouTube link. He had written:

Brace yourself.

A second text from him followed:

Where are you? You need to come home.

With a twist of dread, I called him. Straight to voicemail. Then I tried Bay's phone. It rang out.

If I watched the film now, I would miss the last train home. If Nell was there, I must not miss the train. But if she was in London, in trouble, I should stay and wait until she called me back. My foot hovered over the top step and I called her one last time.

Again there was no answer, and I charged down the stairs into the Tube.

CHAPTER FIFTY-THREE

Nell

My coughing is drawing attention from the other passengers. I move along the carriage and go through the connecting door. The window of the carriage door is open. I stand near it, but the stale city wind seems to hoover more air out of my lungs. The train is moving so damn slowly out of the station. I wonder if I should tell the guard I don't feel well, that I want to get off. I could catch the last train instead.

I go back to my seat and try to keep my coughing under control. Mum still hasn't texted back. I wonder where she is. I'm terrified she's seen the film and is ignoring me. Leah and Tally have Snapped me, but I can't bear to read their texts, knowing they will be angry with me, as though I was in on it. And more messages from Bay keep on coming. I will never respond to her ever again. She has ruined my life.

I scroll Instagram. Her post about the film on her @BayShoots page has got 1,579 likes. She has directed her followers to 'see link in bio' for direct access to it. I switch my phone off.

When the train trundles into Milford – one stop away from my station – my chest tightens and I begin coughing again.

The sighs and dirty looks are making me feel awkward. I go through the connecting door again and slide down to the floor, trying to catch tiny, wheezing breaths. A vice seems to tighten around my ribs. I begin to panic. My throat feels like it is closing, as though my windpipe is narrow as a stripy straw clogged with milkshake. Iris loves those stripy straws. The thought makes me want to cry, but it helps me to regulate my breathing, to stop the panic. I will be home soon.

But Bay will be at home too.

I can't breathe. I can't breathe. I want Mum. I need to find a guard.

Am I having a panic attack? It feels worse than that. At school, they told us that counting down from ten helps.

Ten… nine… eight… seven… Oh my God, I can't even breathe long enough to count. When I stand up, I can't balance, I am so light-headed. I sit back down again.

Ten… nine…

The doors open and the guard sees me.

Concentrating on what he is saying is less important than breathing. I try to understand him, but the need to breathe is more urgent.

A lady appears. She rubs my back and tells me not to panic, asks me if I have an EpiPen or an inhaler. I shake my head, wiping my nose and eyes. My whole face is wet.

I catch snippets of their conversation and flashes of their concerned faces.

'Only four minutes to go… Will she be okay?… Yes, the ambulance will wait… Can we borrow your phone to call someone for you?… Panic attack… asthma attack… allergic reaction… Breathe, darlin', that's right, count and breathe… That's right, you're doing grand.'

I try to tell them that I want to go home but that I can't go home. I make them promise that they won't take me there. I try to tell them about Matthew and how he's lent me a bike. I try to tell them that he is the only safe place in the world. But I don't think they hear me. I am never really heard. Not about the things that matter.

CHAPTER FIFTY-FOUR

Anna

The train guard who had found Nell had called my mobile before Dom's, and I had been able to get off at Guildford and take a cab straight to the hospital, ten minutes away. Dom had agreed to stay with Iris at home, and be there for Bay, just in case she showed up.

Nell was now propped upright, cross-legged and holding her shoulders unnaturally high around her ears. Her chest was expanded fully, still working hard to get the air in. It was agony watching her. She was talking to me for the first time since I had arrived by her curtained bedside two hours ago.

'Sorry…' she began, through the nebuliser, taking more breaths from the oxygen that was being delivered by a thick blue tube to a rigid face mask. 'I…'

'Don't be sorry, sweetheart, don't be sorry. Don't talk at all. Conserve your breath. I'm here now. I'm the one who's sorry,' I said, kissing her forehead, holding her shivery, cold hand, the one without the cannula, wishing I could scoop her into my arms and hold her close to my heart. Hospital tubes and wires and beeping machines surrounded her like a barrier, leaving untrained, inexpert laymen like me on the periphery, but I was reassured that she was finally, and officially, cradled and protected.

'But the film…' she began, taking more in-breaths.

I pushed aside my complicated feelings towards Bay and her film and said, 'Let's not worry about that now. Let's get you better, see what the X-ray says.'

In the light of her ongoing cough, the A&E consultant had said he wanted to check for pneumonia, but he suspected the breathing problems were an asthma attack brought on by acute sinusitis, for which they were going to run a chest X-ray. I had been told that the scariest, life-threatening minutes had taken place earlier, in the ambulance up the A3, where the paramedics had administered intravenous medication to open up her airways. When I thought of her struggling to breathe, alone, without me or anyone she knew to hold her hand, my own throat constricted.

I consoled myself that I was with her now, at the very least, and that the immediate danger had passed, as long as her stress levels remained low.

She began to talk again about the film. 'Have you...' she puffed, 'seen... it?'

'Yes, I have, sweetheart,' I said, stroking her fringe from her clammy forehead. 'Dad's trying to find a way to take it down.'

I had clicked on the link on the train and been initially pleased to see that Bay already had 421 thumbs-up likes, wondering how this film could possibly be the source of Nell's upset. By halfway, I could barely see straight for the angry tears that had gathered in my eyes. If it had been technically possible to close down the internet, meaning that the whole world's power grid would go down with it, I would have tried. Anything to stop that film from being watched by one more person.

Nell frowned and shook her head. 'He...' she breathed into her mask, 'won't... be... able... to.'

For my generation, it was impossible to fathom the power of unregulated social media platforms, and Dom had fixated on the idea of being able to take the film down. When I had called him with updates from the doctors about Nell's condition, he had quickly returned to the problem of the film and the phone calls he had made to troubleshooters at YouTube. He had been told, in call operator lingo, far removed in Bangladesh, that the film was there to stay unless Bay wanted to take it down, which we knew she wouldn't.

'Don't worry about all that now, Nellie. Daddy sends you a big hug,' I said, maintaining the authenticity in my voice, relaying a hug that Dom had not in actual fact communicated.

A shaft of light in my mind exposed Billy's face smiling down at me, and deep shame eclipsed the joy I had felt at the time. But my guilt about this afternoon did not cancel out my anger towards Dom, as maybe it should have done. A ball of fire spun in the pit of my belly. It had been gathering momentum over several months. However hard I tried to smother it now, by remembering my own culpability, and Bay's, I could not extinguish my hateful feelings towards the man I was supposed to love above all others. At the core of it, I believed that Dom was to blame for everything: for marrying Suki, for abandoning Bay, for resenting her, for ignoring her; for encouraging Nell, for being greedy; for Francis Ray's attack. For not being on my side. Bay's lurid film had exposed much more than the sexual exploitation of vulnerable young models; it had brought to light how remiss we had been as parents. Dom's encouragement of Nell's career was almost as bad as the lasciviousness of the men depicted in the ironically titled film.

To give Bay her due, if I were able to step back from how wounding it was for Nell, she had made a film that represented all my original fears about modelling – all the fears that I had shoved away to accommodate Nell's naïve wishes and Dom's vicarious dreams of a better, more exciting life. As much as Dom had wanted to be an entrepreneurial spirit, which I had liked once, he wasn't; he was a plodder. He had not had the career he thought he could have had, and he was not the exceptional man his parents had told him he was. His unmet desires had been realised through Nell's modelling career, at her expense. I didn't think I could ever forgive myself for failing to spot his underlying motivations.

The porter and a nurse arrived at Nell's bedside to wheel her to X-ray.

In the blue room, I put on my radiation vest and chatted to the young radiographer, standing in the corner as he held the big machine in front of Nell's ribcage. It was a challenge for her to remain still for the required few minutes. I imagined the rays travelling through her body, right inside her, to be absorbed by her tissues. It seemed intimate, somehow, and I feared what they might find.

When it was finished, I watched through the glass as the radiographer wrinkled his brow at his screen and called a colleague over. The young professionals both seemed unsure of what they were looking at. A third colleague arrived. I hid my worry from Nell, whose gaze had followed my own. Images of malignant masses on her lungs went in and out of my head, too frightening to dwell on.

I called over to them. 'Everything okay there?'

'Sorry, Mrs Hart, the consultant will analyse the results shortly.' The radiographer returned to our side of the divide. 'Let's get you back to the ward,' he said, seemingly more engaged with us than before.

I noted from his badge that he was called Mahmood, and I wanted to be able to read his mind in the way he had read her X-rays. Something was wrong, it was obvious.

Within ten minutes of our return to the cubicle, Dr Ward was at Nell's bedside.

'Mrs Hart, before we talk about the X-ray, I'd like to examine Nell's chest area, if I may. Is that all right, Nell, if I take a little look at your chest?'

Nell shook her head and I was confused.

'Of course you can,' I said.

She began to take off her nebuliser, protesting.

'Nell, it's okay,' Dr Ward said, gently insisting she replace her mask. The rate of her breathing began to increase.

'Is it necessary? Right now?' I asked inanely, knowing that he wouldn't do it unless he had to.

'We've identified something on her X-rays that concerns us.'

Nell lay back and closed her eyes. She flinched when he touched her.

'Sorry, I've got cold fingers.'

He prodded gently while her chest continued to heave up and down, stretched to its capacity.

'Nell, can you tell me what the cause of these scars is?' His fingers swept the air above her chest, in the area underneath her breasts and between them.

She didn't answer; just shook her head, still with her eyes closed.

'Does this hurt at all?' He pressed down.

Again she shook her head.

'Is the scar tissue sensitive to the touch?'

She shrugged.

'Is that the scar from the wax?' I asked, standing up to look. She suddenly twisted away and I stepped back, feeling a chill through my bones. I remembered her at Take One, and her explanation for the minor scarring that Collette had seen.

'Do you have any strange sensations in these areas?' Dr Ward asked.

She nodded. 'When… it's… cold…' she replied breathily.

'Hmm. Yes. Have you ever experienced any pain or swelling or seeping from these scars?'

She made no reply, as though she was humming a tune in her head.

'Nell?' I said, embarrassed by her rudeness.

Dr Ward pulled up her gown. 'You can't tell us anything about them, Nell?'

She turned her head away.

'Can I have a word with you outside, Mrs Hart?'

'Of course,' I said, glancing at Nell, who stared stubbornly at a spot on the floor.

'We'll be back in a minute, okay, Nell?' the doctor said.

Outside in the corridor, next to the nurses' station, he pinned two X-ray photos onto a mounted light box.

'This is Nell's chest area. You see these?' He pointed to a series of thin white lines, about a millimetre thick and an inch long, that were placed, wonkily, about an inch apart. They were arranged in an eerie formation of two curved lines, leading from the middle of her chest and sweeping underneath and across her ribs, where her bra would sit. I didn't know what I was looking at.

'My exam of her chest just now revealed some mild scarring, which concurs with these foreign bodies findings on the X-ray.'

My whole body began to tremble. 'What foreign bodies?'

'It seems these white lines resemble some kind of metal object, but we're not sure what, specifically. Retained needles in patients with a history of drug abuse are by no means unheard of, and there have been cases of acupuncture needles left under the skin, but the location and shape of the foreign bodies in Nell's X-rays are not consistent with drug use or acupuncture—'

I interrupted. 'No. Neither is possible.'

He continued. 'Hmm. Yes. Well, it looks to me and my colleagues as though they might be common sewing needles. Do you know how this might have happened?'

My voice wouldn't work. I shook my head as I stared at the strange lines across Nell's X-ray. I couldn't associate those lines with my daughter's body lying in a bed along the corridor. There must be some kind of mistake, but I couldn't seem to say it out loud. 'She told me she had scars there from hot wax,' I said finally, in disbelief at my own stupidity.

'Hmm. Okay. Well, we'll be calling the CAMHS team, which is the Child and Adolescent Mental Health Services, and social services, who will want to have a little word with her about it.'

I stared at Dr Ward, right into his tired coffee-coloured eyes. 'Social services?'

'It's protocol, I'm afraid,' he said kindly.

We both returned our gaze to the X-rays. 'So horribly neat – the lines, I mean,' I said, feeling nausea rise up my gullet.

'Hmm. Yes.' He folded his arms over his clipboard. 'Has she any history of self-harm?'

'No. Never!' I said, adding, 'Or not that I know of.'

'Foreign body insertion can be a form of self-harm,' he said, pausing, waiting for me to say something. 'And Nell seemed distressed and reluctant to explain just now.'

'I just can't believe what I'm looking at,' I said, barely audibly.

'Self-embedding behaviour is unfortunately something we're seeing more of lately, in teens specifically. Sometimes post-trauma, or if they have a history of depression.'

I thought of the trauma of Francis Ray's sexual assault.

'Can you tell how long they've been there?' I asked.

'No, I'm afraid not. The wounds don't seem fresh. There's some entry point scarring, but I couldn't tell you how long ago it happened, I'm afraid, not based on a superficial exam. For now, Nell is the only one who can tell us that.'

'But wouldn't needles work their way out, like when you get a splinter? Wouldn't the body reject them?'

'In some cases, patients can develop haematomas or fibrosis, but not always. And if the objects are cleaned properly and cause no infection, there's no reason why the body would reject them. Theoretically, they could remain there for a whole lifetime without being detected.'

'Like shrapnel,' I said vaguely, remembering my mother's stories about the embedded fragments scattered through my grandfather's thigh.

'Yes, just like that.'

'Is this anything to do with the breathing difficulties?'

'No. Her tests have confirmed asthma, which can be triggered by stress, and we will talk to you about that as well.'

On top of what I was seeing in Nell's X-ray, the diagnosis of asthma didn't seem so serious.

'Will you take them out? I want them out of her.' I blinked wildly at him, knocking back confused tears.

'Yes, we would recommend removal. Under general anaesthetic, because of the number of needles and the scar tissue, and the length of time they might have been in the body. And there might be a need for further exploration for internal damage.'

'Internal damage?'

'They'll carry out a full skeletal survey, just to make sure there aren't any others.'

'There might be *more*? More than…' I stared again at the strange white lines and began counting them, as though a specific number would change anything.

'There are twenty-four,' he said.

Twenty-four horrible sewing needles had been inserted into Nell's body and I had no idea how they'd got there. The shock of it. My God. I couldn't even unscramble it to make sense of it.

'Would you like someone to get you a cup of tea?'

I shook my head, 'No thank you, no. I need to talk to Nell.'

Nell looked paler than before. Paler than I had ever seen her. She caught my eye briefly before looking down at that same spot on the floor.

I sat down on the chair next to the bed, unable to hide the misery I felt on her behalf. I reached out to touch her ribs, wanting to transfer all her anguish to me. However the needles had made their way into her body, I knew the process must have come with terrible suffering, and I braced myself for what I was about to hear: had it been self-harm? Or a sexual game gone wrong? Or a weird friendship ritual with Jade and Mint? Or maybe the injuries were more recent? One of the men in Bay's film, perhaps?

'I've seen the X-ray,' I said. 'They think they're sewing needles. Is that what they are, Nell?'

Her blue eyes were peeled in fear. 'They're still in there? Inside me?'

'You didn't know?'

She let out a small cry.

I whispered, 'What happened to you?'

A stream of tears worked its way down her cheek, and I wiped it away, again and again, despairing, feeling my own tears fall.

'I can't say it,' she whispered.

'You can say anything to me, anything. You know I'll always be here for you, whatever the truth is.'

'I'm sure she's sorry…' she said, before taking a breath and holding it.

'Who's sorry? Who is she?'

'Bay,' she said suddenly.

'Bay?' My brain couldn't catch up.

'Bay did it to me.'

My stomach caved and I clutched it as though winded. 'What?' I breathed.

Strangely, her breathing regulated. When she spoke again, her voice was calm and straightforward, as though her story was well worn in her head. 'When we were little, she used to force me to be her patient on a pretend operating table. The games started out okay, but then she ended up bringing all these horrible things into it, like rubber bands and pliers and lighters. She used to push the needles inside me, like she was sewing me up.'

Her words felt like a backdraught of fire across my whole being. 'My God,' I rasped.

'Sorry, Mum,' she said, beginning to cry again. 'I never thought she'd left them inside me.'

'Nell,' I said, crying with her, clutching her hand, 'how can *you* be sorry?'

'You wanted me to be kind to her, and I tried so hard. I really did,' she said, her chest heaving again.

'Shh, shh, of course you did. Of course you did. You must look after your breathing,' I said, smoothing her hair, my face close to hers.

'She lied all the time, about everything, and she kept blaming me for things and you'd never believe me because she was so small and sweet and Suki had been so horrible to her.' She broke down into her hands, pulling her nebuliser away to wipe her tears.

I secured it back onto her face, ashamed of myself, allowing the truth of the past to slowly filter into my consciousness, remembering all the times I had not believed my own daughter when she had come crying to me during their fights.

'How long did these games go on for?' I asked, terrified of her answer.

'When I was about ten, I went to her and said I wanted it to stop, that it wasn't normal. And she did stop. It was so strange. I remember how simple it was and how she accepted it without a fight. And I was so annoyed with myself for not asking her to stop before then.'

Nell had been six years old when Bay had come to live with us. For years, she had lived with Bay's torture games and I had never known.

'My God, Nell, it went on all that time?' I squeezed her thigh and thought of Bay's film, realising it was *still* going on. Nell had trusted her big sister, while Bay had pretended to have Nell's best interests at heart, ingratiating herself with me. I was engulfed with disgust and regret. With Bay. With myself. 'When you were little, I thought you were struggling to accept her. I thought you felt usurped, which I understood, but I had no idea you were going through that. No idea.'

'How could you have known?' Nell asked me, stroking my arm. She was making excuses for me, trying to make it easier for me to forgive myself. It was what she had been forced to do as a younger child: hide the truth, make it better for me, for Bay, and for the rest of the family. In return, she must have accepted that she would endure Bay's spitefulness. *Take one for the team.*

'This is my fault,' I said, holding one side of her face in my palm, looking right into those vulnerable blue eyes of hers.

Nell's teenage rebellion began to slowly slot into place. It had context, beyond the rhetoric of hormonal changes. Her destructive behaviour had a deep, awful source. It was no surprise she had shown me such anger: both displaced and deserved.

'No, Mum. This is Bay's fault. I *hate* her,' she said. 'I *hate* her so much.'

It pained me to hear the words, but no more than it had pained me to learn this new truth about our past and see the cause of her upset. I understood why she felt this way; in the face of those needles, it was healthy to manifest anger towards Bay. Appropriate. In Nell's mind, at least, it should be cut and dried. Less so in mine. Both Bay and Nell had been children. The responsibility and the blame rested at my feet. In spite of Dom's protestations, I had insisted we take Bay in and I had grown to love her. I had loved another woman's child. I had loved a grubby, wounded child. I had loved a child who had hurt my own. Like an echo of Suki's abuse, Bay had become the abuser, unconsciously perhaps, but harmfully. In her envy, she had shoved Nell into a cold, dark place and Nell's screams had not been heard by me or by Dom or by anyone who could have put a stop to it. And the two of them had lived with an unforgiving secret for the whole of their childhood.

Sickness spread through me, leaving me dry-mouthed and wet-palmed. 'I'm so sorry,' I repeated, inadequately. 'I'm so sorry.'

I had failed to protect her, even though it was the one promise I had whispered to my pregnant belly in the early weeks of her existence. 'I'll keep you safe and cosy in there,' I'd said, believing my love alone could ensure it, inside the womb and beyond; it had been my only job as her mother and I hadn't been up to the task.

'That's okay, Mum,' she said simply, and I loved her in that moment more than I had ever loved her, if that was even possible. How kind-hearted and courageous she was, and how little I deserved it.

That's okay, Mum. Three brave words. I could only guess at how much it took out of her to say them, to both acknowledge the guilty role I had played in her ordeal and forgive me for it. I wanted to extricate those needles from her chest, figuratively and literally.

The problem of Bay loomed. Her whereabouts was unknown. Since posting her film, she had been radio-silent. Part of me feared for her, part of me wanted her to suffer. The latter made me feel like a bad person, and I took it back. She was only seventeen years old. I would continue to be the grown-up. We had to find her.

She would be sorry for what she had done. She would take down the film. Nell would forgive her. Our family could survive this.

CHAPTER FIFTY-FIVE

Bay

Badger's jaw was plonked on my thigh and he was drooling onto my pyjamas. Ty had placed a croissant on a blue plastic plate in front of me. Ty's mum didn't allow real china in the pool house.

I picked at a flake while Ty opened up the laptop.

'Shit, Bay. It's blowing up.'

'How many views?'

'Two thousand five hundred and six.'

I should have been over the moon. This was about a thousand more than I had ever received for my other films, and it had only been up for a few hours.

'Likes?'

'Six hundred and thirty-two.'

'Thumbs down?'

'One hundred and three.'

Dad would be one of those hundred and three thumbs down. He had called almost as many times.

'Femo reposted it,' I said, pasting a good thought on top of a bad one. Femo was a feminist social media influencer. She was fierce and respected. In any other circumstances, Ty and I would be dancing around the laptop.

'You serious?' he said. He scratched his lower back.

'This was the whole point, Ty. I wanted it to go viral, right?'

'Sure.'

I shoved Badger off my thigh. 'I *wanted* it to shock Dad.'

'I'm guessing that's worked.'

'I wanted it to stop Nell from modelling.'

'Depends. It might have the opposite effect. The exposure could make her hot property.'

'Everyone knew I was making an exposé. I spelt it out to Anna. What did she expect?'

'Maybe she didn't know how good it would be.'

'That's the point,' I said again, standing up. 'Everyone's shocked because it's good and because it shows the truth.'

'They can't handle the truth!' Ty said in an American accent, mimicking Jack Nicholson in *A Few Good Men*. Badger looked up and tilted his head at Ty as though questioning his behaviour.

'Shut up, Ty,' I said.

I shoved the crummy old window-door to the side and stepped into the early-morning sunshine. The air gave me goosebumps. The hot-pink roses bounced around on their stems. The glare from the plastic pool cover blinded me. Everything around me was perfect. When I had been small, cramped in Suki's flat, tiptoeing around her drinking, I had dreamt of living in Dad's house in the country, which I had pictured as a large, ramshackle farmhouse just like this, with flowers crowding up its flint walls and horses in the stables and chickens laying eggs for breakfast. The disappointment of seeing Anna and Dad's terraced house had been lead-heavy. I had feared it would be as claustrophobic living there as it had been at Suki's.

I kicked off my flip-flops, just like Suki always used to. When she came in late from a night out, she would flick her slip-ons off her tiny feet and they would land willy-nilly around the flat. The next morning, she would cry over her lost shoes, and I would dash around reuniting the separated pair and physically place them on her feet. Sometimes she would kick her foot up into my chin and then pretend she hadn't meant to. But she had always been sorry for being cruel.

'You okay?' Ty said, joining me outside.

'Can I stay here again tonight?' I asked, winding the cover back from the pool as though it were mine already. Badger barked croakily.

'Course.'

'Thanks.'

'Your parents will definitely come looking for you here.'

'They'll be happier, just the four of them again. I was never meant to be there.'

'Don't be daft.'

'Believe me, it's better this way,' I said. 'Do you have any sunglasses?'

He scuttled inside, and I imagined staying with Ty until university started in three months' time. In many ways, it was a dream come true to live in this house with someone who had chosen me as their friend.

Dad and Anna and Nell and Iris would regroup after the shock had worn off. Nell would give up modelling and men, pass her GCSEs and stay at school to take her A levels. Maybe she would even date Matthew. Eventually, I guessed, she would tell Anna about what I had done to her when we were small and she would be released from the secret. Strangely, I never imagined myself being released from the secret, whether it was out in the open or not.

I thought back.

When Nell had been ten, she had come into my bedroom and said, 'I think we should stop playing those games.'

'Okay,' I had replied.

All at once, the unpleasantness of what I had been doing to Nell had hit me. I had been horrified and embarrassed in front of her, like an alcoholic who had been caught out secretly drinking; the games had been a bad habit that I had not been able to give up and that I had almost kept as a secret from myself. Nell's confrontation had been like an intervention, a whoosh of air blowing everything out of me, leaving me hollow and ungrounded. Previously denied feelings of shame and self-hatred had thickened the air outside my head, almost to the point of suffocation.

Ty and Badger had been the only ones there for me. The following day at school, I had found Ty in our lunch break, telling him I'd had a horrible argument with Nell, only revealing so much. Ty had not known the facts, but he had hugged me as I rocked with sobs, taken me home and let me sleep with Badger. My feelings had settled back down inside me again, safe and small.

Ty had probably imagined that Nell and I had shouted and thrown things and sworn at each other. He hadn't known that the real scenario had involved one simple demand from Nell and immediate acquiescence from me. It would not have been obvious to anyone else that the exchange had been life-changing. A complete role reversal. But it had been. It had been a day of reckoning. What I had done to Nell was evil, and she had been brave enough to call me out, but she had not rejected me in the way Suki had. I would always be grateful to her for that.

My feet were hot in the sun now. I rolled my pyjamas up, sat on the side of the pool and lowered my ankles into the water. The cold stunned me. I hadn't expected it to be that icy. Enduring the burn on my skin and the sharpness in my ankle bones felt like repentance.

Nobody would ever believe me if I told them the film had been a gift: for Nell and for Anna. A thank you for everything they had given me. An apology. My love for them went beyond what I expected back. My love was unconditional, unlike theirs for me.

CHAPTER FIFTY-SIX

Nell

We are sitting in the car outside Ty's house.

I had never thought teeth chattering together was an actual thing. Turns out it is. The thought of seeing Bay has set them off, big-style. It has been three weeks since any of us have seen her or spoken to her, three weeks since it all came out.

In my nightmare last night, her face was like a beast's, with black whiskers and large incisors. Every night since the operation, I've been having nightmares. As I lay there on a real operating table, about to go under, I relived Bay's games and imagined that the surgeons in their masks were multiple Bays, gleefully cutting and tugging and sewing the skin over my bones, relishing that little ping of the needles dropping into kidney dishes, laughing at me as they hung over my body. At the memory, my armpits tingle and I feel light-headed.

'You don't have to do this,' Mum says.

I am trying to shake off the image of Bay as a beast. It is weird: having lived with her for most of my childhood, having loved her as a big sister, I am now petrified of setting eyes on her, as though she is capable of doing it to me all over again just by looking at me.

'Yes, I do,' I say. It is as important to me as having the needles removed from my chest. Terrifying but necessary.

I get out of the car, wincing. The wounds on my chest are still sore through the painkillers. Mum follows me up the path. I ring the doorbell. It is a long, rambling house, but the window frames need a lick of paint and the path is overgrown, and there is an orange swing out front that has half fallen off its ropes.

Ty's mum is small – strangely, a bit like Bay – and her cheeks are hollow. She doesn't say hello. She nods and stands aside, as though this is not her house. 'They're in the garden. I haven't told them you're coming.'

'Thanks, Rose, I appreciate it,' Mum says.

Being here is weird. The smell of the house is horrible. Ty's parents' divorce is lingering in the air still. Mess is everywhere. Bay had described Ty's house as ramshackle and rather romantic. The reality didn't match her description.

There is a frilly pink and white striped swing seat at the bottom of the overgrown lawn. The metal hinges creak as it rocks back and forth, ringing out across the fields. It is like a rusty cradle in a horror movie.

Neither of them has noticed us come out of the back door of the kitchen. I walk across the grass as though I am flying. My legs are working but I have no say in it. My entire focus is on Bay.

Her small face is nothing like a beast's. She is on the seat, cross-legged like a child, while Ty's foot pushes them from the ground. Her black Ray-Bans make her look paler than ever and are too large on her face. Her lips are painted bright red and her hair has a quiff. She looks so like Dad, with the high forehead and small mouth.

The squeaking stops when they see us.

Ty stands up and his head hits the canvas canopy, flinging it back vertically, flooding Bay with sunlight. She pulls her knees to her chest.

I stand in front of her and Mum stays back a little.

Everyone says hi to each other. I am actually relieved she is wearing her shades.

'I just came here because I want to sort this out,' I say. My voice comes out all shaky.

'Uh-huh,' Bay says.

'I want you to take the film down,' I say. 'I hate it being out there. It's so humiliating. And I won't get any work.'

I'm not sure I even want to be a model any more. Ian was chilly and professional on the phone. I spoke to him a couple of days after Bay posted the film, and sent him a heartfelt email apologising on her behalf, making sure he knew I had nothing to do with it. Mum sent him a separate email explaining that I was finishing my exams and having 'a minor operation' and that I wouldn't be able to work for a while. He sent 'get well' flowers to our house, even though Bay still hadn't taken the film down. The film is a reminder of all the mistakes I have made. I want a clean slate. To start afresh. While it's still up on YouTube, I can't move on. Surely, if she has felt any love for me ever, she will understand that. I still have hope.

'No,' she says.

Mum steps forward and speaks up. Her voice is scary, low and really unlike her. 'Bay, you've made it clear that you don't want anything to do with us any more, and I'm very hurt by that, but I really do believe you are better than this. I really do believe you can make the right choice here. Surely you can see how distressing it is for Nell to know that the film is out there, gathering more and more viewers every day?'

I love Mum for standing up for me and realise how rare it is when it comes to Bay.

'I never expected you two to understand why I did it,' Bay says, reaching for Ty's hand. Ty holds it on his thigh.

'We don't *understand*?' I say. 'Are you kidding me? We've spent our whole lives trying to understand you and stepping on eggshells and making sure you know how much we love you. Every fricking day of my life I've bent over backwards to make you fricking happy!'

'I'm sorry it was so hard for you to love me,' she says, standing up. 'Don't worry, you don't have to bother trying any more.'

It is the sarky tone and the ingratitude that goes right through me. Stupid tears spring into my eyes. 'Always the victim, aren't you? Take a look at these, then tell me who's really the victim here.' I pull up my T-shirt and show the twenty-four weeping sores sliced across my chest.

Ty's hand goes straight to his mouth. Bay's skin turns see-through. Then she collapses, literally just collapses, right there in front of me.

Ty falls on his knees next to her. 'Bay? Bay? Are you okay?'

Mum's reaction is delayed, but she bends down to see how Bay is. 'She's fainted. Turn her on her side, Ty. She'll be okay.'

I don't budge to help them. I just stare down at her, feeling sick, then I walk away up the garden and through the kitchen and out through the front door and shut myself in the car. I wait, stony-faced and dry-eyed. I feel nothing. I wouldn't care if she swallowed her tongue and died.

Mum's arm is suddenly around me. I didn't even register that she had got into the car.

'Let's get you home, sweetheart,' she says, kissing me. 'Are you okay?'

'Yeah,' I say, staring out of the window.

'Bay's fine. It was just the shock. Rose and Ty are looking after her.'

Like I care.

Mum starts the engine and drives us away. I look behind me and I think I see Bay through one of the windows, but I am probably imagining it.

'I didn't mean to upset her,' I say, even though I did. It is habit to say it.

'It's okay, sweetheart. She needed to see what she did to you.'

There is anger in Mum's voice and I like hearing it.

She goes on, 'She can't go through life thinking she can behave how she likes and then act all upset when people react to what she's done. I'm sure she's sorry and she'll do the right thing. She's trying to push us away because she doesn't know how to be loved. Give her time.'

Mum still believes that Bay will change. It is unbelievable. I've given her enough chances.

'She'll never understand, Mum! Don't you get it? Stop trying to fix her! She's a total sociopath. Anyone normal would have taken down that film by now. So yeah, okay, she had a shitty time of it with Suki, but Jesus, when do the excuses run out? There are people in the world who've had it far worse than she has, and not all of them are total bitches to the people who love them. Some of them are probably caring for sick people or doing loads of good stuff because they don't want to treat people how they were treated. Some fucked-up people are just being nice fucking people! But Bay is still saying "poor me, poor me" and shitting on everyone she loves and you're still defending her! It's un-fucking-believable!'

I can't believe I said so many 'fuckings' to Mum, but I don't care. She needs to hear it. I'm sick to death of her overprotective-ness towards Bay. My whole body is now shaking with the injustice of it. I want her to prioritise my feelings for once, to put her own daughter ahead of Bay. I want her to choose me. For once in my life, I want her to choose *me*! Is that so much to ask?

Mum goes silent for a while, probably trying to think up a way to disagree with me. I wait for her to tell me off.

Then she pulls over in a lay-by and turns to me and says, 'You're right, Nell. In defending her, I lost sight of what you needed from me, and I'll regret that for the rest of my life.'

All at once, it feels like a mass of darkness is sucked from my soul; it feels like I just got my mum back.

Her eyes tear up and I hug her so tightly, and we both cry for a bit. Mum chose my truth, and everything feels right in the world.

God, I love her. I love her so much it hurts.

CHAPTER FIFTY-SEVEN

Anna

I stacked the food into Mum's fridge in a hurried, rather haphazard way. If I didn't leave in the next five minutes, I was going to be late for Dom. It was date night, which was a new thing. Every Tuesday night, we went out. And every Tuesday night, I dreaded the pretending.

Over the past few weeks, we had been fully occupied by the girls: failing to coax Bay home, helping Nell get through her GCSEs and supporting her emotionally after her operation. Poor Iris had been confused and upset throughout most of it. She was not old enough to fully understand the fractures in our family and it had left her tearful and cross. Getting through the last month had been tough on all of us, but things had finally settled down in the past week. Bay was living with Ty until she went to Norwich – albeit still not talking to any of us – Nell had finished her last exam and her chest was healing as it should. Now that school had broken up, Iris had been easier. There were fewer diversions, leaving the state of our marriage laid bare. Yet continuing as we were, limping along, was bearable. Pretending I could imagine spending the rest of my life with him was a less challenging path than any of the alternatives. Dom seemed to be happy with that. He wasn't trying to prise open my heart or reveal his innermost thoughts or sort through our resentments. We were coasting. Giving it time. Hoping we could ride out the storm.

'There weren't any decaf coffee pods, I'm afraid,' I said to Mum. In my haste, I dropped the ham.

'Oh, I never use them anyway, dear,' she said.

'Don't you?' I said. I stopped stuffing the fridge and stared at the expensive coffee machine we had bought her for her seventieth.

'It's too noisy and fiddly,' she said.

'All you do is put the pod in that bit,' I said, demonstrating.

'Oh well, I prefer my instant.'

'Have you even tried the pods?'

'No, dear.'

'What have you been doing with all the ones I've been buying you?'

'You sometimes have a cup when you come over, don't you?'

'But I must have bought you a packet of twelve every week for months!'

She tugged one side of her cardigan over her chest. 'I give them to Jeff next door and he buys me a jar of my instant.'

'Oh, right.'

I had no right to tell her what she liked and no clue about why it upset me so much.

'I've always drunk instant, Anna,' she said, in a tone that suggested I should have known better than to force her to drink good coffee.

'You should have said. I'll stop buying them for you then.'

'I never asked you to spend all that money on a fancy machine.'

No, she had never asked me for anything. She had only expected everything. She would never change. She would drain me of everything I had and still want more. Nothing I did was ever going to make her happy.

I squeezed the mayonnaise onto the top shelf and closed the fridge door.

'Well, I'd better get going.'

'When will you come again?'

'Thursday? Is that okay?' I said.

'It's just, you missed the other week.'

'Mum, Nell was in hospital that Thursday, remember?'

I had told Mum what had happened, but she had fixated on the asthma attack, saying, 'Oh, Nell is so like me! Remember when I had that awful asthma attack?' Mum had not had an asthma attack. It had been a chest infection that had caused wheezing for a few months.

'Oh yes,' she said now. 'How *is* Nellie?'

Mum hadn't been involved in my agony and self-flagellation following Nell's disclosure about the games of torture she had been subjected to as a child. But Nell and I were doing well, or better, at least.

'The stitches are out, which is good, I guess,' I said.

Mum sat down on the sofa and switched the television on. 'I have terrible asthma too, you know.' Plainly the stitches in Nell's chest were too much for her to think about.

'Okay, Mum. I'll say goodbye.'

She waved the remote in my direction. 'Bye, dear.'

I took my handbag and left, feeling sad for her but disconnected.

There are people in the world who've had it far worse than she has, and not all of them are total bitches to the people who love them.

Nell had said that.

I drove home thinking about what else Nell had said.

Some fucked-up people are just being nice fucking people.

Nell was wiser than I was.

The pub was almost empty. There was a couple in the corner. They weren't deep in conversation, but they looked comfortable together, focused on their food, offering up the odd comment to each other, smiling as they took a sip of wine at the same time. They were enjoying their evening, it was obvious.

'Bay got in touch,' Dom said, tutting.

'What?' I couldn't believe he had saved this information until now.

All Dom's blame and anger had been directed at Bay, exclusively, which was unjust. His lack of interest in her was half the reason she had felt unloved and in need of attention in the first place, though I didn't say so. My own guilt about Billy lived on quietly in the back of my mind, but there had been too much else going on to dwell on it.

'She wants to meet up.'

'With both of us?' I asked. I wasn't sure how I felt about seeing Bay.

'No, she only wants to meet me.'

I was relieved, in a shameful sort of way. 'It's good she wants to see you, Dom,' I said.

I was now more honest with myself about Bay. It was hard to admit, but I could not love her as my own, could never love her as I loved Nell and Iris. I had tried to replace her mother, when I should have tried to be a good stepmum instead, a good carer, and more realistic about her position in the family. My love for Bay would always be conditional, and perhaps she had always known it, deep down, better than I had. This did not sit comfortably inside me, and I felt sad for her, but I could no longer hide from the brutal truth that she was not mine in the way that Nell and Iris were.

'I told her I needed time.'

I choked on my mouthful of fish. 'You did what?'

'I can't face her. I'm still too angry about what she did.'

I took a sip of wine to help the food go down. I had done my best, but Dom couldn't change the fact that she was his flesh and blood just as much as Nell and Iris were. 'I think it's really important you find a way to forgive her, Dom.'

'Why?' he said, like a child.

I couldn't believe I had to spell it out. 'Bay's your daughter too.'

'But she's so like Suki.'

'It'll be hard to confront her about all this. I really do understand that.'

'I wouldn't know what to say to her.'

'You'll know when you see her. You should have seen Nell at Ty's. She was so brave. She went straight in there and told Bay what she wanted from her and showed her the scars. It was incredible, honestly. It took real courage.'

'I'm not avoiding her because I'm scared.'

'Okay?' I said, sceptically.

'I'm not.'

'She needs you, Dom. She's always needed you.'

'She should have behaved better then.'

What did he expect? He had abandoned her to Suki and then resisted taking her in. At best, he had been ambivalent about her. At worst, he had actively disliked her. Either way, he had a responsibility towards her now. 'Dom. She's your daughter. You have to love her just the way she is. Warts and all.'

'You're better at all this stuff than I am,' he said.

I was dumbfounded. 'I'm not better at it! Look at the mess I've made! It's not about being good at it. It's about a child needing love.'

'You can't tell me how to love my own daughter,' he said.

Anger spread through me, right to my fingertips, and I spoke without thinking. 'If you'd loved her more, she might not have done all those awful things to Nell,' I hissed, shocked that the words had come out of my mouth. I looked around the restaurant, checking whether the strangers on the other side of the room might have heard me utter such a vile truth.

Dom's jaw fell. Nobody had ever spoken to him like that. And maybe I shouldn't have, but I hadn't been able to keep it inside any longer. He said, 'You were the one who made us take her in.'

'I still don't regret taking her in. What choice did we have? But I should have handled it better and I wish with every bone in my body that I had. But at least I recognise I made mistakes. You can't even see where you went wrong!'

He held his knife and fork up as if ready to dig into his food, but he didn't eat; he spoke at his plate. 'I think some kids are just born a certain way,' he mumbled.

'You're seriously not going to take any responsibility for this situation?'

He threw his cutlery down and the couple across the room glanced over. 'Why the hell should I?'

I tried to keep my voice down. 'Jesus Christ, Dom. I've spent my whole life trying to give you the benefit of the doubt. But you're just not capable of thinking beyond all your self-pitying crap, are you? You're just like Mum and just like Bay. Stubborn and pissed off with everyone else all the time. Don't you realise that what you put into life, you get out? Why can't you see that? I know I've screwed up, big-time, and I'm trying bloody hard to make it right, but you're just sitting in the shit and folding your arms with a big sulk on your face, like a baby, waiting for someone to pull you out. It's pathetic, quite frankly.'

'How can you blame me for everything?' He was crestfallen, but I wasn't falling for his vulnerable victim act any more.

I stood up, knowing that everything had changed, that nothing could go back to how it was, that I would never want it to. 'For Nell's sake, I blame you, and for Nell's sake, I blame myself. I'm sick of living a lie and pretending that our messed-up marriage doesn't affect the kids. If I'd spent less time making sure your daughter was okay – *your* daughter from *your* fucked-up marriage – while you moped around wishing you had more money or whatever the hell it is you want, I'd have been able to protect Nell. At least that bloody film exposed the truth about how much she's been hurting!' Tears fell down my cheeks and I stormed out, only realising when I was outside that he had the car keys.

I decided to walk instead. I would do anything rather than go back in and see him.

As I made my way through the woods, I dialled Billy's number. After some tearful retelling of what had just happened, I calmed down.

Billy said, 'I feel responsible.'

'No! You're *not* responsible. You're more like the symptom.'

'That's romantic.'

'You know what I mean. Dom and I have been so unhappy for so long, but we love the kids and so we've just muddled through.'

'How's Nell doing?'

I started crying again. 'The operation was horrendous.'

'Poor, poor Nell.'

'She's going to be okay, though. I know that now. She's her own person with her own journey, and I've got to stop trying to own it and control it. I used to think she was mine, but she's not mine, she doesn't belong to anyone. She's just Nell, and she's going to have an amazing life.'

'Will you remind me of all that when Dixie is a teenager?' he said.

'Yes.' I cried some more. 'Oh, Billy. You're going through so much too, with Dixie and everything, but it'll all be worth it, I promise. Even though this past year has been hell on earth, I wouldn't take any of it back.'

'None of it?'

'Okay, quite a bit of it, but you know what I mean.'

'Who'd be a parent, right?'

'Right!' I laughed.

'I wish we were going through it together,' he said.

'Me too,' I replied, in a semi-whisper.

I walked on, and was surprised that I wasn't scared in the woods alone, not while I had Billy's voice in my ear.

He spoke again. 'You have to leave Dom and be with me.'

'Yes,' I said. I knew this was true.

Pretending to be the perfect family didn't seem possible any more. Staying together all those years for the sake of the girls had been counter-intuitive: the damage had been eating away at us anyway, but it had been more dangerous, suppressed and insidious. Facing up to it was not going to be easy, but I couldn't see any other way forward. Not now. I couldn't hide from the truth any longer. I loved Billy. I had always loved Billy, and I had run away from him because I'd been scared. Scared to live a life that broke through my neuroses, that halted the generational trauma passed down to me from my parents. In turn, much to my shame, I had married Dom, as second best, and passed the pain on to him and the girls.

No more. I refused to be scared like my mother was.

I wanted to drink better coffee than she had! What was so wrong with that?

'I love you, Billy,' I said.

Like putting an oxygen mask to my face and breathing into it first, I would save myself in order to save my children's lives; inhale the happiness, so that I could blow it back over their heads like invisible sprinkles of dust.

'I love you too, Anna,' Billy said.

Simple as that.

Love would conquer all.

EPILOGUE

Two years later

And it had. In a way. Love and anger and truth and empathy and kindness and forgiveness had conquered all.

'You are beautiful,' Matthew said, lying next to Nell, naked, tracing a finger around each and every scar on her chest. The nerves were damaged still, and Nell didn't like to touch them herself, but Matthew's finger was healing where Bay's had been destructive. She let him feel her healed wounds, amazed that he wasn't disgusted by them.

Matthew did not care about the beauty of Nell's face and body, although he accepted the power of it; he was more interested in the beauty of her scars – although he accepted they would not be beautiful to most – because they represented what she had been through and what had shaped her and who she had become.

'You're beautiful too,' Nell said, grinning at him with her trademark smile. She wasn't shy about telling him. His beauty was in his intelligence and his kindness.

It had been her mother who had taught her to recognise love and to grab hold of it. In spite of all the heartache of her parents' separation, Nell had seen how much her mother loved Billy and how much Billy loved her mother, and how you couldn't force love if it wasn't there.

Anna lived with the guilt of the mistakes she had made. She saw how destroyed Dom was by her love for Billy, but she understood that she could not find a way out of his misery for him. He had to do that for himself. Just as Nell was finding ways to heal after her own traumas.

As difficult as it had been to admit, Bay's film had changed their lives for the better.

Anna had started her own millinery label, Anna B., with a website and an Instagram page, and Nell had given up modelling, given up partying, given up being used by men. She had been offered a conditional place at Exeter to study psychology.

Little Iris, who wasn't so little any more, had grown three inches and had finally been allowed to have a kitten. Two, actually. A black rescue with one white paw, and a ginger tabby with a torn ear. They hadn't made up for her dad's absence in the house at Lower Road, but they had helped. Iris felt sorry for her dad when she stayed in his flat near the leisure centre.

Poor Dom was yet to benefit from the changes, but he would. One day. One day he would find love with a woman who didn't mind cleaning the dried porridge off the bowls he left in the sink.

Bay had done them a favour, not that Nell would ever tell her that – that would be going too far. Did the end justify the means? In Nell's mind, there had been too much pain caused for that. Bay knew what she'd done, both the good and the bad. Bay was smart. Bay was a survivor. Bay's film had given her celebrity status at Norwich. In Bay's world, it was all about Bay still.

According to Granny Berry, who was the only member of the family Bay still spoke to, she was getting firsts and being asked to all the parties. She was thriving. She was finding her own way. And secretly, she credited Anna for every positive step forward that she made. Anna had rescued her and cared for her and accepted her and shown her how to find her own way. Bay would tell her that one day.

But not yet.

On the outside, she might be fine. On the inside, she still had some working-out to do, and some more mistakes to make.

A LETTER FROM CLARE

Dear Readers,

Thank you for reading *The Pretty One*. I feel unbelievably lucky to have you with me. This book was written during the first Covid lockdown of 2020, and the more anxious part of me wondered if it would ever see the light of day. But here we are again, still connected.

If you have enjoyed it, I'd love to hear from you. Please keep in touch by clicking on the sign-up link below, where you'll hear about what I'll be writing next:

www.bookouture.com/clare-boyd

This year, I have had more time than ever to write my book, thanks to fewer school runs, fewer nights out and fewer shops to browse in. Although I hated being locked down, I think this story needed my undivided attention. Testimony from my youngest daughter in her post-lockdown school essay confirmed how one-track I became: 'I was so lonely during lockdown,' she wrote. 'All I could hear was the tap-tap-tapping of Mum's keyboard in the distance'. Not my proudest mum moment! Like Anna's character, I have always tried to be a good mum and prioritise my children, but it often goes horribly wrong. Anyone else relate?

When step-siblings or half-siblings, like Bay and Nell and Iris, are thrown together under the same roof, it becomes even more complicated. Us parents often expect them to get along and to love each other. Many families achieve this, but it is not easy. You might be surprised to hear that the prevalence of sibling bullying and abuse is higher than that of spousal or parental abuse, yet it has been called the 'forgotten abuse' by experts and it largely goes unreported. Sadly, stories like Nell's are not uncommon.

Bay wasn't Nell's only problem. The modelling world did not provide a safety net for her. Like Nell, I started modelling at fifteen, and there were a few experiences I'd rather forget about. Thankfully, my career was short-lived. I was *literally*, as Nell would say, the worst model ever known to the fashion business. In front of the camera, I was stiff as a board and was therefore rarely rebooked by clients, and I survived the tedium of shoots by reading books and chain-smoking fags (in the nineties, you could smoke indoors and under-sixteen models didn't have chaperones). One of the few good things to come out of my debt-ridden, directionless period in fashion was meeting my husband, who has had a surprisingly long career as a model and is represented by brilliant agents who are not corrupt and exploitative like Ian in the book. Still, between you and me, getting out of the business was the best thing I ever did!

Lastly, for those of you who have enjoyed *The Pretty One*, please do write a review, and follow me on social media. A new 'follow' or hashtag or DM on Instagram from a happy reader really does make my day. See below for details.

Again, thank you very much for reading my book.

With very best wishes,
Clare

 clare.boyd.14

 @ClareBoydClark

 claresboyd

ACKNOWLEDGEMENTS

First and foremost, my thanks go to my dream team, Jessie Botterill and Broo Doherty, for their brilliant editorial instincts and sensibilities. A big thank you to the whole team at Bookouture. I want to hug every single one of you individually at the summer party next year.

On the research side of things, I want to thank Hannah Sneath at Select Model Management. She brought me up to date with the new safeguarding measures for models aged under eighteen. Hannah is the polar opposite to Ian's character. She cares passionately about the safety and well-being of the girls she represents.

In almost all of my books, I'm sure I have thanked Nanci Doyle for her medical expertise, and here, once again, I want to thank her for taking the time to read my manuscript and correct my errors.

I want to thank my first readers, Bex, Clare and Mum, for their emotional intelligence and acumen. The headspace they gave to this book was more valuable than anyone will ever know.

Lastly, to my moon sisters, Alice and Jessi. I wouldn't have been able to survive those crazy years – you know the ones! – without you.

Made in the USA
Monee, IL
03 April 2021